Just one more kiss can't hurt. It will be the last.

Venus's fingers caught in his hair, pulling his head down, their mouths meeting in a searching kiss, deeper and deeper until his breathing changed.

A shrill phone ring and the dogs barking tore them apart. The second ring broke tonight's strange spell . . .

Looking into his eyes, she knew Connor had shut down, closed himself off from her. Somehow he'd turned off the raging emotion she'd felt in his body when they kissed.

I'm trying to do the same thing. Am I hiding it as well?.

"I didn't want to leave without saying good-bye. No one will make another attempt to break in here tonight." Connor's formality seemed ludicrous to her since mere moments ago they were pressed chest to breast in multiple passionate kisses.

Tension beat in the air between them, but she followed his cool cue. "I hope this proves to you that I'm right and the real thief is trying to retrieve the brooch."

At last she saw a spark of emotion in his emerald eyes. "It proves you're in danger . . ."

SUIT UP FOR *A BLACK TIE AFFAIR*

"A second-chance-at-love thriller . . . fans will enjoy Ms. Bodine's entertaining joy ride."

—Midwest Book Review

"*A Black Tie Affair* is a charming romantic romp I thoroughly enjoyed . . . Sherrill Bodine has found a way to open a glamorous world everyone can delight in."

—Blogs.PublishersWeekly.com

"A light, little romance . . . a fun way to pass an afternoon."

—*RT Book Reviews*

"Great read . . . fast, and oh so romantic . . . I'm a fool for romance, so I fell under the spell of Sherrill Bodine immediately."

—TheReviewBroads.com

"Wonderful characters . . . I can't wait to read about what's happening in Chicago with Ms. Bodine as my guide!"

—NightOwlRomance.com

"Simply fun . . . This one will bring a smile to your face and perhaps bring up a memory or two."

—BookJourney.wordpress.com

"*A Black Tie Affair* is a light, fast read with several moments that made me laugh out loud . . . a light read with bit of love and romance lightly sprinkled with mystery."

—FictionVixen.com

"If you like fashion, romance, mysterious toxins, erratic and funny behavior coming from otherwise staid people, and two people who are meant to be together, then you probably will enjoy reading this novel."

—CoffeeTimeRomance.com

"Ms. Bodine's readers will appreciate the buildup of this romance and the time that she spends pulling us into her tale."   —SuspenseRomanceWriters.com

"I highly recommend this book with a 5/5 rating. It has some adventure, romance, and fiction based on factual incidents and places."   —SAHMReviews.com

"A light, frothy romance with enough substance to keep the reader interested. Fashion history can be fascinating and Bodine makes that the center to *A Black Tie Affair*."
          —JandysBooks.com

"Filled with intrigue and intricate details and real emotions . . . and enjoyable read."   —MiddayEscapades.com

"What makes this book stand out for me was the author's ability to use internal thoughts and punch them into stellar one-liners. It made the characters so much more dimensional, complete with lovable flaws. You really found yourself relating to them and rooting for them. Recommended!"   —BookPleasures.com

"Oh, but I loved this book. Ms. Bodine has a way of bringing you into the world of high fashion couture dresses and making any girl feel all giddy inside. This was a light, fluffy romance, with great characters, witty banter, and an underlying mystery to solve . . . a very enjoyable read."
          —BookWormyGirl.blogspot.com

TALKING UP THE *TALK OF THE TOWN*

A Cosmopolitan Red Hot Read

"4 Stars! A funny, energetic, and charming story that's sure to entertain many readers . . .The depth and reality of Bodine's characters make the story come alive, and readers will finish the novel with a happy feeling inside."
—*RT Book Reviews* on *Talk of the Town*

"Fun, fresh, and entertaining, Bodine's work sparkles for those who like a little dish and a little romance."
—*Parkersburg News and Sentinel* (NC)

"I love this book! Fizzy, frothy fun expertly blended with sexy romance, powerful friendships, much warmth, and lots of laughter. Don't miss this witty and wonderful page-turner."
—Barbara Bretton, *New York Times* bestselling author of *Casting Spells*

"Charming and a fun escape."
—JandysBooks.com

"What a hoot! Laugh-out-loud rollicking romance . . . Juicy gossip, fashion advice, delish recipes, and sexy romps; *Talk of the Town* is destined to be the talk of romance readers everywhere!"
—SingleTitles.com

"I thoroughly enjoyed *Talk of the Town*."
—ArmchairInterviews.com

ALL I WANT IS YOU

SHERRILL BODINE

FOREVER

NEW YORK   BOSTON

This book is a work of fiction. Names, characters, places, and incidents are the product of the author's imagination or are used fictitiously. Any resemblance to actual events, locales, or persons, living or dead, is coincidental.

Copyright © 2012 by Sherrill Bodine
Excerpt from *Talk of the Town* copyright © 2008 by Sherrill Bodine
Excerpt from *A Black Tie Affair* copyright © 2010 by Sherrill Bodine

Forever
Hachette Book Group
237 Park Avenue
New York, NY 10017

www.HachetteBookGroup.com

Printed in the United States of America

First Edition: January 2012
10 9 8 7 6 5 4 3 2 1

Forever is an imprint of Grand Central Publishing.
The Forever name and logo are trademarks of Hachette Book Group, Inc.

The publisher is not responsible for websites (or their content) that are not owned by the publisher.

ATTENTION CORPORATIONS AND ORGANIZATIONS:
Most HACHETTE BOOK GROUP books are available at quantity discounts with bulk purchase for educational, business, or sales promotional use. For information, please call or write:
Special Markets Department, Hachette Book Group
237 Park Avenue, New York, NY 10017
Telephone: 1-800-222-6747 Fax: 1-800-477-5925

To my friend Susan Grimm for opening her home and her heart to talk about her unique jewelry designs

and

To my critique partners, Laurie DeMarino, Cheryl Jefferson, Jude Mandell, Rose Paulas, and Patricia Rosemoor for always so generously sharing their wealth of knowledge.

When you get into a woman's closet you get into her life; who she was, who she is, and who she hoped to be.

CHICAGO JOURNAL & COURIER

Talk of the Town, *by Rebecca Covington-Sumner*

Darlings, love is in the air!

It seems wild mischievous Eros, God of Love, aka Cupid, has cast his sights on our windy city. I have been reliably informed of five engagements and six weddings in Lincoln Park alone and at 1220 Lake Shore Drive, in a mere three days, four engaged couples bought condos, and one glorious wedding took place on the rooftop garden of that very same building. Truly, Chicago is bursting with *amore* from the lake to our suburbs, north, south, and west!

We all know Eros's greatest delight is to zip around shooting arrows of desire into innocent and perhaps not so innocent victims who instantly fall in love, whether they want to or not.

Methinks Cupid aimed well when one of Chicago's most eligible bachelors, Drew Clayworth, finally realized exactly who he wanted when he wooed and won the heart of Athena Smith.

As you know, beautiful Athena runs the divine vintage boutique Pandora's Box, along with her sisters, Venus and Diana.

Only the finest treasures find their way to this store

from the Smith sisters' mini treasure hunts through the closets, attics, and basements of Chicago's elite. To all you blissful brides—no doubt the perfect wedding dress awaits you in their house of vintage beauty.

While shopping there please feel free to flaunt your engagement rings, because not only is Venus an expert on vintage couture costume jewelry but she is also a consummate jewel lover. She informed me that in the Orient and the West, diamonds, "stones of light," symbolize both the hidden riches of the gem and a spiritual connection to the giver of the jewel.

Darlings, I've found that no matter how much time has passed since my beloved presented me with my ring, I only have to gaze at the diamond and I'm flooded with emotion. Yes, I appreciate its beauty, but, more important, it instantly conjures up my feelings of bliss at being married to the man of my dreams.

May it be true for all of you.

Speaking of the delights of marriage, the union between Drew Clayworth and Athena Smith is much anticipated by friends and family and destined to be the nuptial of the season. It is my fondest wish their marriage will heal the painful, deep rift between these two wonderful families. Where Cupid is concerned, who knows?

And who knows where the mischievous fellow may strike again.

Beware, Clayworth men! If your confirmed bachelor Drew can succumb to love, how far behind can you be in finding your soulmates?

When it happens it will be the Talk of the Town and I promise to share every romantic detail with all of you!

Chapter 1

Venus Smith saw her father, Alistair, waiting for her at a table next to the flower boxes at their favorite outdoor café in Lincoln Park.

The sunlight gleamed off his white hair as he bent over a thick tablet of paper.

He was still writing fast and furiously when she came up behind him.

"Happy Saturday," she whispered into his ear and bent over to place a white pastry box on the table in front of him.

Squinting, he looked at it and then up at Venus.

"What is this?"

She dropped onto the chair across from him. "Open it."

Meticulous as always, he slowly slid a knife blade along the tape holding the lid closed. Raising one eyebrow, he lifted out a small, white cake shaped like an open book.

Goddesses Rock was written out in pink frosting across the top.

"Do you like it, Dad? It's to celebrate you starting to write your children's book on goddess mythology."

A gleam of joy lit his eyes. This was the first time she'd seen him happy since he'd been fired and disgraced by the Clayworth family eight months ago.

"Thank you, Venus. I love it."

Ready to cry, she blinked hard and bit her lip to get a grip on herself. "It's your favorite—white cake with fresh strawberries and whipped-cream filling. We probably should wait for Diana, but if you want we could cut it right now."

"Cake for breakfast?" His chuckle warmed her in a way she hadn't felt since that fateful, horrible day.

"Of course, cake for breakfast." Laughing, she leaned across the table toward him. "It has all the food groups. Eggs, milk, flour, butter, even fruit. When you think about it, cake is perfect."

"Just like my daughters."

She wanted to savor this moment, with her father's face alive in a way it hadn't been since he'd been forced out as treasurer of John Clayworth and Company, Chicago's iconic department store. The September sun bathed them in a warm, comfortable glow, and she felt herself relaxing in a way she hadn't in months.

Please let this be the ending of the bad times and the beginning of good things for Dad.

But a deep, husky laughter rang out across the open-air restaurant and sent an icy shiver down her spine, as if a bucket full of ice had been dumped over her head.

Oh, no! It can't be!

Hoping it might only be her overactive imagination, Venus shifted around in her seat, afraid that her weekly breakfast date with her father and this perfect new beginning was totally spoiled. If that voice belonged to the man she thought it belonged to...

The shiver shifted to her stomach as her eyes focused on Connor Clayworth O'Flynn pulling out a chair for his aunt at a table located near the geranium-festooned boxes that lined the sidewalk café. This had always been one of Venus's favorite spots. So much for that.

The sun shot streaks of light through Connor's thick black hair. He must have felt her gaze on him, because he turned his head and glanced toward her.

Deliberately, and with disdain, she swung away, ignoring him. She had been doing her best to avoid laying eyes on Connor for months, and even before he'd proven himself to be totally judgmental and without an ounce of loyalty, he'd always made her feel strangely...uneasy.

Across the small table, her father sat up straighter and stared over her shoulder.

She watched her father's face change, hating the look of disappointment and hurt again etched across his bones and the tight lines of his mouth.

"Do you want to leave, Dad?" Waiting for the usual lecture, she met her father's eyes.

"No, I do not want to leave. Connor is simply having breakfast with his aunt and uncle. As I plan to enjoy time with you and Diana this morning. These encounters are bound to occur. Chicago is a small town in many ways. Which is one of the reasons I have asked you and your sisters to put all our difficulties with the Clayworths in perspective and move forward."

Hearing the defeat in his voice, she couldn't bear it another moment. She'd really tried to honor his wishes, tried to still her burning desire to dig for information to help him. Now, unable to stop herself, she leaned across the table to clasp his hands.

Her father's grip was strong and tight on her fingers.

"Please talk to me, Dad," she urged, as she'd wanted to do for months. "I know being fired as treasurer of John Clayworth and Company after so many years hurt you. I'm not sure I'll ever be able to forgive any of them, even Drew when he marries Athena, if you don't explain the reason they fired you. Why you didn't fight them. Why you didn't defend yourself. Why you won't talk about it with any of us."

His deep sigh seemed more like a shudder. Guilt burned hot and bright through her but still she gripped his fingers, hoping *this time* he'd reveal the truth.

"Venus, you know all the Clayworth men and I signed an antidefamation agreement. I cannot and will not discuss it with you or your sisters. I'm sorry, but my decision is final."

The slight breeze off Lake Michigan again carried the sound of Connor's laughter and a snatch of his conversation, "...*work at Clayworth's*...," seemed to hang in the air over her table. She saw pain flicker like a blinding light through her father's aquamarine eyes.

That's it. Someone has to take Connor to task for what he's done. Make him explain himself.

"Dad, you worked so closely with Connor and you always spoke of him so glowingly. His betrayal must have hurt you more than the others," she said softly, almost afraid her words might cause him more pain.

He pressed a kiss on her knuckles and released her hands. "Yes, Connor and I became very close running everything together these last ten years since his father passed away. That is the only information I can share with you, Venus. You must let this go."

I tried, I really did, Dad, but I can't any longer. I'm going to defy your wishes and learn the truth to exonerate you.

"You look exactly like your mother."

The warmth in his eyes brought a rush of emotion settling at the back of her throat. "You're being silly, Dad." She laughed, her voice husky with unshed tears. "You know Mom was tiny like Athena and Diana. *I* have your bone structure."

"What did we always tell you?" he asked, his voice soft and loving.

"That I am the perfect combination of both of you," she repeated, as she knew he wished her to do.

"Yes. And when you get that particular look on your face you're the image of your mother, determined to solve a problem no matter how long it took her or what she had to do."

"Then my tenacity is a good thing, right?" She laughed so she wouldn't get weepy.

"I'm here," Diana gasped, rushing up to kiss their father on the cheek. "What did I miss? What's a good thing?"

He smiled between them. "Your sister's tenacity."

Diana flicked a look past Venus to where Connor sat behind her. "It depends on what Venus is up to."

"To getting us all breakfast now that you've arrived, right on time as usual."

"Afraid I might break my record this morning." Diana slid into the chair next to their father. "I had to stop by my office at Clayworth's to pick up some sketches."

Not wanting to spoil their weekly breakfast together by opening the hot subject of Diana's still working for John Clayworth and Company, Venus jumped up. "I'll go ask the waitress to get our orders started."

Trying to be patient while waiting in line, she couldn't stop glancing out the window to where Connor sat with Bridget O'Flynn and Tony Panzarella.

Remembering her father's pain, his words kept pounding through her head "...Connor...became very close running everything together these past ten years..."

How do I get Connor to tell me what happened to change everything and cause him to fire Dad? And how do I get him to admit he's made a horrible mistake?

The crazy idea that she was the only one who could end this travesty of justice took root and wouldn't stop growing. As if the power of her plan reached him, Connor rose slowly to his feet and turned toward the café door.

Warm air caught in her lungs. *If he comes into this restaurant I swear I'm going to confront him right here and now.*

He held the door open for his aunt Bridget to walk through.

Venus released her breath in a long sigh of relief. *Okay, so I'm not quite sure yet what I'm going to say to him.*

She smiled at Bridget, the only member of the Clayworth clan she still trusted. Except maybe Drew, for Athena's sake.

"Venus, this is kismet." Bridget's wide grin split her narrow face. "I've been wantin' to call you about my closet. Tony and Connor are always sayin' I haven't thrown out anythin' in thirty years. Today they both threatened to clean it themselves because Connor is at the brownstone all day helpin' Tony. Can you find the time soon to take a look? See if I have anythin' for your store or to donate? I'd hate for them to toss out somethin' of value or somethin' that might find a good home with someone else."

Firmly convinced this must be an omen that the cosmos had picked up her thought and was giving her a shove to make something happen to help her Dad, Venus lied. "This *is* kismet, Bridget. I happen to be free today."

"Can't believe my luck." Bridget laughed. "We're headin' home now. Can you make it soon?"

Mentally going through the list of appointments she'd need to cancel, she nodded. "Very soon. Actually, as soon as I finish having breakfast with Dad and Diana I'll come right over."

From the moment Bridget strolled happily away between Connor and Tony, Venus could think of nothing but how quickly she could follow them.

She tried to be patient while she waited for their breakfast and carried the tray back to the table. Tried to listen to her father and sister while she pushed her scrambled eggs around on her plate and nibbled on the edges of an English muffin, but her wild scheme kept twisting through her head, blocking out everything else.

Connor and I have always been like oil and water. What could possibly be my first move here?

Ideas bounced around in her head, ways to coax information out of Connor, but everything felt too obvious. And Connor was anything but stupid. Determined to put the pieces of the puzzle together herself somehow, she didn't realize her sister was staring at her.

"Venus, you've hardly eaten any breakfast. And you haven't touched your piece of cake. What's wrong?"

Diana's soft but firm voice broke through Venus's plotting and she came back to reality with a thump of her heart against her ribs. Her baby sister had an uncanny way of knowing when Venus wasn't exactly telling the truth.

Resisting her powerful urge to play with her hair, which would totally give her away, Venus folded her hands in her lap. "You know I'm always on a diet."

"You don't need to be. You're beautiful." Her father

patted his lips with a napkin and rose slowly to his feet. "I must get back home to my writing. Love you both."

He kissed their cheeks and Venus watched him walk away, his tablet of notes on his book tucked under his arm and the leftover cake in his hands. His shoulders weren't as square as they'd once been, nor was his stride as long and strong. Seeing it felt like a blow to her heart. *It's more than time for me to end this one way or another.*

"All right. Dad's gone. Now tell me what was going on with you and Bridget. After you came back to the table you were totally preoccupied."

Venus shrugged. "I'm just helping her with her closet this afternoon."

Diana's aquamarine eyes, so much like her own, widened. "I know Connor won't be at Clayworth's today because he's helping Tony. Did Bridget tell you he'd be there?"

"Yes," Venus said as nonchalantly as possible. "Aren't you the one always telling me I need to be at least cordial to *all* Clayworths no matter how I feel about them?"

Wise Diana was not fooled, and Venus knew it by the stern look on her sister's usually angelic face.

"I've never understood why you've always seemed to dislike Connor. Even after he rescued you from Lake Michigan when we were teenagers."

Remembering the embarrassment of being hauled up onto the Clayworths' sandy beach like a soggy bag of extra-large potatoes, her bathing suit askew, exposing way too much of her overblossoming curves, Venus shook her head. "He didn't *rescue* me. I was perfectly fine. He always took his unofficial lifeguard duties as stupidly rigidly and seriously as he does everything else. Including thinking he's always right. "

Diana stared her down while rising slowly to her feet. "Venus, I know since the troubles with Dad you've gone out of your way to avoid Connor, even at Athena and Drew's engagement party. So why are you spending the afternoon with him now? What do you want from him?"

To charm him, maybe even befriend him, so that he'll reveal everything I need to know to help Dad.

Of course she couldn't confess such an outrageous plan to anyone, especially her sister. She had no idea how she could ingratiate herself with Connor, but after her talk with her dad this morning and after seeing the look in his eyes, she *knew* Connor had the key to the truth.

Venus hugged her and decided to tell her *part* of her plan. "Stop worrying. All I want is to help Bridget clean her closet."

Chapter 2

"Venus, thank God you could come on such short notice. I can't face this without your help." Bridget flung open the doors to her expansive walk-in closet in her equally impressive neat-as-a-pin bedroom.

Bridget's look of utter gratitude made Venus feel so guilty for being here under false pretenses that she felt a need to leave immediately and come back when her motives were pure and her head wasn't full of crazy plots.

"Are you sure you really want to do this today?" Venus asked with real hope. "I could come back next week. Give you more time to really think about it."

"Gotta do it now." Bridget nodded with vigorous determination. "You bein' free today is a Godsend. Tony's thrilled. But drivin' me crazy with helpful suggestions. I made Connor take him to lunch. They'll be back soon."

Good. That's why I'm here. Venus tensed, feeling even guiltier.

She watched Bridget peer longingly into the closet. The light cast a halo around the cloud of strawberry hair piled high on her head, and her still-twinkling eyes looked like narrow slits of emerald above her sharp, ivory cheekbones.

A rush of true affection for Bridget washed away some of Venus's guilt. Okay, she might be here for the nefarious purpose of ingratiating herself with Bridget's adored nephew, despite the fact she considered him Smith family enemy number one, but Venus *would* help Bridget with this closet.

Smiling, Bridget glanced back at her. "Please hurry, Venus, before I change my mind. If you don't find anythin' suitable for your store, maybe there are some items I can donate to that charity you support for needy women goin' back into the job market."

Venus gave herself a sharp kick to do her job for the good of others. This didn't need to be all about her and her plot to get Connor on her side.

"Thanks. Your donation would be much appreciated by Dress for Success. I'm ready if you are."

Venus stepped into the closet, which looked as large as her first studio apartment had been, and came eye to eye with Connor's undeniably handsome face framed in a portrait perched on the middle shelf.

"See what I mean? I have hundreds of pictures of Connor." Bridget sighed behind her. "I should have put this one away years ago. But he looks so darn handsome in it. I can't bear to part with it even though I think it was taken the day Connor got kicked off the Northwestern swim team for breakin' Brad Evans's nose in a fight in the locker room. Remember that?"

Venus nodded, her gaze glued to the picture of Connor climbing out of the pool after winning the Big Ten hundred-yard butterfly championship.

Remember? Like yesterday.

The smell of chlorine. Connor's thick black hair slicked back. A faint smile curling his full lips. His six-pack abs glistening with beads of water. He'd reminded her of the statue of David she'd studied in Florence during her junior year of college abroad.

She hadn't liked Connor even in those days, but she'd felt a twinge of *Oh, my God, he is so hot* before the team surrounded him, slapping him on the back. Including his best friend, Brad Evans, the object of her youthful passion.

The timing of their fistfight on the heels of her and Brad's getting together had given her the totally illogical idea that she'd had something to do with the fight. When she'd found the courage to ask Brad, he gave one harsh laugh through his bandages and murmured, *"Connor's a jerk who thinks he's better than everyone else."*

Over the years it had become clear that Connor being a jerk was the one thing Brad *was* right about, she thought as she resisted the powerful urge to turn the picture to the wall.

"I was there. I went to Northwestern, too, don't forget. It turned out to be a bad day all around."

"Then it's high time we put it away once and for all."

To Venus's relief, Bridget swept the offending picture off the shelf and dropped it with a heavy clank into a cardboard box already half filled with items destined to be put into storage.

"One down. What's next, Venus?"

She waved Bridget deeper into the labyrinthine room filled with rods hung with clothes and shelves neatly stacked with countless velvet and satin boxes in all shapes, sizes, and colors.

Gazing around, Bridget shook her head. "I don't know where to begin. Start wherever you want, Venus. Tony and Connor will be back soon, wantin' to give us advice."

The thought of staring Connor in the eyes and actually implementing her plan made her shiver and her heart thump faster.

She tried to ignore her galloping pulse by slowly moving through the closet, but she couldn't stop worrying about how horrified her father would be if he knew she planned to somehow convince Connor to reveal the evidence he had against him. Her sisters would be even angrier, since they'd decided to respect their father's wishes and accept his firing as treasurer of John Clayworth and Company by his lifelong friends and employers, the Clayworth men.

But Venus had never been saintly like her sisters. She wouldn't rest until she found out the truth. Just as her mother would have done.

Today's the day I begin.

She sucked in a deep, strengthening breath.

Roses.

She should have known Bridget wouldn't use a heavy, powdery sachet, or worse, essence of mothballs, which unfortunately permeated the storage closets of other Chicago grandes dames for whom Venus had performed similar services.

She pushed up the sleeves of her cashmere sweater, sans jewelry, to ensure there was nothing to catch on any delicate lace or silk she might come across. She felt naked without her bangles, necklaces, and big earrings. Fashion as armor, her sister Diana called Venus's baubles. She'd need all the armor she could get when Connor showed up.

"Bridget, let's start with the items you've had for a long time. Stuff you might have forgotten was in here."

Determined to get this job done, Venus walked to the very back of the closet, dropped to her knees, and pulled out a long, sturdy white dress box. She lifted the lid and gasped at the rich cream satin and delicate lace of one of the most beautiful gowns she'd ever seen.

"It's my mother's wedding dress," Bridget said, a gentle, sweet smile curling her wide mouth.

The look on her face made Venus go all gooey and warm inside. "It's a perfect dress for a bride," she sighed, fingering the weighty fabric. "Did you read Rebecca's latest *Talk of the Town* column? She's right. Nearly everyone I know has either just gotten engaged or just gotten married. And who wouldn't want to walk down the aisle in something as exquisite as this? I mean, look at this lace." She gently lifted the gown up across her breasts, smoothing it down to its tiny waist. "It's handmade Alençon, probably more than a hundred years old. See, you can tell. Look at these tiny, tiny little knots, all tied by hand. And the thread is linen..."

"Bellissima, Venus!" Tony Panzarella's booming voice interrupted her.

Venus started and for a second she couldn't breathe. She looked up to find the closet door filled by Tony and Connor, staring at her as she clutched the wedding dress to her breasts. Burning with surprise, she met Connor's eyes and his oddly appealing almost-smile. She gripped the gown even tighter, like a shield. *You're back too soon. I'm not prepared yet.*

"What are you two doing back so soon?" Bridget demanded.

Tony gazed adoringly at her. *"Il mia cara,* Connor and I made a wager about whether Venus could convince you to truly clean your closet, and I insisted on seeing which of us won. I willingly surrender my fifty-dollar bet to you, Connor. You were right about Venus. You said she is stubborn as a mule and it is impossible to change her mind once she's decided on something. What a woman!"

Tony threw her a kiss and Connor reddened, making his emerald eyes, so like his aunt's, blaze.

Venus sucked in a sharp, painful breath. "Well, I am known for my persuasiveness. But I prefer to think of it as tenacity, not stubbornness," she purred the words with such forced sweetness she nearly choked. She'd rather faint from lack of oxygen than let Connor see her confusion. Tony might be charmed by the idea of Venus as strong-willed, but she knew Connor had not meant it as a compliment. It was part of her plan to change his mind about her.

"Hello, Venus." Connor nodded.

"Hello, Connor." She nodded back with equal, if not superior good manners.

Hands on her hips, Bridget faced the men. "Both of you out. No, wait. Before you go, Connor, would you please take down those brown boxes from the top shelf?"

The closet seemed to shrink around Venus as Connor stepped toward her, reaching for the high shelf. Trapped, she had no choice but to stay put, the exquisite wedding gown on her lap, and pretend she wasn't bothered by Connor's powerful torso looming over her, reminding her again of Michelangelo's statue of David.

Of course the David statue is gloriously nude.

She pictured the David in a Speedo like the one Connor wore in the photo. Given the size of the tiny Speedo in the picture, it didn't take much of her fertile imagination for that image to give way to a vision of Connor as magnificently nude as the David.

Willing the image to vanish, she blinked, bit her lip, and literally stopped breathing.

The lace wedding dress slithered out of her fingers.

Lip throbbing, chest aching, she sucked in some oxy-

gen while gathering the dress tightly to her breasts.
Hoping she appeared utterly nonchalant and not at all flus-
tered, she flicked Connor a bored glance as he hunkered
down beside her to place two boxes on the floor. One was
a wooden chest with a heart and two doves carved on
the lid.

Bridget laughed. "My God, it's my hope chest. I'd forgotten where I'd stored it."

Tony took a step closer. "Your hope chest? I thought
they were much bigger. This is too intriguing. I cannot
leave now. I must see what's inside."

"No, you don't." Bridget stopped him with her palm on
his chest. "Out. You too, Connor."

Connor straightened, brushing against Venus. She felt
a pull on her hair as her tortoiseshell clip caught on the
arm of his navy blue cashmere sweater.

Her hair fell heavy and hot around her shoulders.

He hunkered back down, quickly found the clip, and
handed it to her.

"Sorry," he muttered, staring into her eyes.

*Perfect time to do something nice. Like say his eyes are
honest to goodness as dazzling as priceless emeralds.*

Instead she simply nodded. She felt utterly stupid not
being able to utter one single friendly comment to the man.

Ridiculously nervous now that the moment to move
forward with her plan was at hand, she sat like a lump,
fumbling with the clip, trying to pull part of her hair back
up. Helpless to stop him, she watched Connor kiss Bridget
on the cheek and urge a protesting Tony out the door.

"Are you all right, Venus? You look ready to jump out
of your skin." Bridget shook her head. "I know this isn't
easy for you. I hope someday you can forgive Connor for
his takin' sides against your dad. Understand his choices.

Move on like your father wants you to do. Like your sisters have done. Perhaps you could even be friends with Connor. You are all goin' to be family."

She'd never in a million years hurt Bridget by being rude and putting her in the middle of this feud with Connor. But she couldn't bear to lie either, especially because of everything Bridget had done for her and her sisters after their mom passed away.

"Connor and I have always been like that old cliché. Oil and water don't mix."

"That makes me sad, Venus. You and Connor are two of my favorite people in the whole world."

Venus tried to sound cheerful. "Well, who knows? Maybe things between Connor and me will change."

They'll have to if I'm going to get any information out of him. But the last thing I want to do is to hurt you, Bridget.

In her heart of hearts, Venus was utterly convinced that learning the truth about Connor's part in her father's disgrace would be good for all of them, that it would finally right this terrible wrong and heal the breach between their two families. She gave Bridget a genuine smile. "Now I don't want you to be sad. Be glad you saved this priceless wedding gown. It stays right here."

Ready to get back to business before she gave too many of her feelings away, Venus carefully placed the dress back in the box and set the lid firmly in place. She could have sold this exquisite gown in a heartbeat to one of the brides who haunted Pandora's Box looking for a totally original wedding dress. But the look on Bridget's face when she'd first gazed down at it told Venus the dress represented memories too precious to be discarded, even if she never opened the box again.

Laughing, Bridget joined her on the carpet, crossing her legs in a classic yoga pose. "I promise I won't be sentimental about much."

"What about this?" Venus ran her fingertips across the top of the hope chest. The inscription *Love and Marriage* was carved over the inlaid heart.

"Hope chests like this were all the rage back in my day. Every girl I knew had one." Bridget shrugged. " I guess you don't get much of a call for them in the store now." She paused for a moment and ran her fingers over the inscription. "So how do you feel about love and marriage goin' together, Venus?" Bridget gave her the *truth and nothing but the truth* look she'd perfected in the years she'd been head of security for John Clayworth and Company. The years when Venus's mother and father had worked at Clayworth's. The years when they'd all been like family.

"Is there someone special in your life, Venus? Are you goin' to be the next Smith sister to be married off?"

Delighted to be finally and completely truthful and to push her guilt about plotting against Connor aside for a little while, Venus laughed. "I'm going to be just like you, Bridget. Gloriously single, thrilled and fulfilled with my career. That's more than enough for me. I'll never marry either. I'll be everyone's favorite adored and adoring auntie."

Bridget's rich, deep laughter was positively infectious. Venus couldn't stop laughing back, but she tried, forcing a stern tone into her voice. "I'm serious, Bridget. Really."

"You're way too young to be thinkin' such a way. You wait. Some tall, dark, and handsome Mr. Right will come along."

"Not everyone can be as lucky in love as Rebecca Covington and David Sumner. Two strangers whose eyes met across a crowded room, making every cell in their bodies go numb." Venus gave a mock shiver of delight. "I love the way Rebecca describes how she felt the instant she first saw David. I'm very sure about the type of guy I want, so I'm betting if my *aha there he is at last* moment hasn't happened by now, it never will."

Bridget gave her another sharp look. "Can't believe there haven't been a few Mr. Rights in your life."

Venus twisted a lock of hair around her ring finger. "Nope."

"Sure about that?" Bridget teased. "I recall your parents and sisters tellin' me that when you start twirlin' your hair you're either confused or tellin' a fib."

"Oh, all right." She laughed, folding her hands primly in her lap and wishing her habit didn't always give her away. "Once I thought Brad Evans was Mr. Right. My type. Tall, blond, and handsome. In college we got pretty *close*. You know the old story. Boy and girl meet. Then boy gets a broken nose. Breaks his promises and his girl's heart by breaking up with her." The tiniest bit embarrassed, Venus blinked and smiled. "Eventually we got back together. And have called it off, gone our separate ways, and reunited dozens of times since then."

A deep furrow appeared between Bridget's delicately arched brows. "But Brad Evans hasn't lived in Chicago since he went east to law school. As you gals say, isn't he geographically undesirable?"

"That's the beauty of it. We get together when it's convenient for both of us." Venus reached for more hair to twirl. "No commitments. No judgment calls. Exactly the kind of modern, fun relationship we both want."

"In my day they didn't call such a thing a relationship. Don't you want more?" Bridget asked, sounding quite a bit like Diana did whenever they discussed Brad.

Venus couldn't deny that Brad had changed and so had she. But she wasn't ready to let go of the nice memories they shared yet. Bridget kept watching her, so Venus forced herself to quit playing with her hair. "Nope. I'm thrilled with the status quo. But I *do* want to see what's in this hope chest. Can I peek?"

As she lifted the lid she glanced at Bridget. Was that regret in her eyes? *Regret for me? Or for herself?*

Worried, Venus stopped. "Are you okay, Bridget?"

"I'm thinkin' I'm a fine one to be lecturin' you when I've been engaged to Tony forever and never married him."

So many times Venus had wanted to ask why Bridget and Tony had stayed perpetually engaged. What changed their mind about marriage?

The pained look on Bridget's face told her now was not the time to get an answer. "We don't need to do this today, Bridget."

"Yes, we do." Bridget smiled and all traces of sadness vanished. She seemed her usual confident, take-no-prisoners, self. "I'm a lot like you, Venus. Stubborn. Let's do it."

The see-through nylon chemise nightgown Venus lifted from the chest told its own tale. The very expensive price tag from Clayworth's still hung from one delicate strap.

"Good lord, I must have been nineteen when I bought that nightgown."

Venus laughed. "Bridget, I never knew you were such a sexpot."

"If memory serves, I fear there's worse to come."

Venus held up a black garter belt and glanced at Bridget's still-slim hips. "Love it! You should wear this."

"God in heaven, Venus, Tony would have a heart attack."

Picturing robust Tony with his mane of salt and pepper hair, flat belly, and wolfish grin, Venus shook her head. "I'm betting he'd *love* it."

Venus dug deeper into the box until her fingertips hit something hard. "Oh, what's this?"

She lifted out a black velvet jewelry box. Every nerve in her body quivered with excitement and every instinct screamed *vintage jewelry find*. Unable to resist, she sprang the lid.

Instantly, tiny pinpoints of light reflected off metal hangers in the closet's dim recesses. Resting gently against the box's cushioned interior lay an exquisite mermaid brooch. About the length of Venus's manicured index finger, the mermaid's body was made from one large rhinestone. Her hair rippled in a cascade of navette-cut aurora borealis.

"I forgot that brooch was in there." Over Venus's shoulder, Bridget's voice sounded strained, as if she'd been running.

Venus stared at Bridget's pale face, then back down at the open black velvet box in her hand.

"Bridget, this is a really rare Eisenberg mermaid pin. They only made a few copies. You must remember how the original was commissioned by John Clayworth to be made of real stones and then it was stolen in that famous heist?"

Bridget nodded and a little color returned to her high cheekbones. "It happened before I started workin' at Clayworth's. Over the last thirty or so years that heist has become a Chicago legend. Like Al Capone's vault."

"Exactly. Even more reason why you should definitely keep this piece. Think of the fabulous history behind it."

Bridget stared at the brooch. "Someone gave me that

on one of the darkest nights of my life. There are too many bad memories attached to it for me to ever want to look at it again."

With that, Bridget jumped to her feet and bolted out of the closet.

Aching with worry, Venus waited, wanting to give Bridget time before she followed her. She'd encountered this kind of momentary emotional shutdown in her clients before.

Hoping she'd given Bridget enough time but too worried not to go to her, Venus rose slowly to her feet. Clutching the jewelry case, she walked out of the closet and into the bedroom.

Bridget stood gazing out the window.

"Maybe we should take a break, Bridget," Venus said softly, wanting to make this easier. "Revisiting the past can be tough."

Bridget turned to her. "I'm sorry, Venus, after I promised not to be sentimental. I'm sure you've had your share of other closet criers with all the society ladies takin' their walks down memory lane."

"Yeah, I've heard a lot of stories. Of heartbreak. Tragedy. Triumph. Deception. But most of all about sweeping, awe-inspiring, fairy-tale-worthy recollections of every possible kind of love."

The pain on Bridget's face suggested something so sad it made tears of sympathy burn behind Venus's eyes. Sensing looking at the brooch was painful for Bridget, Venus snapped the lid of the black velvet box closed. "Are you absolutely sure you don't want to keep this? This is a book piece. Highly, highly collectible."

Bridget took such a deep breath she seemed to shudder. "The truth is, there are certain hurts that leave a lingerin' sore point, no matter how long ago they happened. I bet I sound like a hypocrite to you after askin' you to forgive Connor's sins. But I had my doubts about why and how I got this gift, so I never felt right wearin' it. And I still don't. Will you sell it for me and give the money to charity?"

Venus held the box close to her breasts, knowing she could never part with it if Bridget didn't want it. The instant she'd gazed down at the mermaid it seemed to belong to her. Maybe because she'd grown up listening to her father's stories about her namesake, the goddess Venus, being born of the sea. Rising out of the water. In her childish mind she'd asked, *"So I'm like a mermaid, right, Daddy?"*

Her father had always been magic to her. Now he seemed broken because of his so-called crime against the Clayworths. And she knew Connor's betrayal hurt him the worst.

She took a long, deep breath, more determined than ever to get the truth from Connor no matter what it cost her.

"Bridget, if you're absolutely sure you don't want the brooch, I'd like to buy it for myself."

Bridget shook her head. "I'd give it to you but I've always had the crazy notion this brooch is bad luck. I don't want it to rub off on you."

Venus laughed and gave her a quick hug. "It won't be bad luck for me. It reminds me of happy times when I was a child. Please, please, will you sell it to me?"

Bridget seemed to be studying her, looking for something. "No, I won't sell it to you. I'll give it to you."

"No way." Venus stood firm. "I can't accept such a gift. This copy is worth twenty-five hundred dollars, at least.

I'll write you a check for that amount. Once I research it a bit more, I'll pay any difference. I won't feel right about it any other way. Honestly."

The tiniest of smiles curved Bridget's mouth. "I'm not takin' your money, Venus. If you want to do somethin', donate the money to Connor's Golden Gloves boxin' gym he built for juvenile defendants and we'll call it even. The brooch was a gift from Tony."

She's giving away a gift from Tony?

"Bridget, my mother always told me never to give away a gift from…" Venus stopped. *I can't say husband like Mom did. Should I say lover, paramour, what?*

"…a close loved one," Venus decided sounded right. "Won't Tony's feelings be hurt if you sell the brooch to me?"

Bridget patted Venus's shoulder. "Don't worry yourself. Trust me, men don't care about this sort of thing. Tony probably won't even remember he gave it to me."

Chapter 3

The door opened on Connor O'Flynn's boxing gym in Lakeside and he looked up from adjusting the Velcro on Gregori Prozument's bag gloves.

Holding hands, Bridget and Tony walked in.

As had been the case for as long as he could remember, seeing them together brightened his mood. Laughing, he shook his head. "This is great. I didn't expect to see you today. What are you two up to?"

"Surprisin' you. We're takin' you for a steak dinner before your mother arrives in Chicago for her yearly visit and wants you to eat organic tofu for the next ten days." Bridget waved. "But no hurry. Don't stop on account of us. We'll wait in the office until you finish." Bridget shot Gregori her *the truth and nothing but the truth* look, which never failed to get answers. "Good to see you here. You keepin' yourself out of trouble?"

The teenager shifted from foot to foot as he did when boxing. "I'm cool here," he shouted back.

Tony gave him a thumbs-up, grinned, and draped his arm around Bridget's shoulders as they strolled through the open office door.

Watching them, Gregori kept swaying with pent-up energy, circling the mat. "Your Aunt Bridget's been real cool since she busted me for boostin' at Clayworth's Department Store. My mom says she's the best thing to ever happen to me 'cause it got me here to Golden Gloves."

Gregori motioned toward the mirrored walls and the four-rope ring with its stained white canvas flooring where two other teenagers were in full gear and sparring.

"The judge says you been with Golden Gloves awhile. That why you started this club, Mr. O'Flynn?"

He'd always been honest with the kids in the program. "Yeah, that's how it started. In college I got into trouble for not being able to control my anger. Got into a fistfight over a girl." *Over Venus Smith, of all people.* "The guy pressed charges."

"Whoa!" Gregori's eyes grew wider. "How come a rich dude like you couldn't get out of it?"

The sharp image of his parents' disappointment and the pained look in Bridget's eyes flashed through his head and again he heard her voice, *You did it. You own up to it.*

Connor shook his head. "Didn't try to get out of it. My grandfather Clayworth was on the Park District Board when they started Golden Gloves to get kids off the street. I chose to volunteer with the program as my community service. And I've never stopped, because it works."

"Fuckin' works for me. Got me out of the gang, didn't it." Gregori knocked his gloves together. "Now I fight fair. By the rules."

"That's the idea. So show me your stuff. Let's drill some combinations first." Connor slipped on red focus mitts and held his hands up at shoulder level. "I want you to aim at the white dot in the middle of these targets. Left lead jab to a right rear cross. Ready?"

Connor circled, moving into position. From the beginning Gregori had been a quick learner. The kid took an orthodox left-lead stance. Jabbed with his left. Then his right.

Nodding, Connor absorbed the impacts. "Just like that. Keep it going." He heard his aunt's and uncle's voices coming from his office but tried to ignore them to concentrate on Gregori getting his rhythm. "Great. Now give me more."

"*Cara,* how could you sell Venus the brooch I gave you for your twenty-fifth birthday?" Tony's deep voice roared through the gym.

Tony never yells.

Hot with shock, Connor turned toward the open office door. At the same instant he felt a sudden sharp pain along his right jaw.

"Dude, you moved!"

Hearing the panic in Gregori's voice, Connor swung his head back. The kid's face looked as white as the stenciled *O'Flynn's Golden Gloves Gym* blazoned across his black tank top.

Wanting to reassure him, Connor grinned. "It's not your fault I dropped my guard." He stripped off the targets to rub his throbbing chin. "Nice cross. Now finish up the circuit yourself. Two-minute jump rope. Three minute round shadow boxing. One hundred crunches. I'll be back."

Connor sprinted across the gym to his small office and pulled the door closed.

Instead of standing close, arms around each other, as they had when they entered the office, Bridget and Tony now stood at opposite ends of the room, each gazing up at the flat-screen TV on the wall.

Venus, her apricot-colored hair tumbling around her shoulders the way it had in Bridget's closet, her body poured into a vee neck black dress with a brooch shaped like a mermaid pinned on the high curve of her left breast, was frozen on the screen.

"What's going on?" Connor asked, carefully studying his aunt's and uncle's tense faces the way he observed jurors in the courtroom.

"We're watchin' Rebecca's show, *Talk of the Town.* She's doin' a segment on all the gowns that have been bought at Pandora's Box for White House events in Washington since the last election."

His aunt sounded calm, but the pained look in her eyes turned Connor icy cold. He knew this look, although thank God he'd seldom seen it. *Why in the hell is she so upset?*

Looking for an answer, he turned to Tony, who pointed to the DVR frozen Venus on screen.

"*Cara,* that is my brooch, is it not? Why would you want to part with it?"

Bridget seemed to be studying her black shoes instead of responding to Tony's normally deep, soft voice cracking around the edges. "I didn't think you'd remember or care, Tony."

"Remember? *Cara,* I gave the brooch to you the night I proposed to you. The night I told you I loved you."

At last Bridget looked up at Tony. The powerful intensity of their locked eyes made Connor feel like a voyeur. He backed up one step and his gym shoes creaked.

They both stared at him, all emotion stripped from their faces. He knew these looks, too. They were the ones used when Connor was growing up and his aunt and uncle were trying to protect him from being hurt.

Now, like then, Bridget smiled too brightly, forcing it for his benefit. "Enough of this nonsense. Ready, Connor? You must be starving. I know I am."

Narrowing his eyes, he studied both of them. "We're not going anywhere until I get some answers. I've never seen you guys fight."

"That you haven't seen it doesn't mean it never happens."

He met his aunt's stern stare, refusing to back down. "You're avoiding the question, Aunt Bridget. Tell me what's going on."

"Now don't you be givin' me your lawyer look and tone of voice, Connor Clayworth O'Flynn. This is a little misunderstandin' between me and your Uncle Tony. Nothin' for you to worry about or try to make right."

"You could make it right, *cara,* if you bought the brooch back from Venus."

With a sharp gasp, she swung to Tony. "I'd never ask Venus such a thing and you know it. I don't go back on my word."

Something raw flashed between them.

Connor stepped closer, wanting to break this tension he didn't understand. *There's more to this than the brooch.* "You two taught me to talk through a problem until it's solved. Let's do that now."

Into their silence the door creaked open. Sweating, Gregori stood, looking at them. "I'm done, Mr. O'Flynn." He glanced toward Venus, still frozen on screen, and whistled. "Man, that chick's smokin' hot!"

Frustrated at not getting answers, Connor sucked in a deep breath.

Before he could answer, he heard Tony's short, hard laugh. "You're a discerning young man, Gregori."

The kid grinned. "If that means I'd like to get it on with that hot chick, then damn straight." His eyes darted between the TV and Connor. "You look kinda upset, Mr. O'Flynn. I mean if she don't belong to you."

"Mine? Far from it," he muttered, staring at Venus in all her glory. The brooch that seemed to mean so much to Tony winked at her breast.

I need answers.

He nodded to Gregori. "Good job today. If you're finished with your circuit you're done."

"Cool. See you Monday for clean-up." Gregori nodded to Bridget and cast one last lustful teenage stare at the TV screen before he disappeared out the door.

"There's hope for that boy." Bridget chuckled. "He knows a beautiful woman when he sees her. And I know when I'm starvin'. Let's go."

"Not before we talk." Connor glanced from his aunt's set face to Tony's stricken one. "C'mon, tell me what's wrong so we can work it out."

"Maybe at dinner." Bridget clutched Tony's hand. "Go shower and close up the gym, Connor. Meet us at Gibson's in about an hour. I'm in the mood for one of their steaks plus their frozen ice cream pie. You need to fortify yourself for your mom's idea of cookin'."

Bridget pressed a quick, warm kiss on Connor's cheek and pulled Tony out the door before Connor could stop them.

He'd been outmaneuvered. No way would they discuss anything personal at the busiest restaurant in the city where they'd probably know half the people in the dining room.

Concern and frustration gnawing at him, Connor fumbled with the remote. Venus, lush, her stubborn spirit sparkling through the still frame, stared back at him.

He couldn't deny Gregori had said what every healthy male must feel when he looked at Venus. Connor had always thought that the fact she didn't seem to *get* her sensuality only intensified her impact on men. Somehow it gave her the kind of honest-to-God power that could wring a sexual response from a rock.

Hell, she actively disliked him, yet whenever they were in the same room he felt a kick in his gut. As he had yesterday at the café, until she deliberately turned away from him. Since the trouble with her dad, they avoided each other whenever possible, which was a logical course of action given the circumstances.

As he shut off the TV, the mermaid brooch gave one last wink.

Why was Venus wearing his aunt's pin? And what did the pin have to do with the pain he'd seen on his uncle's face?

He'd talk to Tony man to man and find out. But first he had to get out of here.

He locked up after the last kid signed out, took a quick shower, and was headed to Gibson's within the hour.

The traffic on Rush Street inched along slower than normal. Hot with impatience, Connor glanced at his watch. "Damn it, move," he muttered and pressed the horn.

Reminding himself to stay cool, he sucked in a deep breath. Growing up with his parents' rigid rules, he'd learned to hide his feelings, but sometimes it felt wrong to always be in such tight control, particularly when it involved someone he loved. And God knew he loved Tony and Bridget too much to not find out what was wrong and fix it.

He tried to be patient, waiting his turn to pull up in

front of Gibson's, toss his keys to the valet, and work his way through the crowd coming and going through the revolving door.

Inside, dozens of businessmen and a few women spilled out of the large bar fondly called the Viagra Triangle by locals. One guy, his tie hanging loose and his face flushed, leaned against the wall, hitting on Kathleen, the hostess, who handled him with her legendary tact and charm.

Once he drifted back into the bar, she looked at Connor and shrugged. "One of those nights. Tony and Bridget are already here. Sorry, I couldn't give them a better table. They're sitting next to a table of ten celebrating a birthday."

"C'mon, Kathleen, I know they requested to be in the middle of the action, didn't they?" He laughed, trying to accept that his aunt had her own plan for tonight. Which without a doubt did not include telling him anything he wanted to know.

"You know I'll never drop a dime on Bridget and Tony." With an apologetic smile, Kathleen handled him as smoothly as she had the tipsy customer. "But if you can wait, I'll find a better table."

"Thanks. That would be great." Determined to get some answers, he headed to where Bridget and Tony sat between a table of eight men and the birthday party of women laughing uproariously as one opened gifts.

As usual the restaurant hummed with conversation, every table full of customers, come for the great food and the atmosphere of energy generated by the city's power players who dined here nightly.

Fresh from hosting her show, *Talk of the Town,* live, Rebecca sat in her usual booth with her husband, David, and their best friend, Kate Carmichael.

Disappointment stung him.

If Venus was with them I might have had an opening to question her...she might have given me some clue to why the brooch is so important to both Tony and Bridget.

Rebecca looked up, saw him, and blew a kiss. He turned toward their table to say hello but was stopped by an alderman and a judge on their way out, but wanting to discuss the new mayor's job performance with him.

As Connor had predicted, he knew half of the diners and had to hide his impatience, shaking hands, until at last he reached his aunt and uncle.

Tony was standing, waiting for him at their table.

"Ah, Connor, at last."

Tony's pale face sent a shiver of fear through Connor. He gripped his uncle's shoulder. "Are you all right?"

Lines crinkled Tony's wide forehead. "Headache."

"Kathleen will get us a quieter table. You can't hear yourself think sitting here."

A wistful smile curling the corners of Tony's mouth, he dropped heavily back into his chair. "As your aunt always says, often our thoughts aren't worth listening to in the first place. That's her motto for tonight."

A full glass of red wine rested in front of Tony, and Bridget stared down into her glass of white.

Concern burned hotter in Connor's gut. "Do you want to stay here or go somewhere quieter for dinner? We should talk, Aunt Bridget."

At last she looked up but didn't meet his eyes. She tilted her head and stared around him.

"Look who's come in. Ed Mahoney and his girlfriend, Maxie Robinson. I'll ask them to join us."

She bolted away and Connor turned to stare at Tony's pale face. "What in the hell is going on between the two of you? Is this all because Venus bought the brooch?"

"We will work out this business of the brooch. I fear it may not be as simple to undo the past."

Puzzled by the firm set of Tony's mouth, Connor shook his head. "It's never too late to negotiate a settlement. If you regret Bridget's selling Venus the brooch, then we'll buy it back from her."

"Yes, the brooch is important, but getting it back may not solve everything." Tony slowly stood. "Maxie and Ed are joining us."

Connor had no choice but to stand, kiss Maxie on her soft, scented cheek, and shake Ed's hand.

"I'm very excited. We've been watching Rebecca Covington-Sumner's *Talk of the Town* show and now here she is right across the room. I think she's wonderful," Maxie sighed while Connor held out the chair for her.

Generally he enjoyed Maxie's company, but tonight he couldn't concentrate on her starstruck gushing about Rebecca's show and how she looked even younger in person.

Ed was the best insurance broker in the city, and Clayworth's had benefited by being his biggest client, but his statistics-riddled conversation with Tony about the necessary cost of insurance for home security systems left Connor bored.

Tonight all his senses zeroed in on the careful way both Tony and Bridget held themselves and the way they picked at their steak dinners even though earlier his aunt had said she was starving.

Tony, his eyes hooded, rubbed at his temples.

Bridget glanced over. "That's the fourth time you've done that. You didn't take your blood pressure pill, did you?"

Tony flashed her an impatient look, a gesture so rare, it seemed surreal to Connor.

"It seems I did forget, *cara*. Perhaps I should leave you the car and cab home."

"Don't be foolish. I'm always sayin' you need to take better care of yourself. We'll both go." Bridget stood up, flashing another of her forced smiles. "Sorry to leave before dessert. Have a piece of the ice cream pie for me. Connor, I'll get the car and meet you both outside."

Watching Bridget hurry out, Maxie's eyes grew rounder.

Puffing out his barrel chest, Ed rose. "Tony, may I be of assistance?"

"No, thank you. All is well." Tony bent over Maxie and kissed her hand. "It is always a pleasure to see you. Please enjoy the rest of your evening. Good night."

It hurt Connor to see Tony's slumped shoulders and slow steps as he maneuvered between the tables.

"I'll be back," Connor bit out to Ed before quickly following his uncle.

By the time they reached the entrance, Tony's black BMW sat waiting at the curb.

With innate courtesy, Tony held the car door open. Avoiding his eyes and Connor's, Bridget quickly slipped in.

"Good-bye, Connor. Need to get your uncle home and make sure he takes his medicine this time. See you tomorrow morning at Clayworth's."

Watching his aunt and uncle pull away, he told himself to think rationally about how to help them.

The image of Venus, the mermaid winking at him from her breast, flashed before him.

Yes, getting the brooch back from Venus is the logical place to start.

Chapter 4

Late as usual, Venus drove past Pandora's Box on the way to the garage. The sun reflected off the large front windows. Even squinting, she couldn't see if Diana had arrived and opened the door.

Of course she has. Diana is never late.

Venus turned the corner, heading into the alley. Passing the small side parking lot she slowed, surprised she didn't see Diana parked in her normal spot.

It struck her as odd, but then she remembered Diana had more than once taken a cab to the store.

Running from the garage, through the small yard to the back door of Pandora's Box, Venus fumbled in her black Croc tote for the store keys.

A stiff breeze carried the scent of late-blooming roses from the yard across the alley. The wind whipped her hair into her eyes as she reached out to unlock the back door.

It creaked open before she touched it.

The cool morning air sent chills down her spine. Her heart pounded so hard nausea welled up in her tight throat, making it hard to breathe.

Diana always uses the front door. Never this one.

Shaking, Venus searched through her tote, frantically throwing out her wallet and makeup bag until at last she found her iPhone.

She punched contacts for Diana's number.

Her fingers trembled so badly *default* came up.

Sucking in a deep, ragged breath, she tried again.

This time the call went through.

On the third ring fear shuddered through her.

What if Diana had arrived early and interrupted a robbery.

On the fourth ring, Diana answered.

Weak with relief, Venus slumped against the wooden post of the overhanging porch. "Where are you?"

"Still at home. Isn't our meeting at eleven before my appointments at Clayworth's?"

"Thank God you didn't get here early like you usually do," Venus whispered, cupping her hand around her iPhone. "I'm at the back door of the store. I think it's been burgled or is being burgled."

"I'll call the police. I'm coming. Don't go in," Diana commanded, her voice deliberately soft and soothing, yet firm.

Willing her pulse to stop pounding, Venus dropped the phone into her tote and bent down to pick up her wallet and makeup bag.

Her body felt heavy, as if she could only move in slow motion. Like in a nightmare when she needed to flee but her legs wouldn't move, only run in place.

Time seemed to stand still.

Too slow for me.

Kicking out with the left toe of her thigh-high black leather boots, she nudged at the door until it swung open.

Silent, half-lit by the sunlight filtering in from the large front window, the store loomed empty and trashed in front of her.

"Oh, no," she screamed, rushing in to turn on lights.

Display cabinets and tables lay toppled on their sides. Broken glass winked on the Oriental rugs where hundreds of pieces of vintage jewelry lay tangled and broken.

Tears of rage nearly blinding her, she twirled around to scan the room. The clothes were all hung as neatly in their closets without doors as she'd left them after doing Rebecca's TV show yesterday.

She dashed into the smaller side room. The art deco vanity table with triple mirrors rested in a sea of crushed hat boxes, delicate hats with their feathers and veils broken or torn, purses yawning open, and balls of white tissue paper strewn across the wood floor.

What were they looking to find?

Through the half-open powder room door, she saw no one could be hiding in the tiny space.

Out of the corner of her eye, she glimpsed the brown velvet dressing-room curtain move.

Anger and fear gave her a rush of adrenaline. Grasping her tote like a weapon ready to swing, she yanked the curtain aside.

Only then did she feel the breeze coming in through the back door she'd left open.

She swung around, her eyes searching the hushed, empty room.

There's only one last place for anyone to hide.

At the top of the stairs leading down into the basement storage for off-season merchandise and items to be repaired, she hesitated.

Hadn't she read somewhere about thieves never going into basements because they had no escape route?

She flipped on the light. The first step creaked under her boot.

A pounding on the front door shot shock and a jabbing fear through every nerve in her body. She gripped the hand rail to keep from falling. Sucking in a deep breath for courage, she turned toward the door.

Two stern-faced policemen with Diana behind them stared through the glass at her.

More relieved than she thought possible, Venus rushed to let them into the store.

Pushing past the men, Diana engulfed Venus in a tight hug.

"I told you not to come in here." Diana pulled back to gaze up at her. "Are you all right?"

Taking a deep, shuddering breath, Venus nodded. "There's no one here. I've checked everything on this floor. I was just ready to check out the basement."

The taller policeman surveyed the wreckage around them while the other officer headed down the stairs.

He emerged a few minutes later. "The perps were down there but it's all clear now."

Remembering the three trays of jewelry belonging to clients she'd left on her work table, Venus rushed down the steps.

The usually tidy, organized room looked like a bargain basement after a sale. All three drawers of her wooden file cabinet hung open. The clothing racks of off-season clothes had been riffled through, leaving dresses on the floor or half off their hangers.

Fresh tears burning her eyes, she picked up the empty felt-lined jewelry trays tossed on the floor.

"There were four Iradj Moini pieces. A fabulous En tremblant rose motif pin. A bouquet-of-flowers pin and earrings with hand-blown French glass petals and carved jade leaves. Plus two Kenneth Jay Lane legendary bib necklaces from the 1960s. They were both coral and turquoise. Highly rare and in demand. Both book pieces. All the K.J.L. and Iradj Moini pieces belonged to our customers and now they've all been lost while under my care."

Her knees felt strangely weak. Venus slumped down on her work chair. She felt Diana's small, strong hand on her shoulder and gripped it with tight fingers.

"I know, I know we'll work through this," Venus whispered, tears and rage burning in her throat. "But Diana, it's all just...so much. Why is all of this happening? All this pain and disillusionment since Clayworth's trashed Dad eight months ago. And now someone has trashed our store. I know they can't logically be connected but it feels like someone is out to get us."

Venus placed her hand protectively over the mermaid hanging between her breasts. "Bridget said she was afraid this brooch was bad luck, but I refused to believe it because it reminds me of happy times with Dad. Do you think she's right?"

Diana knelt in front of her, staring up with her clear, steady gaze. "No, I don't. And if Bridget didn't want the brooch, it should be yours if you love it so."

Wanting to believe her, Venus nodded. "Thank God I'm never taking this mermaid off or she would be gone, too."

Connor sat in front of his office computer, ready for his weekly Skype visit with Drew and Athena.

They came onto the screen, laughing, as Drew pulled Athena down onto his lap.

Even through the wavering images Connor saw happiness on their faces.

"Good morning. Everyone looks a little like Yoda on Skype, except the two of you."

"Thank you, Connor." Athena blew him a kiss.

"I received the sales figures from last week you sent me. Looks good heading into the holiday season." Drew's voice sounded serious and his face was intent, but Connor noticed how his fingers were slowly stroking Athena's shoulder.

Hearing his office door open, Connor looked up. "Aunt Bridget is here." He pulled the extra chair closer so she could see the screen.

"Hi, you two. You're lookin' good. Havin' fun?"

"The best." Athena smiled. "How are you, Bridget?"

"Better since Venus helped me clean my closet."

Athena's startling aquamarine eyes widened, just as Venus's had done when she'd looked up and seen Connor standing in his aunt Bridget's closet door.

Athena sat up straighter. "Venus helping you is really, really good news, Bridget."

"Sure was good for me. Tony and Connor were threatenin' to do it themselves."

The surprise on both Athena and Drew's faces made Connor smile.

"You . . . you were there, too, Connor?" Athena sounded breathless.

Drew leaned closer to the monitor, cheek to cheek with Athena. "I don't see any battle wounds, buddy."

Wait until I ask for the mermaid brooch back. "Both Venus and I were painfully polite."

"That's a start." Drew kissed the top of Athena's shining golden head. "See you both same place, same time next week."

Beside him, Bridget laughed. "What do you call your holiday again?"

"An engagement-moon," they shouted in unison before the screen went black.

"Seein' the two of them like that warms my insides." Bridget sighed. "I couldn't be happier today."

Connor tried to read his aunt's flushed face. "How is Uncle Tony feeling this morning?"

She stood up so quickly the chair hit the desk. "Now don't start in again, Connor. Tony's fine. I'm fine. Now I have an appointment. I'll see you later."

The way she hurried out of his office, avoiding his eyes, told Connor all he needed to know.

Ten minutes later he climbed into his car. Walking through the executive parking lot, he noticed Diana's spot was empty.

Maybe she's at Pandora's Box. I hope so. We usually need a referee when Venus and I clash.

Connor saw the flashing blue lights on the two police cars before he realized they sat parked in front of Pandora's Box.

Three women, one pushing a double stroller, and two men stood on the sidewalk peering through the large picture window of the store where one mannequin lay toppled on her side.

What the hell has happened now?

Adrenaline pumping, Connor ignored the tape across the entrance and ran into the store.

Venus and Diana stood with a policeman, staring down at the wreckage of tables and cabinets. Jewelry pieces in all colors and shapes lay tangled across the Oriental rugs.

Venus glanced up, her aquamarine eyes opaque with tears. She seemed to recoil when she saw him. "What are you doing here?" She turned to her sister. "Did you call Clayworth's?"

"No, I only called Dad." Diana shook her head and cast Connor a look that burned his skin.

It feels like she's trying to read my mind.

The feeling vanished when Diana cast her eyes around the room and finally settled on him. "Connor, obviously you can see that someone broke into the store last night or early this morning."

"They took all our most expensive pieces of jewelry." Venus wiped away tears. "Plus several pieces belonging to our clients that we were repairing or sending to New York for repairs."

He'd always hated to see anyone upset. Now Venus looked more upset and vulnerable than he'd ever seen her. She struck the same protective chord in him that she always had since they were kids.

Diana put her arm around her sister's shoulders. "I know it will be an insurance nightmare, but we'll handle it."

What the hell, I've got to help her. "You need professional help with this." He took out his phone. "I'm texting Ed to come over here."

Blinking away tears, Venus stared up at him. He steeled himself against her unveiled contempt.

"We can handle this without any Clayworth help. We don't want or need it."

The policeman cleared his throat, and they all looked at him. "Sorry to interrupt, but I need to ask how you knew about this situation, Mr. O'Flynn."

He'd been so focused on Venus he hadn't recognized Jack from the Addison Street Police Station. "Sorry, Jack. I didn't know about the robbery. I came here concerning another problem. Do you have any clues so far?"

Jack shook his head. "I've questioned the neighbors.

No one heard or saw anything. Looks like the perps were pros. Disabled the alarm, and it's not an easy one. My partner has filed the report while I finished questioning the ladies." He nodded toward them. "I appreciate your cooperation. I've got everything I need for the moment."

"Thank you," Diana said softly.

"Yes, thank you so much." Venus blinked hard, more tears flicking down her pink cheeks. "I'm sorry to be weeping like some drama queen, but the pieces in this store represent people's lives. They're all precious to me."

"I understand, Miss Smith. Someone will be in touch." Jack turned away, giving Connor a sympathetic squint. "Hope you get your problem solved."

No chance. Aunt Bridget's brooch is gone and I've got another Smith mess to sort out.

He felt Venus watching him and he stared back, determined to do the right thing, even though he knew in his gut this would be trouble.

She twisted a thick piece of apricot-colored hair around two fingers. "*I* can certainly handle this without you or any Clayworth help. But I'm not saying no to Ed's help. I'm *thinking* about it." Twisting more hair between her fingers, she stared him down with her usual thinly veiled dislike. "The insurance papers are in the file cabinet in the basement. I'll go find them. Diana, watch the store until I get back up here."

He'd swear Venus's hand trembled when she gripped the stair railing.

The worried look Diana shot after her fired Connor's admittedly inflated sense of justice, his need to right wrongs. "I know Venus hates my guts because of your father, but I need to convince her to accept help."

Again Diana seemed to be looking through him, and

then she nodded. "Yes, go convince her to accept your help. It's the right thing to do."

Venus heard the stairs groan under heavy footsteps. Not Diana, who moved as lightly as the proverbial feather.

Connor.

She curled her fingers around the drawer of the wooden file cabinet to stop them from trembling. Sure, she'd been angry and frightened by this horrible violation of her store. Didn't think she could feel any worse until Connor walked in and added confusion to the mix.

He's only been in the store once. With Drew. How did Connor arrive on the heels of the robbery? Could he have something to do with the break-in?

She took a deep breath, telling herself the idea was crazy even though *she'd* put nothing past him after the way he'd so coldly treated her father.

Feeling him hovering behind her, she swung to confront him. "What do you want, Connor? Why are you here in the first place?"

"I want to help you." His voice rang rich with sincerity and his emerald eyes bored into her as if nothing mattered more than she did.

For one surreal instant she believed him. The next she remembered that lawyers learned early to fake sincerity.

"Please, Venus, for your sake hear me out," he asked with that same note of concern.

Again, the feeling that this moment must be an omen, like what she'd felt in the café with Bridget, rushed into her numbed mind. Someone had committed this horrible act against her, but because of it she now had this opportunity to get closer to Connor.

Only by getting close to him do I have any chance of learning the truth and helping Dad.

She took a deep breath, hating when it sounded so ragged. "I'm listening."

"Ed Mahoney has been Clayworth's insurance specialist for years. And his father before him. You'll need his expertise when it comes to your clients' stolen property and your liability."

"Venus!" Her father's deep voice called to her from the top of the staircase before he started down the steps.

"Dad!" she screamed, and flew into his open arms.

"I was at home working on my goddess book when Diana called. I'm so sorry. I know how much Pandora's Box means to you."

Venus untangled herself from her father's warm, loving embrace. Sensing he hoped she'd behave well and *needing* to be nice for her own reasons, she forced herself to smile up at Connor and bat her eyelashes. Tears she hadn't realized were still there flicked hot and stinging on her cheeks.

"Everything's a mess, Dad. But Connor...Connor has offered to help us."

The tenseness across her father's shoulders seemed to relax. Seeing it made her sacrifice worth it.

He turned to Connor. "Thank you. Ed has arrived. He told me you've asked him to help with the insurance. He's waiting upstairs for you."

Her father's coolness couldn't be more different from his manner toward Connor before this whole mess started. Venus felt his sadness in every cell of her body.

"Thanks. I'll go talk to him now." Connor stared into her eyes with the same open, intent look that earlier had momentarily thrown her off balance. "Venus, I promise this will work out."

Determined to wipe the defeated glaze out of her father's eyes by uncovering the truth, Venus focused on making it happen. Hoping she looked like a damsel in distress Connor needed to rescue, she smiled faintly at him and then watched him bound up the staircase.

Her father pulled her tight to his side. "I know this is difficult for you because of me. Despite the trouble between our families, I believe you've made the right decision in allowing Connor to help."

More confused than ever by his feelings for the Clayworths, Venus twirled a piece of hair around her fingers. "I don't understand how you can still trust any of them after what they did to you."

Sadness settled in the depths of his eyes and etched itself on the strong bones of his face. "Venus, I wish I could tell you more. I can only say again that I became entangled in their troubles. Which are deep." He pressed a kiss on the top of her head. "Trust me, my impetuous Venus, Connor will help with your problem if he can."

Thinking of her father's problem and not the store's, she laid her cheek on his shoulder, fingering the mermaid hanging on a chain between her breasts. "Oh, I hope you're right, Dad, and Connor will help me."

Torn by her love for her father and her absolute heart-and-soul certainty that he would try to stop her from finding out the truth through Connor, she vowed to do it regardless of the cost to her or the Clayworth family.

Trust me, Dad, I'll do whatever it takes to convince Connor to absolve you of all wrongdoing.

Even after all these months, when Connor saw Alistair it still felt like he'd been punched in the solar plexus, the one blow guaranteed to bring a man to his knees. The way he'd felt when he'd finally realized how Alistair had betrayed him and his family. He'd never trust anyone again as much as he had Alistair. Connor had hated what he'd had to do as much as Venus appeared to hate him for doing it.

Now I have a different Smith problem to solve.

Putting on his lawyer facade, he walked to where Ed stood talking to Diana near the large front window. Through the glass Connor saw a few people were still curiously peering inside.

"Thanks for getting here so quickly, Ed."

"I came as soon as I received your message." Ed's face appeared ruddier than usual above his tight white starched shirt collar and he sounded out of breath.

"This is most disturbing," he declared in a deep rumbling sigh. Frowning, he clasped one of Diana's hands between his wide palms. "I deeply regret this violation of your beautiful establishment. My dear Maxie is one of your most devoted clients. I'm sorry my first visit must be under these circumstances. With your permission I need to examine the premises before I review your insurance documents."

"Thank you. Do whatever you need to do." Diana smiled as Ed headed to the broken back door.

Watching Ed, Connor tried to reassure her. "Don't be fooled by his flowery manners. He's the best and tough as they come."

"I know." Diana sighed. "Calling him in was a great idea. I really do appreciate it. And I know Venus does, too. She feels responsible for finding good homes for all the treasures here. She thinks of them as the discarded dreams of others that are getting a second chance at making people happy."

Yeah, I get it, and now she's under my skin in a different way.

He shrugged, trying to rid himself of the way Venus made him feel. "Glad I'm here to help you both. What else do you need?"

Diana glanced around the wrecked room. "A cleaning crew."

Remembering his meeting with Gregori about his doing additional community service by cleaning the gym, Connor smiled. "You've got it. I'll go take care of that now."

"Before you leave I need to know why you came here this morning, Connor."

Diana's eyes seemed to grow larger, filling her tiny face. Again, he had the craziest feeling she could read his thoughts.

"Did you come about Bridget's mermaid brooch? It's so beautiful and old it must be a family heirloom."

He jerked back his head in shock. *How did she know?* "I did come about the brooch. Yes, it is special. I'm sorry I'll have to tell Aunt Bridget it was stolen."

Diana shook her head. "It surely would have been stolen if it had been here. It's safe. Venus is wearing it as a pendant under her blouse. She swears she's never taking it off."

Chapter 5

Bridget walked into Connor's office at Clayworth's while he was still on the phone ordering clean-up equipment to take to Pandora's Box.

"Why is Gregori workin' out in your private gym? I thought it was you in there punchin' away at that bag, makin' all the racket."

Connor hung up the phone and moved quickly around the desk to her side.

"He's going with me to help clean up Pandora's Box. It was burgled last night or early this morning. The thieves took all their most expensive pieces. Plus jewelry belonging to customers left there for repairs." He watched for her reaction, hoping to get a clue to what in the hell might be going on. "Your mermaid brooch is safe, by the way. Venus is wearing it."

Abruptly, Bridget dropped down into the black leather chair in front of the desk. "I knew Venus wanted the brooch for herself. It seemed special to her. I'm glad it's safe." She shook her head. "This is awful news. Tony's company installed the security system in their store. It's top of the line. He'll want to know about this. How are the girls takin' it?"

Remembering Venus's eyes luminous with tears, Connor shook his head. "Venus is taking it hard. I'm going over there now to help get the place back in order. The thieves trashed it."

His aunt tilted her head, studying him. "You're goin'? Why don't you send a cleanin' crew from the store?"

"Drew would expect me to help Athena's sisters." If he had other reasons he needed to keep them to himself for now.

"And you always do what's expected of you." Sighing, Bridget rose slowly to face him. "I'm not disagreein' about helpin' the girls. They're all three dear to my heart. But you're goin' to be busy the next few weeks. Your mother called to arrange for the corporate jet to pick her up in Palm Beach and fly her to Chicago. She's bringin' a friend. Mugsy Osborn. And her daughter, CeCe."

"Perfect." Sighing, he leaned against the edge of his desk, recalling his mother's last visit. "At least she's only offering up one candidate. Last year she brought home twin sisters." He smiled. "I must admit they presented some interesting moments."

Bridget gave him one of her stern looks, but her mouth curled up. "You know your mother and I have never agreed on much. God forgive me but I understand her wantin' you to find a wife. But I'm for lettin' you do the choosin'. She has her idea of the right type for you and nothin' will change her mind."

"Thank you, Aunt Bridget, for finally trusting me to be old and wise enough to find my own mate."

After last night, it felt good to hear her rich *real* laughter.

"Don't try to be funny, Connor. Save your sense of humor for your mother. You'll need it. She's bought a table for the Service Club Gala next Friday at the Four Seasons Hotel. You're to escort all three ladies." She kissed his cheek and chuckled. "But don't you worry. Tony and I are also her guests. You know how we love to run interference for you."

Resigned to the inevitable, he straightened, flexing his shoulders. "I look forward to it. But now I have a more important date to keep, with Venus."

Venus sent Ed away with a thick folder of insurance papers clasped to his chest. But her dad resisted her efforts to be alone.

He cupped her face with his palms. "You've always been my staunchest helper. I want to be here for you."

She gazed up into his dear face, determined to say and do what she thought best for him.

"Dad, I *know* you're always in my corner. But remember, *I'm* the expert on vintage jewelry, so I must inventory the damage myself. There is nothing you can do here. Honestly."

He kissed her nose, as he'd done for as long as she could remember when she frustrated him but he was giving in. "You got your stubbornness from your mother."

"Remember, you told me that's good." She laughed.

Sighing, he stepped back. "Yes. Very good indeed. All right, I'm leaving. But I'm only a phone call away. Love you," he whispered.

"Love you so much," she whispered back, watching the door close behind him. "Okay, you, too." She turned to her sister. "We set our meeting early this morning so you wouldn't miss your appointment at Clayworth's to work on the windows. Go before you keep your staff waiting. You hate that."

Diana gave her a quick, tight hug. "I know you want to be alone. I'll be back as soon as I finish. Promise."

Venus locked the door against the curious people who still stopped to peer through the window. Turning her back, she moved deeper into Pandora's Box. She didn't want anyone to hear her sobs or see tears dribbling down her hot cheeks while she wandered between the two rooms.

The first item she picked up off the floor was a small black velvet hat by local milliner John Koch. His little designs, all handmade and unique, were customer favorites. Everyone called them happy hats because John's creations made everyone smile. Now this little confection of lace, veil, and velvet looked sad. She untangled the twisted fine netting, being careful not to tear it. Pleased she'd restored the hat to its elegant state, she placed it carefully back on the shelf.

A brown alligator bag from the 1960s lay half hidden under balls of white tissue paper. Before she stuffed more tissue back into the handbag to help it keep its shape, she examined it for any damage. She repeated the same routine with a small black beaded evening bag.

Inconsequential actions compared to what lay in wait for her in the next room.

Knowing she had to face the disaster that had been her jewelry displays, she turned back to it.

Trying to view the wreckage as dispassionately as possible, she made a mental list of what she'd need to clean up the mess.

Number one. Rent an industrial-strength shop-vac to get the glass off the rug.

But first she'd have to carefully pick up every single piece of jewelry and examine and gently clean them all.

Rummaging through the back room, she located latex gloves and thick towels.

Determined to get started, she slipped on the gloves, placed two towels on the rug, knelt on them, and heard glass crush under her knees.

She untangled a gold-plated 1970s Dior necklace, picking tiny shards of glass from the settings of paste cabochons and faux pearls. Holding her breath, she checked the clasp and links. If broken, the metalwork could rarely be resoldered. Soft base metals couldn't be reheated.

At last, satisfied that this piece hadn't been damaged, she sighed and placed the necklace on the extra towel beside her.

Amidst the colorful jewels strewn across the Oriental rug, a semimatte Russian gold bracelet by Joseff of Hollywood, a copy of one worn in her favorite Cary Grant film, *To Catch a Thief*, caught her eye.

How appropriate!

A loud rap on the front door again sent a hot wave of fear through her. She swung around to face it.

Shock rooted her to the towels.

Why is Connor back?

Completely ignoring the tape she hadn't yet removed, he stood outside with a young man, a monster red shopvac, and huge padded blankets like those movers used to wrap furniture.

The second time he knocked and motioned to the shopvac, she forced herself to scramble to her feet and yank open the door.

"Hi. This is Gregori. He works out at my Golden Gloves Gym. We've come to help clean up."

Too stunned to stop him, Venus allowed Connor, carrying the padded blankets, to stroll past her into the store.

The teenager dragging the shop-vac stared at her, his

mouth open, a tiny diamond winking at the tip of his tongue. "You're the lady on Mr. O'Flynn's TV."

Utterly confused, she turned to Connor. She'd never noticed before how his blush started at the tips of his perfect ears.

"Gregori saw you on Rebecca's show last night at the gym."

"Yeah, you looked smokin' hot." He shifted from sneaker to sneaker. "That's a compliment, you know."

"Thank you." She smiled. Needing to understand why Connor had come back, she looked at him rolling up the sleeves of his blue striped button-down shirt.

"Tell us where to begin. We need to pick up jewelry first, right?"

"*We?*" she gasped.

"Sure. I told you, Gregori and I are here to help. I would have sent a cleaning crew from Clayworth's but I know how delicate some of these pieces must be and how much they mean to you."

A strange, powerful warmth filled her chest and she caught her breath. "What's going on, Connor?" Regardless of the fact that she felt a little light-headed, she stared him down.

He shrugged, staring right back at her. "I asked Diana what I could do to help. She said clean up. Here we are."

For reasons Venus would *never* understand, Diana still insisted on working for Clayworth's and loved it. Given that Diana owned as much of Pandora's Box as Venus did, how could she refuse?

"We're cool, right? Me and Mr. O'Flynn brought gloves and everything. Want us to start where you were workin'?" Gregori threw the thickly padded large mover's blankets on and around her towel.

"Sure," she muttered, feeling as if she should pinch herself to make sure she wasn't dreaming that Connor Clayworth O'Flynn, one of the most powerful men in the city, was down on his knees picking up jewelry in her ransacked store.

He glanced up, his eyes a bright green in the beams of sunlight streaming through the large window. "Where should we put these pieces?"

For one insane moment he looked so sweet and sexy she felt such a tug of attraction she needed to run away.

"I'll get trays." She fled to the basement, retrieving jewelry trays and her sanity.

I'm supposed to make him like me, not the other way around.

Deliberately picturing her father's face, calling up all her old feelings of dislike and betrayal, she put them on like armor. She staggered back upstairs, laden with confusion and trays.

If she'd had a third hand she'd have been playing with her hair, a dead giveaway that she hadn't figured this out yet.

Gregori jumped up to help her. "Let me take this stuff. Me and Mr. O'Flynn been talkin'. Don't want you to cut yourself or nothin'. We'll do the dirty work, but we'll be real careful. Then you can wash your stuff off and put all the pieces nice and pretty on the trays."

Did Connor know she could read the plea in his eyes not to rain on Gregori's chivalry?

As if I would.

"What a fabulously kind idea, Gregori. Thank you so much. Please place only a few pieces on each tray so nothing becomes tangled." She pointed to the brown velvet swag beyond the counter. "I'll be back there cleaning while you pick up."

Presenting it like a gift, Gregori held out the first tray, with two brooches, one bracelet, and two pairs of earrings spaced neatly apart. "Cool. I'll bring the trays to you as quick as we fill them up."

She gladly fled behind the curtain to escape Connor's grateful smile. Obviously she must be in shock or having some kind of meltdown. Why else would she have this warm, fuzzy feeling watching Connor on his knees, talking softly to Gregori while they helped her? If Connor wanted to charm her he was close to succeeding despite her armor of protective dislike and distrust.

But why would he bother? He never has tried before.

Those questions ran over and over in her head while she took a very small soft brush plus water mixed with a tiny amount of gentle liquid cleaner and gave each piece of jewelry a few strokes, then rinsed and patted each dry with tissue paper, making sure none were left damp to rot the foil backing behind the stones.

"Mr. O'Flynn, did you cut yourself through the gloves?"

Gregori's alarmed shout reached her behind the curtain.

Her stomach knotted.

I may want to kill Connor but I don't want him to hurt himself helping me.

"I'll get the first-aid kit," she called, swooping it out of a drawer.

When she reached him, Connor was sucking on his index finger.

"What are you doing?" She fell to her knees beside him and took a sterile wipe out of the kit.

The tips of Connor's ears turned red. "Hell, Venus, it's nothing."

"Let me see." She grabbed his hand, cleaned his long

finger with the wipe, and examined his smooth, tanned skin for cuts.

Gregori snickered. "When I get hurt my ma kisses it to make it better."

She dropped Connor's hand as if she'd been burned. "You're fine."

"I told you it was nothing." He slid Gregori a stern look and handed her another tray. "Here."

Taking it, she scrambled to her feet and escaped back behind the curtain.

Two hours and four trays full of salvaged jewelry later, she still hadn't figured out Connor and why she'd felt almost *close* to him. The second time Gregori presented her with a new tray and she heard his stomach growl and saw his embarrassed grin, she knew it must be more than time for a break, both from work and from her curiosity about why Connor continued to be positively charming. And why she hadn't thrown him out in an indignant huff of pent-up anger toward him, instead of being, well, *almost* attracted to him. This perfect opportunity to get closer to him had fallen into her lap and she couldn't seem to make the first move.

For heaven's sake be creative!

The old adage, *the way to a man's heart is through his stomach,* popped into her head. "It's two o'clock. Who wants lunch?"

Gregori's arm shot up. "Me."

"I'll go." With absolutely no apparent struggle, Connor sprang to his feet. He flexed his shoulders and she saw muscles rippling under his shirt. "Anything close?"

Since she'd first thought about Connor looking like the statue of David, she couldn't get the picture out of her mind every time she saw him. She blinked to get her focus away from his bare chest glimpsed where his shirt hung open two buttons. "Yes. Sola. Around the corner. They have great food. Especially their short rib sandwich."

"Got fries?" Gregori asked.

Venus laughed. "Their truffle fries are to die for."

Connor glanced between them. "Short rib sandwiches and fries all around?"

Of course she should order a simple salad with dressing on the side but really she needed comfort food. "Absolutely."

She swore she saw Connor's almost-smile before he strolled out the door.

"You got pretty stuff in your store."

She watched Gregori roam around the shop and stop in front of the vintage day wear. "My mom would like these dresses."

"Oh, does your Mom like vintage?"

He shrugged. "Don't know. She likes pretty stuff. Don't have much since my dad left us. That's why she's lookin' for a job."

Her heart ached at the sadness in his young eyes. "I know it's tough right now. I hope your mom finds something soon."

"Me, too." Gregori stretched. "Hey, got any soda?"

"Oh, no, we forgot drinks." She hurried around the counter. "I'll run and tell Connor."

"You're leavin' me here alone?"

The shock on his face stopped her. "I don't think there's any danger now."

"Fu..." he stopped, flushing. "...I ain't afraid. You trust me to stay with all your stuff?"

Of course she knew if he worked out in Connor's gym he had had problems, but she nodded, wanting to reassure him. "Absolutely. I know you'll keep everything here safe, right?"

Venus swore he seemed to grow taller before her eyes. "Ain't nothin' goin' to be gone from here."

"Great! I'll be right back."

Around the corner, she found Connor, a breeze ruffling his thick dark hair, where he sat at one of the tables on the sidewalk outside Sola.

When he saw her, he frowned and stood up. "What's wrong? Is it Gregori?"

She tried to read his face as Diana would have done.

Except Diana is like a psychic, usually figuring it out. Not like me.

"Nothing is wrong, except I forgot drinks. I came to tell you to bring some soda for Gregori."

Connor gave her the oddest look. It seemed to her to be a combination of sweetness, surprise, and gratitude.

The same warmth she'd felt earlier curled through her chest.

"You trusting him will mean a great deal to Gregori," Connor said softly.

Embarrassed by this startling feeling of intimacy, as if they were sharing something special, she started playing with her hair. "It means a great deal to me that the two of you are helping. Why are you doing this, Connor? Not just because Diana said we needed help with cleanup."

He seemed to stiffen ever so slightly. "Since Drew and Athena are off on his yacht celebrating their engagement, I feel it's my responsibility to help you."

Maybe it was the odd intimacy she'd felt holding his hand and now again standing a shade closer than she would normally have done, or maybe it could be delayed shock from the robbery, or maybe her reckless nature finally broke through her guard. The question she needed answered burned in her throat.

"If you really truly want to help me you'll explain what happened at Clayworth's and why you fired my father and ruined his reputation."

The air became very still around them. Even the noisy traffic on Lincoln Avenue faded into the distance.

Connor narrowed his eyes until they were emerald slits. "You know both your father and the Clayworth family signed an antidefamation clause."

"Drew has already broken it by telling Athena Dad made some questionable investments that put Clayworth's in jeopardy. But I know that isn't reason enough for you to destroy his life," Venus snapped, unable to stop herself.

Connor shook his head. "Legally Drew should never have divulged any details of this situation, but I've given him a pass. A man in love doesn't always use his head."

Liquid fire ran through her veins. *If you like me, maybe you'll tell me what I need to know.*

"Everyone has agreed to this." Connor watched her, as she imagined he must study his opponents in the courtroom, but his words seem to come from far away beyond the pounding of her heart. "Why can't you, Venus?"

"I can't because my father deserves better and you know it," she whispered, fighting back tears.

The blaze in his wide-open emerald eyes gave her one answer, his silence another.

Shocked and trembling at her core, she twirled and ran back around the corner.

She saw Diana, Tony, and a man with what looked like a tool box walk into Pandora's Box.

Her heart kept pounding in her chest, not because she had run so fast she felt breathless, not because she'd tried the straightforward approach and it hadn't worked, but it pulsed through every cell of her body because of what she'd been able to read at last in Connor's eyes.

Reaching the door to her store, she rushed in and swayed to a stop behind the tool guy.

Legs braced apart, Gregori held everyone back from entering Pandora's Box more than a few feet.

"But I told you, I'm her sister," Diana said softly, peering up at Gregori.

"It's all right." Venus slipped around the two men to reach Diana's side.

Gregori's quick gaze darted between them. "I get it. You got the same eyes."

"You did a great job, Gregori. Mr. O'Flynn will be here in a few minutes with lunch."

"Connor is here?" Tony asked, a note of surprise in his deep voice.

"Yes. He and Gregori are helping me clean up."

"We're also here to help you." Tony held her hand. "My assistant and I will determine how your security system could have been compromised."

"Uncle Tony!" Connor called, elbowing his way through the door carrying two bags from Sola.

Knowing what she'd seen in his eyes, as if for one moment she'd been physic like Diana, Venus felt insanely grateful that her sister, Tony, and his helper were here to act as a buffer between her and Connor until he and Gregori finished and she could send them away.

Her skin tingled and her stomach burned with excitement and dread. She should be happy. Relieved. Not too terrified to be alone with him.

My crazy plan may work. Connor is as confused by me as I am by him. Now what do I do?

Chapter 6

In the John Clayworth and Company executive offices in their flagship store in the Chicago Loop, Connor paced back and forth from his desk to the windows overlooking State Street.

What in the hell should I do about Venus?

He threw himself into his leather desk chair and stared down at his notes. *It makes sense to stay away from her until I figure out why Tony and Bridget are upset and whether or not it's all about the brooch. If it is then Venus could get hurt.*

Remembering how his aunt and uncle had stonewalled his every question with poker faces even though tension quivered between them, Connor headed to the butler pantry next to his office to pour himself a drink.

He knew it was their problem and they wanted him to back off but he couldn't get past the idea that if he retrieved the mermaid brooch he could "make it right," as Tony had said.

He tossed back the neat scotch, feeling the burn down his throat. Like the burn in his gut trying to figure out how to get the brooch back when Venus supposedly had sworn to never part with it and only a real bastard would try to retrieve it from her when she seemed vulnerable.

Is vulnerable, you bastard.

Again, he paced to the window, factoring in her kindness to Gregori, which had complicated Connor's feelings toward her. He stared out at the traffic in the street below, seeing her face, and ached again for her disappointment when she'd point-blank asked about her dad and he couldn't in good faith answer.

Hell, she already hates my guts because of her father. Why am I so damned worried about making her dislike me even more over the brooch?

Decision made, he stalked out of his office toward Bridget's.

She met him in the hallway. "Your mother and her guests are on the way up here."

"Hell, I forgot they arrived today." Guilt and his mother were synonymous. Her guilt and his.

At the end of the hall, Victoria Clayworth O'Flynn appeared as she always had to him. Distant, fit, tanned, her hair as light as his was dark.

"Connor, my dear boy." She strolled toward him to offer her face for kisses.

He pressed his lips briefly to each cheek. "You look well, Mother."

"As do you. The image of your father." She stepped back, urging an older and a younger woman forward. "You must meet my dearest friend, Mugsy Osborn, and her ravishing daughter, CeCe."

His mother gave him a coy side glance. "CeCe has an MBA in finance from Stanford and has an important position with her family's financial firm. You two have much in common."

Mugsy looked like a clone of his mother, but with dark hair, which didn't swing quite as perfectly under her chin.

Looking at CeCe, surprise flashed through him like a warning.

Mother is getting serious about matchmaking.

As tall, willowy, and blonde as all her other candidates for his affection, CeCe had a glint of humor in her crystal-blue eyes that the others had sorely lacked.

"Clayworth's is magnificent, Connor. I may need to apply for a credit card to do some serious shopping."

"Consider it done." He smiled into her pretty face, relieved his mother's yearly two-week visit might not be as grueling as usual.

Beside him, his mother sighed, and behind her, his aunt cleared her throat.

"I'm Bridget O'Flynn. Victoria's sister-in-law."

Mugsy gave her a limp handshake, CeCe a stronger one.

"My apologies, Bridget. I was overcome with seeing my handsome son again after such a long time apart." Not a quiver of any emotion colored his mother's voice or showed on her face. He expected nothing else.

"If you want to spend more time with your son you should come back to Chicago more than once a year like you've been doin' since he was eight."

Wanting her to stop, Connor tried to catch Bridget's eyes. He knew from years of experience that she'd never forgive Victoria for what his aunt considered neglect of him even though he'd long ago accepted his mother's nature.

A bright flush crept across his mother's face, the one trait they shared and the one flaw she could never hide, although she tried. How many times had he heard her lecture him as a kid about its being unseemly to show emotions.

"You know I've always preferred the Clayworth Compound in Palm Beach and Connor and his father loved Chicago. Connor refuses to budge from here." With a blinding smile, she turned to Mugsy. "We had such a time convincing him to go to Groton for prep school."

Mugsy nodded. "Excellent choice. CeCe's brother went to Groton. Then on to Harvard."

The sharp look his mother flashed him reminded him of her disappointment when he'd chosen not to stay in the East. She masked it with a flutter of her eyelashes and a smile, but he'd seen it as she meant him to. He knew it was her way of showing she'd cared about his future. Her way of showing her affection in the only manner she felt comfortable.

"Connor refused to go anywhere but Northwestern for undergraduate and law school. Naturally he was editor of the law review."

"Northwestern is an excellent school, Victoria. The Stanford of the Midwest, they say." CeCe's smile caught all of them and lingered on his mother.

"How kind you are, CeCe." Sighing, her hand fluttered to the blue-and-white Hermès scarf around her throat. "We're exhausted from traveling. Connor, I trust you're coming to Lake Forest tonight for dinner. I'm preparing a new recipe to give to the cook."

The look passing between CeCe and Mugsy told him they'd been victims of his mother's dinner parties. If you didn't leave hungry, you left with indigestion.

"I have a better idea, Mother. Why don't you have the driver take you to Lake Forest and bring you back to the city. We'll have dinner in Club International at the Drake Hotel."

An avaricious gleam filled his mother's eyes. "I do enjoy their Bookbinder soup. And their special Club International salad is divine. Completely healthy, except for the quarter of hard-boiled egg," she assured Mugsy.

"Sounds wonderful." CeCe jumped at the offer. "It's a date, Connor. Seven-thirtyish?"

"It's a date." He watched the three women disappear into the executive elevator before meeting his aunt's eyes.

"I must say CeCe's an improvement over previous contenders your mom has dragged home. I'm impressed. How about you?"

"She's beautiful. Obviously bright. And has a sense of humor. What's not to like," he shrugged.

His aunt narrowed her eyes. "But…?"

She's not Venus.

"God in heaven, Connor, if you could see your face," she said, laughing.

Fighting to conquer the mindless urge to go to Venus *and do what?* he stared at his aunt. Then laughed, too, trying to cover his confusion. "It should be an interesting two weeks. Beginning with dinner tonight. Will you and Tony join us?"

Tilting her head, Bridget continued to watch him. "Sure, I wouldn't miss this for anythin'. Besides, I like their Red Snapper Bookbinder soup, too. Tonight I might even put in the full shot of sherry."

In the end, Connor put two full shots of sherry in his soup.

Seated at a round table between CeCe and his mother and across from Mugsy, he felt the full-court press coming from all sides.

More than once he met CeCe's amused eyes when the conversation veered dangerously close to a checklist of his eligibility as husband material, naturally delivered without a trace of unseemly emotion by his mother.

He leaned toward CeCe. "I promise you if my mother tells the story of my spelling my name in alphabet soup when I was two I'll plot our escape."

"I'm sure it will be as charming as your school pictures Bridget showed me during cocktails."

Surprised, he glanced over his shoulder at his aunt, who obviously must have heard because she shrugged innocently.

What he'd always liked about the low carved wood ceiling of this club was being able to actually have a conversation. Even as a kid it had seemed like a kind of Old World oasis behind the long windows facing North Michigan Avenue, Chicago's Magnificent Mile.

His dad and his Clayworth uncles had called it a hideaway to get business done. Nothing had changed. At a corner table the new mayor held court with his supporters. At another corner table near the windows, David Sumner seemed in deep discussion with other local media moguls.

"This Veuve Clicquot champagne is perfect with my salad and dover sole meunière, " his mother sighed, having eaten a real meal, possibly for the first time in weeks. "Would anyone care for more champagne?"

Mugsy waved her hand. "Please, Victoria, more for Tony and me." She beamed up at him, leaning closer. "We are having the most fascinating discussion about Friday's gala and about security." She stroked his arm. "Now tell me the truth, Tony, aren't dogs the best deterrent against home robbery?"

Tony's robust laughter caught Bridget's attention and she flicked a stern glance at Mugsy's hand on his arm.

"Bad for business to confess you're right, Mugsy. A large dog with a loud bark."

Connor avoided his aunt's eyes so he could control his urge to smile. Given the tension between her and Tony, it might not be bad for her to feel an innocent twinge of jealousy.

Connor reached into the ice bucket and found a fresh bottle of champagne.

The hovering waiter leaned over. "Mr. O'Flynn, Mr. Mahoney sent you the second bottle of Veuve Clicquot with his compliments."

From across the room, near the door, where Connor hadn't seen him, Ed saluted and strolled over.

His ruddy face split in a smile, Ed greeted each woman with flowery gallantry. "It is always a pleasure when you grace our fair city with your presence, Victoria. Your usual two-week visit, I hope."

Shivering, his mother glanced out the long windows. "If it begins to snow I confess I won't be able to get back to Palm Beach fast enough."

"Then let's hope for a very late Indian summer. I also hope to see all of you at the Service Club Gala on Friday."

"Tony has assured me we shall have several dance partners on Friday. Do you dance, Mr. Mahoney?" Mugsy asked, finally pulling herself away from Tony, who bore the look of a man under siege. Connor knew the feeling.

"I do indeed, Mrs. Osborn. I hope your dance card is not so full you can't honor me."

Looking pleased, Mugsy nodded. "I look forward to dancing with both you and Tony."

"Until then, ladies, enjoy your week in Chicago." He leaned down to Connor. "I'll have those insurance reports you requested done by tomorrow. I'll deliver the packet personally."

The burn in his gut hadn't gone away even after he'd

made his decision. Tomorrow he needed to make his next move.

The bell tinkled over the front door at Pandora's Box and Venus tensed.

Oh, stop hoping it's Connor, you idiot.

Annoyed beyond belief with herself, Venus strolled out to find a perfectly lovely young woman looking for a birthday present for her mother. She quickly decided on an Elsa Schiaparelli lava rock necklace with staggered rows of shocking pink lava stones suspended from a rhinestone-studded collar circa 1940s. Ten minutes later, she left with her mother's birthday gift beautifully wrapped.

Now I can go back to my embarrassing preoccupation with Connor.

Really, how could she *not* be confused by his flat-out refusal to tell her the truth about her father, countered by the look in his eyes telling her he wished he could because...

She shook her head, trying to rid herself of the possibility that the world had gone crazy because she and Connor were actually *attracted* to each other.

The door opened once more, and resisting the urge to twist her hair in confusion, she rammed her hands into the pockets of her long cashmere sweater.

Head held high, just in case it *might* be Connor, Venus swept around the brown velvet swagged curtain to the counter.

Maxie swished toward her. "I'm meeting Edward here when he comes with your insurance report. I apologize for arriving early but I couldn't wait another instant to give you my deepest condolences."

Disappointed way beyond what she should have been,

Venus had to force a smile. "Thank you, Maxie. I confess it's been grim, but having Ed's help has been a life-saver. May I get you something to drink while you're waiting?"

Maxie clutched her hands over her heaving bosom. "You are too kind but no, I'm much too concerned to take a morsel of food or drink. It's my fondest hope the signed Tess necklace and earrings I admired were not stolen."

"They're safe. I'll get them for you." Venus hurried back behind the heavy velvet swagged curtain to the shelf where she kept lay-away items. For some reason the thief had missed these treasures.

Listening to Maxie made her think about how some couples seemed to look alike after spending years together. Not Maxie with her big hair and trim but voluptuous body and bald, pudgy Ed, but they *sounded* so much alike.

Still smiling at the thought, Venus carefully placed the 1980s signed Tess pieces on a felt-lined tray. The milky white opaline, similar in color to opals and pink rhinestone necklace and earrings, glistened up at them.

"Yes, as beautiful as I remember." Maxie sighed. "I told Edward I wanted to wear the set to the anniversary dinner of our first date. It's our seventh wonderful year together." She whipped out her checkbook.

Again the tinkling bell and the door opening filled Venus with a hot eagerness that shocked her to her core.

Rebecca waltzed in, looking ravishing in a cobalt blue dress. The color made her skin glow as if she were lit from within. Beside her strolled her best friend, Kate, in her signature black.

"Hi, darlings," Rebecca called.

Maxie swung around. "Mrs. Covington-Sumner, I love your column," she gushed, wringing Rebecca's fingers.

"And Ms. Carmichael, you are a genius." Maxie rolled her eyes. "I never make an investment without reading your stock tips. And I never miss Rebecca's television program when you're on it."

Kate's apple cheeks grew positively rosy. "I'm pleased you've been helped by my work."

"Thank you, Maxie. We both truly appreciate your support and so do our sponsors." Rebecca's blinding smile seemed to transfix Maxie.

"Speaking of work, I must get back to mine." Kate nodded toward Venus. "I stopped by to say how sorry I am about your burglary. If I can do anything to help, please let me know."

"I will, Kate." Venus blew her a kiss as she slipped out.

Accustomed to Rebecca's effortless charm in fielding Maxie's questions about Chicago gossip, Venus kept smiling and finished writing up the receipt for the Tess pieces.

Startled, she gazed down in awe at Maxie's signature, almost like calligraphy, on her check.

"Wow, Maxie, you have beautiful penmanship."

She beamed. "I grew up in the Italian neighborhood around Taylor Street. The nuns were adamant about perfect penmanship. Now it's a hobby of mine."

"It's lovely. I had good penmanship once. Now I'm sloppy. I wonder what that says about me." Rebecca laughed, looking at Maxie's elegant scroll.

"I took an extended course on handwriting analysis. It would be my honor to do you," Maxie offered.

"Thank you, but I'd be afraid of what you'd learn about me." All at once Rebecca swayed, color draining from her cheeks to make her skin blue white. "That's odd. I feel really lightheaded."

Concerned, Venus rushed around the counter to

urge Rebecca down onto the cream settee. "Did you eat breakfast?"

"Never." Rebecca looked sheepish. "I know I should but I'm never hungry until lunchtime."

"Me either." Maxie smoothed her skin-tight dress over her trim hips. "It's a struggle to maintain our girlish figures."

"Well, you need food now." Happy to do something positive, *everyone should eat breakfast,* Venus hurried to the small refrigerator in her office alcove and retrieved a small bottle of orange juice. "Here. Drink it."

Rebecca sipped delicately. "Really, I'm fine. David will be coming to pick me up soon. When I tell him I feel lightheaded he'll no doubt make me see the doctor. Men!"

She said it with such intense emotion in her voice that Venus got a tight feeling in her chest.

"It's because he loves you so much," Venus said, happy for her.

"I know," Rebecca sighed, her eyes misty. "I've never been happier in my life."

"I'll wait right here to keep you company until your David arrives." Maxie plopped down on the settee. "I feel the same way about my Edward. Mark my words, when my Edward arrives he'll make Venus happy by making everything right for her."

Again Venus fingered her mermaid talisman, wishing for luck with Ed and torn between hope and dread that Connor might be with him.

Connor glanced at his watch. *Why in the hell is Ed taking so long to get those insurance papers to Venus?*

Accustomed to making a decision and taking action, he felt uneasy about this one. Thinking of Venus always put him on edge. Now more than ever.

Restless, he headed down the hall to try to get answers from his aunt one last time.

When he walked into her office, she stood at the window, staring out.

"Aunt Bridget, can we talk?"

She twirled around. For a split second her guard slipped and he saw the pain she'd been trying to hide from him on her face. Then she covered it and smiled, walking toward him.

"Sure. What can I help you with? Business or pleasure? You're not cancelin' our weekly Wednesday night pizza date because your mom's in town, are you? Tony made the crust this morning."

He shook his head. "Wouldn't miss it. Tony makes the best pizza on the planet. Maybe tonight we can talk about what's bothering both of you."

The look she gave him made him feel ten years old again, knowing he'd screwed up and waiting for the lecture he knew would come.

"Now, Connor, I told you this is a little misunderstandin' between me and Tony. Nothin' for you to be concerned about." She headed toward the door. "Concentrate on Venus's problems, where you can make a difference. Ed's ready to head over there. Let me get him for you."

Connor heard her in the hallway calling to Ed and a minute later he leaned in through the open office door.

"I'm leaving now for Pandora's Box. I've completed my report for Venus."

"I'm going with you."

Ed puffed up his chest. "I assure you I will handle this situation with the utmost delicacy."

"I know you will, but I'm still going with you." After

this latest failed attempt to talk to his aunt, Connor knew he had his job to do whether he liked it or not.

In the small lot around the corner from Pandora's Box, Connor pulled into a parking space next to Ed. Walking toward the store, he saw a solemn-looking David Sumner help Rebecca into the passenger seat of his Bentley.

By the time Connor reached the car, Rebecca had the window open, waving at him.

He leaned down. "Is everything all right?"

David's face looked rigid with worry. "Rebecca's not feeling well."

She sent David such a blistering smile even Connor felt the heat. "You're such a worrywart. I'm perfectly fine." She blew Connor a kiss as David started the car. "I'm sure Venus will be delighted to see both of you."

Not me, when I ask for what I've come here to retrieve.

Venus looked up as the bell jiggled above their heads. Her smile sent a heat wave through him.

Hell, she can't be happy to see me.

From years in the courtroom he'd learned to read faces, but with her he had a history of guessing wrong.

No question about Maxie. With a cheerful yelp, she sprang up from the settee. "Edward, look, the Tess pieces I wanted for our anniversary dinner are still here." She held pink and opal-like earrings up to her ears. "I told Venus you would have good news for her, too."

Glancing between him and Ed, Venus widened her eyes. "Or is the news so bad Connor had to come for moral support?"

"On the contrary, Venus. I have prepared a full report, which I believe will reassure you."

Venus blinked at the thick folder Ed placed in her hands.

"I'll help you go through it," Connor offered, wanting to be alone with her to do what needed to be done.

She hesitated so long that both Maxie and Ed cast him embarrassed looks. He stood his ground and stared unblinking into Venus's luminous eyes. He saw the second she made her decision.

"Thank you, Connor. I'd appreciate your help."

He motioned for Ed to get lost.

Looking relieved, Ed gripped Maxie's arm, moving her toward the door. "Have a good day. We'll leave you to your task."

When the door closed behind them, Venus heaved a huge, deep sigh. Her blouse opened with the movement of her breasts and he caught a glimpse of the mermaid.

"This could take some time." She lifted the thick folder as if she were weighing it in her hands. "I guess we should get to it."

Guilt ate at his gut but the memory of the tension between Bridget and Tony, plus the look on her face today, bit stronger.

"First, I need to ask you for a favor, Venus."

Tossing her hair over her shoulder, she seemed to tense. "What is it?"

"I want to buy back my aunt Bridget's mermaid brooch."

With a thud, she dropped the folder onto the counter and clutched the brooch in the valley between her breasts. "Why?"

"Because Bridget regrets selling it to you. She wants it back." *It's a lie, she didn't say that, but I know it's true.* "It was a gift from Tony," he added, hoping to cinch the deal.

He might be lousy at reading her, but only a fool couldn't see she didn't believe him.

"Oh, my God, *this* is why you've been so nice to me. *This* is why you swore you wanted to help. *You wanted the mermaid brooch back!*" She laughed, but it broke at the end in a little gasp.

The disgust in her eyes hit him harder than it should have given their history of confrontation.

"All these years I thought you were totally devoid of the legendary Clayworth charm and here you are the absolute champ. The very best. So good at faking sincerity even *I* bought it." She flung back her head and glared into his eyes. "If Bridget really wants the brooch back all she has to do is ask me herself. Now I want you to leave."

As he always did when his emotions burned too strong to control, Connor felt his defenses snap into place to give nothing away.

"I promised to help you with the insurance papers."

"I believe you've *helped* me quite enough, thank you very much."

She marched to the door and flung it open. "Good-bye." She glared at him, her eyes blazing.

I've blown this big-time.

He knew it made sense to leave. She looked too angry to listen to reason and he held his emotions in such tight control he couldn't identify the feelings churning in his gut.

"Good-bye, Venus. We'll talk later."

"I doubt it," she said before slamming the door behind him.

Walking back to his car, the feeling he couldn't identify crystallized into regret.

He couldn't get Venus out of his mind. Hell, even while flirting with a beautiful, desirable woman he'd been thinking of her.

Another emotion surfaced. How many times had he told the kids at the gym that there was no substitute for desire?

Yeah, this hadn't been his finest hour, but he wasn't finished. He had every intention of picking his moment and trying again for the brooch and Venus.

Chapter 7

Hot, and a heartbeat later, shivering, Venus watched Connor walk away, replaying over and over in her head why she'd let her anger, *no, admit it, my disappointment*, get in the way of her plan to use her so-called feminine wiles on him after she'd waited in breathless anticipation for days to do it.

I should have been able to finesse my way through his being a jerk about the brooch to stick with my plan to help Dad.

Instead, the atmosphere when Connor left almost gave her frostbite. Shivering from the cold lump still in her stomach, Venus wrapped her arms around her waist. Only a fool wouldn't have figured out he was using his charm on her because he wanted something, just as she planned to use her supposed allure for getting information to help her dad.

So much for thinking Connor might be lusting after her. The only lust he felt was for getting back the mermaid brooch.

She pressed her palm against it, feeling its warmth between her breasts. *Well, he can't have it.*

She marched back to her office, threw herself onto the desk chair, and stared at her computer screen. There was a new email from Brad. He thought he probably wouldn't make it to Chicago for the Service Club Gala on Friday night.

She should feel disappointed or even angry at Brad for backing out of their plans, but she only felt relieved. Well, relieved and a little guilty, and it immediately cooled her anger at Connor. Relationships naturally run their courses but she could never seem to find the right words to end this one with Brad.

She might know everything about jewelry, but obviously she knew nothing about how to deal with men.

Sure, ever since she bloomed early, she'd been fielding jokes and lewd comments about Venus, Goddess of Love, while fending off guys eager to grope her assets. But obviously she still had a thing or two to learn about being persuasive and honest when it really, truly mattered.

Trying to keep busy, Venus dusted all the shelves in the store, vacuumed every inch of the floor, even glanced through the ream of paper Ed had left her, although all the facts, figures, and explanations blurred together. All the while she couldn't stop beating herself up because in her heart of hearts she knew why she'd never give the brooch to Connor, and it had nothing to do with her father and everything to do with her almost falling for Connor's fake charm.

Exhausted from confusion and anger, mostly at herself, Venus headed home to come up with a new battle plan. Obviously using their *mutual attraction* wasn't an option.

The minute she arrived at her town house she raced to the small loft she'd turned into a jewelry studio. The soft cream carpet and heavy luxurious crimson velvet drapes were like her own private jewel box.

Perching at her work table, surrounded by her personal collection of vintage costume jewelry, made her feel better. There was so much she loved about all these pieces. Their beauty reflected the era they were produced in, when workmanship and sometimes materials were often as good as or better than those used in "real" jewelry.

From the trays placed in careful rows in front of her, she lovingly picked out different pieces of broken vintage jewelry she'd found in her hunts through antique and junk stores.

A diamond and emerald paste gilt metal heart, which had once been part of a twin-hearts-and-bow pin. A silver cupid. A faux ruby serpent with its tail in its mouth.

That represents eternal love.

She dropped it back into the tray.

Realizing all the pieces she'd singled out were hallmarks of love in Victorian jewelry, she put them all back.

She quickly chose a Miriam Haskell chain and Trifari flowers from the dozens and dozens of fine vintage costume pieces she'd saved from destruction and restored to their former glory.

Giving them new life by putting them together in her own designs gave her such pleasure. Creating these designs was her private passion, a secret she couldn't bring herself to share with anyone yet.

She placed two Trifari flowers on the gold Miriam Haskell chain. Moved each piece to a different link, added a burnishing gold watch fob, and changed their positions again and again.

Tonight nothing caught her imagination.

Tonight nothing gave her the usual thrill.

Tonight it all made her think of Connor and Bridget's mermaid brooch.

Okay, so I'm thoroughly humiliated, but what if Connor is telling the truth?

Given how much she mistrusted all Clayworths and that Connor had just given her another reason to do so, her instincts said he lied.

But what if he isn't lying?

Hard as she tried, she couldn't get past the same nagging worries. Why else would he want the mermaid brooch back if not for his aunt? What if Bridget truly regretted her decision because Tony's feelings were hurt, just as Venus feared?

Maybe they were fighting about it. Maybe Connor could honest to goodness be trying to do something thoughtful for his aunt. After all, his devotion to Bridget and Tony was one of his few redeeming qualities.

Wistful about possibly returning it, Venus slid the brooch off the heavy chain she used when wearing it as a pendant.

She ran her fingertips across the perfect workmanship, the delicacy of the mermaid's face, the cascade of her aurora borealis hair, the magnificent facets of her rhinestone body.

She knew the trick with rhinestones was in the cutting to make them sparkle and here in the pure light of her studio this one had such brilliance it looked like a...

Shivers of shock ran along her skin.

No, it can't be. I must be imagining it.

Her fingers trembled, trying to focus her intense light and her most powerful magnifying glass directly on the brooch.

As it had outside the back door of Pandora's Box on the morning of the robbery, time seemed to stand still while she studied the mermaid.

A diamond. Her body is a diamond.

Disbelief burning her skin, Venus slowly turned the mermaid over. She focused her strongest lens, searching for the tiny unique marking she'd never in a million years thought to look for when she'd first found the brooch in Bridget's closet.

The mark is here.

She stared down at it for what seemed like hours while shock filled every cell of her body.

Still not believing, wanting to study the brooch from a different angle, she turned the mermaid face up.

She fell back in her chair, nearly hypnotized by the mermaid brought to all her true glory in the pure light of the studio.

This isn't a copy of the mermaid brooch stolen from Clayworth's. It is the original Eisenberg brooch, made of precious stones worth a small fortune.

Her heart banged against her ribs and nausea welled up in her throat as Bridget's words rang over and over in her ears.

"The brooch was a gift from Tony."

Waves of heat paralyzed Venus in her chair. The light bathing the mermaid blazed too bright, too revealing. The diamond at the heart of the brooch began to shimmer around its edges. Tormented by questions, she couldn't stop staring down at it, trying to find answers.

I need to tell Bridget the truth.

Venus jumped up, pushing away from the work table so hard the chair banged against the wall of the loft. The sound vibrated along her frayed, tingling nerves.

But what is the truth?

Did Connor know Tony stole the brooch, and did he want it back before Venus discovered the truth? But why would Tony steal? If for the money, why wouldn't he have sold it years ago? Did Bridget suspect the truth? And was that why she seemed so desperately unhappy? Would Connor turn on Tony, as he had turned on her father when he was accused of wrongdoing?

Afraid her trembling would cause her to drop the brooch, she picked it up with both hands, resting it on her palms.

Its beauty still enchanted her, but now the secrets it might reveal made her sick with raw dread.

A part of her despised what she planned to do. Another part accepted she had no choice.

As hard as she tried to stop shaking, it took her several failed attempts to slide the brooch back onto the chain and attach it around her neck.

The brooch burned against her skin and she placed her hand protectively over the mermaid.

I promise to keep you safe until I learn all your secrets.

Chapter 8

I need to tell Bridget the truth. Now.

Venus repeated it again and again, making herself believe it.

Sick at the thought of what this might reveal about Tony, Venus stared blindly out into the frosty night, hesitating on the front porch.

All at once she felt as if no one was who they appeared to be. Earlier, Connor had totally fooled her. Now Tony might be unmasked as a thief.

Is this how people feel about my dad?

She shook her head, hating the thought.

I'm thinking like a crazy person because I'm terrified to hurt Bridget and Tony. But I need to find out the truth for everyone's sake.

Turning slowly, she sucked in an icy breath and rang the bell at Bridget and Tony's Astor Street brownstone.

A moment later Connor flung open the door.

Her heart felt as if it fell to her toes, leaving her empty and cold inside.

"What are you doing here?" she blurted out.

"Eating pizza." He looked surprised. Then on alert. "What's wrong?"

She saw Bridget behind him, and beyond, Tony, slowly rising from a table in front of the living-room fireplace.

"What's wrong is you lettin' Venus get a chill standin' on my porch." Bridget stepped in front of Connor and pulled Venus inside.

"What a nice surprise. We're sittin' down to Tony's famous pizza. It's chicken breast and mushroom tonight. There's plenty for you. Won't you please join us, Venus?"

Gathering her courage, Venus shook her head. "No, thank you. I'd just like to talk to you alone for a few minutes."

Venus felt Connor's gaze scalding her face and tried to avoid looking at him. The heat and tension became so intense, so unbearable she held her breath and gave in to turn to him.

"You've come about the mermaid brooch, haven't you, Venus?" he asked softly, as if they were alone.

Now she honest to goodness couldn't look away from his emerald eyes pleading with her, even when she heard Tony's deep, ragged sigh.

"Connor Clayworth O'Flynn, I told you not to interfere in this," Bridget gasped, breaking the spell.

Connor glanced away and at last Venus could draw air into her starving lungs.

"I'm sorry, Aunt Bridget, but it's obvious the brooch is important to both of you. I asked Venus to sell it back to you."

Chilled to her soul by what she needed to do, Venus stepped closer to Bridget. "And I said I wanted to talk to you myself. Just the two of us."

"Whatever you need, Venus." Bridget clasped her hand

and squeezed her fingers. "I'm sorry my nephew failed to honor my wishes."

Oh, my God, I'm doing the same thing with my dad by not letting go of my feelings for the Clayworths and now I'm more involved than ever.

All at once new fear pounded through her. Again she told herself they all needed to know the truth. Now more than ever.

Believing she had no choice didn't make Venus feel any less heartsick as she ignored Connor to follow Bridget into a small den and shut the door behind her.

The walnut-paneled room felt warm, cozy.

Then why am I shivering so much my teeth are chattering?

Every tabletop and the stone fireplace mantel held framed pictures of Bridget and Tony, and more often than not, of the two of them, smiling, with Connor beside them.

Feeling worse by the second, Venus forced herself to look away from the signs of their happiness and give Bridget the news that would change everything for her.

"Venus, it can't be as bad as all that. Please sit down before you fall. Never seen you so upset. Except about your dad." Bridget patted her shoulder. "Don't fret about this mermaid brooch business."

"We have to fret about it."

Oh, Bridget, please don't hate the messenger. Please be able to explain all this away, for your sake.

"Your mermaid brooch isn't worth the twenty-five hundred dollars I donated to Connor's Golden Gloves Gym. It's the original brooch stolen from Clayworth's and now worth conservatively a quarter of a million dollars," she blurted out, not knowing how else to do it.

All the color drained from Bridget's face as she

recoiled, backing into a side table. Two picture frames tottered and one fell onto the wood floor with a crash.

They both stared down at the photo of Bridget and Tony smiling through shattered glass.

An instant later the door burst open and Connor rushed in, Tony a few steps behind him.

"Venus, what happened?" Connor's eyes searched her face.

"*Cara,* are you all right?" Tony hurried to Bridget to clasp her shoulders with his hands.

The look Bridget gave him froze Venus's blood. Connor seemed to turn into a statue beside her. He must have also seen the way Bridget recoiled from Tony's touch. She and Connor both seemed paralyzed by the emotions erupting between Bridget and Tony. Not wanting to watch, but unable to drag their eyes away.

"*Cara,* for the love of God tell me what's wrong." Tony dropped his hands and fell back one step.

"Venus, do you have the mermaid brooch with you?"

Bridget's voice sounded full of emotion, like a dam ready to burst, and she looked tense, coiled so tight if she broke she'd spin out of control. Hot tears welled up in Venus's eyes, feeling her pain.

Slowly, Venus pulled the chain out into the open to cradle the mermaid on her palm. "Yes, it's here," she whispered through a scalding pool at the back of her throat.

Bridget's gaze never wavered from Tony's face. "Is that the brooch you gave me for my twenty-fifth birthday? The one you told me you bought from an antique dealer?"

Tony glanced at the mermaid and quickly back to stare into Bridget's eyes.

"If it is the brooch you sold Venus from your hope chest, then you know it is, *cara.*"

"Then Venus says it's the original brooch that was stolen from Clayworth's decades ago."

"That's not possible!" Connor exploded beside her.

Despite wanting to throw up, Venus turned, determined to see this through with him. "It is true, Connor."

"When did you make this great discovery, Venus? You've had the brooch for nearly a week."

His heavy edge of sarcasm wasn't wasted on her. In this instant, with this subject, his lawyer persona and Clayworth confidence didn't intimidate her. This was too important for all of them for her to stop now.

"I'm an expert on vintage couture jewelry. *That* is what I *assumed* I found in Bridget's closet." Their eyes locked and the hot ache in her throat spread down into her chest. "Why would I think any different? Especially after Bridget told me Tony gave it to her."

"Today after our *talk* I started thinking." She heard the sarcasm in her voice and took a deep breath to stop it. "Started thinking about the brooch and how maybe Bridget really did want it back. If that was true, I would of course return it."

Encouraged by Bridget and Tony's rapt attention and the speculative gleam in Connor's eyes, she plunged on.

"So I took the brooch off the chain to really look at it for the last time. I was in my design studio at my town house."

"Sometimes I repair jewelry at home, so I have all the tools. Magnifying glass. Jewelry loupes and special lens. High-powered lights. All the standard equipment needed to distinguish real gemstones from high-quality faux."

It cut Venus to her core to see the shock and pain intensifying across Bridget's face as Tony's stony visage grew even sharper, but she had no choice but to finish what she'd started.

"I'm so sorry. I know this is...this is difficult to believe. At first I couldn't believe it myself." She cradled the mermaid in her hand. "*This* is for real. After the Eisenbergs made the original they signed and dated it in a unique way because they never used real gems, except this one time. Then they destroyed the mold, so there is no way this can be anything *but* the Eisenberg mermaid brooch they designed for Clayworth's."

All the air seemed to have fled the room, leaving a vacuum that felt so crushing she could hardly draw breath.

"*Cara,* believe me, I did not steal it." Tony's words filled the room like an explosion.

"No one believes you did, Uncle Tony." Connor flicked her a glare as if daring her to disagree.

"You lied to me that night about where you got it, didn't you? Tell us the truth now, Tony." Bridget's quiet voice silenced any attempt Venus might have made to say anything.

"Some man gave it to me. A stranger. On Taylor Street. I swear that is what happened."

Bridget closed her eyes, and when she opened them, tears hung on her lashes. "From the moment Venus found the brooch I haven't been able to stop thinkin' about the night you gave it to me. What we both said. What we both did." All the emotion Bridget had held back now poured out in her voice and in the tears cascading down her cheeks. "Earlier that night you swearin' on your mother's grave you would never go down to Taylor Street to gamble again. And me swearin' that if you did go, if you didn't stop gamblin' we were through. I'd never marry you," Bridget ended in a deep shuddering sob.

Beside her, Connor moved. From deep inside Venus some primal feminine instinct forced her to reach out to clasp his arm, stopping him from going to his aunt. She knew this moment belonged to Bridget and Tony alone.

"*Cara,* I admit I lied that night. I did go down to Taylor Street one last time to gamble. I was young. Foolish. Desperate to win enough money for your engagement ring." Tony stretched out his hands toward Bridget in such a beseeching gesture that Venus's heart broke for him.

"After I lost, I sat dejected on the curb and a man approached me. He said he'd been watching me and could see that I needed help. He pulled out the velvet box and told me he had won the brooch at a high-stakes poker game from a man who didn't deserve such beauty. He sensed I would give it the home it deserved. I was afraid you wouldn't believe me if I told you the truth."

Bridget's harsh bark of laughter sent a chill prickling along Venus's skin.

"You expect me to believe that urban legend about 'the Saint of Taylor Street' goin' around helpin' strangers in need? He gave you a brooch worth a fortune because you were upset?"

Tony placed his palms over his heart. "I confess to lying to you about gambling that night and about how I received the brooch. Now I swear I am telling the truth."

All the color drained from Bridget's face and she swayed. "That whole night is a fabric of lies between the two of us. I've always known you went down to Taylor Street only hours after you swore you wouldn't."

Tony's whole body tensed. Venus could see it in his rigid shoulders and clenched fists.

"I was so angry and upset that night I followed you. When I saw you go into the restaurant I knew you were goin' to that illegal club underneath the parkin' lot. Then I realized my word meant as little as yours. I loved you too much to leave you, although I'd sworn I would. But somethin' inside me closed off. I loved you but my trust in you was gone." Bridget took a long shuddering breath. "After a while I thought I'd buried those feelings. That maybe it didn't matter, but in my heart I knew it did. Now there's even more secrets about that night. How can I believe this feeble story about how you got the stolen brooch when everythin' else about that night was a lie?" She squeezed her eyes closed, more tears glistening in her startling green eyes.

"*Cara*, why would I steal the brooch and then leave it languishing in your closet for decades? This whole scenario is madness. I never dreamed the brooch could be the original. How can you not believe me?" Tony pleaded.

"Because you've been lying to me for years and I've loved you too much to stop it for fear I'd lose you completely." Bridget's deep ragged sobs were too much to bear.

Connor tore from Venus's weak grasp and moved to stand beside his aunt.

"Aunt Bridget, you know Tony's not a thief. There's another explanation for all of this. There must be."

Venus agreed, nodding so hard her neck ached. She wanted to believe Tony the way she wanted everyone to believe in her father's innocence. Somehow she *knew* Diana would believe Tony's story. Deep inside she sensed it was true.

"After all these years, after all our shared memories, how can you think he might be guilty?" Connor asked ever so gently, as if Bridget might shatter like glass if he wasn't careful.

"Because he's been sneakin' off behind my back and goin' to Taylor Street every week for years and years."

Tony aged before Venus's eyes in the slump of his shoulders, his slack-jawed shock and stricken eyes.

"You knew and yet you never said a word?" Tony breathed in a whisper.

"Think about it, Tony," Bridget sobbed. "Over the years I asked you in a thousand different ways for the truth. I can get others to tell me the truth with a look, but not you. Not the man who professes to love me. Finally I chose to live in denial, like all deluded women do. But now that Venus has unearthed the brooch again and she found out the truth it's the catalyst I needed to finally end all our lies."

Deep sobs racking her body, Bridget reached out toward Connor and he gathered her to his side.

"Connor, please don't say anythin' more. What I want now is for you to take me back to your place. I need time alone."

The Connor she thought she knew had always seemed as cold and emotionless as a statue. Now the loving way he watched Bridget and his fiercely protective grip on her slight body as he helped her to the door told Venus how very wrong she'd been.

Maybe he's not who I thought he was, but will he turn his back on Tony?

At the last moment Connor swung toward her. "Venus, keep the mermaid brooch safe until we figure out what the hell is going on."

"I will." She nodded, closing her fingers around it.

"I'll be in touch with both of you tomorrow." His eyes vulnerable in a way she'd never imagined possible, Connor nodded to Tony and closed the door behind him.

The instant they were gone, Tony collapsed on the sofa as if his legs could no longer hold him upright and hung his head in his quivering hands.

She'd once read that terror was what one felt before the explosion and horror after, viewing the carnage.

She felt both as she sank down beside Tony. *If I hadn't found the brooch, none of these pent-up feelings would have erupted.*

"I'm so sorry, Tony. For what it's worth, I believe you," she said softly, resisting her impulse to pat his back.

He lifted his head and gripped her hand, kissing it. "I don't know why. It sounds like the tale of a guilty man. But I swear I am not guilty of stealing the brooch."

God knew she'd caused enough damage by seeking answers, but she had to ask one more question.

"Don't you think, if you told Bridget why you've been going to Taylor Street all these years, it might be easier for her to believe you about the brooch?"

"I cannot tell her."

The defeat in his voice and in his eyes reminded Venus so much of her father, a need to protect them both congealed inside her into a fierce determination.

"If I'm the catalyst, like Bridget said, then I can be the catalyst to fix this. I'll go talk to her for you."

Tony shook his head. "When she is this upset only Connor can reach her. Only he can plead my case."

"But will he? I know he loves you like a father, but will he walk away from you? Does he give anyone a second chance if he thinks they've made a mistake? Even someone he cares deeply about? He didn't with my dad."

Again Tony grasped her hand. "Connor is full of passion, which is why he keeps such a tight rein on his emotions. He's been that way since he was a child." Tony's sigh seemed to come from deep inside him. "How could it be different with a father who kept his own emotions in check his whole life? And Victoria is an aloof mother who has always spent more time away than with him. Connor feels deeply but has been reared not to show it. I know he felt much pain over your father's troubles. Like he is feeling tonight for Bridget and for me. When you know him well, you, too, will be able to see it in his eyes. The vulnerability he hides well."

I saw it and I'm utterly confused by it.

"Beautiful Venus, I thank you from the bottom of my heart for believing in me but now, with your permission, I would prefer to be alone."

He stood, helped her to her feet, and led her by the hand to the door.

Worried about leaving him, she dug in her heels. "I don't want to go. I'm not sure you should be alone."

"I promise you I shall be fine alone." His face hardened. "You may find it impossible to believe because of the revelations of this night, but I am a man of my word."

Tony watched from the front porch until she'd safely reached her car and pulled away.

Now what do I do?

Aching sorrow for Tony and Bridget ripped her apart. Guilt at her part in this tragedy felt like a heavy chain squeezing her chest.

She *needed* to do something.

If Bridget would only listen to Connor then *he'd* better listen to Venus and help her find a way to solve this problem.

She turned left, heading to Lake Shore Drive and Connor's penthouse.

Chapter 9

The austere doorman at Connor's building didn't smile when he asked her name and who she wished to see.

Nor did he smile while he dialed the penthouse to announce her. Venus felt hot and queasy with unease.

"Miss Venus Smith is here to see you," he declared in a solemn tone. His long hesitation brought real fear pounding through her.

What will I do if they refuse to see me?

His furled brow gave Venus a tight, hot cramp in her stomach.

I may throw up in the potted plant next to him.

He looked up at her and Venus held her breath, waiting for rejection.

"Go on up." He nodded.

"Thank you," she breathed in abject relief, her pulse pounding. She flashed him her brightest smile before rushing past him to the elevators.

The ride up to the penthouse gave her a precious few minutes to plot her next move. Too soon the elevator doors slid open onto Connor's foyer, all black lacquer walls and gray wool rugs.

Bridget waited in the open door.

She looked tiny, swallowed in a huge Clayworth blue terry cloth robe with the sleeves rolled up several turns.

"I didn't want to send you away, Venus, but I can't talk to anyone tonight."

Venus glanced past her into the penthouse, a blur of black marble floors and a huge expanse of windows overlooking Lake Michigan. In the distance she heard several sharp, short barks of a dog and the loud deep woof of another one.

"Bridget, please talk to me. Is Connor here with you? You shouldn't be alone."

"No. His hoverin' and worryin' make the situation worse. I sent him away to work out in his gym." Bridget wrapped her arms around her waist as if she felt suddenly chilled. "Now, Venus, you need to know none of this is your fault."

She'd seen this strength in Bridget before. Had heard her say she hated to be *mollycoddled*.

So Venus resisted her powerful urge to engulf Bridget in a hug but couldn't stop the plea in her voice. "I'm so sorry, Bridget. I wish I'd never found the mermaid brooch. Never found out the truth and told you. It *is* my fault that you and Tony are so miserable."

"Now you listen to me, young lady," Bridget said in her no-nonsense voice. "This is Tony's doin' and my choices for years. I don't want you worryin' yourself sick or beatin' yourself up the way Connor is doin'. The situation is bad, I know. Tony and I have had our troubles before. I won't lie to you and tell you this isn't the worst to ever happen. It is. I don't know yet how we'll handle it. But we will somehow."

Still consumed by guilt and worry, Venus shook her head. "Please let me do something to help. *Anything* to fix this problem between you and Tony."

Bridget's lips curled into an ever-so-slight smile, but her eyes remained stark with worry. "What you need to do, Venus, is to go home and get some rest. It's late." She stepped back, gripping the door to close it. "Good night, Venus. And thank you. Your carin' is enough help."

"No, it isn't enough," Venus whispered to the closed door and black lacquer walls before twirling back into the waiting elevator.

Tony's words rang in her ears, *Only Connor can reach her.*

Well, Venus knew where to find Connor—in his gym—and once she did she'd force him to listen to her plan to help both of them.

Connor's Golden Gloves Gym on Sheffield couldn't have looked any darker or more deserted.

Disappointed and frustrated to the point of screaming, she waited, parked in front, for twenty excruciatingly slow minutes.

She shifted in her seat and kept glancing at her iPhone to check the time.

I'm too wound up not to do something to help!

She got out of the car, cupped her hands around her face, and peered through the glass window, hoping to see a light at the back. Anything to give her hope.

Maybe he hasn't arrived yet because he's walking here to work off his frustration.

She hurried back to her car and started slowly cruising down the street looking for him.

The only sign of life was five young men standing on the corner of Belmont. All but one had short cigarettes in their mouths. That one was gesturing with his hands, his arms firm and well muscled.

It's Gregori. A little red flag of danger reared its ugly head and she pulled to the curb.

The distinct aroma of marijuana wafted through her open window.

"Hi, Gregori. Need a ride home?" she shouted, and waved to get his attention.

He turned, squinted toward her, and then a grin split his face. "Whoa, Miss Smith."

A chorus of catcalls and whistles at his back, he swaggered toward her and knelt to peer into the window. "What you doin' here so late?"

"Looking for Mr. O'Flynn. His aunt Bridget told me he was at the gym working out. Have you seen him?"

"Naw. He wasn't there tonight with the rest of us guys. Maybe she meant the gym at his office. He took me there once. The day we came to your place."

One of his friends yelled something she couldn't make out.

Snarling, Gregori turned his head. "Shut your stupid-ass mouth," he shouted back.

His face grim, he stood. "Gotta go, Miss Smith."

"Yes, you do need to go. Home. Please get in the car." Her firm *don't mess with me* voice stopped him and he stared down at her.

"What you mean, Miss Smith?"

"I mean I'm taking you home, Gregori. Mr. O'Flynn wouldn't want you here with your friends smoking pot."

"Trying to tell them they're gonna get their asses busted." He shook his head. "I'm not usin' the stuff. Never have. Never will. Costs money my ma doesn't have."

"Good to hear you don't partake. I'm still taking you home."

Shifting from sneaker to sneaker, he glanced at his friends and back to her. "Can't do that, Miss Smith."

Realizing he needed to save face, she leaned out the window, toward him. "Tell them I'm a cougar trying to pick you up," she whispered.

She hoped he saw the determination on her face not to take no for an answer, because she had every intention of sitting here until he got into the car.

Gregori hesitated, looking over his shoulder.

Finally he laughed and made some obscene gesture toward his friends she'd rather not contemplate too deeply. "Hey, dudes, when a beautiful lady wants me what can I do but go with her."

He swaggered around and slid into the passenger seat. Once he had fastened his seat belt, she gunned the motor and roared out onto Belmont heading west.

Happy to have him safe beside her, she smiled at him. "Where to?"

"Cicero and Irving Park," he mumbled, staring out the window.

"What were you doing out so late? Isn't tomorrow a school day?"

Still staring out the window, he shrugged, like all the other sullen teenagers in the world when they wanted to annoy their elders.

Feeling quite old and more than a little annoyed with him, she ignored him for several blocks, until she had no choice and her already frayed nerves quivered. "Okay, time to acknowledge I'm in the car with you. I can only turn right on Irving Park. Then what?"

"Belle Plaine, first street on the left. Fourth house on the . . . Shit! My ma's out lookin' for me."

A thin dark-haired woman stood, wringing her hands

and peering both ways down the street. Venus made the turn and pulled to the curb.

The car hadn't come to a full stop when Gregori jumped out. "Ma, I'm here. I didn't do nothin' wrong."

Mrs. Prozument gave a little scream, clasped Gregori to her bosom, and began shouting in what Venus believed to be Polish.

"Ma, I didn't take nothin' this time. I promise. Miss Smith, she's a friend of Mr. O'Flynn's."

Everything about his mother's body language changed. She stood taller, gave Gregori a stern look, and said something sharp that made him hang his head.

Venus climbed out of the car, waiting while Gregori shuffled to her.

"Thank you for the ride home, Miss Smith." He shuffled back, kissed his mother on the cheek, and bolted into the tiny bungalow behind him.

Mrs. Prozument began to wring her hands again. "Thank you. Thank you for bringing my boy home safe. He has been worried about me finding job." She blinked several times as if she might be fighting back tears. "He thinks my clothes aren't good enough to find a job and I'm afraid he might steal again for me. He's a good boy. Truly. Mr. O'Flynn knows. He is such a fine man."

In a night of being heartbroken and anguished for friends, this was yet another dose of sadness.

At least this time she knew exactly how she could help. She reached back into the car, searching in her purse until she found a business card.

"Here's my card. Please come to my store. Gregori knows where I'm located. I can help you with clothes for your job interviews."

Again Gregori's mother rapidly blinked her eyes,

studying the card. "Gregori says we must not take charity. He has such pride. Refused more help from Mr. O'Flynn." She looked up into Venus's face. "You bring my boy home safe so I'll take help from you when you ask. Tell my son so. Thank you. Thank you. You are very good person. Like Mr. O'Flynn. I wish all good fortune will come to you."

Venus watched until Mrs. Prozument had safely entered her bungalow before she climbed back into the car and pulled away.

In an endless night of seeking answers, her emotions at a fever pitch, she knew she couldn't rest until she found Connor and convinced him to help her.

But first she needed some help from her sister.

Venus pounded on Diana's duplex door until it finally opened.

Her sister stood wearing a white velvet robe, her face scrubbed clean for bed.

Venus rushed in. "Oh, my God, how late is it?" She fumbled for her cell phone to check the time, vowing to start wearing a watch again.

"It's not that late. I'm going to bed early because I have a big day at Clayworth's tomorrow. Time to start planning the windows for the holidays."

"I need to get into Clayworth's tonight to talk to Connor. I think he's there working out in his gym."

The look Diana leveled at her made Venus squirm.

Nope, not getting into my head tonight, baby sister.

"You want to talk to Connor alone tonight? Sit down, Venus, and tell me what's going on."

Exhausted, Venus threw herself down on Diana's chintz sofa with just the right number of pillows to make it *too* comfortable. *If I stop to rest I won't be able to get up to finish this.*

She sat up, perching on the very edge of the sofa, and Diana curled up beside her.

"So tell me everything, Venus."

"I can't tell you everything that's going on because it involves others, but suffice to say it's *huge*." She rubbed her fingertips across the mermaid body visible where her blouse gaped slightly open.

"A lot of this horrible mess I caused. But I truly believe if Connor and I work together we can make *everything* right."

It honestly appeared as if Diana's eyes grew larger. "Does this have anything to do with Dad?"

Venus knew from years of experience that Diana possessed an uncanny knack for knowing when she lied.

"Maybe. Partially. This whole thing started because I wanted to help Dad."

"Tell me. You know I'd do anything for him."

"I wanted to get closer to Connor in the hope that he'd tell me what happened with Dad at Clayworth's."

It felt as if a weight lifted off her shoulders to actually admit her folly. But for the first time in her life, Venus knew from Diana's pale, still face she'd truly shocked her baby sister.

"Don't just stare at me like I've grown another head. Say something."

"I understand pillow talk between lovers like Drew and Athena. And I've been watching guys drool over you for years trying to get you into bed with them. How close were you planning to get to him? Sleep with him?"

"My God, I wasn't going to try to *seduce* him!" Venus shouted to relieve the scalding heat coursing through her veins at the very thought. *But what would it be like to make love with Connor?*

"What then?" Diana sat up straighter, an unusual frosty glint in her eyes. "Tell me how you really feel about Connor and why you think you can do this."

Still warm, her heart pounding, Venus leaped up to pace the wood floor in front of the sofa.

"You mentioned it yourself, Diana. Connor's overzealous knight-in-shining-armor complex, like the time he pulled me out of the lake."

Diana's eyes softened. "I know you think you were fine, but you did look as if you were in trouble that day. Grey and Ric even dived into the lake to go help."

Venus shrugged, but still felt a twinge of her old embarrassment. "You know how I *hated* blooming so early and so abundantly. I was mortified when Connor clutched me in his arms and crushed me to his manly chest." Venus shook her head. "I know my plan is crazy but Connor and Dad were so close. It makes sense he knows better than the others exactly how Dad became entangled in this mess. I wish I could be like you and Athena and simply accept the situation like Dad wants us to do, but I can't."

"I can't stand the defeat in Dad's eyes any more than you can, Venus. But I'm trying to respect his wishes for us not to interfere. Are you sure you want to continue with this insane plan?"

"Honestly, I don't have a choice." She forced a smile, feeling not an iota of joy. "Now the situation has become much more complex."

Diana watched her with the intent look that always made Venus feel like she heard her thoughts.

"It sounds serious and I can see how important it is to

you. But can't it wait until morning? Give yourself more time to think about what to do."

Venus shook her head, hair flying wildly against her hot cheeks. "No. Now's the moment to resolve this. I know it. I *feel* it."

Curled up on the sofa, her moonbeam hair cascading over the white robe, Diana looked like an angel. Pure and omniscient.

"Okay, Diana, here's the deal. I know I'm impulsive and sometimes too passionate to see beyond what I think is best. While you're wise beyond your years and I swear sometimes positively *psychic*. So if you tell me *not* to go tonight to talk to Connor, it will kill me but I'll obey you."

For an instant Diana narrowed her aquamarine eyes, so like their father's and her own. Ever so slowly she uncurled from the sofa and seemed to float to the small cherrywood desk in the corner.

She wrote on a piece of paper and then handed it and a plastic keypad card to Venus.

"Here is my employee number and key card. They'll get you into the private parking area next to the loading dock. When I go to Clayworth's at 6:00 A.M. the guard is already on duty so I sign in. He won't be there tonight. Employees rarely go to the store this late. Except Connor. If his Ferrari is there, he'll be up in the executive offices."

Overcome with relief, Venus engulfed her tiny sister in a hug that swallowed her. "Thank you, Diana. Helping me see Connor tonight is not a mistake."

"I know or I wouldn't be doing it." Diana's serene voice made Venus feel a rush of confidence.

Now if only she found his red Ferrari still parked in the garage she could at last end this night of painful revelations by moving forward with her plan to help them all.

His car sat alone in an area designated for the Clay-worth family and select employees, Diana included. Venus pulled her blue Prius into her sister's parking space.

The store looked surreal at night, as if she walked through a dream. The escalators motionless. The display cases ghostlike in the filtered pale moonlight from the glass dome several stories above.

All lay silent except for the thumping of her heart in her ears and the swoosh of the elevator carrying her to the ninth-floor executive offices.

This part of the store she knew well from the years when she came here with her mom and dad. She passed the offices of the Clayworth brothers, Greyson and Ric, off in Asia and Europe overseeing their far-flung empire.

On her right was her father's old office. She stopped to peer inside. Seeing it emptied of any evidence of his life spent dedicated to Clayworth's made her throat ache with unshed tears.

Taking a deep breath, she kept walking past the smaller office of Ed Mahoney, who used it the days he was at Clayworth's rather than in his larger office on LaSalle where he saw other clients.

She knew the light falling out into the hall came from the twin offices of Drew and Connor, separated by a but-ler's pantry, boardroom, and now, according to Gregori, a small gym.

A rhythmic high-speed sound led her to a small room crowded with a pull-up bar, dip stand, power rack, and crunch board. From the ceiling hung a large black bag that resembled a giant sausage, and a worn-out brown leather puffy ball rested on the floor.

These all look like instruments of torture to me.

Lost in his own world, Connor stood, stripped to

black shorts and tank top, wearing some kind of thin black gloves and striking a tear-drop-shaped red bag with a rolling hand-over-hand motion between his fore-head and chin. The rat-a-tat-tat sound was positively hypnotic.

"Connor," she shouted, desperate to get his attention.

He looked up and Venus saw the shock and, yes, the newly recognized vulnerability before Connor narrowed his eyes.

"Which one helped you get in. Bridget or Diana?"

"Diana." Defiant, Venus tossed her hair over her shoulder. "Is she in trouble?"

His mouth curled into his almost smile. "What do you think?"

"I think you know you're lucky she decided to stay working for you despite what happened with Dad. And you want to keep having her award-winning décor and window displays in all twenty of your stores. So, no, she damn well better not be in trouble."

"Come to put on the gloves, Venus?"

"No, Connor. I've come to take them off."

Waiting for his answer, her heart pounded like a hammer against her ribs.

At last he nodded. "Wait in my office. I'll shower and meet you there in a few minutes. And for the record, you don't need to worry about Diana's job."

Excitement and fear roared through her in such a hot blast she couldn't stand still.

It's true the world has gone crazy. I was right the other day on the sidewalk outside of Sola's. Connor and I are attracted to each other.

Confused beyond anything she'd ever known, she paced the Clayworth blue carpet from large window, to fireplace, to heavy walnut desk, which her artist eye recognized as a priceless antique.

Two files rested on its neat-as-a-pin surface.

Her stomach in one big knot, she stopped to stare down at the one labeled *Eisenberg Brooch Robbery.*

Is there a clue in there? Something that might help Tony?

This file appeared much thinner than the fat one marked *Shoplifing and Robberies in Last Decade.*

The urge to flip through both files, looking for answers, took every ounce of her willpower to resist.

Hearing Connor coming into the room, she twirled away from the desk and temptation.

His hair lay wet and slicked back on his perfectly shaped skull the way it had years ago when she'd watched him climb out of the NU swimming pool. Then, like now, despite her good intentions, she couldn't ignore her powerful sexual attraction to him. Even though tonight his open-neck shirt and khakis hid his powerful physique, she still pictured him in the Speedo.

His vulnerability seemed hidden now, too.

He swept the files off his desk and into a locked drawer.

Curiosity got the best of her. "I thought everything was computerized these days."

"At Clayworth's we're creatures of habit. We use both computers and hard copies. I was looking through the records of the heist when the brooch was stolen. Other fine pieces of jewelry were also taken that night."

His narrow-eyed gaze, she decided, must be a lawyer's trick to throw off the opposition. Tonight she knew what she needed to do.

She stared right back at him. "Tony didn't do it."

Although he tried to cover it, she saw him square his

shoulders as if he had himself in a straitjacket, utterly in control.

"Venus, I'm an officer of the court. In the end the evidence will determine Tony's guilt or innocence. Not me or my feelings."

Frustration and raw disbelief at his matter-of-fact tone burned so bright she almost lost it. Remembering how high the stakes were in this for all of them, she took a deep breath and stepped closer to him.

"How can you stand here and pretend to be so calm? At Bridget's I saw in your eyes how you want to come to Tony's defense. Or have you rushed to judgment on Tony like you did with my dad? How *could* you, Connor, when Tony's like a father to you?"

Connor's face seemed to soften, yet his stare felt as intense and powerful as ever, still totally devoid of vulnerability. "Why can't you understand that facts are facts with your father, Venus? You can't change them. Like I can't change what happened between Bridget and Tony. I can't change the fact Tony had the stolen brooch in his possession." A glimmer of vulnerability sparked in his eyes. "Even if I wish like hell I could."

Seeing a chink in his armor urged her on. "Don't *wish* it, Connor. *Make* it happen. Open yourself to the possibility you could be wrong. And the facts actually lead to another conclusion. There are so many different explanations for Tony's actions." She heard the hoarse plea in her voice and cleared her throat, fighting for control. "I know you can't or won't talk about what happened with my dad, but I know there must be just as many other explanations for his actions besides guilt."

He shook his head. "I'm sorry, Venus. I know that's the story you want to believe, but the overwhelming evidence indicates otherwise."

The sudden gentleness in his voice might have been her undoing if she wasn't driven by feelings beyond her control. Her involvement had started with her father's troubles and her need to right that wrong. Now, with Tony under suspicion and Bridget miserable, her plan seemed to have a life of its own, drawing her and Connor closer and closer.

This is what I wanted.

She stepped so close she smelled the fresh lime scent of Connor's soap. "Forget your damn vaunted logic. What about this, Connor?" She placed a hand over her heart. "What I *know* to be true no matter what the facts or the evidence may appear to be about my dad—and now I feel the same way about Tony."

Slowly, fear a tiny flame in her chest, she placed her other hand over his heart and felt its beat beneath her fingers. "You must feel it, too. Tony is like a father to you. I know you love him as much as I do my dad."

He tensed, the accelerated pace of his pulse telling her he felt the tension between them just as she did.

Their eyes clashed and she refused to be frightened into looking away.

"To live by your emotions leads to mayhem, Venus. Life has taught me that people are innocent or guilty by their actions. The world is black or white. Right or wrong. Why in the hell can't you understand that life isn't always fair and events don't always turn out the way you want no matter how much you try to make it happen. You can't change any of it, Venus. Leave this alone before you get hurt even more."

Weak with her need to convince him, she swayed closer, placing both palms against his warm, hard chest. "I don't believe the world is black and white. To me it's a fabulous color of gray. Full of endless possibilities, if you'll only let yourself go and not be afraid to think outside the box. Like now. A few days ago I would never have touched you. Now I am and you're letting me. *Please*, Connor, let yourself go further and help me. Together I know we can find out the truth about Tony and my dad."

Their gazes seemed to meld together, creating a wave pulling her toward him.

"Venus, don't play this game. I can't let go. It's not who I am and you know it," he said, his voice hoarse.

Every stinging instinct she possessed urged her on. "Yes, you can and I'm proving it to you right now."

She slid her hands up to cup his face. Closing her eyes, she pressed a kiss on his mouth.

The feel and taste of his lips ran like liquid fire through her blood.

Burning with shock, she tried to pull away.

He stopped her, sliding his fingers into her hair, pulling her tight against his body to deepen their kiss.

As if lightning had struck between them, they both jerked back, but their eyes locked.

Desire pulsing through her, she stared up at him, terrified but determined.

"You see, anything is possible." Her voice sounded so breathless, she took a deep strengthening breath to steady it. "We don't even...like each other, yet we kissed as if we cared. We let go of our preconceived notions and look what happened. Please let go again, Connor. Work with me to prove Tony is innocent. And when we discover the truth isn't what you believe it to be, then you'll know logic doesn't always work. Go with your feelings about my dad and Tony. Then anything is possible.

"I know Tony is innocent." She pulled out the mermaid brooch from between her breasts. "And this is our bait to find out who is really guilty."

Chapter 10

His gut clenched. *What in the hell is wrong with me.*

A night of pain and worry wasn't excuse enough for his lack of control. He shut down his throbbing desire to pull Venus back into his arms and tried to act like a Clayworth should.

"This was a mistake, Venus. I apologize."

"You're apologizing for kissing me?"

At least he had the willpower not to smile at her guileless indignation or touch her soft, flushed cheek. Her hair had felt like silk, her skin warm velvet.

"Venus, often in intense emotional situations people act and think irrationally." He needed to move away from this personal quicksand and back to the fact that she wanted to do something ill advised. "Like your idea of using the brooch as bait. Totally illogical."

Her skin flushed even pinker, making her extraordinary eyes blaze brighter.

"No, it isn't illogical. I didn't see the connection at first either but now it makes perfect sense to me. On Rebecca's TV show I mentioned this is a rare Eisenberg copy of the mermaid brooch made of real stones, stolen in the famous heist. I even said I recently found it forgotten in a Chicago closet."

Again she stepped closer to him. He steeled himself not to react.

"Connor, don't you see, only the thief would want to know if my brooch could possibly be the one made of precious gems he lost to the Saint of Taylor Street in a poker game."

Why in the hell do I want to believe her far-fetched theory?

He shook his head, trying to clear it of her and the way she made him feel.

"The most logical explanation is a basic robbery."

"The day after I wore the brooch on Rebecca's show? Now who's not being logical? I don't believe in coincidences," she taunted him.

Concentrating on convincing her to be reasonable, he focused his gaze on her face the way he did with witnesses in the courtroom. "No coincidence. It's obvious the thieves targeted Pandora's Box after they saw the quality vintage jewelry you carry in the store. You said they took all your most expensive pieces. They were pros."

He saw defiance blaze in her eyes. Knew it meant trouble.

"You are so wrong, Connor. I've been wearing the mermaid on a chain hidden under my clothes all week. But now I'm going to wear it openly everywhere I go in public. If you're right, I'll be perfectly safe. If I'm right, we'll capture the real thief and exonerate Tony."

He'd never understood why she instilled such a need in him to protect her. Still didn't understand. *Did* know no way would he allow her to turn herself into a target for any thug on the street. "Venus, that idea is criminally reckless. If you're right you're putting yourself in real danger."

She lifted a strand of hair off her shoulder to wrap around two fingers. "I suppose I could hire bodyguards, but that might put off the thieves."

Concerned, as any rational person would be under the circumstances, he broke the promise he made to himself, way back when he'd fought for her, to never do it again. "There is no way I will allow you to do this."

Eyes wide in defiance, she laughed up at him. "Connor, I don't believe you can stop me from going home and doing exactly what I please. After all, I paid for the brooch. Well, underpaid," she admitted with a shrug. "But it's mine to do with as I wish until I decide what I should do with it after we solve this mystery."

Her eyes were aquamarine flames beckoning him to join in her game. No one frustrated or excited him more than Venus. The feelings welled up from his gut. "Listen to me. Whether I'm right or you're right about the robbery, all your wandering around in public wearing a fortune will get you some small-time hit-and-run purse snatcher, not the guy you're looking to find. It's too dangerous for you to continue wearing a fortune in jewelry, and you know it."

Smiling, she swayed closer so he smelled her sultry perfume, felt the warmth of her body.

"When your customers buy expensive pieces in your fine jewelry department, do you give them a disclaimer that they might be in danger if they actually wear their new jewels?"

Ignoring the jab of truth, he tried again to reason with her. "It isn't the same and you know it."

She twirled another curl around her fingers. "Well, if you're so concerned that I'm in danger, then become my knight in shining armor and help me slay the real dragon. It's what you really want to do and you know it. But if you're afraid to admit it, I'll have no choice but to do it on my own."

Anger rolled through him at her reckless disregard for her own safety. "This isn't a game, Venus," he roared. "If you don't come to your senses about this crazy plan to make yourself a target, I'm calling your father. He'll stop you."

Their eyes clashed. All playfulness gone, she flashed him such a look of loathing it felt like a blow.

"I can't believe you have the nerve to threaten me with my father like I'm a child. How dare you use him in such a way. But I shouldn't be surprised considering how you've already trashed him."

Once he would have called Alistair without hesitation to help protect Venus. The anguish over his betrayal burned fresh in Connor's gut.

"Venus, you need to listen to me about your father and understand."

"Never! I'm leaving. You're an arrogant ass who thinks he is always right. I was a fool to hope you were capable of change or of actually lifting a finger to help me or your uncle!" She spun around on her towering heels and pushed past him to run down the hall into the waiting elevator before he could stop her.

Instead of following her, he sprinted over to the private executive elevator and took it down, knowing he'd arrive at the employee exit before she did.

Hell, she confused him more than any woman he'd ever known. Why couldn't she be rational?

Because she feels so passionate about everything in her life and the people she loves. She's addictive.

Breathless, eyes flashing, breasts heaving, she appeared like a vengeful goddess out of the dim store.

In that instant he knew he'd go along with her crazy plan. His flawed reasoning that he was doing it for his aunt and uncle he'd deal with later. The rational part of him believed if he went along with her he could convince her to not only give up the mermaid brooch for her own safety, but also finally come to grips with her father's guilt.

"Get out of my way. I'm going home." She tried to push past him.

He blocked the door with his arm, stopping her. "Leave your car. I'll have it delivered to you tomorrow. I'm driving you home. We need to discuss our next move in your plan to exonerate Tony."

She flung back her head and glared up at him. "Our next move? Are you insane? Why this sudden change of heart?"

"You," he stated with blunt honesty. "Tonight you made me realize I feel as passionate about helping Tony and Bridget as you do about your dad. However, my wanting to go along with this plan doesn't mean it will turn out the way either one of us want in the end. Can you let go and accept whatever happens, whatever we uncover?"

Unflinching, she met his eyes. "If you can do it, so can I."

Relief made him smile. "Then let's go."

Silent, she paced beside him to his Ferrari and opened the passenger door before he had the chance.

He glanced at her profile. Her perfect nose, long lashes, high cheekbones, lush lips, all the Smith sisters' undeniable beauty etched in the stonelike clenching of her jaw. Her defiance brought a rush of concern.

Damn it, here I go again feeling like I need to protect her from her own stubbornness.

"Venus, we need to talk if we're planning to work together."

At last she turned toward him. "So talk."

"I believe we can reach an equitable agreement about how to proceed with this problem if we can negotiate a compromise."

"For heaven's sake, Connor, stop talking like a lawyer." She glared at him. "Just tell me what you have in mind."

"We can't rush into anything before we first start an investigation into the original robbery and other thefts at Clayworth's that may implicate Tony. His father's company had recently installed a new security system when the famous heist took place. Tony has updated and maintained it since he took over the business years ago."

"I understand how that could look bad for him." She stroked the pendant visible at her throat between the open buttons of her blouse. He forced his eyes back on the road.

"I bought this brooch in good faith. But is it really mine? Or does it belong to the insurance company, which must have paid Clayworth's claim years ago?"

He glanced at her softer profile. "I *should* immediately notify Ed of the situation. He needs to contact the insurance company that the brooch they paid us for has been found. However, I'm willing to *go gray* instead of my usual black and white and hold off telling anyone for now."

The fact that his feeble attempt to lighten the tension made her lips curl slightly in amusement gave him a kick of pleasure.

"Is there some statute of limitations or something on it?"

"Or something. That's a negotiation Ed and I will get into later." He was much more interested in his present negotiations with her. "Now we need to decide what our next step should be."

"I'll wear the brooch to the Service Club Gala on Friday night at the Four Seasons. If we don't get a bite I'll wear it again at the Dress for Success benefit at the Drake Hotel the following week. There'll be lots of media there plus Rebecca's doing a segment on the charity. I'll make sure I mention I'm adding this to my personal collection I keep at home."

"Hell no, Venus! I said we need to take it slow, not give every damn thief in the city carte blanche to break into your town house."

"I have a state-of-the-art security system your uncle Tony installed. Stop worrying so much. I'll be perfectly safe at home and at both parties." She patted his arm and her smile dazzled him.

His pulse pounded. He tried not to think about the feel and taste of Venus in his arms. The way he'd reacted to her was like the feeling of lightning about to strike he'd once experienced with Drew while sailing. He'd felt the electricity along every inch of his skin and every instinct registered danger and the need to escape.

Now he didn't want to escape. "One compromise. Don't wear the brooch on Friday. Give us more time to set our plan into place. Hold off until the Dress for Success benefit. I'll accompany you to be sure you're safe."

She hesitated, watching him. Finally she nodded. "Okay. Just to prove I'm reasonable, I'll agree not to wear the brooch on Friday. But you don't need to escort me to the Dress for Success benefit. I may have a date. If he's in town, which he may or may not be."

Jealousy wasn't an emotion he often felt. It came hot and sharp and hard to control. He'd been stupid to think a kiss had changed the fact that she hated his guts. "Then I'll attend alone to be there if you need me."

"It will probably be all right if you want to go with me as part of our plan." She twisted another curl of hair and flicked him a smile. "My date probably won't make it. Meet me at the Drake in the Palm Court for cocktails at six-thirty on that Saturday. If anything changes I'll let you know." She stretched out her hand toward him. "I think it's best if we keep this whole plan our little secret. Deal?"

He touched her cool fingers in a quick handshake. "Deal. But with conditions. Here's my phone to get my number. From now on if anything suspicious occurs, or if anyone even *looks* questionable, you call me day or night."

Before he could get her promise, and sooner than he liked, he pulled up in front of her town house on Schiller.

Needing one more answer, again he grabbed her fingers, tighter this time, keeping her from sliding out of the car.

She became still but her eyes blazed, watching him.

He didn't flinch. "Venus, why are you so intent on helping to clear Tony?"

She stared at him so long the heat in his gut rose slowly to fill his chest. Still silent, she pulled out of his grasp and he let her go.

"I want to clear Tony because I feel partially responsible for all the pain he's going through. And Bridget. My finding the mermaid brooch started this whole chain of events. I need to finish it by proving Tony innocent despite the evidence against him. Then even someone as pig-headed as you will have to admit it's possible my father is innocent, too, despite the evidence. Then you'll know I'm right. Once you let go of your preconceived notions, anything can happen."

Confused by his desire to believe her and his iron-clad

belief she was wrong about her father, Connor watched her walk away from him into her town house.

Venus glanced out her living-room window for the fourth time. What she'd *never* believed possible stared her in the face.

Connor Clayworth O'Flynn was standing guard outside her door.

Well, *sitting* in his car, being her knight in a shiny red Ferrari.

To her it had always seemed out of character for someone as controlled as Connor to drive such a sleek, fast car.

Remembering his kiss, the taste and feel of him, she understood how wrong she'd been. She rubbed the goose bumps on her arms.

His kiss had been so expert, so sensuous, his fingers combing through her hair to rest at her throat as if he wanted to feel the changing rhythm of her pulse.

What would happen if he ever let go of the tight leash he holds on his emotions?

Her imagination sent hot erotic images through her head of Connor letting go completely. Taking their kiss to the next level...then the next...then...

Stop it! This is crazy!

Trying to rid herself of Connor, she soothed herself with chocolate-covered orange peel. *The endorphins will be good for me.*

Munching on a second piece of chocolate, she wandered into her jewelry bower, hoping her passion for design would completely banish him from her head.

She stared at all her favorite jewelry pieces and felt no thrill, no desire to create.

I can't concentrate.

She went back out, too restless to sit down. Sure Connor would have given up by now and left, she rushed to a window.

Oh, my God, he's still here.

She peered out, watching him rest his head back on his seat.

Confusion and an odd tension drove her away from the window and to her bathroom. She ran a hot bath and threw in scented oils. Surely her ultimate panacea for stress would finally help her to fall asleep.

Sipping at an icy cold flute of champagne, she lazed in the hot bubble bath until her fingertips looked as puckered as prunes.

Limp as a noodle, her eyelids drooping with exhaustion, she wandered back into the living room to look out the window one last time.

He's still here protecting me.

Her heart banged against her ribs and she felt so weak she dropped down on the padded window seat with the oddest warm feeling in her chest.

Should I go offer him coffee, tea, a drink, a bed?

The last idea reminded her again how her body had tingled and burned during his expert kiss.

No. Definitely not offering him a bed in the guest room.

She stared out the window until the sky seemed a little lighter toward Lake Michigan. A police car cruised slowly down the street and stopped at Connor's car. She watched him and the policeman chat through their open windows.

She heard her morning paper hit the front door before she saw the delivery guy. As the city stirred to life, Connor pulled away in his Ferrari.

Falling back against the window, she closed her eyes,

telling herself it must be fatigue and champagne making her forget why she disliked him, why she didn't trust him.

Pulling herself together, she sat up. Every woman admitted it was possible to feel physical attraction to a gorgeous guy even if she thought him a jerk.

But what she'd never thought possible before this moment was that, jerk or not, she felt sad when Connor left.

Chapter 11

The next morning, groggy, admittedly not on his game, Connor sat at his office desk staring down at a pile of memos and appointments.

The first one of the day had been demanded by Diana.

Closing his eyes, he leaned back in his chair.

Hell, I feel like I've been on a week-long bender.

Sure, he'd been out all night carousing with his cousins more times than he cared to count, but those tense hours sitting in his Ferrari waiting to do battle with some thief if necessary had been a first.

Why in the hell did I do it?

Hearing his office door open, he blinked several times trying to wake himself up to confront Diana.

Carrying a steaming mug of coffee, his Aunt Bridget strolled in.

Surprised, he stood at his desk and took the cup from her outstretched hand. "How did you know I needed caffeine? To what do I owe this unexpected pleasure? I usually get you coffee."

Her face inscrutable, Bridget marched to the disc

player. "You'll need a jolt of somethin' stronger than caffeine when you see this."

The security camera had caught Venus coming in the employee entrance.

The steely glint in her magnificent eyes and the determined set of her jaw made him smile.

Lady on a mission.

Desire shot through him, as it had last night.

Then he saw himself on tape, barring Venus's furious attempts to leave.

Last night he'd felt the hot energy between them. Now, seeing their body language and the expressions on their faces brought an even more powerful confusion about her effect on him.

"Seen enough?" Bridget pushed stop and turned to look at him. "Don't worry. I removed this before any of the security guards saw it. You know, you and Venus look like lovers havin' a hot and heavy quarrel. Are you lovers?"

The question should have shocked him. It didn't, because the thought had planted itself in his head from the moment they kissed. "You know Venus hates my guts."

Bridget shrugged. "So? They say there's a fine line between love and hate. Are you and Venus an item and you didn't want the rest of us to know because of the problems between our families?"

He'd never been more grateful that no security camera existed in his office to record their kiss. *If we were two other people, last night would have ended differently.*

"No, Aunt Bridget, we are not lovers. Situations are not always what they appear to be."

"She came to talk to you about Tony and me, didn't she?" Bridget dropped down into a deep brown leather chair.

He leaned against his desk to watch her face. He needed answers. "Aunt Bridget, Venus is concerned. So am I."

"I know. She came to the penthouse lookin' for you. Diana help her get into the store?"

He nodded.

"Those Smith sisters were always a handful." She chuckled. "Venus means well. Got a heart bigger than the outdoors." Bridget straightened her shoulders and slowly pushed herself up. "I do not want the two of you worryin' yourselves sick. I'm doin' enough of it for all of us."

From childhood he'd seen this strength in his aunt. He understood she didn't want him to comfort her, but it took all his willpower not to do it today.

Worried about her stark paleness and the fragility in her eyes, he chose his words carefully. "Will you at least talk to me about your feelings? About Tony?"

"What do you want me to say? My heart is broken." She shook her head. "I can't believe Tony stole the mermaid brooch or knew it was real when it was supposedly given to him. I'm all mixed up inside tryin' to figure out how it truly came into his possession and why. And why he went down to Taylor Street that night. And why he continued to go and keep it from me. And why I let it go on for all these years."

Bridget took such a deep sigh her entire body shuddered.

Unable to stop himself, he reached out to her.

She stepped back. "No mollycoddling me, Connor. I understand the implications of that brooch being the real Mermaid stolen from Clayworth's and Tony's admission that he gave it to me and his flimsy story of how it came into his possession. I know there were other gems stolen that night of the heist. What do you plan to do with the evidence you have against him?"

After a lifetime of being honest with his aunt, lying to her now felt strangely right.

"I'm taking the situation under advisement."

She cocked her head, squinted, and studied him as she'd done when he was a kid and she wanted to know what trouble he was planning to get into so she could stop it. "Best to tell me what's going on. Your inflated sense of justice and need to right wrongs is part of who you are, Connor. This isn't like you, not to take immediate action."

He forced himself to remain impassive even though he saw the pain in her eyes and it twisted his gut.

"I'm sorry if I appeared to rush to judgment on Tony last night." He heard himself repeat Venus's words. "I don't want to believe he's guilty of stealing the brooch. I will eventually begin a thorough but quiet investigation for Clayworth's, but first I'm laying some necessary groundwork of my own. Have you talked to Tony today, Aunt Bridget?"

She shook her head. "Fair enough, Connor. I get you won't tell me what you'll be doin'. And I don't want to talk about it now. Certainly I'm not ready to talk to Tony. All I can do is keep movin' forward until somethin' changes with the facts as they look now." Again she cocked her head to study him. "You're the handsomest young man I know, but this mornin' you're lookin' the worse for wear. Did you get any sleep last night?"

Remembering where and why he'd stayed awake watching over Venus, he smiled. "Not much."

"Me either. I'll make a fresh pot of coffee for both of us."

The door had barely closed behind her when Bridget opened it again. "Brace yourself, Connor. Another Smith sister is comin' down the hall to accost you."

Diana glided into the room with her angelic smile,

dressed in cream and the ballet slippers she liked when working in the windows and carrying a black portfolio nearly as big as she was.

He instantly went on alert.

They'd all learned as kids never to be fooled by her ethereal beauty. Angels had tempers.

"Relax, Connor," she said softly, seemingly gauging his reaction. "I'm here to say mea culpa. Last night I know I broke every rule in the book by giving Venus access to the store."

Wanting to reassure her, he shrugged and took the portfolio to lay it on his desk. "I understand there were extenuating circumstances."

She widened her eyes and put her hands on her hips. "Since when do you so easily disregard your own iron-clad rule?"

"Since last night." Again, he leaned against his desk. This time he folded his arms across his chest in a classic protective gesture. His gut told him he'd need it. "Diana, do you think I'm pigheaded?"

Her laughter sounded like melodious chimes.

"Now I understand why you're on red alert. Here I am, another Smith sister come to cause you trouble."

The portfolio between them, she perched beside him. Her angelic smile should have made him feel less tense. Today it didn't.

"I would have chosen a different term than Venus did. Yes, Connor, you are rigid in your beliefs. But I've also found you to be extremely fair and to have a deep desire to right wrongs. Something you share with Venus."

An instinct of self-preservation warned him he shouldn't be discussing last night but his desire to talk about Venus overrode his normal good sense.

"Did she tell you why she came here or anything about what happened when we talked?"

Diana lowered her eyes, the sweep of dark lashes hiding her expression. When she looked up she seemed to be peering through him.

"Hell, Diana, why is it sometimes I feel like you know what I'm thinking before I do?" He laughed, but part of him believed she was doing just that.

"I can't read your mind or anyone else's. All I read are nuances."

She slid off the desk and opened the portfolio. "Like now. You want to talk about Venus but whatever you've decided to do together is secret. So you can't really discuss her. I'll put you out of your misery and change the subject. Here are my sketches for the holiday windows."

Glad to have something to focus on besides Venus and their deal, he spread out the sketches across his desk.

Each detailed drawing built on the others to create an artist's mural of the joys of the holidays.

He picked up a drawing of a woman dressed in a short, glittering gold evening dress, stirring a pot on the stove with one hand and opening her black leather briefcase with the other, while watching two small children reading on a plush cream carpet.

"I agree with Grey and Ric, your imagination and grasp of what will draw in shoppers is always on target."

"That's why you pay me the big bucks. I like this one." She tapped her fingertips on a sketch of a man and woman dressed in elegant royal blue velvet robes. They were dancing in front of an evergreen tree lit with thousands of tiny lights, surrounded by piles of colorfully wrapped gifts, toys, and a long table laden with a ham, turkey, trays of pastries, bowls of nuts, and bottles of their most expensive champagnes and wines from the food halls.

"In this one I'm showcasing all the most sought-after toys of the season, the lingerie department, and the food hall. The most important aspect is presenting the joy of taking a few moments out of the busy season to steal a dance with your lover."

"I'm escorting Venus to the Dress for Success benefit next Saturday night." Shocked at his own stupidity, he shook his head. "Why in the hell did I bring that up now?"

"It's obviously on your mind." Her serene gaze urged him on.

"Yeah, it is. Do you know the name of her no-show date?"

"Brad Evans."

His name conjured up the long-ago brawl and all the anger he'd felt in that locker room. Now an odd unease settled over him. "Have they been seeing each other all these years?"

"Absolutely not. About five years ago they reconnected. On and off. Thank goodness mostly off for the last year or so."

The frosty glint in her eyes made him smile. "I take it you don't care for him. You know I once broke his nose. Back in college."

"I'm sure he deserved it."

If you only knew it was all about Venus.

All at once Diana sucked in a deep breath and quickly gathered the sketches back into her portfolio.

"You know, Connor, in fairness to Venus I shouldn't be discussing her love life. Not that she's in love with Brad," Diana added quickly, smiling. "Whatever happened last night I'm grateful it put you in such a good mood that you forgive me. And I know Venus will be grateful, too."

The truth hit him like a body blow. *Grateful is not what I want Venus to feel for me. I want much much more.*

Pandora's Box teemed with customers, which on any other day would have had Venus tingling with excitement and gratitude.

Today she had a devil of a time keeping her focus *off* Connor and *on* helping customers choose the perfect evening gown and the jewelry and accessories to go with it.

The fifth time she made what she considered mediocre to downright bad choices with trusting clients, she sent a frantic text to Diana.

I'm losing it. Help if your flex schedule permits. Please tell me you still have a job.

The instant she sent it she knew deep inside she was being silly, because Connor would never go back on his word. She shivered, wrapping her arms around her shoulders as if to protect herself, momentarily pushing the past to the side so she could reach her goal with Connor.

Because there are now two reputations to save and other aspects of my plan have taken alarming, shocking turns.

Rationalizing this mess didn't make it any less scary. Determined to focus on *anything* else, she reorganized the jewelry table twice between helping customers.

An hour later, the sight of Diana entering the store with a serene smile and a thumbs-up confirmed Venus's fledgling trust in Connor and there he was right back in her head, which deeply disturbed her on several levels of her emotional well-being.

What if I'm wrong? What if he's trying to charm me again for some reason?

Ignoring her twinges of self-doubt as best as she could,

she helped a customer choose between a 1940s Walborg beaded bag hand-made in Belgium and a 1950s Lucite bag by Willardy, while Diana showed two women a whimsical hat by local milliner John Koch and a larger, more flamboyant creation by young designer Loreta Corsetti.

Several minutes later, the problem solved by the customer deciding to take both bags, the two ladies leaving with the perfect hats for them, and Diana watching the store, Venus slipped behind the brown velvet swag curtain to return phone calls.

Exhausted, she threw herself into her desk chair and glanced at the memo sheet. Maxie's name jumped out at her. Curious, she dialed the number.

"Hello, Maxine Robinson."

Maxie's abnormally morose voice sent a hot wave of worry to the pit of Venus's stomach. "Hi, it's Venus Smith. Are you all right?"

"Thank you for returning my call." Maxie's voice changed to a breathless almost whisper. "I have a matter of grave importance to discuss. I know you find many of your treasures through estate sales and on consignment. I would like to discuss such a possibility with you."

Hearing the door open, Venus glanced around the curtain to see three women entering the store. "We're swarmed with customers right now. Could you stop by around six when we close?"

"Yes. I'd prefer to conduct our business in utmost privacy."

"Of course." Venus kept her tone deliberately light, sensing Maxie's embarrassment. "I'll look forward to seeing you around six."

In the back corner, the grandfather clock she'd inherited from her mother struck five-forty-five when the last customer walked out the door. Venus's stretched nerves felt every bong of the chime.

Relieved to finally have a few minutes alone with Diana, even if she couldn't reveal *all,* Venus found her sister redesigning the display of hats and gloves.

"Thanks for coming in. Everything all right at Clayworth's? Did Connor say anything about last night?" she asked, as nonchalantly as possible, considering she'd been thinking about him all day.

Diana's smile told Venus she hadn't fooled her sister despite her best effort.

"Obviously neither one of you is talking about last night, which means something profound must have happened."

Deliberately avoiding Diana's keen gaze, Venus fussed with the feathers on a Loreta Corsetti hat. "Well, what *did* he say to you?"

"He told me he's your escort next Saturday night and asked the name of your no-show date."

Surprised, but oddly pleased, Venus looked up. "Did you tell him Brad? You know, years ago Connor broke his nose in a brawl in the locker room at NU."

Strangely, now Diana looked away, wandering over to the triple-mirrored dressing table.

"Yes, I know. Obviously Connor knew years ago that Brad is a jerk. Just like I do now. In the past Brad may have had spurts of deserving you but they were long ago, even if you won't admit it."

"Oh, my God, please tell me you didn't discuss my love life with Connor." Feeling slightly ill at the very thought, Venus followed her sister's ceaseless wandering around the store.

"No, I did not discuss your love life, beyond the fact

that you haven't seen Brad often in the last year." At last Diana stopped to look her in the eyes. "Venus, please don't underestimate Connor. I hope you know what you're doing."

"Of course I do. I promise you." Venus sounded more confident than she felt, considering her shocking change of plans and feelings. "I'd tell you everything, but it would be divulging someone else's private business."

She glanced at her watch. "Speaking of which, a client who asked for a private meeting is coming in at six."

"It's almost six now." Diana looked at the grandfather clock as she glided past it toward the basement door. "I saw the shipment arrived from R&Y Agousti. I've been dying to unpack the python and water snake clutches and minaudières we ordered. They're incredible works of art. I'll be in the basement drooling over them. Call me when the client leaves."

At the stroke of six Maxie walked in carrying two blue shopping bags with the Clayworth clock logo and name printed on both sides.

She glanced around furtively. "Are we alone?"

Venus locked the door. "Diana's in the basement unpacking a shipment of handmade purses from Paris."

"Your dear sister is like an angel. Like you, she can be trusted." Maxie sighed as she laid three silk jewelry bags on the counter.

Slowly, she carefully opened the first one.

It contained a 1960s Hobe Bib necklace, bracelet, pin, and earrings parure in gilt metal with strings of faceted faux topaz and red aurora borealis beads with overlaid spherical blue and pink Venetian glass beads.

"Beautiful," Venus breathed, arranging the pieces carefully on a felt-lined tray.

The second bag revealed a Miriam Haskell floral

necklace and earrings. "This is a costume jewelry classic," Venus gushed, placing the pieces on the second tray.

The last jewelry bag held a Kenneth Jay Lane multiple pendant "catwalk" necklace of silver-gilt base metal set with clear rhinestones.

Venus couldn't miss the sadness in Maxie's eyes as she gazed down at it.

She'd seen this look before in other clients when they were parting with objects they loved. Always she felt the aching need to make them feel better.

"I can see you've taken excellent care of these pieces. They're all in pristine condition."

"I try." Maxie dabbed at her eyes with a white linen handkerchief monogrammed in pink stitching. "My dear Edward has been most generous. Now I must rise to the occasion and help him in his hour of need. There are more treasures at home. Would it be possible to make an appointment for you to come to purge my closet?"

Seeing Maxie's distress, Venus quickly glanced through her date book. "I have time in about three weeks. I can call you with an exact date."

"Please do so at your earliest convenience. It's of the utmost importance." Maxie leaned across the counter. "Meanwhile, please tell no one about my efforts to help my dear Edward since his investments went south." She rolled her eyes. "If only he had taken the sage advice in Kate Carmichael's column as I did, he would not be in this predicament."

"I understand." Venus patted Maxie's soft hand. "It will be our secret."

Unable to contain her burning curiosity another second, Venus peered down into the huge shopping bags. "What else do you have in there?"

"Paintings. I very much hope you can tell me where to sell them." Maxie reached into the smaller bag and pulled out a copy of Leonardo da Vinci's *Mona Lisa*.

Venus's first glance at the stunning oil made her body tingle in disbelief. Then disbelief morphed into a burning shock along every nerve.

She knelt in front of the painting. "I *know* the original is in the Louvre but this is an *incredible* copy. I mean really amazing. The use of light. Everything. Oh, my God, Maxie this painting is unbelievable!"

Maxie puffed out her impressive chest. "I'm flattered you find it worthy. Where can I sell it?" she asked bluntly.

Still reeling in admiration, Venus blinked up at her. "My degree is in fine arts with a major in jewelry and textile design, but Diana has a master's in art history. Would you mind if I asked her to look at this?"

Maxie nodded. "I'd be honored to have your dear sister's expertise."

Venus rushed to the stairwell. "Diana, would you please come up?" she called down.

When Diana reached the top step, Venus pulled her close to whisper in her ear. "You won't believe what Maxie has brought in."

They both turned and Venus saw two other masterpieces had been whisked out of the bigger shopping bags.

Diana glanced at her and then, and as if in a trance, she moved to the *Mona Lisa*, Rembrandt's *Young Girl at an Open Half-Door*, and Georgia O'Keeffe's *Black Iris* propped against the counter.

Diana slipped to her knees in front of the three paintings, her eyes widening. "Venus, please give me your jewelry loupe."

She quickly retrieved it from behind the desk and stood

in silence with Maxie watching Diana slowly, carefully examine each painting. She appeared to be paying particular attention to the signatures.

Venus felt ready to burst with questions when finally Diana looked up. "Where did you get these, Maxie?"

"I painted them."

"*What!*" Venus gasped, trying to grasp the fact that Maxie possessed such unexpected talent. "You could be an art forger."

Maxie clasped her hands to her heaving chest. "That's illegal."

With her angelic smile, Diana stared up at them. "What Venus meant is that these copies are good enough to fool some experts. You have an amazing talent, Maxie."

"I've always had a photographic memory." She glanced between them, pleasure a warm glow on her face. "If I see it, I can reproduce it down to the tiniest detail."

"Have you ever thought about painting your own vision, instead of copying masterpieces?" Venus asked gently.

"No. Do you think I could?"

"Yes." Diana nodded as she rose gracefully to her feet. "If you leave these canvases with me I'll look into the best auction house to place them."

"You're ever so kind." Maxie clapped her hands together. "Perhaps you may have some news when I see you both at the benefit for Dress for Success next Saturday night." She flashed a small smile between them. "I trust my paintings will also be our little secret."

"Of course, what's one more." Venus smiled back, thinking of Connor.

"Wonderful. Now would you please be so kind as to summon me a cab." Smiling, Maxie touched the Tess

necklace at her throat. "I'm meeting dear Edward to celebrate the seventh anniversary of our first date at our favorite restaurant on Taylor Street."

At the mention of a restaurant on Taylor Street Venus
positively quivered with interest. "We'll drive you."

As if she had picked up her thought, Diana nodded.
"Yes. We were planning to go down to Greek Town for
dinner. Taylor Street isn't much farther."

Clasping her hands to her chest, Maxie smiled. "How
generous of you both. I'd be delighted for the ride."

Remembering every word Tony and Bridget had said
about the infamous illegal casino, Venus had a hard time
driving and trying to listen to Maxie's exuberant listing of
Ed's many virtues all the way to Taylor Street.

"There!" Maxie pointed out. "There it is on the north-
east corner."

Pulse pounding, Venus pulled in front of a low gray-
shingled building with a small, discreet sign saying *Fine
Italian Cuisine* and a parking lot roped off by red flags.

"Thank you." Maxie slid out of the passenger seat. "I look
forward to seeing you both very soon." In a few steps she
disappeared behind heavy-looking dark oak double doors.

Playing a hunch, Venus jumped out of the car, released
the flag-draped rope barricade, climbed back in, and
pulled into the black asphalt parking lot.

"What are you doing?" Diana asked from the backseat.

Before Venus could answer, a red-vested attendant ran
toward them, waving his arms and shouting.

"Move! You can't park here!"

With a hopefully innocent-looking smile, Venus rolled
down the window. "I'm sorry. What's the problem?"

"You can't park here," he shouted again.

"But isn't it the parking lot for the restaurant?"

"Paved it recently. Park on the street," he said, motioning her away.

"But I just want to go in to make a reservation. Can't I park here long enough to do that?" she asked, trying to still the excitement pounding through her and ignoring Diana's pointed silence.

Looking harassed, the valet shook his head. "No, not here. You can park in front of the door long enough to make a reservation."

Obeying, she backed up. "I'll only be inside a few minutes," she muttered to Diana.

"I hope you know what you're doing," her sister replied, in a tone that spoke volumes.

"So do I." Venus climbed out of the car to follow Maxie through the dark double doors.

It took a few blurred seconds of blinking to adjust to the dim lighting in the narrow, low-ceilinged restaurant.

All dark wood and lined with banquettes of red velvet, the room looked nearly empty except for a few diners nearly hidden at tall chairs around white-clothed tables in the middle of the room.

Nowhere did she see Maxie or Ed.

Thinking Maxie must be in the ladies room and Ed hadn't arrived, she waited, studying the black-and-white photos on the wall. They were all of Chicago's inglorious gangster past in the 1920s and 1930s.

I swear two of these pictures look like they were taken in this room.

A tuxedoed maître d' appeared and peered down his long nose at her. "May I help you, Madame?"

"Yes, I just dropped off a friend, Maxie Robinson." Again, Venus glanced around the room. "But I don't see her."

"Ms. Robinson has joined a private party. Is there anything else I can do to help you?"

Not wanting to disturb any special anniversary celebration Ed might have arranged for Maxie, but sensing she was on to a clue, Venus flung her hair over one shoulder.

"Yes. I would like a reservation for next Monday night."

"I'm sorry, Madame. The restaurant is closed on Monday evening."

Determined, and not liking his very thinly veiled superior attitude, Venus gave him *her* haughtiest look. "Then Tuesday will do. And I'd like to make the reservation in the name of Connor O'Flynn."

At last she had the full attention of the maître d'.

"Connor Clayworth O'Flynn?" he asked.

Flicking him a bored glance, she shrugged. "Really, in Chicago, is there another?"

All at once oozing helpfulness, the maître d' grinned. "Madame, what time on Tuesday and how many in your party."

"Two at seven."

His smile widened. "May I inquire if this is a special occasion?"

"But of course it is." She turned on her heel and strolled out the doors, hoping she looked confident.

Now all she had to do was convince Connor to go along with her plan to check out the hidden casino she *knew* must be under the forbidden parking lot.

Chapter 12

Trying to call Venus for the tenth time, Connor walked slowly up the grand staircase at the Four Seasons hotel. "Where in the hell are you, Venus?" he cursed under his breath.

He hated to bring his phone to black-tie affairs, but after two days of missed calls and cryptic text messages from Venus he felt a thin edge of desperation cracking his calm exterior.

He gave it one last try. Got her voicemail again, cursed, and shut the damn phone off.

Good manners dictated he spend the next four-plus hours on duty with his mother and her guests.

The hell with good manners. Venus, if you show up at this party I'll have to drag you out of here to discover what in the hell is going on.

Knowing he was already late, he hurried through the gathering room, where only a few security guys roamed the silent auction tables, and walked on into the ballroom crammed with people.

Venus's face jumped out of the crowd.

At a table next to the dance floor, she sat, laughing,

between David Sumner and Kate Carmichael and across from Diana, Alistair, and Rebecca.

Ignoring his mother's table on the other side, he headed directly to Venus.

What in the hell is she up to now to get herself into trouble?

Rebecca saw him first and waved him to her side.

Turning her head toward him, her eyes gleaming in the dim light, her hair half-up, the rest falling around her bare shoulders, Venus looked so beautiful he honest to God felt his heart miss a beat.

Rebecca laughed. "Connor, from the look on your face I believe the Stanley Paul Orchestra is playing your song."

"I beg your pardon?" He bent to kiss Rebecca's cheek, controlling his real need to drag Venus from the ballroom to talk.

"The orchestra is playing 'Bewitched, Bothered, and Bewildered.' That's how you look." Rebecca gestured across the small dance floor to where his mother sat with Mugsy and CeCe. "Is it because of that delectable creature in pale mauve? CeCe Osborn?"

"No." He straightened, his eyes lingering on Venus's interested face. "It's because I'm late."

"Darling, you are very late." Rebecca laughed. "We are already through our salad course. Go make up with your mother. I know she's like the Sphinx and would never show it but I'm sure she's fuming. Good luck."

Rebecca was right. He needed to leave, despite his desire to confront Venus here and now.

He nodded to the group around the table, noting with a pang of sharp anger how tense Alistair looked. *Does he know how much he's hurting his daughter by not admitting his guilt?*

Connor allowed his eyes to linger on Venus. "I'll talk to all of you later."

She nodded, twisting a piece of her hair around two fingers.

He hesitated, knowing that meant trouble. But when his mother met his gaze and gestured to his seat, he forced himself across the room.

Glad he'd become expert at hiding his feelings, counting the minutes until he could somehow get Venus alone, he kissed his mother's cheek and slid into the empty chair beside her.

"I apologize for being late. I had to deal with some problems at the store."

"You're exactly like your father and your uncles. Clayworth's always came first. As it should." His mother sighed as deeply as her horror of drama would allow. "As you can see we've been deserted by Bridget and Tony, for some reason. I'm not pleased to be a table of four."

"This is a lovely size table, Victoria," Mugsy offered with a small smile.

"Yes, it must do under the circumstances." She glanced across the dance floor. "We could have joined David and Rebecca Sumner's table and made it a ten top if Alistair hadn't been their guest. Much too awkward."

Mugsy leaned closer. "Alistair Smith is such a distinguished looking man. Now tell me more about the scandal involving him and Clayworth's."

Knowing how hurt Venus would be to hear her father discussed like this, Connor abruptly stood. "Would you like to dance, CeCe?"

"I thought you'd never ask." She took his outstretched hand and he led her onto the dance floor.

Her mauve jersey gown hugged her tall, slender body.

She smiled up at him. In another time and place he might have felt a stir of interest.

"I assume the two beautiful women with the extraordinary eyes you're watching are Alistair's daughters."

"Yes," he said quickly, turning CeCe so he could no longer stare at Venus. "Their sister, Athena, is engaged to my cousin, Drew Clayworth."

CeCe's eyes widened in surprise. "Isn't that an impossibly awkward situation for both families, considering the circumstances?"

Once he'd felt the same way.

"Drew and Athena have been in love since they were teenagers. Long before the trouble with Alistair. They'll make it work."

"Still, how difficult it must be for all of you. Victoria told us the story. Look. Ed Mahoney has finally arrived. My mother will be pleased to have a dance partner at last."

Grateful CeCe had changed the subject, he twirled her around the dance floor, trying to keep Venus in view.

The music ended and so did his patience. *To hell with waiting. Time to find out what trouble you've gotten yourself into this time, Venus.*

He caught sight of her getting up from her table to stroll toward the door.

"CeCe, would you like to take a look at the silent auction?"

"Please. I adore them."

Relief and a burning ache to reach Venus drove him to hurry CeCe into the gathering room.

He saw Venus strolling along the tables of jewelry items and urged CeCe in the same direction, trying to pull her along to finally intercept Venus near the auction item from Pandora's Box.

CeCe gasped, staring down into the velvet-lined jewelry box. "What an elegant pin."

His eyes locked with Venus's. Then she looked away to smile at CeCe.

"That is a rare swan and bridge pin with blue and dark ruby red enameling and clear rhinestones on a sterling silver casting from the 1940s. I donated it from my store."

Venus is never so polite when she speaks to me.

CeCe nodded. "Wouldn't it be perfect on any dress or suit."

"Absolutely. If you're starting to collect it's best to begin with a brooch like this. You'll find the most use for it. It can be pinned on a suit lapel, collar, or pocket, or a hat, belt, or evening dress."

"Thank you." CeCe laughed. "You've convinced me. I'm going back to my table to use my Bidpal to own this."

"Good luck. I hope you get it. Have a nice evening."

Venus's voice sounded husky to him. She smiled, flicked him a look—he had no idea what it meant except to frustrate the hell out of him—and strolled back into the ballroom.

"I truly do want to bid on this piece. Could we go back to our table?" CeCe slipped her hand around his arm.

"Definitely, we need to go back in." *And this time I'm talking to Venus whether she wants me to or not.*

He found her chatting and laughing with Ed at the edge of the dance floor.

CeCe released his arm and stretched out her hand to Ed. "This is the dance you promised me. No excuses."

Puffing out his chest, Ed bowed, took her hand, and led CeCe onto the dance floor.

Not believing his luck, Connor pulled Venus into his arms and followed them.

"Why, thank you, Connor. Yes, I would love to dance.

Etta James's 'At Last' is one of the most romantic songs ever. What a shame you aren't dancing with your date." Venus smiled up at him. "She's lovely and nice. Much better than last year's twins."

"To hell with my mother's matchmaking. What's this plan you can't tell me about on the phone? We have a deal. We're in this together."

"Yes, we do have a deal." She tilted her head to look up at him through her dark lashes. "Have you noticed I didn't wear the brooch tonight? Just like you requested."

The raw emotions and confusion she inspired made him a little crazy. He pulled her tighter, her breasts round and full above her strapless gown where he pressed her against his chest.

"Thank you, Venus. Now what do you want in return?"

"Very clever of you to figure it out, Connor." Venus flung back her head and laughed up at him.

His gut clenched with desire.

"On Tuesday night I want you to take me to dinner at the restaurant on Taylor Street where I dropped off Maxie for a date with Ed. I'm sure it's the place Bridget and Tony told us about. We need to see it for ourselves. Maybe there's still a hidden casino under the parking lot. Maybe there's a clue there. Something that might help us find out who gambled the mermaid brooch away that night."

Relieved she hadn't gone off alone to the restaurant, he gave in to his need to draw her even closer and whisper into her ear. Her hair smelled of apricots and felt like silk against his lips.

"Why, thank you, Venus. Yes, I would love to take you to dinner Tuesday night."

He felt her stiffen in his arms. Anxious, he slid one hand to her throat, feeling the accelerated beat of her heart.

"What's wrong, Venus?"

"Nothing." Still not meeting his eyes, she pulled away. "The music has stopped. I'll text you the address and meet you there at seven."

She turned away so quickly, her hair fell forward, hiding her face.

She didn't go back to her table. Then he could have watched her to figure out what the hell had changed in a split second to make her run away from him.

If Venus could have run in her tight black sequin and silk dress, she would have kicked off her stilettos and made a dash for the door.

Instead, she forced herself to glide as gracefully as possible away from Connor.

Her body felt on fire.

The playful way he'd whispered in her ear had sent goose bumps down her spine and induced a swirling heat in regions of her body which should feel *nothing* for him, of all people on the planet. Just as she shouldn't have felt a twinge of jealousy when she saw him with CeCe Osborn, who was so exactly his type.

These feelings are wrong. Absolutely positively wrong.

Venus hid in the ladies lounge, pretending to be fixing her hair, but actually trying to stop shaking.

Diana found her there.

"Are you all right? Dad's getting worried. You've been gone so long."

Not wanting her sister to read her face, Venus ducked her head to rearrange the antique diamond comb in her hair.

"I'm fine. Just having trouble with keeping my hair up. I'll be back to the table in a few minutes."

"They're ready to serve the main course. No one will start eating without you."

Knowing she had no choice, Venus nodded. "I'll be there shortly. I promise. Run interference for me just a bit longer."

Diana squeezed her shoulder. "Always."

Grateful, Venus glanced up to watch her glide out the door.

Alone, Venus stared at her reflection. She blinked, hoping to rid her eyes of confusion, and she practiced her normal smile. It looked strained and fake even to her.

I need to get a grip and remember who I am. Remember who Connor is. Remember there is nothing I won't do to help prove my father is innocent, no matter what it costs either one of us.

Talk of the Town *by Rebecca Covington-Sumner*

Darlings, I'm delighted to report romance is still in the air in Chicago!

Never more so than at the Service Club Gala at the Four Seasons hotel where the fabulous women of this venerable organization re-created El Morocco.

Sometimes nicknamed Elmo, this twentieth-century Manhattan nightclub was frequented by the rich and famous in the 1930s and 1950s.

So it was in Chicago this week with the civic and social leaders of our fair city in attendance.

From the dinner music, "low enough for guests to chat yet loud enough to enjoy," to the last bite of the delectably sinful chocolate dessert, the evening was perfection.

Seen dancing from Lady GaGa's "Bad Romance," to the Black Eyed Peas "Got a Feeling," to Etta James's dreamy "At Last" were Alistair Smith, too long absent from the social scene; finance columnist and author Kate Carmichael; insurance mogul Ed Mahoney there with a table of fellow brokers; Victoria Clayworth O'Flynn gracing us from Palm Beach along with her friend Mugsy Osborn and her daughter, CeCe Osborn; often-seen-on-the-scene Smith sisters Venus and Diana; and Connor O'Flynn.

Our eligible Clayworth bachelor and the lovely Miss Osborn were also seen earlier in the week dining together at the Drake Hotel's Club International.

Could the mischievous fellow, Cupid, be at work once again?

Certainly there was romance in the air, but exactly who the arrow of love may have struck remains to be seen.

Stay tuned, Darlings. I promise more good news to come very soon!

Chapter 13

On Tuesday, before she left to meet Connor at the restaurant, Venus tortured herself by rereading Rebecca's Sunday *Talk of the Town* column about the Service Club Gala to relive the night in her head.

Her odd hot jealousy at seeing Connor with CeCe Osborn looking like his perfect match, tall, slender and elegant. The twinge of jealousy again while reading about his dinner date with the beautiful Miss Osborn.

Venus's icy self-doubt giving way to shivering, she closed her eyes, letting the sensations she'd felt in his arms, pressed against his chest, his breath tickling her ear, wash over her one last time. She hadn't been mortified, as she had been as an awkward teenager the day he'd pulled her out of the lake.

This time, crushed to his body, she'd wanted him.

Okay. Enough. Reality check.

She opened her eyes and threw the paper in the trash.

Face the truth. Connor and I have an uneasy truce, nothing more.

And they had a deal she hoped would help Tony and Bridget and ultimately her father. It all seemed to be run-

ning amuck because of her confused libido, and that needed
to stop. Now. Tonight she and Connor had a job to do.

Defiant, she fastened the mermaid brooch to the scoop
neck of her black wool dress.

Impatient, Connor glanced at his watch again. *Hell!
Another hour before I can meet Venus at the restaurant.*

Restless, he got up from his desk and paced down the
hall to Bridget's office.

He found his mother in deep discussion with Bridget,
while Mugsy appeared confused and CeCe concerned.

Bridget looked up, saw him, and relief softened her
pale, tense face.

His mother glanced over her shoulder at him. "There
you are, Connor. We were coming to see you. Help me
convince Bridget and Tony to have dinner with us this
week. I've hardly seen anything of the dear man and
Mugsy found him an interesting dinner companion."

Bridget's eyes pleaded with him to help.

"Isn't Tony still fighting off the flu, Aunt Bridget?"

"Yes. He had a slight fever last night and he's still
coughin' up a storm," she fibbed, knowing his mother's
aversion to anyone sneezing around her.

"Why didn't you say so in the first place?" His mother
stepped back. "Connor, can you join us tonight for
dinner?"

"No, I'm sorry. I have an important meeting." He sent
an apologetic smile between Mugsy and CeCe.

"Then I insist on tomorrow night at home in Lake
Forest."

Willing to agree to anything to get out of here, Connor
nodded. "Yes. I look forward to it. Now I need to go. Have
a nice evening, ladies." Sending a loving look to his aunt

Bridget to forgive him, he turned and stalked out of her office.

No way could he be late for Venus. God knew what trouble she might get into without him. At least investigating an old speakeasy from Chicago's notorious prohibition years turned private club with possible illegal gambling was a hell of a lot safer than her making herself a target by wearing the damn mermaid brooch all over town.

Venus pulled up in front of the low, shingled restaurant on Taylor Street. The parking lot remained roped off with red flags and the same valet came running out.

She watched him park her car across the street in the lot of another restaurant.

"Asphalt still not dry?" she asked with what she hoped sounded like innocent interest.

He shook his head. "Nay. Had to do it again."

I'll bet. Smiling, she strolled inside to wait for Connor.

A few minutes later, he came in, and frowned when he saw her pacing the entryway. "Am I late?"

"No. Did the valet park your car across the street?"

"Sure. He said the parking lot has just been resurfaced," Connor stated in his usual calm, reasonable voice.

"That's what they told me three days ago." She leaned closer, pretending to kiss his cheek. "I think the asphalt's been drying for decades because there is still an illegal casino under there."

"Then let's find out, Venus." He helped her off with her black cape and handed it to the attendant in the coat room.

Venus felt him tense and knew he'd seen the mermaid pinned to her shoulder.

"Why in the hell are you wearing the brooch tonight?" he muttered with an edge of anger in his voice.

Smiling, she turned and slid her arm through his, hoping they looked to anyone watching to be a devoted couple.

"I'm wearing the brooch because it was won here in that poker game Tony told us about. Someone might remember it."

Obviously going along with her ruse, he leaned closer. "Venus, the alleged poker game took place thirty years ago."

Continuing to smile up at him, she stroked the lapel of his dark suit. "Connor, you know as well as I do there are several restaurants in Chicago where waiters have worked for decades. They know everything and everyone."

His gaze slid slowly over her. "Do you have any other ideas up your sleeve I need to worry about?"

"Of course. Just follow my lead." She urged him farther into the dark interior until they reached the maître d'.

He stood in regal attention to greet them.

"Mr. O'Flynn, we are delighted you chose to dine with us this evening. We have a quiet corner reserved for you."

She glanced at the back table set for two and then gazed up, fluttering her eyelashes at Connor.

"Oh, I'd love something a bit more private for our celebration. Didn't Ed arrange something special for Maxie here?"

The gleam in Connor's emerald eyes curled that forbidden heat through her again.

"I'm sure there's a private room available for us tonight," he purred, kissing the tip of her nose.

She took a deep breath, holding her grip on his arm to keep herself steady.

The maître d' hesitated for one sharp beat of her heart.

Then nodded. "I'm sure something can be arranged. Please. Give us a moment."

He stepped away and Connor looked down at her. "How did you know there were private rooms?"

"When I came in here looking for Maxie and Ed the maître d' told me they were at a private party. Which I assumed must be behind one of these paneled doors."

The maître d' reappeared. "This way please."

Excitement a hot band around her breasts, she clung to Connor's arm to cross the room. The maître d' slid open a dark door, which had looked a part of the paneling.

"Please, both of you be careful. These steps are steep."

The staircase led down to a wide hall lined with brass art deco wall sconces and discreet doors set into the paneling in such a way as to be almost invisible.

"Here you are." He opened the second door on the right into a small wine cellar, filled floor to ceiling with racks of bottles. Piped-in music was playing Puccini's *Madame Butterfly* and a round table arranged with china, silver, and crystal for two rested in the center of the room.

"I hope this meets with your approval. I understand you're celebrating a special occasion."

Without missing a beat, Connor pulled her closer to press a kiss on her forehead.

"Yes. We're celebrating the first night of the rest of our lives. We'll need a bottle of your finest champagne and your most experienced waiter. I want everything to be perfect tonight."

Overcome with a totally inappropriate desire to melt into his arms, Venus buried her face in his shoulder, wanting to hide her reaction. "Oh, Connor," she sighed, trying to play her part.

"I'll see to it," Venus heard the maître d' say, followed by the click of the closing door.

She spun out of Connor's arms. "All right, you can stop pretending." Feeling him watching her, she prowled around the wine cellar trying to read wine labels.

"I think you're on to something, Venus."

Startled, she stopped and stared at him. "Really?"

"Yeah. Let's see how this plays out. I hear someone coming."

In two strides he stood beside her, his arm draped around her shoulders, his fingers tantalizingly close to her breasts.

An older gentleman with a neat salt-and-pepper mustache came in carrying an ice bucket.

"My name is Joseph. It will be my pleasure to help you this evening. Does this bottle meet with your approval?" He held up a frosty bottle of Cristal.

Connor studied the label and nodded. "Yes. Why don't we follow this with antipasto."

"Very good. I'll get that started, but first let me pour your champagne."

Connor pulled out a chair and before her knees gave out on her, she dropped into it. He sat so close their thighs touched under the table.

Joseph popped the cork on the champagne bottle and poured a small amount into Connor's glass.

He drank it and nodded. "Excellent. Thank you."

Her nerves quivering, she beamed at Connor while Joseph poured them each a glass and left the room.

"A toast to getting answers?" Connor asked.

"I'll drink to that." She clicked his glass and gulped down the icy champagne. Ever so carefully she inched away, breaking contact with his warm thigh.

He leaned closer. "Don't you trust me?"

"You know I don't. Well, maybe a little at the moment," she murmured, "What are you doing? We're supposed to be investigating, not having a four-course dinner."

"We are investigating. We're looking for the information you believe we might find here. Trust me, this is the way to go about it."

"Well, when should we start asking questions?"

There was a discreet knock on the door.

"Now," Connor whispered in her ear as Joseph came in carrying what looked like tiny paper-thin pizzas. He placed a plate in front of each of them.

"This is our famous flatbread with our special blend of cheeses and herbs. Compliments of the chef."

She took one bite. "Delicious," she lied, too nervous and confused to taste anything. It might as well have been sawdust.

"How long have you been here, Joseph?" she asked as calmly as she could muster.

"Forty years last month."

"Then you should choose our next courses." Connor stroked her neck where her pulse pounded with excitement. "Unless you want a particular dish, Venus?"

Putting a shrieking halt to her traitorous libido and wanting to give him a reality check, she stared deep into his eyes. "Tonight all I want is you."

At last he looked as startled and confused as she felt.

Joseph smiled. "I'll see to your dinner." He backed from the room to leave them alone.

"What in the hell was that all about?" Scraping back his chair, Connor stood to pace the room. All at once the intimate wine cellar seemed to be shrinking around them by the second and vibrating with tension.

"Just playing your game, Connor," she said, hoping she sounded calm and he couldn't hear how loudly her heart was pounding. "Are you ready to get serious about this now?"

Swinging back to the table, he poured himself another glass of champagne. "Yes, you're right. We need to move this along."

He dropped down in his chair, moving it slightly away from her.

A few minutes later, with another discreet knock, Joseph came in with an antipasto plate of roasted artichokes, peppers, asparagus, and Italian sausages.

Connor held up his hand, stopping him. "Could you please cover that dish, Joseph? I understand there may be other activities we could enjoy tonight besides your fine cuisine."

Venus held her breath.

Not by a flicker of an eyelash did Joseph give anything away.

"If you'll excuse me a moment." He stepped from the room.

Venus met Connor's eyes and counted six thumps of her heart against her ribs before Joseph returned.

"I believe your Clayworth uncles enjoyed our services in the past, and we are happy to offer them to you tonight, Mr. O'Flynn. What's your pleasure?"

"Poker," Venus blurted out, rising to her feet.

"I apologize. There are no games arranged for this evening. However, there are other games of chance available. Craps. Roulette. Blackjack. Baccarat."

Connor rose to stand beside her. "Let's take a look."

Joseph led them to the end of the hall and opened nearly invisible heavy-looking dark double doors she'd thought were paneling.

Hidden behind them she saw an elegant room with two tables of blackjack and craps, a roulette wheel, and baccarat in the corner. Every table was surrounded by men and a few women. Waiters moved among them with trays of drinks.

"Where are the poker tables?" Connor asked.

"Through here." Joseph motioned them to a short hall and yet another dark, heavy door. "This is one of our two private poker rooms."

Shivers ran down Venus's spine looking at the deep green-painted walls, the low-hanging art déco chandelier over the octagonal oak table.

She could almost smell the cigar smoke. *See* the piles of money, the mermaid brooch placed on the table in wager.

"Who arranges games?" Connor asked with an emotionless poker face.

How does he do it? I'm burning up with excitement.

"Alfredo will take care of whatever you need, Mr. O'Flynn."

"Has he been here a long time, like you, Joseph?" she asked, not able to hold back her feelings.

"No. He took over from Mr. Marco, who had been here for years before I started."

This is exactly what we came here to find out.

"How fascinating," she gasped, deliberately stroking the mermaid brooch pinned on her shoulder, and pleased when Joseph's gaze rested briefly on it. "When did Mr. Marco retire? I'd love to meet him."

"Sadly, he passed away three years ago."

Limp with crushing disappointment, she sagged against Connor and he held her steady.

"I'm sorry. I'm sure he had wonderful stories to tell."

Joseph's mouth curled ever so slightly beneath his neat mustache. "Mr. Marco had seen and heard it all but remained to the end the soul of discretion."

"Did he ever talk about the Saint of Taylor Street?" Venus asked, hoping for any tidbit of information that might help them.

"As I said, Mr. Marco was always discreet. But yes, he knew about the good the Saint does." He shrugged. "The Saint of Taylor Street is a phantom. No one knows his identity. I'm sorry I can't be of more help."

Connor's arm tightened around her. "Thank you, Joseph. I'm sure our dinner is ready."

"Yes, indeed, Mr. O'Flynn. All is ready."

In a daze of disappointment Venus walked back to the small table in the intimate wine cellar with the faint scent of fermented grapes.

Her hopes dashed, she watched through a filter of tumbling thoughts about what to do next as a plate of pasta primavera appeared before her.

Going through the motions, she picked at the pasta and the grilled bronzini that followed.

Once Joseph removed the plates and left the room, Venus looked pleadingly at Connor.

"Can we go now? I'm sorry I wasted your evening."

"You didn't waste my evening." He leaned closer and stayed there as Joseph came in carrying dessert cheeses, strawberries, raspberries, and small Italian cookies, some with almonds on the top.

The minute the door clicked shut again behind Joseph, Connor picked up a piece of soft cheese stuffed with apricots. "Here. Eat this. You've barely touched any food tonight."

Too emotionally bruised to defy him, she opened her

mouth. "This is a first. No one has ever force-fed me before. It's usually the other way around, encouraging me not to eat."

Shaking his head, he watched her.

Burning with embarrassment for enjoying the positively sexual gleam in his eyes, she tried to chew as daintily as possible. "There. Satisfied?"

"Not quite. Give me your car keys," he demanded.

She eyed the champagne bottle. "I haven't had that much to drink."

"No, but you've had a lot of disappointment. When the limo comes to take us home, a staff member from Clayworth's will be with them to drive your car home."

"When did you arrange that?"

"I sent the texts on my iPhone under the table."

The idea of Connor texting like a teenager made her smile.

"Good. That's better." He nodded. "Let's go."

Too beaten down to argue with him, she let him lead her up the steep steps and to the front door.

She mustered a smile for Joseph, who waited for them in the entry with a small box of cookies, compliments of the restaurant. "Thank you. It was a lovely evening," she said as Connor helped her into her black cape.

He shook Joseph's hand. With a jolt of warmth, she saw Connor press a hundred-dollar bill into the waiter's palm.

"Thank you, Joseph. And if you ever remember any stories about the old days with my uncles I'd like to hear them."

Exhausted from disappointment and trying to keep her feelings about Connor under control and out of his sight, Venus climbed slowly into the limo.

"What do we do now?" She sighed, tilting her head back against the leather seat.

Connor leaned back, too, and turned his head to meet her eyes. They were mere inches apart.

"Venus, we learned a great deal tonight. The existence of the casino and the fact people here know about the Saint lends strength to Tony's story."

"I agree. But it's not at all what I'd hoped to discover," she gulped.

His eyes were wide and very green in the dim light. "Did you really believe it would be that easy to find someone who would simply lay out the truth neatly before us?"

"Yes," she admitted without shame. "With me, hope springs eternal. You know that."

His slow smile and the way his gaze caressed her face and lingered on her lips brought a rush of tingling warmth to her numbed-by-defeat body.

I want him to kiss me.

She sat straight up in the backseat and shifted as far away from him as possible.

"We're almost to my place." She looked out the tinted window, wishing it were true. "We need to decide what we should do next."

He reached across to stroke her arm under her cape. "Give yourself a little time, Venus."

With no way to escape, she sucked up the courage to face him. "Okay. We'll go ahead with our plan for me to wear the brooch on Saturday night at the Dress for Success benefit. Until then, I'm sure you're busy with your mother and her guests. I'm sorry I took you away from them tonight."

He shrugged. "I'll be with the family tomorrow night."

Again the little twinge of unreasonable jealousy burned along her skin.

"Good. Bridget needs you. I know how terrible this is for her. How is she holding up?"

"Aunt Bridget is hurting. I think it best not to tell her what we did tonight. Don't worry, Venus. Bridget has an iron will."

So do I, but I think it's rusting.

"Here we are at my place." The relief in her voice sounded so strong she felt guilty. "Thanks for the ride."

She opened the door and bolted up the steps to her front door.

Needing to escape from him, not wanting to wait for him to retrieve her keys, she reached deep inside the free-standing antique replica mailbox for the spare she kept hidden in a tiny secret pocket.

"Venus, here are your keys. Your car's in your parking space." Connor loomed beside her.

Startled, she dropped her spare key and they both knelt at the same time to pick it up.

"Let me put it back in for you." His fingers were dry and warm taking the key from her. His smile hypnotic. "We sell these mailboxes at Clayworth's."

I need to do something to break his spell on me.

"I know you sell them. That's where I bought it. Before I stopped shopping there the day you disgraced and fired my father."

All at once the porch seemed too small for the two of them.

Connor must have felt the wall she had thrown up between them. He backed down one step. "I'll see you at the Drake on Saturday, Venus."

"Good night," she muttered, not looking at him before she closed the door.

She leaned back against it, thankful to be alone at last with her confusion.

Tonight they hadn't learned much about the mermaid brooch but she'd discovered a great deal about herself. Now she needed to figure out what to do about it.

Chapter 14

Connor's office at Clayworth's had always been like a sanctuary. Here he knew what he needed to do and did it without hesitation. Today his responsibilities caged him in.

He paced to the window and stared out, trying to figure out what the hell to do about his feelings for Venus.

He'd done his duty to Clayworth's by firing her father and Venus had bluntly reminded him on her front porch exactly how she felt about his actions.

It's illogical to want someone who hates my guts.

Looking over his shoulder, he stared at the locked drawer of his desk.

Could Venus be right? Did I miss some piece of evidence with Alistair?

He unlocked the drawer to take out her father's file once again.

Bridget's abrupt appearance in his office made him look up and snapped him back to reality.

"I'm done moping around," she declared with her old fire.

"Good." Flexing his tense shoulders, he stood and moved to her side. "Are you seeing Tony to talk?"

"Not ready for that yet. Don't know what to say." She shook her head. "I have some appointments. Already called your mother to cancel dinner at the house tonight. She's not happy. Sorry to be puttin' that on you." Bridget kissed his cheek. "Have a nice time. At least your mom's idea of your perfect mate is improvin'. That CeCe isn't hard to take."

As his aunt Bridget had said, CeCe's willowy blonde beauty wasn't hard to take. Nor were her dry wit, her intelligence, and her kindness to his mother during the long, tasteless meal.

After dinner, while his mother and Mugsy sat gossiping over sherry, Connor followed CeCe into the library.

"Here's your brandy, CeCe."

She looked up from the computer usually hidden behind carved cherrywood doors in one of the dozens of bookshelves. "Sorry. I had to check some emails for work." She stood, taking the brandy snifter. "Thank you, Connor. I forgot to ask how your business meeting went last night."

A vision of Venus looking into his eyes, murmuring *All I want is you* and Venus again reminding him of the truth of their situation on her porch flashed through his head.

He looked down, swirling his brandy in the glass. "Not as well as I had hoped."

"I'm sure you'll work it out."

"I'm not." He glanced up and for the first time noticed she was wearing the swan and bridge pin from the Service Club silent auction.

"I see you were the winning bidder."

"Yes. I nearly lost it when I was dancing with Ed." CeCe smiled at him over the rim of her brandy snifter. "But I knew you needed a few minutes alone with Venus."

He studied her, choosing his words carefully. "I apologize. I didn't realize it was obvious Venus and I needed to discuss some family business."

"Don't worry, Connor. Maybe it was obvious to me you were both eager to talk because I'm in the midst of my own personal drama."

Liking her even more for her candor, he smiled. "Since you helped me, let me return the favor. Do you want to talk about it?"

Laughing, she glanced at the computer and back to him.

"The emails are from a colleague at our office. We don't have the same difficult obstacles as you and Venus have to overcome." She took a long sip of brandy and sighed. "My parents don't approve of him. I'm the boss's only daughter and he's not Episcopalian. Not exactly insurmountable."

No, not betrayal, family loyalties, and years of active dislike.

He clicked her glass. "He'll be a lucky man when you convince him nothing is more important than being together."

"Excuse me for interrupting your conversation." His mother stood in the open door. "CeCe, your father is on the house phone. Your mother thought you'd like to speak with him about a business question."

"I do. Thanks." Smiling, she hurried from the library.

"Such a lovely girl," his mother sighed.

"Yes, she is." Sipping his brandy, he watched his mother over the rim of the glass. "She's witty, intelligent, and beautiful."

"And you have no interest. I see." Without obvious judgment, she nodded. "Connor, I know I am not the most maternal of women, but you are my only son and I want you to be happy."

Watching her, he nodded. "I know you do, Mother." It wasn't the kind of love he felt from Bridget but he knew in her own way his mother cared for him.

"This visit has shown me that my efforts to introduce you to the kind of women I think would suit you have been futile. I only hope a woman will come along who can break through the barriers around your heart the way your father broke through mine. We're not so different, you and I."

A flush rose from his mother's chest to her cheeks. "I apologize if my being so forthcoming has made you uncomfortable."

Feeling more affection then he'd ever experienced coming from her and a real warmth toward her, he took her hands in his. "On the contrary, Mother. I'm pleased you shared your feelings with me."

"Then my visit hasn't been in vain. I look forward to being apprised of developments with the young woman of your choice."

On Saturday night as he paced the foyer of his penthouse waiting for Bridget to come out of her bedroom, Connor kept thinking of the young woman of his choice and his words to CeCe, *Nothing is more important than being together.*

Again, he glanced at his watch, impatience eating at his gut.

Usually he wouldn't mind being late, but not tonight.

Tonight he wanted to be on time. To see Venus. Touch Venus. Use any flimsy excuse to talk to her about their next move in this crazy plan, which sure as hell wasn't getting them any closer to finding the real thief, but *was* keeping him close to Venus.

Relieved to hear the bedroom door open, he turned to see Bridget gliding down the hall toward him.

Gazing at her new haircut and the green silk gown matching her eyes and the emerald earrings dangling from her ears, he knew they were both keeping secrets about their feelings. Obviously she'd made some decisions, just as he had.

It wasn't time yet to tell Bridget about his visit with Venus to the casino. He needed to discover some concrete evidence to completely vindicate Tony. Something positive to lift the haunted look from Bridget's eyes, which no makeup could conceal.

"You look beautiful, Aunt Bridget." He pressed a kiss on her warm forehead. "At least ten years younger."

"Don't be cheeky, Connor." She laughed, smoothing down her sleek, burnished chin-length bob. "Nothin' like a bit of straightener and a bit of color to lift a gal's spirits."

The transformation went deeper and Connor knew it. "Will Tony be at the benefit tonight?"

"We'd planned to go together, but that was before everythin' happened." She shrugged. "I don't want you to be tryin' to play matchmaker tonight. Or I might do the same with you."

She reached up to redo his tux tie. "You never get this quite right. So who is the lucky young woman you're plannin' to dazzle tonight? CeCe?"

Yes, he had secrets to keep from her, but at least he could be honest about this.

"No. Venus."

His aunt stopped redoing his tie to stare up at him. "I guess oil and water do mix after all."

Not understanding, he narrowed his eyes, studying her. "I beg your pardon."

"Never mind." Smiling, she patted his bow tie and stepped back. "Perfect. Now you're ready for what promises to be an interestin' night for you."

"More like confusing," he muttered, glancing over her head to look into the mirror at his now straight tie. He remembered to take his cell phone out of his pocket and place it on the foyer table.

Tonight he wanted no distractions.

Thinking of what the next few hours might bring in his quest to protect Venus, his head sent him one message, his body another.

Venus stood in her tiny dressing room staring at her body in the triple mirror.

She turned back to front and side to side, constantly adjusting the mirrors to critique herself in the rich sapphire Grecian-inspired one-shouldered Carolina Herrera gown with the mermaid strategically pinned for maximum exposure.

Visions of CeCe looking paper-thin in her evening gown last week flashed before her eyes.

I'd look thinner in black.

"Stop it!" she scolded her reflection. "That Connor usually goes out with zero-body-fat model types doesn't mean you should get more neurotic than usual about your curves."

I can't believe I'm actually going out on a date with Connor again.

Multiplied three times, the eager look on her face scared her. "Stop feeling more excited than you should be under these dire, totally weird circumstances. It will probably be more confusing and uncomfortable than it was Tuesday night."

The chime of the doorbell interrupted her one-way conversation with her reflection.

Connor forgot he's supposed to meet me at the Drake.

The thought that he was here to pick her up sent warmth rushing from her flushed cheeks to her toes.

Forcing herself to walk slowly, *well, honestly there's no other way to move in this dress*, she reached the front door on the second chime.

She took a deep breath, pasted a quizzical, not too eager smile on her face, and opened the door.

"Hello, gorgeous. Surprise. I made it to Chicago after all." Brad laughed, flinging open his arms.

Chapter 15

Frozen in shock and disappointment, Venus stared at Brad's ruddy face, with the wave of honey-brown hair that always fell across his wide forehead.

She couldn't move to walk into his open arms as he expected. As she probably would have done a mere few months ago.

He lifted one eyebrow and dropped his arms. "Not much of a greeting," he drawled, strolling past her.

Still reeling in disbelief at finding him on her porch, she shut the door and whirled to face him. "Brad, what are you doing here?"

"Taking you to a party." He pinched her chin, tilting her face up as he loomed over her. "Aren't you glad to see me?"

Thinking of Connor and what might have happened tonight and what she should do now, she forced a smile until her face ached.

"I'm surprised. The last time we spoke you said there was an important expansion deal for your firm being negotiated and it might not be possible for you to get away. Then I got your email saying you couldn't commit to coming tonight."

He ran his palm slowly along her bare shoulder. "Some things are more important."

This time her smile and laughter were real. "Brad, we've been playing this game for years and you've never put our relationship before business."

"Priorities change." He crinkled his eyes in the charming way she'd once found totally irresistible.

"Oh, *that* I know. However, yours have not. Why are you really here?"

"God, you know me well, Venus. I've always loved that about you." An incredibly self-satisfied smile curled his long mouth. "We're opening an office in Chicago and I'll be the managing partner. Deal inked this morning and I was on the next plane. Booked into the Peninsula until I decide where I want to live."

A sinking feeling in her stomach, she shook her head. "This is all so sudden. It must have been in the works for ages. Why didn't you say anything?"

"Hush-hush deal." He put a fingertip to his lips and then touched hers. "We haven't had any quality time together in months."

Definitely no pillow talk. It isn't that kind of relationship any longer and we both know it.

Getting uncomfortable with Brad's playful attitude and desperate to call Connor, she backed up. "Well, Brad... my plans changed... and..."

"Hey, I came all the way from New York and put on my tux to celebrate with you." He crinkled his eyes and twisted his mouth in a pout. "Don't disappoint me on my big day."

It's official. I not only inherited my mom's stubbornness, but her soft pudding heart.

Sighing, she nodded. "Okay, since you're here we might as well go together."

"That's more like it. Now any time you're ready, gorgeous. The car is waiting outside. I'll lease myself a Bentley tomorrow."

"Oh, my," she glanced toward the window. "I don't want to keep the driver waiting. I'll just get my evening bag and wrap. Be right back."

She climbed the staircase as quickly as possible in a floor-length gown, fled down the hall into her bedroom, grabbed her phone off the dresser, and punched in Connor's number.

"Please answer, please answer, please answer." She counted the rings until his voice message came on.

"Oh, no," she groaned.

Footsteps in the hall warned her before Brad reached the door. The thought of him in her bedroom drove her to grab up everything she needed and rush out.

They nearly collided on the threshold. "I'm ready. Don't want to be late."

He draped his arm around her shoulders as he'd done dozens of times and kept it there until they both slid into the backseat of the town car. Tonight it felt strangely awkward to her.

She immediately shifted away and pulled out her phone to text Connor.

"You don't usually bring your phone to black-tie affairs." He lifted one eyebrow. "What's so important?"

"I need to let Diana know I'm coming with you to the benefit after all."

"Don't tell me you were going to this party with Diana. Only in Chicago would two of the most beautiful women in town be dateless." He threw back his head in loud, annoying laughter.

She opened her mouth to tell him she had planned to

meet Connor there. Just as quickly she pressed her lips together. Somehow it seemed like a betrayal of Connor to discuss him with Brad.

Wanting to warn Connor of the change in plans, she sent a text to Diana asking her to find him and tell him what happened.

The more she thought of Brad's just showing up on her doorstep, the more she realized that it had been his growing arrogance over the last few years that had pushed her further and further away from him and those memories of when she'd been young and infatuated with him.

Glaring at him, she dropped her phone in her evening bag. "Stop being so mean. You know Chicago is a fabulous city."

Looking bored, he shrugged. "I have no choice but to get used to it again, since I'll be based here."

Worry and impatience burning a hole in her stomach, she could hardly wait for the car to come to a full stop in front of the Drake Hotel. She flung open the door and slipped out. "I'll meet you inside, Brad."

The doorman looked startled as she ran past him, the hem of her gown clutched in her fists to keep from tripping on it. Not caring if she looked clumsy, she took the steps two at a time up to the lobby.

Dozens of guests milled around, blocking the three wide, sweeping steps leading up to the Palm Court.

"Excuse me," she muttered repeatedly, pushing her way through the crowd as politely as she could, considering how desperate she felt to find Connor and explain what had happened herself.

Trapped between couples on the top step and on the one below her, she felt as if it took an eternity for her to finally reach the entrance to the Palm Court.

Instantly she met Connor's eyes where he stood just beyond the beautiful center fountain decorated with silver-tipped boughs for the upcoming holidays. He nodded toward her as if he'd been watching the entrance, waiting for her.

She swayed toward him.

Suddenly she was pulled back against a tall, hard body.

"Hey, gorgeous, what's the hurry," Brad whispered behind her as he gripped her shoulders. "Wait for me."

What in the hell is Venus doing here with Brad Evans?

Hot with searing disappointment and anger simultaneously, Connor forced his eyes away and looked straight into Diana's angelic face.

"Good. Don't watch them. Don't let Brad see your anger and disappointment," she commanded. "I know you've been watching for Venus to arrive tonight."

"I thought you couldn't read minds." He hoped he sounded normal, sane, considering he irrationally wanted to break Brad's nose again.

"Connor, anyone in this room watching you could tell you're not happy. Venus tried to call you. She sent me a text to warn you Brad arrived unannounced on her doorstep."

Relief and pleasure felt sweet. "She's not happy to see him?" Unable to resist, he glanced over his shoulder, searching for Venus in the crowd.

"Hell, what is she doing now?"

He swung completely around to watch Venus being interviewed by Channel 7 for their ten o'clock local news segment. Every one of her gestures suggested she must be talking about the mermaid brooch.

Diana gripped his arm. "Shall we wander over to where Bridget is talking to PR wiz Cathy Post and, look,

I see Maxie and Ed have joined them. They're close enough to hear what's going on with Venus."

By the time they reached them, Venus and Brad had disappeared.

"I did the PR for tonight's event. What do you think?" Cathy asked, giving Diana a quick kiss on the cheek.

"Fabulous as always." Diana smiled.

"You're fabulous, too, Diana. I've never seen gowns more beautiful than yours or your sister's," Maxie gushed. "You look like a shimmering moonbeam."

"Thank you. It's from Nazia, a local designer."

Diana's gentle hand on his arm and the serenity of her voice couldn't soothe his burning desire to know what Venus had done that might get her into trouble. "Did any of you hear Venus's interview with Channel 7?"

"I did." Maxie nodded. "Venus is such an expert on jewelry. She talked about the rarity of her magnificent mermaid brooch. Remember, Edward, I pointed it out to you the night she wore it on *Talk of the Town* with Rebecca. And you remarked on its beauty. I don't blame Venus for keeping it for her private collection at home."

"Yes, indeed I remember. The mermaid is even more beautiful when seen close. Maxie has a great eye for fine jewelry." Ed's chuckle rumbled up through his barrel chest. "Please excuse us. We recently arrived and are in need of liquid refreshments."

"I'll join you. I need another Diet Coke." Cathy waved and followed them.

Bridget waited until they all disappeared into the crowd before turning to him and frowning. "What happened with Venus's being your date for tonight, Connor?"

He tried to make light of being stood up. "I switched sisters."

"Connor and I are working the room together." Diana pressed a kiss on Bridget's cheek. "I see Tony. I believe he's looking for you."

"Then I should go powder my nose before he sees me." Bridget bolted off in the opposite direction.

Connor watched Diana's eyes widen, huge in her tiny face, and then her lashes sweep down to hide her reaction.

"I know. Nuances. Don't worry about it. I'm working on solving the problem."

She lifted her lashes to peer deep into his eyes.

He braced himself to not give anything away.

"I know you and Venus are in collusion. I don't need to tell you how much is at stake here. I hope you both know what you're doing, for everyone's sake."

"We do." His gaze searched the room, looking for Venus as he'd done all evening. *Where the hell did she go now?*

"Come with me." Diana wrapped her arm around his to lead him across the crowded room toward one of the giant urns full of tall, fat palm leaves.

Half hidden behind it, Venus and Brad stood, talking.

"Here you are at last. I've been looking for you all evening." Diana's light musical laughter cast a spell, freezing them all staring at one another.

Brad, with a frown and a calculating squint at Connor.

Venus, eyes wide, lips parted in . . .

Hell, why can't I ever read her?

"It's so warm in here." Diana fluttered her delicate hands in front of her face. "I need a glass of champagne."

"I need one, too," Venus added too quickly.

At last a nuance he could read. *Smith sisters have one another's backs.*

"Would you mind, Brad?" Venus asked sweetly, batting her eyelashes.

"Sure. Anything for you, gorgeous. Stay here. I'll be back." Turning, Brad flicked Connor a warning glare.

He ignored it.

"I'm buying you two more time to chat." Diana floated after Brad, leaving Connor alone at last with Venus.

"Why did..." he bit out.

"Connor, why didn't..." she whispered.

They both stopped interrupting each other and glared into each other's eyes.

"Ladies first," he muttered through clenched teeth.

"Why didn't you answer your phone or respond to my text?"

"Because I never bring my cell phone to these black-tie affairs. Why did you make yourself a target by broadcasting that you keep the brooch at home when I told you not to do it?"

"I told you what I planned to do to draw out the real villain. I had to do something to move things along after Tuesday night's fiasco at the casino."

"And I *told* you not to make yourself such an obvious target for every petty thief in the city," he reminded her, trying to sound calm, when he felt concern boiling up in his chest.

"I'll be perfectly fine." She smiled at him as she'd done in his Ferrari.

Now he felt even more dazzled by the curl of her lush lips and her luminous aquamarine eyes daring him. Daring him the way she had that night with her kiss.

"Connor, don't forget your uncle Tony installed an excellent alarm system in my town house. No need tonight for you to sit in your car till dawn to protect me."

"I'm not planning to sit in my car to protect you." He wasn't lying to her. At the moment he had no time to tell her the whole truth and argue about it with her.

A coil of her hair hung provocatively over her bare shoulder. She twirled it around two fingers. "I'm glad to hear you've come to your senses. But we do need to talk. Oh, no, here comes Brad."

Connor watched Diana delay Brad every few steps by stopping to introduce him to someone, but very soon she'd run out of options.

Jealousy eating at his gut, Connor shrugged. "He showed up without warning. He can't expect you to drop everything for him. Tell him we need to talk."

Eyes wide, she blinked up at him. "Connor, he knows what happened with my dad and the Clayworths. Our talking would seem suspicious to him. Remember, the plan is our little secret. Besides, he's never forgiven you for breaking his nose. It's never been quite the same."

Connor flicked a glance at the slight bump on Brad's formerly perfect nose.

"It gives his face some needed character."

Her eyes light and bright, she gasped, swallowing a laugh.

Using iron control, he resisted his powerful urge to pull her into his arms to kiss her full, lush mouth.

"Trust me, Venus. We *will* be talking very soon," he muttered as Brad reached them.

"Here's your champagne. I saw your father talking with Kate Carmichael and Rebecca and David Sumner. I need to connect with all of them. Let's go."

Seeing the way Brad so easily draped his arm around Venus's shoulder to lead her away bothered Connor on a level far beyond anything he could have imagined possible a few weeks ago. His body went cold, empty, and he felt alone.

"Your feelings are showing, Connor. Come with me. I have one last good deed to do for you tonight."

Diana took him by the hand, strolling to where Tony stood, holding a scotch on the rocks and watching Bridget wander around the Palm Court talking to everyone but him.

Standing on her tiptoes, Diana kissed Tony's cheek. "You look magnificent in a tux." Her warmth could melt a glacier.

To Connor she gave a sterner, cooler look. "Now do what needs to be done."

As she seemed to float rather than walk away in her shimmering silvery white gown, Tony sighed. "That child is like an angel."

"Maybe. But I wouldn't cross her." Connor looked his uncle in the eyes, man to man, the way Tony had taught him as a kid, and held out his hand. "I'm sorry, Uncle Tony."

His uncle's grip felt as strong as ever, but his grave eyes gave away his true feelings. "Thank you, Connor. I know you are taking care of your aunt. How is she? She won't take any of my calls."

He followed Tony's gaze to where Bridget stood talking to Rebecca and David. His aunt's forced smile made his chest ache. "She's miserable. Like you are." He stared into his uncle's eyes. "Is there anything else you want to tell me? Anything else you remember about that night? Anything at all that might lead us to the real thief?"

"No, Connor. Nothing more I can say about that night or why my visits to Taylor Street continued." Tony looked away and the ache in Connor's chest shifted to his gut.

Tony is hiding something more than how he got the brooch.

Sighing, Tony shook his head. "I'm at a loss to know what to do to make all of this right for everyone."

"There's only one way to make it right. We find out the truth." Connor watched Venus, all at once fearful that neither of them would like what they discovered.

Tingling all over, Venus *felt* Connor watching her. Using every ounce of her willpower she pretended to listen with rapt attention to Brad trying to impress her father and David.

Tucked into the curve of David's arm, Rebecca smiled beside her husband.

"This is all utterly fascinating, Brad." Rebecca tilted her head back on David's shoulder. "Would you mind if Venus, Kate, and I sat for a few minutes?"

"Do you feel all right?" David nearly carried Rebecca the four steps to a cocktail table with three chairs. "Do you need anything? Are you ready to leave?" he asked, frowning, his gaze searching her face.

"I'm perfect." Rebecca sighed. "Stop worrying. Go back and solve the problems of the world with the men while we ladies catch up."

Openly reluctant to leave her side, David walked slowly back to Brad and Venus's father, who were deep in conversation.

"You do look tired, Rebecca. Something is going on. What is it?" Kate asked in her crisp matter-of-fact way.

"Yes, something is going on." Rebecca leaned closer. "Kate, would you help Alistair with his children's book on goddess mythology if I need to take a break? And, Venus, how do you think your father would feel about that?"

Rebecca didn't flinch when Kate cast her a long, piercing look. "You're scaring me," she said bluntly.

"Me, too," Venus added. The fact Rebecca and David had found each other gave shimmering, blissful hope to other women to believe in second chances at love.

"No, no, darlings, trust me. There is nothing to fear." Rebecca reached out to clasp their hands. "I'll know in a few days if I'm taking on a very special project with David. If so, I may not be able to give Alistair's book the time and attention it richly deserves."

"Have you discussed this with him?" Kate glanced up to where Venus's father stood with the younger men.

She knew her father's mane of white hair, long-lashed aquamarine eyes, and straight back made him every bit as attractive to women as men nearly half his age. She'd seen it in the years since her mother died.

"I wanted to discuss it first with the two of you to get your permission before I talk to Alistair." Rebecca looked pointedly at Venus.

Instantly, as if she'd finally been granted some of Diana's psychic gift, Venus understood Rebecca might also be doing a little matchmaking between Kate and her dad and wanted her approval.

She felt a rush of sadness, thinking of her mom's short illness and her loss and how working hard at Clayworth's had been her father's salvation for all those years.

Until it was taken away.

She had every intention of righting that injustice just as her mother would have done.

She looked into Kate's kind face and thought of the other voids in her father's life that could be filled. "Dad has always said Kate is one of the smartest women he knows. I think it would be a lovely partnership."

"Fabulous. I'm so happy." Sighing, Rebecca leaned back in the chair. "Now let's discuss the delicious fact that Connor can't take his eyes off you this evening, Venus."

Kate glanced across the room to where he stood, propped against a pillar, and smiled. "Indeed he can't. I've noticed it, too."

Proud of herself for not following suit and looking at him again, Venus blinked, feigning innocence. "I'm sure I don't know what you're both talking about."

Rebecca patted her hand. "Never fear. Your secret is safe with us."

Venus knew it was true, but still felt relieved when the waiter walked past hitting the chimes, announcing dinner.

Although Brad walked beside her, his attention remained firmly on talking with David, which was fine with Venus, who needed to center all *her* attention on not giving away her desire to talk to Connor.

In the crush going into the ballroom, Maxie sidled up beside her. Venus stopped, letting Brad go on without her.

"I wanted to show you this earlier, but I didn't want Edward to see." With furtive glances in all directions, Maxie opened her gold, egg-shaped Judith Leiber bag just enough so Venus could peer inside.

A ring set with an emerald surrounded by mounds of diamonds sparkled out at her.

"Wow. He has great taste." Venus glanced at Ed, walking ahead of them talking to her father. "If you really want to sell this ring it needs to go to a fine jeweler."

Nodding, Maxie clicked the bag shut. "Edward thinks the ring is too flashy for Chicago. I only wear it when we go to Vegas. I'm not sure I can bear to part with it. I wanted to share with you some of the treasures I have in my closet."

"I can't wait to get in there." Venus smiled and hurriedly waved, following Brad to their seats.

As he pulled out her chair, she glanced two tables over to where Connor sat between Bridget and Diana.

I also can't wait for this night to be over so I can talk to you.

Chapter 16

All the way home, not wanting the limo driver to hear more of their personal business than necessary, Venus sat like a lump, saying nothing, just nodding while Brad talked endlessly about his plans for the expansion of his firm in Chicago and all the contacts he needed to make as soon as possible.

At her door, he literally had not stopped talking and had one foot inside before she could turn to stop him.

"Brad, you must be exhausted after closing such a big deal, traveling, and then going to the gala with me."

"Aren't you asking me in for a nightcap? One for the road?" His signature crinkly-eyed grin *did* make her laugh.

"As you say, I *do* know you well, Brad, so I know exactly why you want to come in. The answer is no."

Not giving up, he nuzzled her neck. "Playing hard to get, gorgeous, because I haven't called lately?" he whispered in her ear.

Yes, I know you and I know it is more than time to end this. All she needed to do was press her palms firmly against his chest for him to back off.

"No, Brad. I'm tired. And so are you. Call me tomorrow if you like."

"Sure?" He lifted one eyebrow. "It's been too long."

"Good night, Brad." When she stepped back out onto her narrow front porch, he had no polite option but to do the same.

"You know what you're missing." He pinched her chin, tilting it up. "Sure about this?"

"Good night, Brad," she repeated without hesitation and stared him straight in his eyes.

"Your choice. I'll call you later," he muttered, as he loped down the steps and out her gate.

Just to be sure he'd really gone, she watched from her front porch until the town car disappeared into the night.

She stared at the spot in front of her town house where Connor had sat watching over her.

If it wasn't so late I'd call him.

"C'mon, Georgia," Connor called softly.

Tingling shock made her shiver.

Did I imagine I heard him because I'm thinking about him?

Looking around, her heart thumping hard against her ribs, she moved slowly down the steps, through the gate, and out onto the sidewalk.

In the shadows at the end of the building she saw the darker outline of a man.

At any other time late at night she would have screamed in terror and bolted into her town house.

I know it's him.

"Connor?" she called.

"Yeah, it's me. I was waiting for Brad to leave." He moved out of the shadows into the glow of the street light.

Then she saw he'd changed out of his tux into jeans

and a sweater, had a duffel bag slung over one shoulder,
and held a huge black Newfoundland and a small pug on
leashes.

"What are you doing here?" she asked, even though
she knew the answer. Pleasure melted through her.

"Atlas, Georgia, and I are spending the night protecting you. Your news segment has already played on Channel 7."

She tried not to smile, tried not to show her feelings.
She tossed her hair over her shoulder and purposely didn't
look at him.

Instead she studied the dogs. "The Newfie is big
enough to scare anyone. He looks like a bear." Unable *not*
to smile, she gazed down at the pug, who stared unblinking right back at her. "But Georgia as a watchdog?"

"The best. If anything moves she barks and Atlas fol-
lows suit."

Still confused, still trying to figure out her next move,
she shook her head. "How did you all get here? Atlas
would never fit into your Ferrari."

"I drove my Jeep. I parked in that garage two blocks
west in an attempt to safeguard your reputation. You know
Chicago is a small town in some ways. If Rebecca doesn't
write about it, someone else will. We're lucky no one saw
me the other night."

His smile, the way his eyes seemed to be caressing her
face, made her shiver. She wrapped her arms around her
bare shoulders, "I know we'd be the talk of the town."

"Hell, I don't care about the gossip but I don't want it
for you."

Again his eyes seemed to be caressing her face, her
body.

"You're shivering from the cold. Let's go inside."

Excitement a blazing flow through her veins, she tried to count the dozens and dozens of reasons why she should never allow him to do any such thing as spend the night with her.

She opened the gate. "This is utterly unnecessary but since you're all here and it's so late how can I refuse?"

To see Connor in her living room, letting his dogs off their leashes, and then giving her his almost-smile, his eyes stroking her, had to be akin to an out-of-body experience.

"Don't worry about me, Venus. I'll sleep there." He motioned to the deep blue velvet sofa loaded with sapphire and ruby red silk tasseled pillows.

"No, you won't." Attempting to be as matter-of-fact as possible, despite the tingling excitement in the pit of her stomach, she motioned him to follow her up the staircase and down the short hall to the guest room.

She flipped on the light. "If you insist on staying you can at least get a good night's sleep in here." Deliberately not looking at the queen-size bed, draped in jade green and mother-of-pearl, she moved right to the bathroom. "There are extra toiletries in here for you to use."

"I brought my own toothbrush."

The fact that Connor was actually trying to be amusing added to the utterly surreal scenario. The *whole* idea of his being fully prepared to spend the night and her letting him do it shook the very foundation of her world.

But this is what I set out to do. Get close to him for pillow talk. Has it always been at the back of my mind even when I denied it to Diana and to myself? Use his feelings for me to get what I want?

The truth hit her over the head.

I can't. I care about him too much.

Needing to get away from him, she backed out of the room. "Good night, Connor. Sleep tight."

As quickly as she could move in a tight dress and towering heels, she closed her bedroom door and leaned back against it.

"Men in love don't always use their heads," he'd once said, and she believed it. Every feminine instinct screamed that if she walked back into his bedroom they'd end up in bed together and she might get the "pillow talk" about her dad she so desired.

The impossible has happened. I want to sleep with the enemy because I'm stupidly attracted to him.

That truth sent her reeling away from the door to pace her room.

Nothing had turned out the way she'd planned in her fervor to help her dad no matter what she needed to do.

Stumbling onto the truth about the mermaid brooch had brought them here to this moment and the shocking realization about her totally confusing feelings toward Connor.

Desperate to get a grip on herself, she kicked off her heels and yanked down the zipper on her dress.

I need to focus on getting into bed and sleeping this madness off.

Slowly, carefully, she hung the evening gown in the canvas dress bag. Locked the priceless mermaid brooch in the small wall safe hidden in her closet. Went through her usual nighttime ritual before settling into bed and closing her eyes.

In the morning my sanity will be restored and everything will look much clearer.

What seemed like hours later, she opened her eyes to glance at the crystal clock beside the bed.

Only fifteen long minutes had passed.

Sighing, she flipped over on her right side, punched the pillow into a more comfortable position, closed her eyes, and tried to will herself to fall asleep.

Almost as if an alarm were ringing in her head, again and again she opened her eyes to glance at the time to find mere minutes had passed.

A low, scratching sound, movement outside her door as if someone was leaning against it, brought her straight up in the bed.

Every nerve quivering, heart pounding in hot anticipation, she watched the door inch open in slow motion.

Should I pull back the covers, inviting Connor in, or throw the clock at him and tell him to get out?

Atlas butted the door open wider with his enormous head and the pug strolled in ahead of him.

The moment rocked Venus in silent laughter.

Georgia jumped up onto the velvet-covered bench at the foot of the bed and then leaped nearly into Venus's lap.

A moment later Atlas flopped down with a thud beside the bed.

They were too adorable to scold. "Okay, you can both stay," she whispered, patting Georgia's head.

Immediately the pug stretched out beside her and began to snore.

At least one of us is getting some sleep.

Sure *she* wouldn't without help, Venus slid out of bed and stepped carefully over Atlas to swing the bedroom door *almost* closed, but not quite, in case the dogs wanted to get out. Then she went into her bathroom.

She poured a generous amount of Jo Malone Pomegranate Noir Bath Oil into the rushing hot water and breathed in its intoxicating fragrance.

Sure this would work to lure her to sleep, she pinned

her hair on top of her head, shrugged out of her night-gown, and stepped into the deep tub.

Sighing, she lay back, allowing the hot water to soothe her jangled nerves.

Just as she'd hoped, at last she began to feel the tiniest bit sleepy and closed her eyes.

In a few more minutes I'll get out and sleep like a baby.

An explosion of barking shocked her eyes open.

She sat up and heard the clicking of the pug's tiny paws on the wood floor beneath the bedroom windows and the Newfie's galloping thumps.

Atlas gave two more deep, loud woofs.

"Atlas, be quiet before you wake up Connor," she called through the open bathroom door.

The pug broke into short staccato yelps loud enough to wake the dead.

"Oh, no," Venus groaned, standing up, reaching for a towel.

"Venus, are you all right!" Connor shouted, bursting half-dressed into her bedroom.

Through the open bathroom door their eyes met.

Every cell in her body went numb. Stark naked, she couldn't move, couldn't look away from the shifting emotions in his emerald eyes.

Without words, he slowly pulled the bathroom door closed.

Only then did reaction sting her to life. Shivering, she sank back down into the hot water. The warmth, the fragrant steam rising around her, and her own over-heated emotions made her feel light-headed. Taking deep breaths, she gripped the side of the tub to keep from faint-ing for the first time in her life. She shook her head, trying to clear away the image of Connor gazing at her in a way that, she swore, made her heart skip a beat.

She laid her head against the edge of the tub and closed her eyes. Burning hot tears stung her skin as the truth settled into her heart and soul.

If it had been any other man on the planet I'd be forever grateful to have looked into his eyes and had my aha here he is at last moment.

Sobbing, more tears streaming down her scalding cheeks, she wrapped her arms around her bent knees and rocked herself.

I know Connor is the one. Just as I know I can't ever have him.

Barefoot, shirtless, Connor raced into the small, enclosed backyard beneath Venus's bedroom window.

The cold November night air didn't touch him. Thinking of Venus, the slope of her shoulders, her breasts, the long line of her legs glistening with water, her eyes wide and frightened, his body felt on fire.

He'd wanted nothing more than to take her into his arms, press kisses on her lips, touch her, show her with his mind and body how he felt. When their eyes met he let go completely to accept that he wanted Venus more than he'd ever wanted anyone or anything in his life. And nothing would stop him from having her.

As he'd learned to do, he clamped down on his feelings to concentrate on what needed to be done.

First, I have to make sure she's safe.

Atlas and Georgia at his heels, he ran across the brick patio toward the wooden fence.

The gate hung open. Beyond it, the alley lay silent and empty before him.

Whoever had broken in, alerting the dogs, had fled.

"Good job." He patted Atlas on the head and leaned down to tickle Georgia under her chin. "Special treats for both of you. C'mon, let's go back to the house."

His gut clenched in anticipation. *Will Venus be waiting for me?*

All at once fear broke through her pain. *Where's Connor? Has he gone after the intruder?*

In a panic of worry, she stood, grabbed her aqua cashmere robe off the hook on the back of the door, belted it tight at her waist, and ran down the stairway.

"Connor, where are you?" she called through the empty rooms.

When she saw the back door in the kitchen wide open, she screamed. "Oh, no, he's running around half-naked in the freezing night to defend me."

She yanked the heavy antique rolling pin off the shelf to use as a weapon and bolted toward the door.

Watching him walking safely back toward the town house, overwhelming relief made her knees feel weak. She sagged against the door frame.

"Did you find anything?" she called, watching him cross the patio.

"Whoever it was broke in through the back gate and escaped the same way."

Again the thought of Connor's getting hurt because of her sent a bone-chilling ache through every inch of her body. "Thank goodness he wasn't waiting for you out there. Come into the kitchen. I'll make you coffee."

Not giving Connor time to respond, afraid she might give away her feelings, she turned and walked to the small galley kitchen. She flipped the switch on the coffeemaker she always had ready for morning caffeine.

She paced the floor. Shivering, she curled her toes into the hard, cool wood floor.

I'm just going to confront this head on. Well, part of what happened anyway.

Hearing him at last, she swung around, poured him a mug of coffee, and handed it to him. "Here. I know you like it strong and black."

"Thanks." He took a long drink and nodded. "It's good."

Even though he'd slipped on his blue vee-neck sweater to cover his impressive chest, it wasn't enough to cool her aching need to touch him.

I should put more distance between us while I do this.

She wandered to the granite countertop and leaned against it to watch him, legs apart, stare back at her.

"Okay, let's just get this out in the open, Connor. If even half the stories about you and your cousins are true, naked women are a common occurrence in your life. I'm surely not the first one you've ever seen."

His lips curved a bit deeper at the corners than usual when he smiled. "No, you're not."

"Exactly my point." She yanked at a curl of her hair hanging on her shoulder. "So there's no reason for either of us to feel embarrassed about this."

"Then why are you playing with your hair?" he asked, firmly placing his mug on the butcher block.

Realizing too late she'd given herself away, she folded her hands primly in front of her. "Your ear tips are beet red."

"Not because I'm embarrassed." Never taking his eyes off her, in three steps he stood mere inches away. She felt the heat from his body. "I know you hate my guts and you don't trust me. But believe me when I tell you I've never in my life seen anyone more beautiful than you. Never be embarrassed about your body."

Is this how Rebecca felt with David? As if a portal opened up inside her that only he could fill?

"I don't hate you, Connor." Hearing a strange quiver in her voice, she cleared her throat. "I don't *understand* or *accept* your actions against my father and never will unless you explain. Since you can't, or won't, where do we go from here when we both want... want to..."

"Kiss," he mercifully interrupted.

Slowly, he brushed his hand against her cheek, trailed his fingers down her throat to rest at her pulse.

"Do you do that so you can feel how my heart is pounding?" she whispered through the hot, tight feeling in her chest.

"No, I do it because I love how soft your skin feels there." He pressed a kiss where his fingers had been.

Tiny shivers running along her spine, her resolve dissolving, she slid her hands under his sweater, her palms cool on his warm, smooth, firm-muscled chest. "Your heart is pounding, too." Unable to resist, she gazed into his eyes. "This time it's your turn to kiss me."

Laughing huskily, he dragged her closer. He touched her lower lip, rubbing gently back and forth with his thumb until she closed her eyes.

His kiss felt so soft, so coaxing, her lips opened to the strokes of his tongue.

Aching to be closer, she slid her hands around to his back, tangling her fingers in the silky hair at the nape of his neck.

Frightened by such powerful erotic feelings when she

knew they were wrong and could only hurt both of them, she pulled away.

With another husky laugh, he brushed his lips over her ear, nibbled at the warmth of her throat beneath the collar of her robe. "Your turn," he whispered.

I must stop.

Her sense of self-preservation rose up to save her, but a primal need she didn't even know she possessed urged her on.

Just one more kiss can't hurt. It will be the last.

Her fingers caught in his hair, pulling his head down, their mouths meeting in a searching kiss, deeper and deeper until his breathing changed.

Still she pressed even closer. Caught up in spinning sensations of desire she'd never known in quite this way, she wanted to melt into his muscles and bones, the hard heat of his body.

A shrill ring and the dogs barking tore them apart.

She saw an echo of her frustrated longing in Connor's dazed eyes and heard it in his breathing, matching hers.

"If someone's calling at four in the morning, something's wrong." Trying not to tremble, she backed up two steps and spun around to look at caller ID.

"It's Brad," Connor said behind her, his hands cupping her shoulders, his fingertips stroking the pulse pounding at her throat. "Don't answer it."

Waves of feeling shook her and she leaned back into Connor's strong, warm body.

The second ring broke tonight's strange spell.

There can't be so little space to pass through from loathing Connor to loving him.

Wanting, needing to believe danger had somehow intensified her feelings and made the attraction between them move so quickly it took on a life of its own, she shook her head. "I need to answer it."

Connor's instantaneous withdrawal left her feeling cold. Shivering, she picked up the phone.

"Brad, why are you calling at four in the morning?" Watching Connor stride out of the kitchen, Atlas and Georgia following, left a frozen lump of longing in her throat.

"I'm too keyed up to sleep and I miss you." It was the whiskey voice of a man after a few drinks accustomed to getting his own way.

With no time for his spoiled antics, she sighed. "Brad, go to sleep. You're tired and you've had too much to drink. Good-bye."

"Wait, Venus!"

His urgency made her hesitate.

"Promise to go to the Black and White Party with me on Friday and I'll be able to sleep like the dead."

Because of tonight, because of Connor, she suddenly had a desperate need to clear away all the shadows from her past. That included Brad.

I'll do this one last thing with Brad to end it completely between us.

"All right, Brad. Now go to bed."

The cold lump in her throat expanded into her chest as she made her way past the empty guest bedroom and down the staircase.

In those few minutes she'd been on the phone, Connor had gathered up his duffel and the dogs and now waited at the front door.

Looking into his eyes, she knew Connor had shut down, closed himself off from her. His striking face looked as controlled and inscrutable as she'd once thought him. Somehow he'd turned off the raging emotion she'd felt in his body when they kissed.

I'm trying to do the same thing. Am I hiding it as well?

"I didn't want to leave without saying good-bye. No one will make another attempt to break in here tonight. I feel sure you'll be safe."

His formality seemed ludicrous to her since mere moments ago they had been pressed chest to breast in multiple passionate kisses. Obviously he didn't want to talk about it and neither did she.

Tension beat in the air between them, but she followed his cool cue, pulling her robe collar higher around her throat. "I hope this proves to you that I'm right and the real thief is trying to retrieve the brooch."

At last she saw a spark of emotion in his emerald eyes. "It proves you're in danger. Since you won't give me back the brooch will you at least promise not to wear it like a damn bull's-eye?"

"Even if I don't wear it, the real thief knows it's here. But that's what we want, isn't it. To catch the real thief. The sooner this is over, the sooner we can get Bridget and Tony back together."

And, I hope, you will either tell me what happened with Dad or realize you are wrong about him like you are about Tony. And all my anguish over you will be worth it.

What she left unsaid quivered between them.

"Venus, I understand what you want from this. I can't make any promises." He took a long, deep breath and squared his shoulders. "What I do promise is that I will get additional police surveillance on this block to keep you safe and, I hope, catch the thief."

"But you won't tell them about Tony or how I got the

brooch?" she asked, wanting to confirm what she already knew in her heart. In this Connor could be trusted.

"No. I can get it done without too many questions being asked."

Knowing the Clayworths had the power to make it happen, she nodded. "That's good. Then you won't feel like you need to be on nightly guard duty to protect me." She forced lightness into her voice when her insides felt like a melting honey pot.

"Yeah, that's right." Solemn, his face like smooth granite, he stared into her eyes. "Do I have your promise not to wear the brooch?"

Tossing her hair over her shoulder, she stared right back at him, hiding her heartache. "Yes, I promise. But I'm not giving up on what I want, Connor."

"I'm not either, Venus," he said softly and walked out her door.

His cryptic words, the flare of emotion in his eyes, and her own bruised and battered feelings kept Venus sitting on her window seat, staring out, watching the sun rise over Lake Michigan.

Her stupid plan to entice Connor into telling her all the secrets about her father scattered around her like a broken strand of pearls.

She needed to restring her life so it was strong again.

I'll never stop wanting to help Dad. But now I want Connor, too. How can I have everything I want?

Chapter 17

Her head fuzzy from lack of sleep, Venus walked slowly toward her dad's house for their weekly Saturday morning breakfast date before she opened Pandora's Box for the day, and noticed the same police car cruising past her four times.

Two blocks farther west she spied yet another police car parked in the alley.

Her insides felt warm and gooey, as if she was melting from confusion, and...*No! I will not put a name to my burning feelings. I'll simply accept that Connor takes his promise to protect me very seriously.*

Finally reaching her dad's beloved "money pit," and running late as usual, Venus rushed up the wide stairway to the second floor.

Hearing Rebecca's voice surprised Venus as she strolled into the shabby, chic library with its slightly saggy wood floor and bookcases lined with his beloved tomes on mythology, history, literature, and a sprinkling of serious business books.

Rebecca and Kate sat on the tartan plaid love seat talking to Diana, who was curled up in front of the fireplace, which, as always for this time of year, had crackling logs warming the room.

"This is a nice surprise. We're all having breakfast together?"

Her father stood behind his desk. "Yes, now that you're here." He reached out and she walked into his arms for a warm hug. The tiny gleam of sadness she always saw now in his eyes reminded Venus again why she'd plotted against Connor to find out the truth.

But what do I do now?

"Darlings, I'm sorry to interrupt your family time but I couldn't wait another second to tell you all my news."

If Rebecca wanted a totally attentive audience, she had it, as they all turned to look at her. Even the logs stopped crackling and spitting.

"David and I are going to have a baby girl," she cried, her eyes filling with tears.

An instant of shocked silence all at once split into shrieks of feminine joy and her father's deep true laughter.

"Oh, my God, how wonderful." Venus rushed to hug her.

Diana rose quickly to her feet to do the same.

Their father held Rebecca's hands in his and looked deep into her eyes. "My daughters are the great joy of my life. I wish the same for you and David."

Intensely private and self-contained, Kate pulled Rebecca close for a second and then smiled in the encouraging, understanding way of a dear, trusted friend who couldn't be happier for her. "You will be an exemplary parent."

"Thank you, darling. David and I are both still in a state of shock." Rebecca dabbed at her eyes with a handkerchief passed to her by Kate. "He is such a worrywart. This is considered a high-risk pregnancy because of my age, which means I'll need to be monitored more often. But I know everything will be fine."

Seeing Diana's smile and nod of agreement gave Venus a profound release from worry. She hoped that Diana had a good vibe from the universe about Rebecca's blessed event.

"Now, Alistair, you fully understand why I'm agreeing to David's request to cut back on my schedule. Kate is a much better editor than I could ever hope to be."

Alistair and Kate exchanged tentative smiles. "Not true," she said briskly. "However, I look forward to working on Alistair's fascinating book. Goddess mythology will be much more interesting than my usual facts and figures."

"Perfect." Rebecca sighed. "Like my life. To think I once thought of David as the new boss from hell. The man who had taken away my identity. Yet in actuality he is the man who has expanded me and my world beyond my wildest dreams. And trust me, I've always been able to dream big." Rebecca laughed through her tears.

Her words struck such a resounding blow to Venus's confusion that she gasped. "How long did it take for David to go from boss from hell to love of your life?"

Completely ignoring Diana's sudden, penetrating stare, Venus watched Rebecca's enraptured face light up the warm, dusty library.

"I'm sure there were many small 'aha' moments along the way. But it only seemed to take an instant when it happened."

"I understand." Venus nodded, twisting strands of her hair around two fingers. Realizing she was giving herself away, she dropped her hands into her lap, twining her fingers tightly together. "Never in your wildest dreams did you think it could happen but somehow, some way, you let go of your preconceived ideas about him and then the possibilities for the two of you became endless."

"Exactly, Venus." Rebecca laughed. "And they call Athena the wise one."

Unable to ignore Diana's stare another instant, Venus met her eyes, knowing full well her sister knew she was thinking of Connor.

Determined for all their sakes to get at the truth, Connor picked up the phone to call Tony.

This morning, he answered on the first ring. "Connor, is something wrong?"

The worry in his voice hit Connor hard. *I should have made this move sooner, for his sake.*

"Someone tried to break into Venus's town house last night. Probably to steal the brooch. It's time we all face this head on. Can you come to Clayworth's, Uncle Tony?"

"I'm on my way."

Her mug still hot and steaming on his desk, Connor took long swallows of caffeine waiting for his aunt Bridget to come for their morning coffee together.

The wary look in her eyes when she walked in warned him this wouldn't be easy.

She dropped into her favorite chair in front of his desk and took the mug between her palms.

"I know you've refused to talk with Tony, but you need to know someone tried to break into Venus's town house last night. This gives credence to her theory that the real thief, or at least someone who knows the true value of the brooch, is trying to get it." Coming around his desk, he leaned against it, watching her. "Atlas and Georgia warned us and scared the thief away. I don't believe for an instant it could have been Tony. Besides, my gut's telling me it's true, you know the dogs only bark at strangers. They know Tony as well as they do you or me."

All the color drained from Bridget's face. "God in heaven, Venus is puttin' herself in danger for us. What are you plannin' to do about it?"

"I've alerted the police to add patrols to Venus's neighborhood. And I got her to promise to stop wearing the brooch. At least she won't be a walking target until this is over."

"When this is over, what are you plannin' to do about your feelin's for Venus?"

As always, his aunt pulled no punches and expected him to do the same.

"Finding the thief and vindicating Tony is only the tip of the iceberg." He sighed, placing his own mug beside him on the desk. "For Venus, Tony and her dad's problems have somehow become connected. If she can prove Tony is innocent beyond the slightest doubt, despite the evidence against him, then it becomes possible for me to be wrong about her father."

All the love he knew Bridget felt for him welled up in her eyes. "How do you feel about the possibility? Can you make this dream come true for her?"

"You've seen the evidence. The money trail to Alistair's new bank account." He shrugged. "Although it contains only a fraction of the funds lost. We've got his signatures authorizing stock sales and crazy risks. All supposedly done by him on the basis of memos from Drew, Grey, and Ric. Plus the transactions he denies ever signing, although he agrees it's his signature."

Frustrated, Connor paced back around his desk. "Hell, he even claimed I sent him a memo authorizing a huge sale, and you know how close we'd become." The sharp pain he'd felt at Alistair's betraying their friendship had a new edge now because of Venus.

Unlocking the drawer, he took out Alistair's thick file and threw it on the desk. "I've gone over and over this evidence every day for the last few weeks searching for something, *anything,* I might have missed."

Palms flat on the desk, he leaned over the file, staring at it as if somehow he'd miraculously find what he needed. "You know company policy dictates all memos are shredded at the end of the day. There is absolutely no proof to substantiate his claims. Besides the crucial fact that none of us sent him any such memos."

"But you keep lookin' and hopin' anyway." Bridget came to his side to pat his arm in a gesture of comfort from his childhood. "I understand, Connor. I'm doin' the same thing with Tony."

Connor looked up, gazing into her eyes. "You need to talk to Tony. If I question both of you together about the night he was given the brooch perhaps something will click to help solve this mystery."

Continuing to pat his arm, she nodded. "I'll do it for you, Connor."

He kissed her forehead. "I knew you would. He should be here any minute."

As if on cue, Tony hurried into the office with his normal long, quick strides. The look passing between him and Bridget scorched the air.

For the first time in his life, Connor understood emotions so powerful they needed no words.

Venus's image flashed into his mind. The taste of her lips and skin. The feel of her body in his arms. They would have made love if she hadn't taken Brad's call.

Why did she? Does she care more about Brad than Diana believes she does?

"Connor." Bridget's voice snapped him back. "You should tell Tony about the attempted robbery at Venus's town house."

"I already did. That's why he agreed to come." Connor's eyes locked on his aunt's face and then on Tony's. "I wanted to tell you both together that Venus and I went to the private casino on Taylor Street. We'd hoped to find someone who had been there for decades. Someone who might know anything that could help us prove your story, Tony. Or lead us to the real thief."

Both his aunt and his uncle became very still. With a deep sigh, Tony settled into a chair in front of the desk.

"Mr. Marco was there that night. He knew everyone."

"He's been dead three years. But you knew that, didn't you, Tony? You need to talk to me, Tony. Now," Connor said, more coldly than he'd intended. "Tell me exactly what happened the night you got the brooch."

Tony sent Bridget a pleading look and she moved to slowly perch on the edge of the chair next to him.

"That night your aunt and I had an argument about my gambling. I thought she was being overly dramatic. Perhaps we both were that night. I was feeling particularly cocky and believed I could beat the odds. At that time everyone went to the private club for gambling. Fortunes in those days were won and lost."

"Who exactly belonged?" Connor asked.

"That you would know?" Tony shrugged. "So many. All the Clayworth men except your father. Ed and his father. Alistair Smith. My father. Some current alderman you know well. All the political power brokers of the day. Even though it was a private club, often high-stakes poker games were in progress. Then outsiders were invited."

His instincts urging him on, Connor leaned closer. "Do you remember who was there that night?"

Across his wide forehead deep frown lines appeared and Tony closed his eyes as if he were trying to see the scene.

"No one I knew well." He lifted his heavy lids, his eyes grave. "I remember I did not go into the poker rooms that night. I lost everything at craps. Then I left and sat on the curb, defeated, until I was approached by the stranger."

"What did he look like?" Connor asked.

"I don't remember very clearly." Tony shook his head. "It was dark away from the streetlight and I was depressed. Feeling hopeless."

Connor and Bridget locked eyes. They both recognized Tony was being vague, not really answering the question.

"Is the stranger the reason you kept goin' down to Taylor Street and kept it a secret from me?" Bridget asked softly.

Tony turned to her. "*Cara,* I was wrong that night to lie to you and it has cost us much. The rest of my actions have nothing to do with my love for you."

Her eyes filling with tears, Bridget stared at him. "If you were doin' nothin' wrong, why did you keep your visits a secret? Why can't you tell me now when it's so important?"

Reaching out, Tony clasped her hands, carrying them to his lips. The fact that Bridget allowed it gave Connor hope.

"*Cara,* I give you my word my actions over the years have nothing to do with the troubles at Clayworth's. Nor have I ever gambled again. Why can't you believe me?"

"I want to believe you, but your choice to keep hiding the whole truth makes it impossible. Like now. Avoiding giving us a description of the Saint, the man who supposedly gave you the brooch." With a little sob, Bridget pulled free and fled the room.

Tony half rose to follow her but then slumped back down. Defeat glazed his eyes.

"How does a man choose between love and his honor? How much must he sacrifice to keep a promise?"

Sadness ate at Connor's gut. He had no answer for himself or for Tony. He believed his uncle was telling the truth about the Saint. Just as he knew Tony wasn't answering completely in order to keep another secret, at great cost to himself.

What price am I willing to pay to give Venus back the father she believes in despite all the evidence against him?

Chapter 18

Working at his Golden Gloves Gym on Sheffield, sparring with the kids, kept Connor's mind off Venus for a few minutes here and there. Yet the same questions kept running through his head.

How can I give her what she wants?

He sparred with Gregori until they were both breathing hard, their shirts dark with sweat. He watched Gregori go through his circuit training and kept the clock on his pushups.

Willful. Beautiful. Unpredictable. Venus drifted back into his head.

I know she is attracted to me. I know her responses to me are real. But does she feel like I do? All I want is her.

He also knew she was safe. His contact keeping surveillance on her town house and the undercover cops working the blocks around Pandora's Box kept him informed.

What he *didn't* know knotted his gut.

Is she seeing Brad?

"Whoa, Mr. Clayworth, where'd you go?" huffed Gregori. "You still keeping time? Ain't that a hundred?"

"Sorry." Connor clicked the timer. "Good job."

"Thanks. Gotta go now and take my shower." Gregori hauled himself to his feet and flung a red towel around his neck. "My mom's meetin' me here to take the bus to Miss Smith's store."

All attention, Connor stared at him. "You're going to Pandora's Box today?"

"Yeah. Miss Smith's gonna style my mom for her job interview at the Polish restaurant close to where we live."

Curious, Connor narrowed his eyes. "How did this come about?"

Shifting from foot to foot, Gregori looked uncomfortable, glancing at the floor, everywhere but at him. "Miss Smith didn't tell you about takin' me home one night and meetin' my mom and offerin' to help her find the right clothes for her job interviews?"

Knowing there was more to the story, but not wanting to press Gregori, Connor smiled. "Miss Smith likes to help."

"Yeah, she's smokin'." Gregori shifted back two steps. "A real nice lady. You know what I mean."

"I do indeed." Connor laughed, feeling better now than he had in days. He had an excuse to see Venus. "You don't need to take the bus. I'll drive you and your mom to Pandora's Box. I need to talk to Miss Smith myself."

In a rare moment in which there were no customers in the store, Venus went over her calendar, noting that she needed to look at two estates next week and she had an appointment to do Maxie's closet. It was hard to concentrate on business when she kept glancing at the phone, trying to come up with a plausible reason to call Connor.

She could thank him for the plethora of policemen patrolling her neighborhood. No thieves with an ounce of the instinct of self-preservation would come near her. Unless they were desperate.

The way I feel.

Her decision to accept Brad's date for the Black and White Party sat like a big hot mistake in the region around her heart.

It gave new meaning to the word *heartburn*.

The sudden swoosh of the door opening and the tinkling bell brought her gaze away from the phone.

Sunbeams streaked Connor's damp, dark hair with shimmering lights. He looked harder, leaner, his eyes even more guarded than when she'd last seen him.

It took her two full, deep breaths before she noticed Gregori and his mother.

"Oh, hello." She rushed around the counter to squeeze Mrs. Prozument's hand. "I'm so happy you're here. I have some outfits in the dressing room for you. Would you like to try them now?"

"Yes. Yes." Mrs. Prozument nodded.

Venus led her to the dressing room and pushed back the heavy curtain. "Let me know if you need any help."

At last she turned to Connor, using every ounce of self-control not to fuss with her hair. "This is a pleasant surprise."

"Mr. Clayworth drove us here so we didn't need to take the bus," Gregori piped up.

"How nice." Foolishly she looked deep into Connor's emerald eyes.

She wanted to throw herself into his arms and sob all over his wonderful chest. Wanted to tell him she was sorry she'd answered the stupid phone. Even though she knew with a deep, painful certainty that making love with Connor would be a horrible mistake from which her heart might never recover.

She turned away before she actually blurted it all out in front of Gregori.

Frightened at how close she'd come to making a fool of herself, she swung back to the dressing room. "Do you need any help, Mrs. Prozument?"

"No. No. It fits good. My favorite color." She stepped slowly from behind the heavy brown velvet curtain to look at herself in the enormous gilt-framed mirror.

The 1960s-style three-piece navy suit with its pencil shirt, jacket with notched collar, and a beautiful navy silk blouse with tuxedo pleating and a tie bow did indeed fit her to perfection.

Grinning from ear to ear, Gregori whistled. "You look beautiful, Mom."

The look of wonder Venus loved to see in clients lit his mother's face.

"I feel pretty. Maybe now I'll get the job at the Polish restaurant greeting customers." She chuckled, her cheeks rosy.

"Absolutely." Studiously avoiding catching Connor's eyes, Venus led her back to the dressing room. "Let's have a fashion show. Please try on the other dresses. I think you'll like them."

In the end Mrs. Prozument left with the suit and a navy and cream shantung dress with a vee neckline and three-quarter sleeve jacket, plus information from Dress for Success to help her with job interviews and smooth her way back into the business world.

There was no point in pretending not to be waiting for Connor to finish paying the cab driver and stroll back into the store.

His mouth curled into his real smile. "That was special for both of them. Thank you, Venus."

Warmed by his words, by *him* standing so close, she flung back her head to watch him. "You know me. Always trying to fix things. Speaking of which, how are we going to trap the real thief with a squad of policemen patrolling my street? He'd have to be crazy."

"Or desperate. Either way we can't take the chance with your safety now that we've put this in play."

He stepped closer and she backed against the counter. Only inches separated their bodies.

Studying the firm curl of his mouth, she wanted to pull his head down to kiss those lips here in the sunlight, in the full exposure of her store where anyone could walk in at any moment and catch them in the act.

It's official. I've lost all sense of right and wrong.

Yet still she didn't move, mesmerized by the look in his eyes.

"You need to know I wanted to believe that Tony was innocent even though he was in possession of the brooch and his story is suspect at best. But now I believe it with all my heart, despite the evidence against him. You helped me to think outside my own rigid preconceptions."

Such strong emotion caught in her throat, she gasped. "Are Bridget and Tony back together?"

The sadness shadowing his face warned her before his words.

"No. I told Aunt Bridget how I feel. I think she believes it, too. But there's more between them than the brooch and his innocence in its theft."

Like there's more between us, keeping us apart.

She gripped the edge of the counter behind her so tightly her fingers went numb. "What happens now, Connor?"

"That's up to you, Venus. As much as I want it for your

sake, I can't make you any promises about your father."
The bones in Connor's face seemed to relax into tenderness. "We're both aware of the attraction between us. Can't we find a way to work this out together? Will you try with me?"

His clear-eyed honesty made her want to sob like an infant. But if she started to cry now she'd drain every cell in her body. She needed him to leave quickly before she made a fool out of herself.

She needed to be honest right back. "I'm going to the Black and White Party with Brad Friday night."

The effect on him hardened his face back to its perfect form and he stepped away from her.

"Why?"

It wasn't the response she'd expected. Off guard, she blurted out the truth. "Because all of this...us...our *attraction* is like a romance novel that can't possibly have a happy ending."

Looking amused instead of being angry, he shocked her out of her tears and into deeper confusion.

"I've never ever in my entire life, even when we were kids, seen you *grin* before."

"I've never felt like it before. You told me to let go and I'm trying."

This new side of him made her nervous in a stinging, pleasurable way.

"You should know that I'm also attending the Black and White Party on Friday night, Venus."

Now the sting became unreasonable jealousy. "Are you taking CeCe?"

The way his eyes roamed over her body gave her goose bumps.

"No, I'm not taking CeCe. I'll be seeing you there, Venus."

He *would* be attending the party if he could convince the right woman to go with him.

He found Diana in one of the store windows creating the frame of a huge space ship, a small conveyer belt curling through its center with toys that seemed to have come alive to play.

"Diana, I need your help."

Her eyes widened, huge aquamarine pools in her tiny face. "I can tell from your face something important has happened." She rose slowly, the top of her moonbeam hair barely reaching his shoulder. "You know I'll do whatever I can to help you."

"Will you be my date for the Black and White Party Friday night?"

For the first time he saw surprise flicker across her face. "You're not into the old boy network and you're not a player in that sense so..." She smiled. "There's only one person I've ever seen who can get beneath your cool facade. It's all about Venus, isn't it?"

"Isn't it always about Venus?" Such a feeling of euphoria rushed through him that he laughed. "She's attending the party with Brad. Which we both know is a mistake."

"Ah, I see." Diana sighed. "Do you know what you want?"

The demanding stare she leveled on him would have driven some men to their knees. Not him. Not about Venus. Not now. Not ever.

"Yes. I know I could invite any number of women. However, I don't want to make Venus jealous. All I want is her."

Tears glistened like diamonds in Diana's luminous eyes. "Thank goodness you've accepted the truth. My sister will fight it. Until you convince her beyond even her capacity for denial."

Diana straightened her delicate shoulders and blinked up at him. "The Black and White Party this year is in the ballroom at the end of Navy Pier. I'll meet you there at seven."

On Friday, eager to begin convincing Venus beyond her capacity for denial, Connor arrived early at Navy Pier.

Waiting for Diana, he paced in front of the entrance to the ballroom. The cessation of all conversation from the milling crowd and an odd tension in the air caused him to glance up.

For an instant he thought it was Venus shimmering in a black gown and diamonds at the end of the hall.

A heartbeat later he realized it wasn't Venus but Diana.

He caught the stunned looks of both men and women and smiled. Forsaking her usual virginal white, Diana had become a creature of tantalizing desire. Her hair, a cascade of silver, fell across her breasts, draped low in black silk. Her full lips reddened as never before and aquamarine eyes shadowed in such a way they teased were irresistible.

"Hell, Diana, you could corrupt a saint tonight." Not at all tempted, Connor smiled down at her as she tucked her dainty hand into the curve of his arm. "I wish Grey and Ric could see you. They'd realize you were all grown up."

"I wish they could see me, too," she purred, her dark tinted lashes hiding her eyes. "Shall we go in and conquer?"

Venus had tried to conquer her misery over Connor

and her aching regret that she'd ever agreed to this date by decking herself out in her favorite white sequin Versace dress. She'd had this same fake smile plastered on her face from the moment Brad arrived for what would *definitely* be their last date.

I at least owe him this much.

Halfway across the vast, round ballroom, Brad bolted off into a laughing group of men.

Well, maybe not. She eyed him with boredom.

"I'm on my way out. Take this." Cathy Post handed her a glass of champagne and motioned to Brad. "I did the PR for the Black and White Party in New York and saw him there. This is his milieu. The pounding music, the powerful men, the yearly influx of beautiful women ready to have a good time fit him like a glove. It gives me a headache. Have a drink. It might help." With a wave, Cathy escaped.

Dutifully, Venus took a deep gulp of icy cold champagne. It didn't help. She still felt miserable and empty.

A stir at the door caused her to look up.

Connor stood in the entrance with a diminutive slinky siren on his arm.

A rush of jealousy made Venus see shots of red around them. She blinked, the beauty's face coming into sharp focus.

Shock tingled along her hot skin. *"Diana,"* she gasped.

As if her sister had heard her, Diana glanced up, waved, and led Connor across the room.

Too stunned to speak, Venus stared at her baby sister in disbelief.

"Don't forget, I'm a Gemini. I'm showing my other side for a change." Diana's delicate laughter was like a siren call drawing every male within hearing distance closer.

As Brad wandered back to Venus's side, Diana placed

her hand in the crook of his arm. "There are some people across the room I want you to meet. I think they could be valuable clients."

He raised his eyebrow. "Great. Let's go."

Over her shoulder Diana glanced between Venus and Connor, her meaning unmistakable.

"Diana is sacrificing herself for us." Connor handed the champagne glass to a passing waiter and took Venus into his arms so suddenly she couldn't resist. "Besides, they're playing our song."

Pressed against his hard-muscled chest, their thighs moving together to the music, she buried her hot face against his shoulder, desperate to keep her feelings hidden.

"Yes, Patsy Cline's 'Crazy' fits us to a T. This whole thing has been crazy from the beginning," she murmured, at last fully understanding what her plan had done to both of them.

"I'm crazy about you," Connor whispered into her ear, moving lower to brush his lips at her throat.

Sexual pleasure weakened her knees, but from somewhere she found the strength to pull away slightly to look up into his eyes. "Have you been drinking? This isn't like you."

His arm tightened her back to his body. "I've let go, Venus. Isn't this what you wanted?"

Her heart aching, she turned her face away and pressed her palms against his chest. "You know what I want, Connor. This is..."

Gently, he turned her head and kissed her. The pressure of his hand at the nape of her neck under her hair and his warm, dry, searching lips were irresistible. Their mouths clung together, burning, broke apart and met again.

A tremor of passion shook her, and, shocked by it here

surrounded by noise and curious onlookers, she turned
her face to bury it again in his neck.

"Oh, my God, what are we doing? We must stop."

"I'm not stopping. Let's get out of here."

"I can't..." Venus peeked over Connor's shoulder and
caught Brad's angry glare. Then she glanced up to see Connor answer it with a rigid jaw and narrowed eyes. The memory of their fistfight years ago flashed through her head.

"Oh, no, you don't. Behave," she gasped as Brad
danced over with Diana.

"Time to change partners," he demanded.

"No thanks," Connor bit out and twirled her away, leaving Brad standing alone, as a tall, handsome state senator
had whisked Diana off in his arms.

The music stopped yet still Connor held her, one hand
at the nape of her neck and the other low on her back
where her hips swelled.

"Let's get out of here," he urged again.

She saw Brad weaving through the crowd toward them.
"My parents taught me to always leave the party with the
date I came with no matter what temptations presented
themselves. I chose to do this tonight. I need to finish it."
She wiggled free but Connor caught her hand, twining
their fingers together.

With a sour look, Brad glanced at their clasped hands.
"Venus, this is our dance."

Ignoring him, Connor slowly smiled and lifted her fingers to his lips. "I'll be waiting," he murmured.

Venus felt his eyes following her as she let Brad lead
her onto the dance floor.

"What kind of game is Connor playing?" Brad glared
back at where Connor stood with one shoulder propped
against a pillar. "Everyone knows you hate the guy."

"I don't hate him," she said through the hot, tight ache at the back of her throat.

Brad lifted an eyebrow. "Since when?"

She tried to clear her voice. "Situations change."

"Has something changed between the Clayworths and your father? Have they vindicated him? Given him back his job and restored his reputation?"

Miserable, she shook her head.

"Then nothing has changed except Connor drooling all over you. I can't stand the guy but I don't blame him. You and Diana are even more gorgeous than usual tonight. I think we should make an early evening of it." He ran his palm down her bare back.

Not wanting to be rude, she stopped herself from shuddering in discomfort. "Fabulous idea." She brightened, wanting to be home to lick her wounds. "Now?"

"I'm flattered." He chuckled. "But I need to circulate another half hour or so."

Brad kept her by his side, a proprietary arm around her shoulder. She knew his attentiveness, the way he kept rubbing her back with his palm, was nothing more than spite against Connor.

She watched Diana extricate herself from three guys who looked crushed with disappointment as she glided over to where Connor stood against the pillar. He'd never taken his eyes off Venus all evening.

Ready to collapse from the stress of pretending not to notice, she nevertheless made an effort to pay attention to Brad's business conversation with a polo player and two money managers.

Out of the corner of her eye she saw Connor and Diana leave. Nearly at the same moment, Brad squeezed her shoulder.

"Ready to go, gorgeous?"

"Absolutely." She couldn't wait to be at home where she could figure out Connor's cryptic, *"I'll be waiting."*

The minute she settled into the front seat of Brad's leased Bentley and he slid into the driver's seat with a self-satisfied smile, she knew she should have handled this differently. Should have handled it differently so many times after she realized they were totally wrong for one another. She was as guilty as Brad of becoming too comfortable to make a move.

Trying to figure out the kindest way to end nearly a four-year "on but mostly off" relationship, she searched for the right approach.

Halfway home, she took a deep breath. "I'm sorry, Brad. I should have taken a cab so you could stay at the party. I know these black-tie affairs are good business opportunities for you."

Still smiling, he reached over to rub her bare arm. "I made the contacts I needed to tonight. Now I'm looking forward to spending quality time with you."

Perfect opening.

"Brad, that is not going to happen tonight. Or any other night." She tried to be as kind as possible. "I believe we both deserve better than to be in a relationship of convenience."

He slid her a long look. "How do you know I'm not ready for more commitment?"

His crinkly-eyed smile left her cold and had for quite some time. "Because I know you so well. Plus I'm not willing."

"Don't I at least deserve the opportunity to convince you otherwise?" He pulled up in front of her town house and slid out to open her door in record time.

Determined to do this as cleanly as possible, she stepped out and shook her head. "Brad, we need to say good-bye here."

"After all these years. That's it? A brush-off on the sidewalk?"

Purposefully, she moved toward her front door. "We haven't seen each other in several months. It's been over for a long time. You know it as well as I do."

"But I'm in Chicago now..."

"And I'm convenient," she finished for him. She was on the front porch with her key in her hand. "I wish you the very best. I really do. Good-bye."

"I refuse to take good-bye for an answer." He chuckled. "I know you don't mean it."

"I do. I really do," she said gently and put her key in the lock.

The door swept open to reveal Connor with his tux shirt hanging open and his feet bare.

She glanced at her mailbox hiding place and back to him.

. The look on his face made it hard for her to breathe.

Beside her, Brad stiffened. "What are you doing here, Connor?"

"Making sure you brought Venus safely home," he replied serenely, opening the door wider for her to enter.

Unable to resist the never-before-seen playfulness in his eyes, she stepped inside and instantly regretted it when Brad followed.

"What's going on here, Venus?" he demanded, spreading his legs, snarling at Connor.

The tension between the two men gave her the oddest impulse to giggle at the absurdity of the male psyche.

I'm no man's trophy.

"Okay, both of you stop acting like teenagers in testosterone overload." She sent her sternest look between them. "You are both leaving," she ordered, feeling deep, painful regret at throwing out Connor.

"Thanks for spoiling my evening with Venus. I owe you one for the last time you felt the need to protect her from me."

Brad swung back his fist and struck Connor on the jaw. He swayed but didn't stagger under the blow.

Stunned, it took her half a heartbeat to scream and step between them.

"What are you doing?" she cried to Brad.

White as a ghost, he shook his hand. "I think I broke my fingers."

"You deserve it for acting like a Neanderthal. Out." She pushed him through the open door. "You'd better go to the ER to get your hand X-rayed," she urged before she slammed the door in his face.

Leaning against the wood to gather her strength, she glared at Connor. "Go sit on that sofa. Your jaw is already beginning to swell. I'm getting ice."

When she hurried back from the kitchen with a plastic bag full of ice, wrapped in a red-and-white dish towel, he lay prostrate on her deep velvet sofa. She slid to her knees on the floor beside him.

The slight curl of his beautiful mouth and the heated look in his eyes were not going to get him off the hook.

"So tell me about the last time you felt the need to protect me from Brad."

Chapter 19

Connor's eyes picked out every detail as Venus leaned over him, pressing the cloth-covered ice bag to his aching jaw—the tumbled apricot hair over her shoulders, the full breasts covered by shimmering sequins moving with her breaths, the rosy flush on her cheeks and the determination in the startling aquamarine eyes.

"My face doesn't hurt much. I'm lying here so you'll be my nurse," he murmured, loving her attention.

"Don't try to change the subject. Tell me what Brad meant."

"There's nothing to tell." Blood pounded through his veins with his lie.

From the sharp intake of her breath he knew she didn't believe him. She pressed the ice bag harder into his cheek, and he winced before he could stop himself.

"Sorry. Really. I didn't mean to hurt you." She sat back on her heels. "Brad hit you because you broke his nose back in college. Please tell me if that fistfight had anything to do with me."

Slowly, Connor brought his hand up and with the back of his fingers brushed tears from her pink cheeks. "Please don't cry, Venus. We're two asinine guys acting like jerks. Not worth your tears."

She stared into his eyes. "You won't tell me the truth about my dad. Will you ever tell me the truth about anything?"

Seeing and hearing her pain, he felt as if he were inhaling fire.

"Come here." His hands on her shoulders, he urged her up onto the soft navy sofa. They fit together perfectly, side by side on the plush velvet, the ice bag forgotten on the floor.

Laying his forehead against hers, he massaged the tears from her hot cheeks. "The truth is you are the only woman I've ever known who looks beautiful when she cries."

"You're changing the subject again," she said in a husky voice. "Although I appreciate the compliment." She tilted back her head and, blinking, watched him. "If you don't tell me, I'll think the worst. Really I will."

Wanting to distract her, he drew a slow line down her throat with a fingertip. "It's not worth talking about. Especially now." He smoothed his thumb over her full lower lip, wet from her tears. "Let's kiss instead."

"Tempting. But you asked for it. So here goes." She sat half up on one elbow, her jaw clenched in the determination he knew all too well. "I confess I've always had a queasy feeling about your infamous locker-room brawl with Brad, because it happened the day after a rather monumental event in my life. That day I asked Brad if I had anything to do with it and he said no, you were a jerk." She took a deep breath, a beautiful flush coloring her cheeks. "I think he told you what happened between us the night before and you socked him in the nose. Although I'm not sure why you'd hit him. Don't men usually fight over women because they're jealous? But you didn't even like me then..."

Connor felt his ears burn.

"You're blushing!" she gasped, sitting straight up. "Oh, my God, it's true."

He had no choice but to follow her. "Venus, I promise you it's not true."

"Which part? The jealousy?" she guessed.

Heat coursed through him, spreading in a hot flush down his neck. "Hell, Venus, this isn't a game of Twenty Questions."

"I don't need twenty. You're as red as a pepper. If it wasn't jealousy then..." Her eyes widened. "Oh, my God, I know! Brad was the one being a jerk. He was going to tell the entire swimming team I'd given up my precious virginity to him the night before and I was horrible at it."

"Quite the contrary," Connor said, resigned. "He said virgin or not, you were the best he'd ever had."

If he'd been dazzled before by Venus's smile, it paled beside the blistering heat of *this* brilliant gleam in her eyes and the lush, deep curve of her lips.

"You stopped him before my reputation could be ruined or enhanced, depending on your point of view." She threw herself against his chest. "Oh, Connor, that is so romantic...so chivalrous, so..." She pressed a gentle kiss on his throbbing jaw. "So loving."

In that instant, he felt the strain of a lifetime of constant caution and iron control release with a long grateful sigh.

Venus felt his deep sigh where her body pressed against his chest.

"Wherever you hurt," her lips whispered along his cheek, "I'll kiss it to make it better."

"Don't tempt me."

His short husky laugh filled her with so much tenderness and heat she pulled back to gaze into his perfect face.

Now she knew denied desire, love, like a wildfire, couldn't be stomped out once the flames took hold, regardless of the cost. In this moment nothing else mattered but this.

"*Please* let me tempt you, Connor."

His emerald eyes lightened, blinding her to everything but him.

"Here," he said in a low voice, pointing to a spot on his throat. "This hurts."

She placed her mouth there, tasting his skin, feeling his pulse pound beneath her lips.

She caught his tux shirt, spreading it open to trail her fingertips down his chest. "Does it hurt here?"

Lying at his side, she nuzzled her face into the warm, tight-knit muscles of his stomach and felt them contract under her mouth. "Does this make it feel better?"

She slid her fingers to his tux trousers, miraculously unfastening them on the first try despite her slight trembling, to explore with her hand and lips the heat of his thighs. "Or this?"

"Venus," he said her name on a ragged breath.

She felt his hand under her heavy hair at her nape, urging her up to kiss.

Gently, he moved her face back and forth to penetrate all the shapes and contours of their lips touching, while his other hand made slow patterns on her bare back where the dress came to a deep vee.

"I'd feel much better if we were closer." He lifted his hands to her shoulders and tugged ever so gently on her gown.

He eased it down her body to her ankles.

Heat oozing out of every pore, she buried her hot face in his smooth, hard chest. "Oh, goodness, all those tales of the Clayworth men's sleight of hand are true. Here we are both naked in the bat of an eyelash."

"Not quite."

The pace of her breathing altered while his fingers slid into her silk thong to ease it off her body.

She tilted her head, brushing her lips against his. "Shall I leave on my stilettos for fun?"

The mischief in his eyes startled her so that a quiver of anticipation began low in her body.

His lips caressed her ankle while his expert hands slipped first one and then the other silvery Louboutin heel off her feet to land on the rug with faint thumps, joining their clothes and underwear.

He pressed soft kisses in the hollows behind her knees, his lips following the line of her thigh.

Anticipation an agony quivering at her core, she gasped in pleasure when his lips and fingers brushed the sensitive side of her breast.

"Yes, tell me what makes it feel better." His breath feathered her aching skin.

She pressed his fingers to the curve of her breast and he lifted the swelling weight in his hand.

Taking her nipple deeply into his mouth, he teased it with his tongue.

"Yes," she moaned softly, trying not to hold her breath.

Then she sucked in a deep gulp of oxygen as he caressed her thighs, the heel of his hand a hypnotic motion in the heat between them.

He scattered hot open kisses onto her throat, her breasts, and her quivering stomach. She tried to do the same to him, but pleasure wove ever tighter so she could only press herself closer to him, moving in erotic need to the rhythm of his body.

Now she knew Connor free of his iron-tight control gave passion and tenderness with his every touch.

She sought his mouth, drinking in his taste, wanting all of him.

His fingers a fire on her hips, he lifted her and she parted her thighs. He eased into her, convulsive warmth inside her tightening to increase the pleasure for both of them.

She felt it in his movements, his breathing, the way he whispered her name, his mouth hot and open against her throat.

She'd never experienced lovemaking like this. It filled her with spinning circles of pleasure, blending to become a kaleidoscope of sensations pulsing together. She clung to him, lost in the colors and feelings of him bringing her to joy again and again. She'd never ever settle for anything less.

Venus whimpered, snuggling deeper into Connor's side. He struggled out of sleep to tighten his arms around her.

She's cold.

The parts of him not tangled in Venus's warm, lush body felt the middle-of-the-night chill.

He brushed silky strands of hair off her cheek. "Love, we need to go to bed," he whispered into her ear, pressing a kiss on the soft skin beneath it.

She didn't wake when he lifted her off the velvet sofa and up into his arms.

He knew the way to her bedroom from the night he'd rushed in, afraid she was in danger, and finally realized why she'd always inspired such conflicting feelings in him.

He tossed back the coverlet and laid her on the pillows.

Sighing, still asleep, she curled onto her side.

Wanting to keep holding her, he curved his body into hers and pulled the down coverlet over them both for warmth.

He buried his face in her silky hair, breathing in its fragrance. It reminded him of apricots, as did the delicate color. Unique. Special. Like Venus.

I've never felt happier.

Refusing to think about Clayworth's or her father or all the other obstacles to be overcome, he gratefully accepted this perfect moment. He closed his eyes, surrounded by the exotic essence of Venus.

She woke to faint almost-morning light in her own bedroom with Connor gloriously naked curled around her.

Disoriented, she sat straight up in bed. "How did we get here?"

He stretched, every muscle knitted perfectly to the next. "I carried you."

"How? I'm not *little*." A sudden stupid embarrassment made her pull the coverlet back up over her spread of hips and breasts.

He caught her hand, carrying it to his lips. "Don't, love."

Love.

The word melted her bones. She slipped back down onto the pillow, her heart doing a dance against her ribs.

He leaned over, pulling the coverlet completely away, his eyes caressing every inch of her body.

"Why do women think men like skinny girls? Studies

prove that looking at a curvy woman can be as addictive and stimulating as drugs or alcohol."

He cupped her hips with his palms, catching her close, cradling her against the heat of his thighs. "Can't you feel how addicted I am to you?"

Overcome with emotions new and startling to her, she swallowed his kiss, heat spinning through her blood. With him she truly felt like Venus, goddess of love.

Burning for him, she arched into his mouth, his tongue drawing scorching circles over her breasts to their aching center.

She sobbed once. "I never thought addiction a good thing before."

His husky laughter caressed her stomach, her thighs. He lingered there, teasing her with his tongue. "I'm addicted to every part of you, love," he murmured between her writhing thighs, sucking gently, his mouth and tongue bringing her to a mindless fever pitch of desire.

His words, his touch melted every inhibition. She opened completely to his body, his touch, eager for him.

He took her face between his palms, gazed into her eyes, his breath as uneven as her own.

"Tell me how I can bring you more pleasure. Tell me what you want, love."

Hardly able to breathe, only able to feel, she wrapped her legs around his body, pulling him deep inside her.

"All I want is you."

Chapter 20

It must be morning. The thought flickered into her half-awake brain as she slowly opened her eyes. Faint light outlined her drawn bedroom drapes.

Without moving any other part of her body, she turned her face to Connor on the pillow beside her.

His perfect nose was buried in bunches of her hair.

The shocking, scalding tenderness she felt turned to confusion and ultimately, although she tried to stop it, to cruel regret.

How could she love Connor, still honor her family, and satisfy her real need to find out the truth and vindicate her father, which she knew with every fiber of her being needed to be done?

We're star-crossed lovers in a romantic story with a sad ending. And I've just made it even worse by experiencing the most tender and erotic lovemaking of my life. How can I resist this?

Wuthering Heights, Casablanca, Witness, every tragic love story she'd ever read or seen ran through her head.

Ready to sob herself into a puddle, she eased her hair

off his pillow, although from the sharp tugs she felt sure she'd left a few strands there under his lips.

Without waking him, she slipped on her robe and padded to her jewelry bower.

Here, she'd try to still the heartbreaking thoughts tumbling through her head, making her utterly miserable with longing for what could never be unless she could clear her father's name.

With a deep sigh, shuddering to her bare toes, she sat at her design table, determined to focus on anything besides her doomed feelings for Connor.

She pulled out the tray with the newest, simplest designs she'd created.

Smiling, she remembered her excitement at finding this early 1900s gilt metal chain with sapphire blue rhinestones, which had long ago lost its clasp and pendant. She'd found a clasp and then been thrilled at rescuing the 1920s glass cabochon and rhinestone pendant from a tray of broken jewelry at a flea market. United, the two discarded beauties had created a delicate, lovely piece.

She fingered the lone YSL 1960s asymmetrical earring she'd found in the same tray at the flea market.

The vendor had laughingly asked what she wanted with one earring and had sold it to her for four dollars. Now the colored crystal rhinestone with turquoise and red enameling had become a pendant on a thick gold-plated chain.

"What are you doing, Venus?"

Cutting through his words and her shock were his hands gently massaging her shoulders.

Embarrassed that he'd discovered her secret, she couldn't bear to turn around. "I'm...I'm fixing pieces of broken jewelry I've found and putting them back together."

He knelt beside her and she saw his hips were wrapped in one of her pale green bath towels.

"You designed all these pieces?"

His gaze left her face to linger on the trays lined with necklaces, bracelets, and brooches spread out on the wide work table.

"They're beautiful, Venus."

Her heart did the same dance it had earlier when he'd used the word *love* and her insides melted, sending the warmth tingling over her skin.

Against every instinct she'd had to keep her creations a secret, now she felt overwhelmed with happiness about Connor knowing.

"I've never told anyone about my designs. Not even my sisters. I wasn't sure they'd understand why I want to do it."

His hair ruffled across his forehead, his eyes shining, he looked at her and smiled. "It's the ultimate 'going green.' Taking beautiful, well-crafted pieces from the past and giving them new life now."

Venus choked back tears of wonder. "You really do understand what I'm trying to do."

Slowly, he stood over her and tilted her head back to press kisses on her eyelids, the tip of her nose, her flushed cheeks.

"Wear one of your creations for me."

His hands at her nape, he fastened the turn-of-the-century sapphire rhinestone necklace around her throat. The pendant fell between her breasts.

He pulled her up against his body, his lips whispering across her ear. "You should call your designs A Touch of Venus. Magical like you. Every piece deserves to be worn."

She could hardly pull air into her lungs. "That would be a dream come true. To give my pieces new homes with people who would cherish them."

She closed her eyes against the intense, powerful look on his face.

Under his deep kiss, the hard, restless feel of his body, Venus ached in the colors of her jewels.

Red heat.

Sapphire sensations.

Aurora borealis prisms of desire.

In this glorious world there was no space, no reason for tragedy or doom. For these precious moments there was only Connor.

With one slow sweep of his hand he freed her of the robe, his fingers smoothing over the swell of her hip.

"Your skin feels like silk here," he whispered. "And here." He lifted the heavy weight of her breasts in his palm, his thumb caressing the nipple.

Weak with desire, she sighed deeply, sagging into his arms.

"Yes, love, let's go back to bed."

He swept her up in his arms and she couldn't find the strength to protest or argue that she wasn't a delicate flower like her sisters. He made her feel as if she was perfect. Perfect for him.

As he laid her on the bed, their eyes locked and his mouth hovered barely above her lips. "I love making love to you, Venus."

Last night in Connor's arms she hadn't believed anything could ever be sweeter. Now her skin and his seemed warmer, the fit of their bodies tighter. Each knew the exact rhythm, the moment of exquisite pleasure for the other. She gave herself freely with no inhibitions, no fear. He returned that tenfold and more, dazzling her senses, completing every dream of desire she'd ever known.

This time Connor opened his eyes to Venus curled up on the pillow beside him. Looking at her profile almost buried in her thick cloud of hair brought such a startling blaze of pleasure that he had to discipline himself not to touch her.

Maybe it felt so strong because of the panic he'd felt earlier when he woke to find her gone and he'd discovered her in her jewelry studio.

Thinking of the unique, beautiful pieces she'd created, it came to him how he could make at least one dream come true for her, if not the one she truly wanted.

He slid slowly out of bed and pulled the coverlet up over her shoulders before he went to her studio. Studying the trays of jewelry, he picked out the pieces that immediately caught his eye. He hesitated, thinking she might want to keep them for herself. Then he remembered her words, *give my pieces new homes with people who would cherish them,* and smiled, his instincts telling him this would make her happy.

Thirty minutes later, showered and with the jewelry safely stored in the duffel bag he'd brought last night, he sat on the side of the bed closest to her.

"Venus," he said her name once. And again, "Venus."

Slowly, she lifted her heavy-lidded eyes. She batted her thick lashes, as if his presence beside her hadn't penetrated her sleepiness.

"Connor," she whispered and sat up, clutching the coverlet to her breasts, covering the lucky pendant tucked between her warm heavy breasts, perfumed with her unique fragrance. "What time is it?"

Unable to resist, he cupped her flushed cheek with his palm. "Time for me to go."

"We need to talk." Now her eyes were brilliant, catching the morning sunlight as she twisted strands of her silky hair around two fingers. "About...this. Last night. Us."

"We will. Come to Clayworth's this afternoon. I have a surprise for you."

Her eyes blazed, questioning him while she twisted more hair. "What kind of surprise?"

"Something I think you'll like. One o'clock. Will you come?"

He didn't realize he was holding his breath until she nodded and he let it out on a long hot sigh.

"Yes, I'll be there. Better to talk about this at Clayworth's than in my bedroom."

Connor would rather stay in the bedroom with Venus, but Clayworth's had always been home to him. He felt the beat of its rhythm every time he walked into the flagship store in the Loop. His legacy. Rebuilt twice by his ancestors after the great Chicago fires. They'd never surrendered to defeat.

Neither would he. He'd pore over the evidence against her father again and again searching for a way Alistair could be innocent, hopeless though it seemed to look for what didn't exist.

He knew how concerned and confused Venus felt about these feelings beating between them, despite all the differences neither of them could stamp out.

For the first time he felt a deep, life-changing regret for the necessity of being *here* when he'd rather be *there* with Venus.

The thought made him smile and hurry to the costume jewelry department.

As luck would have it, the department manager stood talking to Diana while she gathered pieces for a window display.

"I'd like a space cleared near the Alexis Bittar display for a new artist."

The manager rushed to the next counter to do as he asked.

Across the top of this glass counter he spread the four necklaces, two bracelets, and three brooches he'd taken from Venus's studio.

"These are lovely." Diana traced the six faux pearl drops hanging from a brooch of sapphire and more pearls. "This necklace with the rose motif and the white on red carved cameo looks like a fine vintage piece. So does this triple-strand bracelet of faux pearls with the gilt metal links and the shields with engraved hearts. But the designs are more contemporary. Who's the designer?"

"They're called A Touch of Venus."

Wide-eyed surprise marked Diana's delicate features with a childlike innocence, very different from the femme fatale of last night.

"Venus designed these? She never said a word to me. But she told you."

Remembering the look in Venus's eyes, the emotion in her voice when he'd discovered her in her studio tapped such deep feelings for her he fought to hide even a small part of them.

"Yes, she told me. However, I didn't tell her I brought some of her designs here for display and to sell."

Again, Diana blinked up at him, shock widening her eyes.

Sure of himself, he laughed. "I know it's a bold plan to take them without her knowledge but I want it to be a surprise. She'll be here at one."

At 1:00 P.M. sharp and not a minute late for a change, Venus walked into Clayworth's on the hunt for Diana. To accomplish what she needed to do today, she required heavy moral support.

Venus found her sister in the children's department, creating a fantasy display of storybook dresses, headbands festooned with ribbons, dainty, sequined Mary Jane shoes no self-respecting mother or grandmother could resist buying for the holidays.

"I need to talk to you. Alone." She motioned toward the storeroom and marched purposefully to it, with Diana following.

Being ready to confess her utter folly and being able to do it without crying were two completely separate things. She burst into loud, sloppy hot tears.

"Tears of happiness. I would be doing the same thing." Diana nodded, watching her with a brilliant smile.

"Happiness?" Venus sucked in a soggy breath. "What are you talking about? I'm more miserable than I've ever been in my life. Or ever likely to be. You should have locked me in and thrown away the key the night I begged you to help me find Connor. I set out to make him care about me but it backfired. *I* care about him too much. It's different for Athena and Drew. They've loved each other their whole lives. Years before the troubles with Dad. So it makes sense they could find a way to be together."

Her lungs nearly empty, she took another deep breath. "But I didn't even *like* Connor for so many stupid childish reasons, and then when he betrayed our family, Dad, everything I hold dearest, I *loathed* him. What kind of person, daughter, am I to now love him?"

Hiccuping swallowed sobs, she drew herself up. "As it stands, there is no way any relationship between Connor and me can possibly work, and I'm telling him so right now before it becomes even more painful."

Her tirade appeared to have left Diana speechless.

"Venus, before you do anything, I think you should come with me," Diana finally said, and abruptly turned on her ballet slippers.

Venus followed her to the first-floor costume jewelry department. Finally Diana stopped in front of a jewelry case and looked pointedly inside it.

"What? I love Alexis Bittar jewelry, too. I own three pieces. What does..." Her throat tightened. The small neat Touch of Venus sign blurred and then focused so sharply it hurt her eyes.

"They've already sold two of your pieces this morning," Diana said quietly beside her.

Mindless, Venus stared at her sister. "How did this happen?"

"Connor brought the pieces in this morning. He wanted to surprise you."

Delirious happiness felt like a monumental betrayal of her intent to be sensible, yet she couldn't contain it. "Where is he?"

"I thought he'd be down here to see your reaction. He must be delayed in his office."

Diana's final words followed Venus, for she was already running toward the elevator.

On the executive floor, she caught a glimpse of Bridget on the phone at her desk.

Breathless to see Connor, Venus didn't stop.

Silence greeted her when she rushed into his office.

"Connor," she called, thinking he must be in the butler's pantry, board room, or his small gym.

When she couldn't find him, she wandered back into his office and over to his desk where a blue mug sat beside folders and piles of papers. She felt its porcelain sides.

Still warm. I must have just missed him.

Then she glanced down at the papers, admiring a sheet with pictures of a two-strand ruby bracelet and an emerald and diamond necklace with a matching emerald ring surrounded by mounds of diamonds. It looked vaguely familiar to her.

Her gaze slid to the thick file beside it.

Her father's name jumped out at her.

Connor's words rang through her head. *At Clayworth's we're creatures of habit. We do both computer and hard copies.*

Almost in a trance she stared down at the folder.

Was this what she'd been seeking all along? The evidence against her father? The *truth* that she needed to know so she could refute the surely flawed evidence and somehow help vindicate her dad?

The need made her ache all over. If only she could find something, anything to make Connor change his mind about her dad, all the barriers between them would disappear.

If I can find something, anything that can make it possible for Connor and me to be together, it will be my gift to him.

Trembling, she opened the file and began to read. The sheet after sheet of numbers, stock transactions, and bank statements made no sense to her but yet a pattern appeared in her frenzied mind.

Her father's signature. Everywhere.

She riffled through the sheets more rapidly, his name flicking before her eyes like an old-time silent movie.

Her jeweler's eye caught the tiniest shade of difference in the image of his name.

Blood roared through her ears.

Was it simply a trick of light? Her overheated imagination?

She separated out two sheets, comparing them to a third. Now they looked exactly the same, no matter how she shifted them side to side and up and down in the light.

Defeat gnawed at her heart. There was nothing new to show Connor.

But I know I saw something.

Her insides quaking, she clutched the three sheets in her fist and walked back to Bridget's office.

Not wanting to involve Bridget any more than necessary, she held the papers behind her back as she peeked through the open door.

"Hi, Bridget. Sorry to bother you."

A frown between her eyes, Bridget glanced up and immediately brightened. "Venus, sorry. I didn't hear you. Connor went downstairs lookin' for you. I'll page him that you're here waitin' for him."

"Great." She forced a smile. "By the way, I...have a problem with a...possible forged check at Pandora's Box. Do you know an expert on that sort of thing?"

"Dr. Carl Potts at U of I. He's the best, but forgeries are tough to prove. In court cases there are often differin' opinions as to the validity of a signature."

"Okay. Thanks, Bridget. I'll give him a call anyway. I'll...just wait in Connor's office for him."

She carefully placed the three sheets of paper in her tote and zipped it securely.

If Dr. Carl Potts could throw even a *shadow* of doubt on any one of those signatures, there might be a glimmer of hope for her and Connor.

All at once he walked into the room, and despite her best, wisest intentions, she said his name once in a voice that sounded shaky to her and walked into his arms.

She stroked the firm muscles of his back and shoulders, kissed his mouth, his hair, his cheek.

Her heart twisting around in her chest, she flung back her head and looked up into his face.

"Why did you take my pieces of jewelry and bring them to Clayworth's?"

"Because I think they're beautiful, like you, and I wanted to make your dream for your designs come true."

The naked emotion in his voice made her ache for him.

Fed by love, by her belief that she'd found a way for them to be together, she pushed away from him and went to lock the door.

She turned back and smiled at him. "Why don't you go lie down on that black leather sofa?"

His eyes lightened and there was that new, playful, totally erotic curve to his mouth.

"This is getting to be a much-desired habit. My lounging on a sofa, waiting to ravish you." Stretched out with his hands behind his head, he watched her walk slowly to him. "You know my uncle, Grey and Ric's father, took his afternoon naps on this sofa for thirty years."

She hesitated. "Oh, dear, it seems a bit sacrilegious to continue with my plan now."

Connor laughed and pulled her down so she sprawled

on top of him. "My uncle had four wives and twice as many mistresses. Naps were a euphemism for what went on in here when the door was locked. This old leather sofa has tales to tell."

"Let's give it another one." She laughed and one by one undid his shirt buttons.

Connor's gaze, open and warm, changed to a deeper emerald when she pulled her sweater dress over her head.

Clad only in a sheer black bra, thong, and thigh-high boots, she slid to her knees beside the sofa and began to tug off his jeans. His loafers followed.

"Venus," he whispered, a question in his voice. Then his breath sharpened as she slid her fingers into his briefs, as he had her thong last night, to pull them off.

Holding his heated gaze, she stood and with deliberate slowness stepped out of her thong, peeled off her bra, and knelt between his thighs.

Leaning into him, she rubbed her heavy breasts against his chest, his stomach, his thighs, pressing soft kisses in her wake. She lingered at the warmth of his inner thighs, loving the tangy taste of him.

Slowly, she took him into her mouth, sucking, stroking him with her tongue.

"Venus ... what in the hell are you doing?" he asked in a thick voice.

"Hopefully making your dreams come true." she smiled against his inner thigh.

She felt his breathless laughter.

"The best dreams are shared ones, love."

He drew her up, rolled her on top of him to meet the unguarded blaze of his eyes.

"Tell me yours so we can find them together." His lips brushed again and again over the aching peaks of her breasts while his hands stroked her hips in the same rhythmic, hypnotizing way.

She closed her eyes, gasping at the sweetness of his hands suddenly cupping her breasts, his thumbs gently rubbing her nipples.

"Tell me how I can bring you more pleasure," he whispered.

"Everything you do brings me pleasure," she whispered, meeting his mouth with an open, burning kiss that exploded passion through her blood.

With an urgency that shook her, she slid down his body, straddled his hips, and settled over him.

Gently, he caught and held her. "Slowly, love. Make it last."

But she couldn't stop.

Her body shuddered with each thrust and she became part of a hot, wet haze of ecstasy. She couldn't think, she could only feel.

From a distance she heard him repeat her name over and over, his fingers kneading her flesh with ever-increasing strokes. Now he couldn't stop, their movements stronger and stronger until he arched hard and tight, their bodies seamlessly meeting.

With tremors throbbing through her, she whimpered his name. Her heart pounding so that she felt light-headed, she collapsed on his chest.

Long moments passed before she could catch her breath. "It must have been the boots," she said, her lips against his throat.

"Promise me you'll never take them off." He chuckled, stroking her back.

She loved the feel of him beneath her, his hand warming her skin, once again giving life to a response.

But all dreams must end. For now.

"Connor, we're at Clayworth's, stark naked, except for my thigh-high boots. There's probably a Chicago city ordinance against this."

"Who's to know?" He nuzzled her throat. "We could do this all day. There are no cameras in here, thank God."

"Cameras?" She glanced nervously around.

The whole idea of being caught on tape snapped her to her senses. With a heavy twinge of regret, she kissed Connor on the cheek and eased off his body.

In record time she gathered up her dress and underwear and slipped into them.

Still gloriously naked, his skin golden and glistening, he smiled up at her. "Where are you going so fast?"

She could hardly resist the playfulness in his eyes. Now she knew she wanted it to last forever, which was why she needed to get the precious documents to Dr. Potts right now.

"If you think lying around naked has any effect on me, you're right." She pressed a kiss on his smiling lips.

"I have an important errand to run. Meet me at my place in a few hours. I promise I'll still have on my boots."

Chapter 21

When his aunt rapped on the door and walked in, Connor was pulling on his jeans.

Their eyes met, hers brimming with humor and a little surprise. "Well, hello there. Sorry to ... interrupt."

"Nonsense, Aunt Bridget. You didn't interrupt a thing," Connor said, buttoning his jeans and hastily reaching for his shirt, a broad smile on his face.

"No need to rush about in false modesty, Connor. After all, I've changed plenty of your diapers—there's little I haven't seen. So I assume you found Venus." She laughed. "It seems to have done you a world of good."

"She always does," he said without embarrassment.

"I've never seen you look happier, Connor. Have the two of you figured out a way to live with the problems between you because of Alistair? Can she honestly, with all her heart, finally let it go?"

"I'm working on it," he said, fastening his shirt and strolling to his desk.

Uncharacteristically, he'd left papers scattered across its surface when he'd heard Venus was in the store. Eager to be downstairs when she saw what he'd done with her designs, he hadn't cared about anything else.

He'd missed that moment. Thinking of her private response and his own, here alone in his office, white-hot need to be with her again made him quickly and efficiently gather up the papers.

"I was going over the items stolen in the original heist with the mermaid brooch in the hopes of helping you and Tony. And for the hundredth time, looking at Alistair's file."

Having relentlessly studied it again and again he knew the contents by memory, so he saw immediately that pages were missing.

Thinking he'd placed them by mistake in the heist file, he slowly went through those sheets one by one.

"What's the problem?" Bridget asked, coming to stand beside him.

"I must have misplaced three important documents from Alistair's file." Connor stepped back, his eyes searching the carpet.

"I don't see anythin' on the floor." Bridget circled the desk. "Sure the documents aren't in one of the drawers?"

But he knew they couldn't be. All the drawers were locked.

Raw disbelief and an edge of panic made him look nonetheless.

Nothing.

Venus was here alone for how long?

"The documents aren't here. I know they were in the file when I left the office."

He met his aunt's eyes, blazing with pain for him.

She shook her head. "But why would Venus only take three documents? What could she hope to…" Bridget gasped. "Dr. Carl Potts. Venus said she had a bad check at Pandora's Box. She asked me for an expert on forgeries."

"Forgeries?" He bit out the word. "Even though Alistair denied signing two transactions, he couldn't deny it was his signature. If there was a chance in hell they were actual forgeries, why wouldn't Alistair have insisted they be examined by an expert if that could prove his innocence? You know he didn't."

The old pain of realizing that a man he'd respected and trusted as much as he had his late father and Tony had robbed him and his cousins roared through him. It felt like nothing compared to the raw agony of Venus's betraying him and what he'd thought they had together.

He'd dropped his guard and this blow finished him. *Had it all been an act to get information from me?*

"Connor, please don't look like…like…" Bridget shook her head, gripping his arm with both hands. "Please let Venus explain why she did it."

He tried to rearrange his facial muscles to prevent Bridget from again catching the privacy of his pain. "I plan to do that, Bridget. Now."

"Think about what you want to do, first. Don't rush to judgment, Connor, you may live to regret it," Bridget said softly before mercifully leaving him alone.

He tried not to see this in black and white. He tried to believe he could be wrong and there could be another explanation for the missing papers, even though the evidence pointed to Venus's being alone in the office when they went missing.

Wanting to believe in any scenario except the one burning up his gut, he called the University of Illinois and Dr. Carl Potts's office.

When he gave his name, Dr. Potts's secretary cheerfully told him Miss Smith had dropped off the documents from Clayworth's and he had only missed her by minutes.

He sat motionless, giving himself time to let the truth, reality, sink in. Gave himself time to shut down to blunt the memories of Venus forever carved in his gut.

Only then did he allow himself to get in his Ferrari and drive to her town house on Schiller.

She opened the door after the first hard jab of his finger against the bell.

Her eyes bright and daring, her hair, which always invited his touch, tumbling across her breasts, she stood clad in a short apricot silk slip and her thigh-high boots.

Laughing, she pulled him inside, shut the door, and leaned against it.

"See, as promised, I'm still wearing my boots." She stretched out one long leg, exposing the pale flesh of her upper thigh, barely covered by the silk hem.

He coldly disguised any trace of his feelings. "Are the boots where you hid the documents you stole from my desk?"

His cool voice rang in her ears as she stared into his even colder eyes. Heat waves of regret and fear washed over her.

This isn't the way it's supposed to be.

Feeling suddenly naked in the silk slip and ridiculous boots meant to bring the newly discovered grin to his perfect face, she pulled on the aqua robe she'd dropped onto the hall chair when she'd heard him at the door.

With his almost smile, he seemed relaxed. But now she knew this was the old, controlled Connor, who saw the world in black and white

"Did you think I wouldn't notice the documents were

missing? Did you even care once you took them? What do you hope to accomplish, Venus?"

"What I've always wanted. The truth about my father. A way to vindicate him, and I may have found it, Connor. Truly," she said steadily, refusing to give in to fear. "I took them without telling you, as you took my jewelry, to surprise you and make you happy."

Slowly, he crossed her tiny foyer until they were so close she felt the warmth of his body.

"God knows I've been looking for weeks for a phantom solution so I could make you happy."

A blast of hope that she could explain her actions so he'd understand caused her to smile and sway the tiniest bit closer to him.

"All I did was take the documents to a specialist for evaluation. I know he'll verify my suspicions. You can't be mad at me for this. Be glad. I wanted my discovery to be my gift to you. Like yours to me."

His eyes still like green ice, he stared down at her. "It sounds good when you say it. But the truth is you don't trust me. If you did, when you found some crucial piece of evidence I missed, you would have shown it to me, instead of lying to me. Trusted me to help you instead of sneaking around behind my back. Hell, Venus, you lied to me about your errand five minutes after we made love in my office. Is there nothing you won't do in your need to prove your father's innocence?"

Remembering how she'd stupidly planned to use him, she twisted a strand of hair around her fingers. "I'll do whatever it takes," she whispered, really afraid for the first time that she couldn't make him understand.

"I thought as much." His short laugh held no humor. "If it wasn't for my colossal Clayworth ego I'd have realized your abrupt change from loathing me to making love with me had to be an act to get what you wanted."

Before when he'd called her *love* it had melted her bones. Now the way he used *making love* froze her blood.

She saw in his eyes and the firm long line of his mouth that Connor had shut down. Realizing with real desperation that this had all gone terribly wrong she determined to right matters by falling back on the unvarnished truth.

"Connor, I may have lied to you. Maybe even pretended feelings I didn't have at the beginning, but not for a long, long time. I …"

"No more lies between us, Venus." His harsh words stopped her. "Your father is guilty. You saw the proof with your own eyes. Nothing you do can change the facts. That's the truth and you have to accept it. Once you promised me that you would accept whatever we discovered. Do you remember?"

Shock ran like acid along her skin at the total loss of the tenderness she'd learned to expect from him.

"My father is not guilty. I'll never accept the horrible things you are saying about him," she whispered through her tight throat.

"So it was another lie, it seems." He brushed past her to the door. "Then there's nothing more to say."

As he opened it, waves of fear and love drove her to call his name. "Connor, please wait. You don't understand."

He stopped, the tension across his wide shoulders evident in the way he held them. Very slowly, he turned, his hand still on the door.

Putting every molecule of her feelings in her eyes and in her voice, she pleaded with him. "You also promised to accept whatever we discovered. The truth I've discovered is that despite everything you've done to my father and continue to do, I've come to love you."

Disbelief as clear as a diamond on his face, Connor turned and walked out the door.

Pain froze her, making it impossible for her to move, to cry out to stop him from leaving her. After months of weeping like a leaky faucet with high emotion because of her dad, and recently for Connor, Venus now felt arid, empty.

As if the flame of passion she felt for life, for those she loved, had been extinguished.

Is this how Connor feels when he shuts down to avoid pain?

She wanted to hide behind a facade of cool control, just as he did.

She tried, locked away in her town house. She went through the motions of living, breathing, and eating but feeling, tasting, nothing. She did her best to keep herself occupied during the day. But when she tried to sleep at night, her mind raced and try as she might, she couldn't shut it off. *What if she was wrong and her father was guilty, just as Connor thought? What if taking those papers from Connor's office and destroying his trust in her had all been for nothing?*

In her darkest hour she even thought if she accepted her father's guilt then perhaps she and Connor could somehow find their way back to each other. In a blaze of pain she knew it couldn't be so.

No! I'll never believe it. There must be something we're missing, and it's probably right in front of our noses.

The next morning she stuck her biggest pair of dark glasses on her nose to hide behind when she went to meet her father at an estate sale where she'd been offered first look.

He was already there, carefully examining old books.

"Hello." He greeted her with his normal tight, warm hug. She had to resist her need to stay in his arms for comfort.

"Did you find anything, Dad?" she asked as cheerfully as she could muster.

"Yes. This is a treasure trove, and I have two more shelves to explore." He laughed.

"Fabulous. I'll be in with the jewelry."

Usually the thrill of an estate sale fired her imagination and energy. Today, finding a twenty-piece collection of Miriam Haskell jewelry produced barely a flutter of pleasure.

Half an hour later, her father found her drifting aimlessly around the jewelry cases.

"Are you ready to leave? I told your sister we would meet her for lunch."

No way could she hide her misery from her baby sister. "Oh, no, I'm so sorry, Dad. I need to do some inventory at Pandora's Box. Have fun." She kissed his warm cheek and fled.

After the third nearly sleepless night even the fact she hadn't heard from Dr. Potts barely registered.

Venus drank gallons of caffeine and put on more makeup than normal to hide the dark circles under her eyes when she dutifully arrived for her appointment at the newly built home Maxie shared with Ed on one of Taylor Street's narrow lots. "Lean out the window and kiss your neighbors," Venus had heard said of these close-set, thin houses with multiple levels to get maximum square footage.

Maxie flung open her front door and Venus stared at her, shocked. Her big hair looked smaller and her smile wobbled around the edges.

Life returned to Venus with a twinge of concern for her. "Maxie, are you all right? Should we reschedule our appointment?"

"No, dear Venus. Please come with me."

Venus followed Maxie, who was dressed in a red silk caftan and high-heeled slippers with matching marabou feathers.

Passing the living room, Venus glimpsed Maxie's stunning copy of Gainsborough's *Blue Boy* painting over the white marble fireplace.

They hurried down a long, narrow hallway lined with painted canvases of Monet's *Water Lilies*, which appeared to be original, down to the artist's signature, but again she knew it was Maxie's amazing talent at work.

At the end of the hall Venus saw a large sunny great-room.

"That is where I paint. It's the best light. Come this way to my closet." Maxie walked up a short flight of steps and Venus followed.

Finally, they arrived in the master bedroom, an opulent rectangle with an enormous brass bed over which hung Rubens's painting *The Toilet of Venus*.

A fizzle of humor returned to Venus as she gazed at the lush curves of Rubens's "Venus," which were once the ideal.

"Maxie, your talent truly is amazing."

"I fear my little paintings must go the way of my jewelry," Maxie said with a deep sigh. "The situation is grim."

Now truly concerned with the high flush on Maxie's round face, Venus walked to where she stood, flinging open double doors.

The wide, deep closet was large splashes of color like a piece of modern art. All blacks together, be they fur coats or transparent black silk nightgowns. So it went with reds, purples, blues, greens, and yellows.

"Most must go," Maxie declared with feeling.

Walking slowly down the long racks, Venus picked out a few pieces. "The fur coats will sell in Pandora's Box, but we don't carry any clothes after the 1980s."

"I know. I've prepared my jewels for your inspection." She opened two built-in drawers, lined in felt. Organized by colors, hundreds of pieces of jewelry sparkled up at them.

The emerald-hued jewelry struck a memory.

Venus picked up a cocktail ring of pavé diamonds and tiny emeralds. The picture she'd seen on Connor's desk of an emerald surrounded by mounds of diamonds flickered through her mind.

Like the ring Maxie showed me at the gala. Like the ring stolen from Clayworth's.

"This isn't the ring you showed me at the gala. I'd love to examine that one," Venus said carefully.

"I'm very sorry, Venus. Edward has liquidated all my most expensive pieces, including the ring and its matching emerald and diamond necklace."

Her overactive imagination flickered to life. Connor had a picture of a matching emerald and diamond necklace that had been stolen in the same heist as the brooch.

Oh, my God, stop it!

The image of pudgy Ed as a jewel thief like Cary Grant in *To Catch A Thief* was utterly ludicrous. She knew she *must* stop looking for clues to solve the burglary. Just as she needed to stop searching for anything that might help her dad. Anything to make it possible for her to totally surrender to her feelings for Connor. Letting her imagination run riot had led to disaster and heartbreak.

She wasn't imagining the teary, anguished note in Maxie's voice. Sympathetic to her unhappiness, Venus patted her shoulder. "I know these are difficult times for many people."

"The worst. Edward has completely cleaned out the safe." She motioned to the home safe, much like the one Venus had in her own closet. "Edward always said he'd never do such a thing because it was our nest egg for the future. He says he did it so he'd have a future."

Something isn't adding up.

Unable to control her pesky imagination and downright curious, she probed more than she should, hoping that if she knew more, she could help more.

"I always thought the insurance business was recession-proof."

Maxie glanced toward the door and with a sigh leaned closer. "I believe there are certain gentlemen to whom Edward owes money and they can be difficult if not paid promptly."

"The bank?" Venus asked, knowing foreclosures were happening everywhere.

"No. Much worse," Maxie whispered.

Studying Maxie's frightened face, Venus thought of her feeling in the poker room of sensing the desperation of another time.

Venus gasped before she could stop herself. "Oh, my God, is Ed in debt to the mob?"

"Venus, in Chicago we call such gentlemen the Outfit." Visibly wilting, Maxie dropped to the zebra-patterned long bench in the middle of the closet. "I fear there are also a few men in Vegas eager for payment."

Trying to be rational about the images and possibilities tumbling through her head and the notion that Ed *could* have been involved in the heist, Venus sat down carefully on the bench beside her.

"Where does Ed gamble?" she asked gently, realizing Maxie had every right to tell her to mind her own business.

"Usually Vegas. He's a high roller. They fly us out and put us up in the most fantastic suites. And he gambles here at his private club."

"On Taylor Street at the restaurant where I dropped you off for dinner with Ed?" Venus asked, trying to find the pieces that fit together, as she did in her designs. "The casino under the parking lot?"

Again, Maxie looked around as if the closet had ears. "It's been around for decades. Very exclusive. Everyone must be very discreet."

"Have *you* ever been there?" Venus asked, still struggling to understand how this all fit together without giving too much away.

"I don't gamble." Maxie sat up straighter. "The odds always favor the house. In Vegas I spa."

She felt guilty for prying when Maxie seemed so vulnerable but she truly believed there might be something here to reunite Bridget and Tony. Even solve the whole mystery of the mermaid brooch.

"Have you ever heard of the Saint of Taylor Street?"

"Heard of him." Maxie sat up straighter, even her hair seemed to puff higher in attention. "He paid for my great-grandmother's wedding after her parents died of cholera, and he helped pay for my uncle Franco's surgery last year."

Calculating the span of years, Venus understood at last. "The Saint has been many different people."

"On Taylor Street, all over the city's Twenty-fifth

Ward, they say the Saint passes it on when he finds someone worthy of the task. But no one ever knows who he is.
Some kind of blood oath of secrecy. They say it started
back in Italy or Sicily or some such place. I don't care who
he is, I could use a visit from him at the moment," Maxie
said wistfully.

Another piece of the puzzle fell into place. *This* one
gave her goose bumps of admiration.

"Well, I'm certainly not the Saint, but I'm here to help
you." She glanced back into the open drawers. "There are
quite a few pieces I can purchase outright for the store and
the others I'll take on consignment."

"Thank you." With a deep sigh, Maxie pulled open two
more drawers. "There is more."

The first drawer brimmed with parures of brooch,
earrings, bracelets, and necklaces, sets in every color of
stones imaginable from bright pink to deepest ruby red,
from citrine to amber. The second drawer was half filled
with creature pins, from birds, to butterflies, to lobsters
to elephants. The other half housed a neat arrangement of
calligraphy pens.

"I've never seen so many beautiful pens." Intrigued,
Venus picked up two, examining their different tips.

"I use them for the writing games Ed and I play with
names. Once he got a copy of the Declaration of Indepen-
dence and he asked me to copy every signature on it and
then he couldn't tell the difference between the original
and my own. I must say I did admire John Hancock's fluid
strokes."

Maxie must have seen the hot shock burning through
Venus. For the first time wariness flickered across Maxie's face. "I have revealed too much personal business,
haven't I?"

"What are friends for?" Venus shrugged nonchalantly even though her pulse pounded with excitement.

Maxie was a world-class art forger, down to the signature. What else could she duplicate perfectly? Another piece of the puzzle fell into place.

"What other writing games do you play, Maxie?"

She shrugged. "I told you I took advance classes in handwriting anaylsis. Sometimes we do that. Edward is fascinated by my little hobby, too."

Looking into Maxie's limpid eyes, Venus wished as never before that she possessed Diana's gift.

"Will you take the furs and jewelry now?" Maxie changed the subject, bobbing up in her high-heeled slippers with amazing energy. "I have cases for the jewelry."

Left no choice at the moment, Venus packed up the best pieces of jewelry and the fur coats to carry to her car.

She might not be psychic like Diana, but even she saw that the pieces created a mosaic of possibilities she needed to show Connor and somehow convince him to believe her.

Surely if she was honest, *trusting* him with what she'd discovered would bring them back together.

It was more difficult to go back to his old ways of concealing his emotions than Connor thought possible.

He'd think of Venus and the deep ache would still even his breathing.

Walking into his office, Bridget caught him. He saw it in her sad eyes.

"Connor, I'm more sorry than I can say. I know how hard it is to accept that Venus took the documents and lied to you."

Not understanding, he blinked. He hadn't been thinking of the papers at all but of Venus pretending while they made love to get what she wanted.

She hadn't faked everything.

The sheen of her skin growing warmer under his touch, her trembling in his arms, her soft sounds were all real.

Those thoughts brought another kind of ache.

"Connor, what can I do to help you? " his aunt asked, patting his arm.

"Talk to Tony," he said quietly. "I want the two of you to be happy."

She nodded. "I understand. I'll do my best to work through all the mistakes Tony and I have made. I don't want you to be makin' another mistake by not talkin' this out with Venus."

She walked out of the office, he hoped, to do as he asked. He wasn't strong enough yet to talk to Venus. As Bridget hadn't been ready to talk to Tony.

A few minutes later Bridget came back in, carrying a large legal-size envelope.

"Dr. Potts had this sent by messenger. Since these are Clayworth documents, he returned them to us and will send an opinion to Venus, since she asked for one."

Quickly, Connor ripped open the envelope and read slowly.

The words sealed any lingering hope for a way to clear Alistair.

"What does Carl say?" Bridget asked, peering over his shoulder.

"He has no opinion that would stand up in a court of law. The use of a different pen could account for any minute variations. On a personal note to me, he says if these two signatures are forgeries they are the best he's ever seen.

"This is no surprise." Connor let the paper drift to his desk and stared at it, realizing he'd give anything to make it different. "This will be a blow to Venus." Even he heard the emotion in his voice.

"Connor, I'm so sorry. What will you do now?"

Unseeing, he stared at his aunt, letting the question and answer sink in. "What will I do now? Nothing. It's up to Venus to finally accept the truth."

Driving to Clayworth's, Venus trembled with excitement and resolve. *Nothing* would stop her this time. She wouldn't keep anything from Connor. She'd tell him everything and somehow convince him to believe her. Never again would she allow him to leave with that look on his face, a look that haunted her day and night.

Yes, she was as stubborn as a mule, as he'd once said. She *would* write a different ending for their tragic love story.

Unannounced, she walked into his office.

He sat at his desk, his hair falling across his forehead, while he stared down, apparently studying a sheet of paper.

"Connor," she said his name softly.

Close as she stood, when he glanced up she saw his eyes widen and his breath catch in his chest.

Then he rose slowly to his feet, the emotion hidden behind the striking bones of his face.

"You've come about Dr. Potts's opinion?"

In the loaded silence, Venus's heart beat so loudly she heard it in her ears. She shook her head. "Has it come?"

"This morning." With two fingers, he slid the paper across the desk toward her.

As she read, the words blurred together but then

divided out to make yet another statement of guilt against her father.

Her stomach a huge knot, she looked up into Connor's steady gaze. "Those two documents *are* forgeries. Done, I believe innocently, by Maxie Robinson. There is a strong possibility that Ed was the instigator of the famous heist when the mermaid brooch was stolen."

"Ed Mahoney as a jewel thief and his sweet girlfriend a forger? Hell, who are you going to blame next in your need to vindicate your dad? Me?" The blaze in Connor's brilliant eyes and his harsh laughter, a slight cover for the underlying anger, should have crushed her spirit.

Strange how desperation made her feel brave.

"I know this is hard to believe, but I just left Maxie. She told me Ed is in debt to the mob. He's desperate to pay off before he gets his legs broken or whatever they do. He's sold all her best jewelry. Including a ring that I glimpsed once, and it bore a striking resemblance to one I later saw on your desk in a description of the jewelry taken during that famous heist. And Ed worked here then and…"

"And you don't have a shred of evidence to prove any of this," Connor interrupted.

Refusing to be stopped, despite his cool, emotionless words, she plunged on.

"And Maxie can reproduce any painting you can imagine. Their house is full of masterpieces that could fool some experts."

"From being able to copy artwork you naturally make the leap to her being able to copy signatures. Notably your father's."

Venus swallowed a tight, hot lump in her throat. "She could probably do your signature too. Mine. *Anyone's.* You must believe me."

Connor narrowed his eyes, studying her with a coldness that broke through her armor of desperation to pierce her heart with fear.

"Venus, you need to accept the truth about your father once and for all. For everyone's sake. Especially your own."

Unable to stop her raging need for him to believe her, she moved around the desk and flung herself against his chest.

Perhaps surprise caused him to catch her close.

"Please, Connor, you must accept I'm telling the truth. For us." She got out the words in a tear-choked whisper.

Abruptly he released her and, shivering, she looked up into his face.

He turned away, tension visible in his back, as if he held something powerful inside that he fought to control.

Tears of frustration and pain dried up in her burning eyes as she watched him stride from the room.

He paused for only a second in the doorway, where his aunt stood, and then pushed past her.

Bridget stared at Venus, with eyes very like Connor's, but hers were full of kindness. "I heard everything. Come with me to my office."

Bridget fed her a cup of tea, placed a box of Kleenex on the black leather love seat where Venus sat and then stared down at her.

"You do know how far-fetched your theory sounds?"

Miserable with pain and worry, Venus nodded. "I know, but I believe with all my heart it's true. I always suspected the truth could be right in front of us. Now I'm terrified if I don't move quickly Ed will make a run for it."

"Because he's in debt to the wise guys?"

Encouraged, Venus blinked up at her.

"I've known Ed for thirty years. Always liked craps and a good poker game, but that doesn't make him an inveterate gambler in over his head. Yes, he worked at Clayworth's with his dad at the time of the heist, but that doesn't make him a jewel thief or a forger," Bridget said with kindness in her voice.

"I'm sure he's using Maxie's amazing talent for his own gain and it's up to us to stop him by trapping him into showing his hand. Pardon the pun."

Venus couldn't miss the indulgent humor in the curling smile of Clayworth's head of security. "How would you be doin' that, Venus?"

"By letting him steal back the brooch he's attempted to retrieve twice."

She saw by the subtle change in Bridget's smile, she was listening with more attention.

Too tense to sit still, Venus sprang up and began to pace the room. "How do you catch shoplifters at Clayworth's?"

"On camera. Leavin' the store with the merchandise."

"Why couldn't we do the same thing with Ed?" Realizing she'd used *we,* she glanced at Bridget.

She nodded. "Yes, we could catch him on camera, say putting the brooch in his pocket. But he'd need to leave the store with it to be finite proof. Clayworth's is a big store. Risky to try this in anythin' but a controllable environment."

Remember lying breathless with sensual satisfaction on Connor's hard, warm chest, his hand stroking her back until he mentioned *no cameras in here, thank God,* she knew what they needed to do.

"Does Ed know there are no cameras in Connor's office?"

"Everyone knows there are no cameras in any of the offices up here, except mine, for obvious reasons."

"Then what if we secretly install some in Connor's office. I'd have no reason to go into any of the other offices but I would his. I leave the brooch there and we tape Ed taking it. Then we catch him and convince him to confess all."

A bit of the amused smile back, Bridget shook her head. "You've been watchin' too many detective shows on television. It's not that easy."

"But it would prove Ed was the original thief or he wouldn't be trying to steal the brooch in the hopes it's the one he lost in the poker game. And from there anything is possible."

Her need to vindicate her father had long been the most powerful and immediate force in her life. Her love for Connor was rapidly keeping pace. She *needed* to do this for all the right reasons for both the men in her life.

She halted in front of Bridget. "Will you help me?"

Trying to still the pulse ramming blood through her veins, Venus waited while Bridget studied her.

"I understand your passion. There's nothin' I wouldn't do for Connor, and you wouldn't know it by my wallowin' in self-pity lately, but the same goes for Tony. Besides, you put yourself in possible harm's way to help me and Tony."

"I think that's a yes, right?" Venus asked with a little catch in her voice. "If I'm wrong, which I know I'm not, Ed will simply find the mermaid brooch and return it to me."

"If he's guilty, in a court of law this borders on entrapment, you know."

"This is why we absolutely can't involve Connor, even if he was willing." Remembering how he'd left, the ache started again low, spreading to every part of her body.

"I agree. And we mustn't involve anyone else either.

Not even Diana. The fewer who know about this the better. But there is someone we need to help us." Taking a deep breath, color flowed into Bridget's pale cheeks. "Meet me at my brownstone. We need to convince Tony to help us."

Chapter 22

Bridget stood waiting for her on the porch of her brownstone on Astor Street as Venus hurried up the brick walkway to join her.

Then, to Venus's utter surprise, Bridget pressed the bell instead of using her key.

A few heartbeats later, Tony opened the door. His glowing gaze swung quickly from Venus to Bridget. After a long pause while he appeared to be studying her face, he smiled.

"*Cara,* why didn't you use your key?"

"Because I didn't know if I'd be welcome, Tony." Bridget's voice sounded strong, but the haunted look in her eyes broke apart something powerful in Venus's chest.

"You are and will always be welcome, *Cara.*" Inclining his head, Tony pulled the door wide for them to enter.

The living room seemed familiar from the horrible night she'd revealed the secret of the mermaid brooch.

She could feel the tension in the air as Bridget took a stance in front of the fireplace where a roaring fire warmed even Venus's shivering skin.

Tony stood a few feet away, watching Bridget with a

quiet longing that only recently had Venus come to understand from her own broken heart.

"Venus, please tell Tony your story so he'll understand why we're here," Bridget commanded in her no-nonsense voice.

Obeying without question, Venus stumblingly at first but then more strongly laid out her story, which presented endless possibilities for all of them. And in the telling, she became even more convinced it all had to be true.

At the end, Tony stared at her, his eyes bright, his shoulders square and still powerful.

"Venus, I will never forget the gift of your belief in me when I needed it most. What can I do to help you?"

"How long will it take you to secretly install cameras in Connor's office?" Bridget said matter-of-factly, although the firelight revealed gleams of high emotion in her emerald eyes.

"With the new technology? Without an assistant?" Tony shrugged. "A few hours at most."

"That works." Bridget nodded. "Connor always goes to his Golden Gloves Gym to work with the kids on Wednesday around noon. And Ed is always in his office at Clayworth's on that day. Tony, come midmornin' and hide out in my office until Connor leaves. As soon as he's safely gone, you move in and do what needs to be done to settle this mystery once and for all. Then maybe we can all get back our lives."

"It is my fondest wish, *Cara*."

The powerful bond beating between Tony and Bridget vibrated in the air. Watching their unhappiness, Venus wanted to cry.

"Venus, you bring the mermaid brooch and we'll lay the trap." With a deep, shuddering sigh, Bridget nodded.

"That's it then. If this madness works then the real thief will be brought to justice and part of this nightmare will be over at last."

"I promise I shall do my part on Wednesday, *Cara*. Will you stay here tonight to talk for a while?" Tony asked.

Bridget shook her head. "Not yet. Perhaps soon."

The helplessness on Tony's face as Bridget abruptly walked out the door broke off another piece of Venus's heart.

Although he didn't look as dejected as he had on the first night, dropping his head into his hands, Tony sank down onto the tweed sofa.

As she had done once before, Venus slid noiselessly beside him.

"Can't you tell her the truth someday?" Venus asked softly, her throat aching for him and her tear ducts ready to spring forth endlessly at his noble sacrifice.

He straightened his wide shoulders with a strength and quickness belying his age. "I am not sure what you mean, Venus."

Overcome with emotion for him, she blurted out the truth. "About the Saint of Taylor Street." Then she clamped her mouth shut.

The long look Tony cast her cut through her last inhibition. Having recently discovered the power of a deep and forever kind of love and the fathomless ache of losing its warmth and tenderness, she felt bold.

"I mean, surely there comes a day when one noble fabulous person gives up a certain responsibility and passes it on to another who might be eager and willing to accept it."

Tony eyed her with a lifted eyebrow and utter silence, but still she struggled on.

"I mean, the noble fabulous person would of course choose someone strong but yet infinitely tender. Someone with an uncanny ability to hide his deepest emotions from those who love him best so he could easily keep a secret. And someone whose honor is totally unassailable. Why hasn't it been done before now? For the sake of the noble fabulous person, of course."

"Perhaps because one party did not believe the other younger party was ready. He hasn't yet been asked," Tony admitted with the deepest of sighs. "Like everything in life, the timing must be correct."

For the first time in weeks Tony's smile looked rich and deep and soothed the rough edges of Venus's wounded heart.

"My beautiful Venus, perhaps because of your stubbornness..." He stopped, his smile deepening. "Pardon me, your tenacity, we will all soon possess our heart's desire."

When a man makes a decision to alter the course of his life he should be sitting in the office that had belonged to his father, in the place he'd always felt at home and spent the most time. The trappings of normalcy, sane thought, might force him to reconsider throwing away the values of a lifetime.

It wasn't working for Connor.

Now on this gray November Wednesday with the feel of snow in the air, and Lake Michigan churning with strong winds, Connor realized Chicago, Clayworth's, this room, *he* would never be the same again.

Because of Venus.

When he closed his eyes he saw her standing before him in this room, seductively removing her clothes, piece by piece, with a joyous acceptance of her beautiful body.

A hope he had helped her understand her power turned his temperature up a notch.

He stared at the space where she'd flung herself onto his chest, pleading with him to believe her far-fetched story of thievery and forgery, which even in his desperate desire to give her what she wanted, he couldn't accept.

Tony's words came back to him.

How does a man choose between love and his honor?

Connor had made his choice.

He rose slowly to his feet to make his way to his aunt's office.

She stood reading a report in the hallway outside her half-closed door.

The oddity of her not being vigilant behind her security screens came and went in his mind, swept aside by his driving need to end this struggle for all of them.

She glanced up. "Off to your gym to work with the boys?"

"No. There's someone I need to talk to and it's long overdue."

Venus watched Connor through the crack in the door and her heart did the funny thing it did in her chest whenever she glimpsed the intent, passionate gleam in his eyes.

Who is it directed at today?

She remembered being innocently curious about what Connor would be like if he'd let go of the rigid control he kept over himself. Her discovery of the truth had changed her life. Now she knew she'd do anything to bask in his passionate tenderness again.

This lurking with Tony behind Bridget's office door was the first step in her road back to him.

Once again wearing the mermaid brooch, even though she'd promised Connor she wouldn't, was another necessary step. When it proved what she knew to be true and swept away all that stood between them, Connor would surely forgive her the broken promise.

Her newfound confidence as a woman because of him fed her certainty she could end any of his lingering doubts about her feelings for him.

"Connor is gone," Bridget whispered through the half-closed door.

Without hesitation, Tony hurried to Connor's office with Venus running after him. While he set up the cameras with quick efficiency, Venus guarded the door.

She could hear Bridget going about her usual business as head of security. Once Diana came up to the executive offices to talk to Bridget and Venus felt a sharp sting of guilt for not telling her sister the plan.

They had two hours before Ed arrived, and she must give the performance of her life.

One nagging thought kept haunting her, getting in the way of her guard duties and interrupting the rehearsal in her mind of the words she needed to say and the actions she needed to take once Ed appeared.

Finally she gave in to the hot, tight tension quivering through her. She wasn't afraid to trap a thief, the person who had heartlessly masterminded her father's disgrace. But she was frightened to her very soul by the passionate, determined glint in Connor's eyes. Who had provoked it and why?

Connor arrived at Alistair Smith's home in Lincoln Park and stood for what seemed like hours on the front porch, taking in the last moments of his old life. Flexing his shoulders, he finally rang the bell. He heard it echo through the large, high rooms of the old house.

The shock in Alistair's eyes at finding Connor at the door reminded him of Venus when she looked confused and at her most lovable. He needed nothing more to remind himself why he'd decided to separate himself from his sense of right and wrong.

Nothing is more important than being together, he had once said. Now he knew how true the words were for him.

Behind Alistair in the wide foyer with its wood floor covered by muted Oriental rugs, Kate stood with her coat on and a thick manuscript in her gloved hands.

"May I come in?" Connor asked quietly.

Alistair hesitated for a heartbeat before stepping back to swing the door wider.

"Hello, Kate." Connor gave her a quick kiss on her cheek.

"Nice to see you, Connor," Kate said briskly. "I'm on my way out." She looked up at Alistair. "Tomorrow morning at the same time?"

"I look forward to it, Kate." Alistair leaned over to kiss her cheek, much as Connor had done.

But this time Kate's skin flushed and her mouth curled into a smile.

As finely attuned as he'd become to his emotions recently, he felt the chemistry between these two. Venus would be pleased.

Alone at last, Alistair motioned him into the living room, where burning logs crackled in the stone fireplace.

Connor took his stance there, legs apart, and watched the man he'd once considered a trusted friend.

"I'll get right to the point about why I've come here,

Alistair. I love Venus and I've come for the two of us to concoct a false story that will vindicate you and make everyone believe you are innocent of embezzling."

Venus and Bridget were deliberately talking too loudly in the hall outside her office when Ed, with a harassed look in his eyes, arrived on the executive floor. He gave them a brief nod before hurrying into his own office.

Behind the surveillance panel at Bridget's desk, Tony gave them the signal that the new cameras in Connor's office were online.

Only then did Bridget and Venus stroll along the hall, all the while talking about their holiday shopping, as they passed Ed's open door and walked into Connor's office.

Once safely out of sight, Venus pulled off the long cashmere scarf from around her neck and dropped it on the floor. They waited four more minutes as planned, and, Venus's heart pounding, Bridget gave the signal for them to stroll back out and down the hall.

Venus hesitated in front of Ed's doorway. "I want to talk to Ed for a few minutes before I go downstairs to spend money." She laughed, giving Bridget a wave.

Ed stood up as Venus walked in.

Now that she knew all, the avaricious gleam in his eyes as he stared at the mermaid brooch couldn't be missed.

"Ed, I want to thank you again for all your help with my insurance problems after the robbery. I couldn't have gotten through it without your help. Honestly."

"It was my pleasure to assist you, Venus."

His smile amazingly jovial for someone obviously so desperate, he wagged his finger at her. "I hope you have that magnificent mermaid brooch fully insured."

With deliberate slowness she traced the body of the mermaid with the tips of her fingers. "It is a beautiful piece, isn't it? I'll put it on my policy soon."

"I would be most happy to take it now for appraisal. Best to have insurance coverage as soon as possible on your prized possessions."

Venus knew it wasn't the tight collar of his white starched shirt making Ed breathe more heavily.

"Thanks, but I'm late for a shopping date with Diana downstairs. Oh!" Her hands fluttered to her shoulders. "I forgot my scarf in Connor's office." She smiled. "I'll see you later. And thanks again."

Walking as fast as possible, she reached Connor's office, carefully took off the brooch, and placed it strategically half under the sofa, which held such pounding sweet memories for her.

Arranging the scarf carefully around her shoulders to hide the absence of the mermaid brooch, she sailed back past Ed's office and waved.

Heart pounding, she looked at her watch. Twenty-five minutes to showtime.

Alistair dropped down into the tall wing chair before the fireplace. Little flames lit his eyes while he studied Connor for long minutes.

"You believe I'm guilty, Connor. However, you are willing to come up with some lie or fake some evidence that will vindicate me. Do you understand what you're saying to me?"

Determined, Connor nodded. "Yes. I'm doing it for Venus."

"I'm stunned by your willingness to forsake your honor for my daughter, but there is no need to concoct any story. I am innocent," Alistair stated softly.

Connor met his gaze, trying to keep anger out of his. "The evidence against you is overwhelming and you know it. Even when you disputed two of the transactions that supposedly hadn't been authorized by my cousins, you didn't insist on having your signature examined by an expert. Why didn't you, if it would have proved you innocent? For the rest and the most damning, my cousins swear they sent you no signed memos and I sure as hell didn't."

The pain in Alistair's eyes reminded him of Venus's, and he had to look away to control his reaction.

"It was then, Connor, when you lied to me, that I knew you were part of the conspiracy." Alistair's voice held threads of pain yet sounded strong.

Not comprehending, Connor shook his head. "What in the hell are you talking about, Alistair!"

"Before you denied sending the memo, I believed it could be one of your cousins sieving money out of Clayworth's. Then when you lied about it I knew you must be a part of the conspiracy."

Hot anger roared through him. "Why in the hell would we steal from ourselves and set you up? And if you believed one of my cousins was behind this why wouldn't you come to me? I trusted you!"

All at once a spark of long-dormant spirit lit Alistair's sad eyes. "The Clayworth family helped build this city from the ashes. Twice. Clayworth's is a symbol of Chicago. A sense of pride, of being a part of something fine for all the hundreds and hundreds of people employed by you. It had always given me a sense of pride to be a part of it. I spend my life at Clayworth's. Your grandfather was a lion of a man and I had great respect for your uncles and your father. I've watched you boys grow into their shoes."

With a deep sigh, Alistair shook his head. "I couldn't believe it at first when I began to see a pattern of embezzlement. I didn't want to believe you boys would destroy your legacy. You wouldn't have believed me if I came to you with my suspicions. Your family loyalty is legendary. Clayworth men always stand shoulder to shoulder. After you denied sending the memo, there was no point. I chose to withdraw without a fight rather than help weaken an institution I spent my life protecting and loving."

His mind tried to make sense of the words as he studied Alistair's face. "You honestly believe the Clayworth family set this whole scenario up to make you a scapegoat?"

"Someone obviously forged my signature on those two documents. It defies logic that someone could have expertly forged your cousin's signatures and your own as well on those memos."

Venus's words rang through his head. *She could probably do your signature, too. Mine. Anyone's.*

Blazing heat filled every cell in his body. Long ago he'd told Tony and he'd repeated, *Venus is stubborn as a mule and it's impossible to change her mind once she's decided on something.* He laughed, harshly and painfully. "She did it. Venus never gave up, and she uncovered the truth despite everything we all did to try to stop her."

Alistair stood. "What did Venus do?"

Reaching out, Connor clasped Alistair's hand in a firm grip. "I hope someday you can forgive me and my family for all you've suffered. I promise you I will spend every day of the rest of my life trying to make it up to Venus."

Confusion washed across the strong bones of Alistair's face. "I don't understand."

"You will soon, I promise. Now I need to find Venus and help her catch a thief."

*   *   *

Eyes as wide as she could stretch them, hands playing wildly with her hair, Venus rushed back into the executive offices. "Help me, Bridget! I've lost my mermaid brooch!" she screamed with high drama at the top of her lungs.

Looking concerned, Bridget stepped out of her office, being careful to close the door, concealing Tony at the panel.

"Venus, calm down. When did you first notice the mermaid brooch was missin'?"

"I don't know." Venus shook her head so violently her hair flew into her eyes. As she brushed it away, Ed came out of his office.

"What happened?"

"Venus lost her mermaid brooch somewhere in the store."

All the color drained from Ed's ruddy face. "Good God, this is terrible."

"Ed, you look around up here. Venus and I are goin' to retrace her steps down the stairs."

Ducking into the stairwell, Bridget and Venus exchanged glances.

"This is it, Venus."

As certain about this as she'd been all along about her father's innocence, she nodded. "Ed will pick up the mermaid brooch and put it in his pocket."

"He did," Bridget gasped, gazing down at her iPhone and Tony's text. "Now let's see what he does."

Her excitement making it hard to breathe, Venus followed Bridget out of the stairwell to hurry back into the executive suites.

Ed strolled down the hall, his face again ruddy and

glowing. "I'm very sorry. I didn't find anything. Did you have any luck?" he asked.

"No." For effect, Venus buried her eyes and nose in the folds of her cashmere scarf. "I can't believe I've lost my precious mermaid brooch."

"We'll look again up here, Venus. It could have fallen underneath a piece of furniture," Bridget encouraged her.

"I looked quite thoroughly and I'm afraid I couldn't find the brooch." Ed appeared solemn. "I have an important appointment. I apologize for leaving you under such stress."

"Nothin' more you can do, Ed. We'll keep lookin'."

Her heart pounding, her eyes filling with tears of joy, Venus peeked out from the scarf to meet Bridget's astonished gaze.

The instant Ed headed to the elevator, they ducked into Bridget's office.

Tony, looking as stunned as Bridget, stared at the monitor, watching the tape of Ed, astonishment and elation in his eyes, picking up the brooch and quickly placing it in his pocket.

Eyes glued to the screen, Bridget shook her head. "God in heaven, you were right, Venus. I can't believe it even watching him do it."

"Wait! Somethin' isn't right. Where did he go?" Bridget began to push buttons on all the screens. "I alerted security to stop Ed from leavin' the store. Somehow he got past them."

Tony's face hardened. "He's making a run for it. We need to notify the police to intercept him either at his house on Taylor Street or at his office."

While Bridget dialed the police, Venus slipped out.

Just as she couldn't wait for the police the day Ed broke into her store, she couldn't wait now. If he was on the run he'd first go to Taylor Street. Maxie would need her help unless she was in on this from the beginning.

Venus knew, from the night she'd come to see Connor, which door was closest to the private parking area near the loading dock.

She ran outside and caught a glimpse of Ed's black BMW turning the corner. She jumped into the first cab in the queue waiting for fares alongside the store.

"Follow that black BMW that just turned on State Street!"

The cabbie looked over his shoulder. "You're kidding, right?"

"No. And there's fifty dollars in it if you catch up and don't lose him. He's probably heading for Taylor Street."

The cab squealed away and her phone rang.

She ignored it to keep her eyes on the prize, several cars ahead of them, heading to Maxie and Taylor Street.

Connor sat stuck in traffic three blocks from the store. His phone rang and, seeing that it was his aunt, answered quickly.

"Aunt Bridget, do you know…"

Her frantic voice interrupted him. "God in heaven, Connor, Venus was right. Ed took the mermaid brooch and somehow got past security. Now Venus is gone and I'm afraid she's goin' to follow him and…"

He tried to piece together what had happened from his aunt's unusually disjointed story, the blood pounding in his ears. "Have you called the police?"

"Yes. Took a bit of explainin' but now they're sendin' squad cars to his office and his house."

Turning at the light, Connor swung around a slow car and gunned his high-performance engine. "I'm heading to Taylor Street now. That's where Venus will go to help Maxie."

Chapter 23

Hurrying up the short sidewalk to Ed's house on Taylor Street, it finally struck Venus she couldn't simply ring the doorbell, demand the return of her mermaid brooch, and make a citizen's arrest.

Ed's car had disappeared into the detached garage in the alley. But had he gone into the house to gather up whatever valuables he might have left before he fled his creditors and the police? And where was Maxie and was she in any danger from him?

The idea of pudgy Ed being a menace would have been laughable a mere few weeks ago. Not so much now.

Thinking of Maxie and what a shock this would be to her gentle soul, Venus changed direction and crept through the narrow passage between Ed's house and its neighbor. She headed to the room Maxie used to paint her fake masterpieces.

Her hunch paid off when she saw Maxie and Ed through the French doors of the family room at the rear of the house. Venus ducked back, pressing her spine hard into the brick wall. She craned her neck to keep peeking through the glass.

Maxie, dressed in a painter's smock, stood in front of an easel with another masterpiece in progress. She and Ed appeared to be arguing while he rushed around placing statues and small pieces of art in a pile on the coffee table.

Hands cupped Venus's shoulders, sending terror shooting through her. She opened her mouth to scream.

"It's me, love," Connor whispered into her ear, silencing her.

Sweet relief and even sweeter sensations of joy at once again hearing him call her *love* turned her into his arms. He kissed her tenderly and long, with an urgency that would have left her limp if she hadn't heard a shout coming through the windows.

She opened her eyes and saw Ed leaving the room and Maxie crying.

"I can't believe I'm saying this, but I don't have time to kiss you right now," she said quickly, swinging away. "I must go in to help Maxie."

She rapped lightly on the glass.

"No, Venus! She could be in on this." Connor's grip on her shoulder tightened.

"I thought about it but decided no. I don't believe she is involved." Venus waved through the glass at Maxie.

Her look of relief as she rushed to open the French doors brushed away any doubt.

"I do believe you, love," Connor said in a husky voice into the hair above her ear. "And I'm here to help you."

"Venus, I believe Edward has had a breakdown over his financial difficulties," Maxie cried, flinging open the door so she could walk in. "He wants me to withdraw all my money from the bank and go to Brazil with him tonight to live forever. I don't even speak Spanish."

"They speak Portuguese in Brazil," Connor said, stepping through the door behind Venus.

Maxie blinked. "I don't speak that either. Why are both of you here?"

"Maxie, where's our other suitcase?" Carrying a duffel bag, Ed rushed back into the room.

When he saw them, he dropped the bag on the floor. "What are you doing here?"

Connor pushed Venus behind him. "Ed, it's over. We know you stole the mermaid brooch. We know everything."

His face nearly purple, Ed puffed out his chest. "I'm sure I don't know what you are talking about, Connor. This is an outrage and I demand you leave my home immediately. Both of you."

For every step Connor took toward him, Ed took two back.

"We have you on camera placing the brooch in your pocket and leaving the store. The police are on their way."

"The police? Edward, what have you done?" Maxie shrieked, and swayed as if she might be about to faint.

Avoiding Connor's lunge to stop her, Venus rushed to Maxie's side. "Those word games you played were a way for Ed to get you to forge signatures on real documents."

"What did I sign for President Obama and Oprah?" Maxie wailed.

"Nothing, I trust. You signed for me." There was the faintest twitch of humor on Connor's beautiful mouth.

Then it hardened. "Don't be a fool, Ed."

This time the hands on Venus's shoulders were rough and pulled her back tight against a rotund stomach.

"Don't come any closer or I'll use this to hurt her,"

Ed warned, holding a marble copy of *The Thinker* over Venus's head.

She saw the muscles bunch in Connor's thighs as he prepared to tackle Ed.

"Edward, stop this at once," Maxie cried. "Why didn't you tell me I was signing real documents?"

"Because you'd never have done it, you trusting fool. You don't have a devious bone in your body. You're even afraid to jaywalk for fear of getting into trouble."

Strangely, Venus felt utterly fearless for herself, but anger roared through her on Maxie's behalf.

Venus stamped down hard on Ed's right foot with the heel of her four-inch Louboutins and twisted out of his grasp into Connor's waiting arms.

"Damn it!" Cursing, Ed hopped back and Maxie beaned him over the head with her unfinished canvas of Custer at the Little Big Horn.

Ed staggered back against the bookcase and *The Thinker* slipped out of his fingers to land on his right foot.

"My foot's broken!" he screamed, falling to the floor, writhing in apparent agony.

"I'm glad, you brute," Maxie cried and swayed again.

This time Connor was there to help Venus urge Maxie down on the white leather sectional sofa.

With the back of his fingers, Connor stroked Venus's cheek and smiled. "Take care of Maxie. I'll see to Ed."

Venus nodded, watching Connor kneel next to Ed, who was blubbering, asking for forgiveness, and cursing the evils of gambling.

Venus heard sirens coming closer, and a few minutes later two policemen came through the French doors. Bridget and Tony were a few steps behind them.

"God in heaven, are you and Maxie all right?" Bridget asked, coming quickly to the leather sectional.

"Yes, I'm fine. And Maxie will be," Venus said, urging her to sit up.

Connor and Tony, standing beside Ed, partially blocked the view of a policeman handcuffing him. Both policemen led him out the door, Ed hopping on one foot between them.

"I trusted Edward. Now will I go to prison with him?" Maxie asked through the monogrammed handkerchief pressed to her red nose.

"No, you won't be going to prison with Ed." Connor knelt beside Venus so he could look Maxie in her watery eyes. "However, you will need to make a statement to the police. I'm an excellent lawyer and I'll be with you every step of the way through this. And afterward, where would you like to go, Maxie?"

"Back here. The house belongs to me. I bought it with the profit I made on my Google stock. If only Edward had gambled on the market like I did instead of the dice he wouldn't be in this pickle."

Venus met Connor's eyes and he grinned in the new way she'd feared she'd never see again. To have it back filled her with lightness.

The whole world seemed to be taking on a distinct rosy glow. Maybe it had been grayer before because of her dad and she hadn't fully realized it. Maybe this was what people meant when they said they were *looking at life through rose-colored glasses*. If so, she was all for it.

It appeared her fears for Maxie were unfounded. Maxie seemed to be bearing up remarkably well, throwing herself into the role of wounded heroine by leaning dramatically on Tony's strong arm when he helped her to the police car. *Not* the one containing Ed in handcuffs, continuing to confess all, including the robbery of Bertha Palmer's priceless vintage couture gowns from Clayworth's secret vault, which had resulted in Drew and Athena getting back together.

Holding her gaze, Connor came across the room at an unhurried pace to stand in front of Venus.

She felt an absurd, jittery uncertainty about what to do. She couldn't just say, *Now the truth is out, there's nothing standing between us. Take me, I'm yours.*

He appeared to be studying her face before he grinned again. Which gave her time to decide she should simply keep her mouth shut and let him make the next move.

"The mermaid brooch is evidence until after the trial. Then it's yours, Venus."

"The brooch is a piece of Chicago history. I'm donating it to the History Museum," she said softly, knowing Athena, as curator, would love the idea.

He lifted his hand and slowly stroked his fingers down her cheek to rest them at her throat where her pulse pounded. "Will you go with Aunt Bridget and wait for us at the brownstone? I'll be there as soon as I can."

The urgency in his low voice shocked her. Her throat ached with love and happiness. "I'll be waiting," she promised.

This time when she and Bridget arrived at her brownstone on Astor Street, she used her key and moved through her home as if it was something infinitely precious to her. Once lost and now found again.

The living room felt cozy, with the roaring fire and the wind whipping snow flurries against the windows.

It should have been peaceful.

Venus seriously doubted if any two women ever waited more anxiously and eagerly for their men to walk through the front door than she and Bridget tonight.

Waiting to discover what their next moves would be.

Yes, Connor was an excellent lawyer, known for his swift and confident moves in the courtroom. But tonight he was also a man deeply in love who wanted nothing more than to get the hell out of the police station and back to Venus.

He saw the same impatience on his uncle Tony's face.

They had both taken on the responsibility of assisting Maxie gently yet firmly through the system, and duty demanded they finish the job.

Ed had been booked and called his lawyer. He would try to get bail set tonight. Connor doubted any competent judge would grant it. If ever someone was a flight risk it was Ed.

Connor should have felt some sympathy for Ed because of all the years he'd known and worked with him, but for what Ed had done to Alistair and through him to Venus, Connor felt only rage and disgust.

Ed would get what was coming to him, which would no doubt be a great deal of time in a white-collar prison.

Maxie bore up well through the grueling hours of paperwork and signed statements about her "writing games" with Ed. In fact, she exhibited more patience than Connor, whose temper did flare once or twice. His excuse to himself was quite simple. Venus was waiting for him.

In a rare few free minutes when Maxie didn't need his legal counsel, Connor sought out Tony in the waiting room.

His uncle looked tired, slumped in a hard chair. He sat up straighter when he saw Connor. "Can we take Maxie home now?"

"No. I'm sorry. We aren't done here." He clasped Tony's shoulder. "Go on home. I know you're eager to see Aunt Bridget. The two of you have a lot to discuss."

So do Venus and I.

"No, I'll stay. You and I also have a great deal to discuss, Connor. I'll wait for you."

The serious tone of Tony's voice, along with the intense look in his eyes, caught Connor's attention. "Is something wrong you want to discuss with me now? I have a few minutes."

"This will take more than a few minutes, Connor. Go. Help Maxie. Then we'll talk."

The nagging feeling that his uncle might need him more than Maxie drove him to hurry the process along as quickly and efficiently as possible without calling in any Clayworth favors.

An hour later, with everything signed and no charges against Maxie, Connor and Tony drove her back to her house on Taylor Street.

With a deep sigh, she settled onto her white leather sectional sofa.

The family room hadn't been touched. The art objects Ed had been gathering up to take with him were still scattered across the coffee table.

Connor picked up *The Thinker* off the floor and placed it on a bookshelf. He knew the fear he'd felt for Venus when Ed had been wielding the statue had been out of proportion to the real danger. He couldn't stop his need to protect Venus from all danger. It seemed to have always been part of him. Even when he hadn't realized what he was feeling and why. He smiled, thinking of all the ways he planned to be there for her in every way for the rest of their lives.

"Maxie, are you sure you wish to be alone tonight?" Connor heard Tony ask, and he turned to find his uncle seated next to Maxie on the leather sofa.

"Yes, Tony, I will be perfectly fine alone. I plan to start a new painting tonight."

"Which masterpiece?" Smiling, Connor strolled over to encourage her.

"My own. I have a still life in my mind I wish to create." Maxie dabbed one last time at her eyes with a white handkerchief. "I believe it is time for me to paint my own vision of beauty."

Sure she would be fine on her own, they left her to her new painting and waved to her standing in the front door as Connor pulled away.

Beside him, Tony turned. "I also believe it is time to make a change. And I require your help to do it."

Hearing the serious note in his uncle's voice, Connor glanced at him. "You know I'll do anything for you."

"Hear me out first, Connor. It is not a task to take on lightly."

He pulled his Ferrari to the curb, parked, leaned his shoulders against the door, and turned to look his uncle in the eyes. "All right. I'm listening."

"You've asked me many times about the Saint of Taylor Street. Tonight, Connor, I want to tell you what I know."

Tony took a long, deep breath, and Connor found his own breathing had changed. There was a feeling of something important about to happen he'd experienced in the courtroom and in the boardroom that made his heart beat faster in anticipation.

"No one remembers how the Saint began his quest to help others. Perhaps in Europe." Tony shrugged. "Perhaps here on Taylor Street. The trust account set up to lend the helping hand when needed. A mortgage paid when a family is in need. A portion of a wedding paid for so the young couple can have a good start in their new life together. A child's operation made possible. A man or woman gotten to rehab for an addiction to alcohol, drugs, or gambling."

"Is someone at the private casino the Saint?" Connor asked, trying to piece together legend with fact. Trying to understand what his uncle wanted him to know.

"No. Mr. Marco often knew who needed help and got word to the Saint. Now Joseph does the same. There are also others."

"I don't understand, Uncle Tony. If no one knows who the Saint is how do they get word to him."

"On the street there are ways. It is part of the promise the Saint makes to remain anonymous to all, even his loved ones. And when it is time to pass on the responsibility he must choose his successor."

I should have known.

His rush of love and admiration for his uncle made Connor feel like a kid again, meeting his hero. He nodded. "I understand, Uncle Tony. You know all this because you are the Saint of Taylor Street."

"Yes, Connor, I am. I have been since the night I was given the mermaid brooch. Now it is time to pass it on to you. If you are willing."

The thought of keeping such a secret from Venus bit at his heart. "I'm not sure Venus wouldn't somehow know."

A slow smile curled Tony's mouth. "Ah, the beautiful, tenacious Venus. You will never tell her, nor will she ever ask, but I believe we both know she will guess."

*   *   *

What seemed like endless, tortured hours later, Venus at last heard Tony and Connor open the door of the brownstone.

Bridget rose from her chair with a calm dignity but Venus swore she heard her heart pounding as loudly as her own.

With long strides Tony reached Bridget and dropped to one knee in front of her.

"*Cara,* I love you. I have loved you from the first moment we met. You must believe my task has come to an end on Taylor Street and always it was for the greater good. Can you trust my word and trust your life to me? Please marry me, *Cara,* and make me the most blessed of men."

"Yes," Bridget stated in her most no-nonsense voice.

Cupping Tony's face with her hands, she kissed his mouth until he rose to his feet and half-lifted her off the floor in a passionate embrace.

The heat of Connor's body came to Venus from behind. She felt his flat stomach, his hips as his arms encircled her.

Her heart skipped two beats and then made up for it.

Tilting back her head, she looked up at him. "Don't you think we should leave them alone?"

His quiet laughter flickered into her ear. "Yes. Let's go into the den."

His face had such a tender, passionate look she felt it low in her body.

Thank goodness he pulled her down onto his lap in the big wing chair before she collapsed from happiness.

Wrapping her in his arms, he buried his face in her hair and she closed her eyes in pure bliss.

"Before you proved the truth to all of us, I went to your father today to fabricate a story of his innocence so we could be together."

Her lids flew open in shock. The last thing she had expected was this blunt admission. "You believed him guilty but you would have lied to make me happy?"

He kissed her eyes, her nose, rocked his mouth over her parted lips.

"You are the most stubborn, loving, beautiful woman in the universe and no doubt beyond. I love you, Venus. I plan to spend the rest of my life showing you how much you mean to me. Can you accept my discovery, love? The hell with everything else. All I want is you."

Feeling cherished beyond her wildest dreams, she curved her body into his in the way two lovers will.

"I do."

CHICAGO JOURNAL & COURIER

Talk of the Town, *by Rebecca Covington-Sumner*

Darlings, that mischievous fellow, Cupid, has struck again!

The wedding we have all been waiting for will soon take place!

These special nuptials are a delightful part of a wonderful fairy tale wherein my fondest hopes have been realized.

Old wounds have been healed and the Clayworth and Smith families have been gloriously reunited. The happy reinstatement of Alistair Smith as the treasurer of our iconic John Clayworth and Company Department Store is the icing on the cake.

You know I always keep my promise to tell you everything, and so I shall, about this sure-to-be-unique wedding party, which will take place next week.

Meanwhile I have another tidbit you might enjoy hearing.

I will very soon be joining the circle of motherhood. Which only goes to prove it is never too late to pursue your dreams.

My beloved and I are currently going through two of

our "Baby Names" books searching for the perfect name for little Miss Covington-Sumner. We absolutely refuse to make an informed decision until we've carefully read through all six volumes. Unless we discover a seventh, God forbid.

Little Miss Covington-Sumner will be auntie to our adorable twin grandsons Kellen and Kyle. Can't you just imagine what fun it shall be when, younger and smaller, she tries to boss those rambunctious boys into obedience as their auntie?

I for one am counting the days.

I wish the same happiness to all of you.

Epilogue

"I always cry at weddings. Is my mascara running?" Venus blinked up at Connor, dabbing at the corners of her eyes with his white handkerchief.

"You're even more beautiful when you cry."

The wealth of love and tenderness on his face melted her bones.

He lifted her hand to press his lips against her palm. "I'll be waiting for you," he said softly.

She curled her fingers over the warmth of his kiss as she peeked into the chapel full of friends and family.

In the front pew, Drew and Athena, back from their sailing trip, looked more in love than ever, if possible, and beautifully kissed by the sun.

Rebecca appeared wonderfully, gloriously pregnant and completely radiant beside David, who held her close to his side.

Wearing an enormous hat of elegant purple feathers, Victoria Clayworth O'Flynn sat beside them. She'd surprised them all by returning to Chicago for this wedding even though there were two feet of snow on the ground.

And in the next pew sat Venus's father, vindicated,

back in his office at Clayworth's but still pursuing his passion for writing. Kate sat comfortably next to him.

A stir at the door as last-minute arrivals came in shook the solemn air with excitement.

Greyson and Ric Clayworth, half-brothers, polar opposites in personality but each possessing the same dark hair and blue eyes, strolled down the aisle.

Even though they had the choice of several empty seats, they squeezed into a crowded pew, insisting Diana sit between them.

"Grey and Ric made it."

Venus turned to Bridget, glorious in the rich cream satin and lace wedding gown that had once been worn by her mother.

"Good. Now the day is complete."

The organ began to play and an expectant hush fell over the room.

"Ready?" Venus asked with an encouraging smile.

Bridget smiled. "At last, I am."

Gripping her small bouquet of cream roses with delicate centers of apricot, the color exactly matching her dress, Venus started down the aisle.

Tony looked magnificent in his tux but Venus's gaze rested on the best man.

Their eyes locked and Connor's slow smile held delightful promises.

No, Venus wasn't saintly like her sisters. But she was the perfect soulmate for the Saint.

New management at the *Daily Mail* means gossip columnist Rebecca has been demoted. Now she'll be doing an entirely different king of dishing . . . in the Home and Food section.

Who does this new—surprisingly sexy— CEO think he is?

Talk of the Town

Available now

Please turn this page for an excerpt.

Chapter 1

Some Monday mornings start out so well.

The cab Rebecca stepped into had her picture advertising "Rebecca Covington's World," in the *Chicago Daily Mail,* plastered across the back of the front seat.

She squinted at the ad. How long had it been since she'd done a new press photo? Her blond hair was so much lighter and shorter now ... her face thinner ... *older.*

"You're lookin' good, Miss Covington. Wife loves your columns," shouted the delightful cabdriver.

Before she looked up at the charming man, she remembered to widen her eyes to smooth out the dreaded lines on her forehead, just as Harry had instructed.

"Thank you," she cooed to the cabbie. "You've made my day." Of course, she gave him a huge tip when she alighted in front of the Chicago Daily Mail building.

Feeling wonderful, and looking forward to seeing Pauline Alper, BFF since they bonded over their divorces only two years apart and shed enough tears together to raise the water level in Lake Michigan, Rebecca swished through the doors and into the small lobby.

Pauline looked up from behind the reception desk, saw

Rebecca, burst into loud sobs, and buried her wet face in two fistfuls of pink Kleenex.

Shocked by Pauline's tears instead of her usual warm welcome, Rebecca rushed across the lobby to offer her shoulder to cry upon. "Pauline, tell me everything."

Instead of being comforted, Pauline jumped up, crying even louder, and ran to the "For Staff Only" restroom.

Her heart pounding, terrified at what could be so wrong, Rebecca raced after Pauline and stood outside the locked stall. "Sweetheart, it isn't your girls, is it?" The thought of any harm coming to Pauline's daughters, Patty and Polly, caused tears to burn in her eyes.

"No," came Pauline's muffled reply, followed by a cacophony of fresh sobs.

Weak with relief, Rebecca collapsed against the cool metal door. "Thank God! Then whatever it is can be fixed. I saw you with the box of pink Kleenex on your desk. You didn't try that ridiculous Kleenex diet and become violently ill, did you?"

"No," Pauline hiccupped.

"Good. Then please come out so I can help you. You're crying so hard you really will make yourself sick."

"I can't stop...I'm...so...so...sad," Pauline wailed between sobs.

"Sweetheart, you're hyperventilating!" Rebecca's voice rose in alarm. She'd never forgotten the day Pauline fainted in her living room after a bout of prolonged crying over the divorce wars. "Please stop."

"I...can't...," Pauline gasped.

Drastic action must be taken.

"Keep breathing, sweetheart!" Rebecca kicked off her black Brian Atwood stilettos. Hiked up her black Carolina Herrera skirt until the top of her pantyhose showed.

Not caring if the expensive Wolford fishnets got bigger holes, she dropped to her hands and knees onto the cold, hard, black and white tile floor. "Pauline, keep breathing and tell me what's wrong," she called through the opening at the bottom of the stall.

An instant later, from beneath the door Pauline peered back, her green eyes swollen nearly shut from weeping. "Rebecca, get up! That's...your...favorite designer outfit. You'll...you'll...ruin...ruin your beautiful clothes," she sobbed anew.

"Sweetheart, I will get up. But you're really scaring me." Rebecca held Pauline's red-rimmed eyes in a steady gaze. "Remember our pledge to always be there for each other. This is one of those moments, but this bathroom floor is no place to have a heart-to-heart. Please splash gallons of cold water on your face and come to my office. I'll shut the door, bring out the chocolate like always, and we'll talk for as long as you need. Promise you'll come up with me."

Pauline heaved a long, ragged sigh and nodded. "I promise. Oh, please don't...hurt yourself getting up."

"I'm fine," Rebecca lied while struggling to her feet. Ignoring the little twinges of pain in her abused knees, she slid back into her shoes. She washed her hands for a good five minutes, all the while staring at the locked stall door, willing it to open. When that didn't work she called through it again. "Are you all right? I'm sure I have enough Leonidas chocolates to handle this emergency. Ready to go up, sweetheart?"

"Not yet...please go on...I promise...I'll be there... soon," Pauline called back in a soft, breathless voice.

Rebecca hated to leave, but she sensed Pauline wanted a little privacy. "All right. I'll be in my office waiting for you."

Knowing Pauline would keep her promise, Rebecca climbed up the short flight of stairs to the *Daily Mail* offices. On the wide landing, the din of voices and noise from the newsroom seeped through the closed glass double doors. Even now in the throes of such powerful angst over Pauline, Rebecca felt a wave of gratitude for having escaped from there so long ago. In the newsroom she'd been just another reporter. She loved being Rebecca Covington, Chicago's most notorious gossip columnist. She loved that she belonged in the quiet executive hallway. Now, if she was having a really bad day, she could shut her door and hide for a few minutes to perfect her confident front for the world.

Her stilettos clicked musically on the tile floor as she hurried to her office, where she'd hide Pauline for as long as it took to calm her down and find out what was wrong. At the end of the short hall, Tim Porter's secretary, Maybella, glanced up from her desk and quickly looked back down, but not before Rebecca spied a smirk on her glossy fuchsia lips.

Something is up.

When Tim stepped out of his office and planted himself in front of her, she knew from the stricken look on his face that something wasn't just up. Something was drastically wrong.

"No!" Rebecca gasped, clasping her alligator bag to her heaving bosom. "Not you, too! What's happened?"

Gently, he ushered her into his office. "Sit down, Rebecca. I have something to tell you."

The aura of doom surrounding him could mean only one thing. She flung herself into the chair before her knees buckled from the shock. "Tim, I can't *believe* you've been fired! You're the finest managing editor in the newspaper business. How could they do this? You have two boys in college and a wife making a life's work of restoring your crumbling mansion in Lake Forest." Devastated for him, she leaned forward to clasp his hand. "How can I help?"

He took a file from his tidy desk and laid it on her lap. "Sign these papers."

She flipped open the file and squinted down at the small, blurry print. She tried holding the papers at arm's length to read. "Darling, if it's that you want me to cosign for a loan, I must tell you my credit isn't any better than yours."

"Here, try these," he said, holding out a pair of reading glasses from his own shirt pocket.

She placed the glasses on her nose, and the letters loomed larger before her eyes.

An unpleasant numbness, like when she slept on her leg wrong, spread through every limb. "These are termination papers. With *my* name on them." Not believing her eyes, refusing to accept it, she kept staring at him. "Is this some kind of joke?"

His face turned a deep crimson. "Damn it, Rebecca. It's your own fault. You shouldn't have run the blind item about that politician. Didn't you double-check your sources? Who was it?"

A rush of scalding anger brought feeling back into her body. Tim didn't need to know that the paper's very own security guard, who moonlighted at several Gold Coast condos, was her most reliable source. Until now. She couldn't believe he had gotten it *so* wrong this time. Something wasn't ringing true. "You know I never divulge my sources!" she snapped, not liking where this was going.

"Well, you might have to divulge it this time in court," he snapped back. "The item struck a nerve with our junior senator, who is damn well connected. He's been in California for weeks trying to reconcile with his wife. He hasn't been anywhere near any Gold Coast condo. He's threatening to sue."

"So what?" She shrugged, relief making her smile. Now she was on safe, familiar ground. "The last time someone threatened to sue, circulation skyrocketed and I received a generous bonus. Tim, darling, you know I'm the queen of naughty gossip in Chicago. That's what sells papers. That's what you pay me to do."

"Not anymore."

She felt the earth shift beneath her in a strange, silent shudder. It started at her toes and rushed up to her brain, just as it had ten years ago when she'd gone home sick from work and walked into her condo to find her husband, Peter, in their bed performing oral sex on his young executive assistant.

Then, like now, every sense deserted her except sight.

She saw Tim's lips moving, but no sound reached her.

She closed her eyes, believing that when she opened them it would all turn out to be a terrible nightmare.

But it didn't work this time, either.

"Rebecca, did you hear me?" She heard Tim shout as his beady eyes nearly popped out of their sockets. "Your position has been filled by Shannon Forrester from the women's page."

"That's utterly ridiculous!" she shouted back, all her senses restored to full furious force. "*I'm* the gossip columnist for the *Daily Mail*. It's been my identity for fifteen years. I'm not giving it up to anyone!"

Tim shook his head. "I'm sorry, Rebecca, but you

don't have a choice. The blind item fiasco in your column brought it to a head faster than I wanted. Regardless of how we feel, there are changes coming under the new owner. He has evaluated the staff and feels Shannon will keep up with the youth market and bring a fresh perspective to the paper. Younger. Sassier. Sexier."

Not caring how many wrinkles she made in her face, Rebecca sneered at him in disgust. "It's ridiculous to think no one over forty has *sexy, sassy* fun! What is going on? I asked you if the rumors were true about the paper being bought and you told me no. How could you lie to me?"

Tim recoiled. "I'm sorry, but I'm not at liberty to discuss anything but your termination."

Wounded to her core by his cavalier treatment, tears choked the back of her throat. She rose majestically onto her wobbly legs. "I'd always hoped that should the worst happen, I'd built relationships along the way so my friends would stand by me."

Tim slumped down onto the edge of his desk. "Rebecca, give me a break. My job could be on the line if you don't cooperate."

His dejected voice and posture caused her to feel a flicker of pity. She doused it with righteous indignation. "I won't be discarded like last year's fashion mistake, Tim. This is blatant age discrimination. I have two more years left on my contract. I'm not leaving without a fight. I'm calling my lawyer." Becoming more furious by the second, she made the ultimate threat. "Then I'm calling Charlie Bartholomew at the *Chicago Journal and Courier*."

At mention of Charlie, all color drained from Tim's face. The nasty rivalry between the two papers was the stuff of urban legend. It had sucked dry more than one managing editor.

"Rebecca, you're trying to kill me," he groaned. "I can't afford a messy legal battle with you right on the heels of the takeover. It's bad PR for all of us. God knows what that bastard Charlie might do if he gets wind of this too soon. He could screw up this deal. He'd like nothing better."

She lifted her chin in defiance and glared at him. "Then give me my column back."

"I can't do that. But I've been authorized to offer you another job." He stood and slid his fingers around his shirt collar to loosen it. Perspiration glistened on his wide, red forehead above his suddenly glassy-looking eyes. "Your salary will remain the same for the duration of your contract. However, the only place for you on the paper is writing a twice-weekly recipe column for the Home and Food section."

Her blood felt like it was freezing in her veins and she hid her trembling hands in her lap. She'd felt this same icy helplessness in her condo bedroom, when she realized her identity as Peter's wife was erased. Hollow with pain from yet another rejection, she'd turned on her heels and quietly walked out the door. Sometimes she fantasized about what she should have done all those years ago. She should have screamed or thrown a shoe at her miserable cheating husband. Better yet, she should have pulled out every follicle of hair *she'd paid* to have transplanted along his receding hairline. The moment of truth was at hand. Had she learned nothing? Would she allow herself to be replaced by a younger woman again?

Anger and pride roared through her in one loud answer. *No! This time I'll dig in my stilettos and fight for what I want.* "I accept the job."

Tim sighed like a balloon deflating. "Thank you,

Rebecca. You'll be working under Kate Carmichael. She's a good egg."

"She's also a Pulitzer Prize winner and a *real* professional." With a last disdainful look at Tim, who deserved every drop of her disgust, she swung away to the door, determined to let no one see how much this blow had stunned her. "I'll clean out my office and move to the Home section."

"Rebecca..." His voice stopped her, but her fierce pride wouldn't let her give him the courtesy of looking back.

"Shannon has already moved into your office."

Rebecca took a deep, steadying breath to calm her raging anger so he wouldn't see it. Then she glanced over her shoulder to smile sweetly at him. "Only temporarily, Tim. Only temporarily."

With her head held high, and ignoring Tim's smirking secretary, who had never been one of her fans, Rebecca forced herself to stroll slowly toward the brown cardboard box with her personal mementos sticking out the top. It was sitting forlornly outside her former office.

She couldn't believe how badly she'd misjudged Shannon's ambitions. Rebecca had believed her when she confessed her goal was to be a *serious* journalist. She'd even helped Shannon with a few in-depth features on society in Chicago and commiserated with her when one of Shannon's pet goldfish had been found belly-up in the small aquarium she kept on her desk.

Rebecca gazed into her beloved sanctuary, ready to confront Shannon, but she was hidden by the high-backed, ergonomically correct chair, which was turned away from the open door.

Everything else appeared the same. The much-coveted window, the oversized desk, and the large-screen

314 OF THE TOWN

computer monitor. But now next to the computer where her silver canister of Leonidas chocolates should be, there was a tiny aquarium with two goldfish and, beside it, a clear glass plate of edamame.

She'd always admired how Shannon embraced healthy eating, and she vowed every morning she would do the same, until inevitably she gave in to her passion for a chocolate-filled croissant. Now it seemed ridiculous to prefer soybeans to chocolate. Shannon would need those endorphins to survive Chicago's society beat.

Rebecca shook her head to clear it of the very thought of someone else doing her job. Shannon would quickly realize she didn't have the life experience to write Rebecca's column, and so would the mysterious, obviously ignorant, new owner. Then Rebecca would be right back where she belonged.

The chair swiveled around and there was Shannon, dead-black hair falling straight around her pale oval face. Did Rebecca see surprise in her slightly bulgy blue eyes?

"Rebecca, I didn't know you were here," Shannon gasped in her soft, saccharine voice and made the little movement with her mouth that somehow always made her appear sympathetic.

Now that she knew Shannon was such a backstabber, Rebecca wouldn't be surprised if the girl practiced the expression in front of a mirror. The ugly thought that Shannon could have had something to do with the false lead flit across her mind.

"Shannon, I'm amazed that you'd settle for this position. I wouldn't think it was *serious* enough for you."

A self-satisfied smile curving her lips, Shannon shrugged. "Circumstances change. I don't know what else to say, except good-bye and best of luck to you."

If her iron will to always appear in control hadn't clamped down like a vise, Rebecca would have given in to her burning desire to toss Shannon's skinny butt out of *her* chair. Instead, she smiled back so hard her face ached. "No need to say good-bye. I'll be right through the newsroom and around the corner in the Home and Food section."

Hoping her calm facade was still in place, Rebecca swept up the box and turned to walk away. Out of the corner of her eye she caught Shannon hastily picking up the phone. If she was calling Tim or the mysterious new owner so they could plot their next move to get rid of her, they should save their breaths.

Let them do their worst—this time I'm not going anywhere.

She held her box of office treasures like a shield. On top, the picture of her with Harrison Ford, taken when he was in town shooting *The Fugitive,* stared back at her.

So we both looked a little younger in those days. But damn it, we still look good today. If I wasn't in the media where they judge my age in dog years, I'd be considered in my prime.

She felt a remarkable connection with her aging hero. Both their careers might be down at the moment, but certainly they weren't *finished.*

With a vow to win whatever battles with Shannon and The-New-Evil-Boss-from-Hell lay ahead, she clutched the picture of Harrison to her breasts, pushed open the glass double doors to the newsroom, and walked defiantly back into chaos.

Fashion curator Athena Smith is
thrilled when she's hired to examine the
Clayworth family's couture collection—
until she suddenly falls ill and
wakes up face-to-face with notorious
bachelor Drew Clayworth.

Please turn this page for an excerpt from

A Black Tie Affair

Available now.

Chapter 1

This was *the day*. The day for which Athena Smith had begged, borrowed, or stolen every favor and debt ever owed her. And now she was so late she might miss it.

On purpose?

The thought stopped Athena cold as she eyed the distance to the elegant doors of the Fashion Institute of Chicago.

No! Nothing will stop me, not even the Clayworths!

Realizing she had no other choice, she hiked up her pencil skirt and ran the last three city blocks in her favorite but impractical heels and burst through the doors.

Her tinted glasses tipped off the end of her nose, and she pushed them back into place, not to see, but to hide her real feelings when stressed. No one needed to know she wasn't like Athena, goddess of wisdom, although she always tried to be. In reality she was more like Athena, goddess of too many mistakes.

Her chest ached from the final one-block sprint as she gazed up at Leonard, the museum's oldest security guard.

"Please tell me I'm not too late," she gasped.

He grinned yet somehow still looked solemn, as befitted his duties.

"Nope, Miss Smith. The Town Car Clayworth's Department Store sent for you and your intern is running late. They called to say they'd be here in ten minutes."

"Thanks, Leonard. You've made my day." She sighed, waved, and headed to the staircase.

The treasure trove of Bertha Palmer gowns the Clayworths had locked away in their Secret Closet danced before her eyes. It was the Holy Grail, the Golden Fleece of Chicago historic costumes.

She *shouldn't* be diving headfirst into their Secret Closet, because if she saw any of them up close and personal she'd just as likely tell them to go to hell as say, "Thank you very much for your support of the museum." But despite the wretched Clayworth men, she *would* get her hands on those dresses for the exhibit and scholarship benefit.

After all, it's my duty as curator of costumes. My duty to help fund Makayla's scholarship fund. My duty to set a good example for her. Thank God she'll be with me to remind me to behave.

Of course today was so much more important for Makayla. An opportunity like this was very rare indeed for an intern. It was one of the reasons Athena had fought so hard to make it happen.

Blissful, despite the Clayworths, that this day had finally arrived, Athena swept into the Costume Collection office.

She loved this room with its heavy carved crown moldings. Sometimes, when she stared upward, trying to brainstorm new ideas for the museum, the wood carvings looked like faces to her.

But today the rich ruby Oriental rugs and antique furniture in front of the stone fireplace didn't give off their usual cozy, old-world vibe.

Something's wrong.

Athena eyed the cup of green tea cooling on Makayla's desk. She should be here, fussing around the office like the perfect intern she'd become.

Worried, Athena headed out to find her.

She stopped when she heard the powder room door across the hall open, then close, followed by sturdy, slow, oddly heavy footsteps coming toward the office.

Makayla Elliott hopped into the room, her right foot and ankle swaddled in a thick Ace bandage.

"My God, what happened to you?" Athena rushed to help her ease down on the red velvet sofa.

"I was working last night at my part-time job at Maggiano's and I dropped a bowl of spaghetti on my foot."

Kneeling, examining Makayla's swollen toes, painted a vivid purple, Athena ached with worry. "Those bowls are big enough to feed a family of ten. Is anything broken?"

"No," Makayla shook her head so hard her black ponytail flicked her cheek. "No problem, Athena. I'm awesome, ready to go when you are."

As Makayla struggled to the edge of the sofa to stand up, Athena saw pain in her kohl-lined eyes.

In that split second, Athena swore the carved crown moldings looked like the laughing faces of those three nasty Greek Fates, Clotho, Lachesis, and Atropos, gazing back at her, secure in their absolute power of deciding everyone's destiny. Lately they'd been doing their worst with her. Well, she wouldn't let them mess with Makayla. Being orphaned, living in a group home, and working two jobs and an internship was enough already.

Laugh away, Fates. No way will I let my dear, sweet, brave Makayla traipse through the Clayworths' closet if she's in pain.

"I'm sorry. I know you're going to be disappointed, but I can't let you go today when you're in so much pain. You might do real damage to your foot. I'll do provenance on the Bertha Palmer dresses alone," Athena informed her in her best boss voice.

"No way!" Makayla wobbled to her feet, hanging on to the sofa's fat padded arm for balance. "No way...I mean..." she stammered, widening her brown eyes like she always did when worried. "I mean, I gotta go. It's an awesome opportunity for me. And what if you, like, run into any Clayworths so soon after your dad's...retirement? And I'm not there to...help you?"

Oh, no, does everyone know I want to tell them to go to hell for dear old Dad?

Disappointment for Makayla burned in her chest, but Athena plastered on her best PR smile. "Please don't worry about me. *We* at the museum *love* the Clayworths for everything they do for us. Plus, we need to convince them by hook or crook to donate the Bertha Palmer dresses to the exhibit and benefit so we can raise more money for your scholarship. *That* is more important than my feelings."

"Excuse me," Leonard called from the open door. "The Clayworth Town Car is here, Miss Smith."

Once again adjusting her glasses, Athena turned and smiled, ready for the glamour and romance of the Secret Closet, even if she must go alone.

"Thanks, Leonard. Please tell the driver I'll be right down."

She swept up the white lab coat, blue rubber gloves, and tape recorder from her desk.

"Wait, Athena." Makayla hobbled toward her, little wisps of fine dark hair clinging to her damp cheeks and her pale lips parted in a grimace of pain. "The Costume Collection manager is on maternity leave for another six weeks. You're already doing two jobs. You've got a meeting with Miss Keene tomorrow, and she's always breathing down your neck. Pandora's Box is opening on Saturday. You've got too much to do. I've gotta help you no matter what."

Gently but firmly, Athena urged Makayla back down on the sofa. "I'll handle the deputy director. Pandora's Box is ready to fling open its doors. You can help me by taking care of yourself. Put your foot up and stop making me feel guilty for depriving you of the joy of examining those beautiful gowns we've been plotting for months to get our hands on." She squeezed Makayla's warm fingers. "I'm so sorry. I know you're terribly disappointed not to go."

"It's a bummer. Everyone I know wants to see the awesome stuff the Clayworths are hiding out there. It's like an urban legend. But I don't feel so great." Makayla's lips quivered into a smile.

"I know." Looking into Makayla's pale face, so young, so earnest, Athena knew this wasn't another mistake. "Tomorrow I *promise* to tell you *everything* about the treasures buried out there."

Sighing, Makayla lifted her foot up onto the sofa. "You're awesome, and so are your sisters and your dad. That Rebecca Covington-Sumner is right on in her column about your dad. I think the Clayworths gave him a bum deal after all the years he worked for them."

Athena blinked and curled her mouth into her "oldest-sister smile." The one she'd perfected to protect those younger and more vulnerable from learning about an unhappy possibility sooner than necessary.

Or Dad made a horrible mistake. Or he's covering something up. Otherwise surely he would have stood and fought like he taught me to do instead of running away.

Like she was fighting now to fix everything she and her dad had messed up.

Which was why, without so much as a blush, a tremble in her voice, or more than a tiny shred of guilt, Athena told the second-biggest lie of her life. "I agree with Rebecca, too."

Athena spied Bridget O'Flynn waiting next to the black Lincoln Town Car and swayed to a stop, nearly toppling off her heels.

Why in the world would the den mother to the Clayworth men and head of security for John Clayworth and Company be driving me out to the Secret Closet?

"I cleared my schedule so I could get the chance to see you," Bridget called, as if she'd read Athena's thoughts.

Before the debacle with her dad, Athena would have loved spending time with her, but right this second she wanted to run and hide like she'd been doing for weeks.

Bridget smiled at her, and Athena couldn't resist. She'd always adored her, so she smiled right back.

Walking slowly toward the car, Athena glanced around, half expecting the Clayworth brothers, who were widely known to be off overseeing their far-flung empire, to have suddenly returned to cause more problems. The way this day was going, Bridget's nephew, Connor, the stuffy lawyer with the body of a Greek god, would probably pop up in the back seat. Or, God forbid, Drew might climb out of the trunk to torment her.

She tried to think back to the days when she'd been *friends* with all the Clayworth men. Well, she'd been more than friends with Drew, but that was ancient history.

Now good manners and real affection made Athena slide into the passenger seat next to Bridget instead of hiding in the back to lick her wounds like she'd planned.

"What's wrong, Athena? Why are you still wearin' those dark glasses?" Bridget's voice held the familiar note of gruff, kind concern that made her so lovable.

"Just a bit of eye strain." Athena glanced over and got caught in Bridget's sharp green stare.

"You've been wearin' those shades since your dad left town. Have you seen a doctor?"

Athena adjusted the offending glasses, painfully aware that Bridget never minced words.

"It's nothing to worry about. I keep straining my eyes at work."

"Humph!" Bridget snorted through her aquiline nose. "Seems to me you've had nothin' but a ton of strain lately. Sure you want to visit the closet yourself today?"

"Absolutely!" Athena said with real feeling. Her fate might be sealed, but she *would* defeat it. If she saw any of the Clayworth men, she'd simply shove them out of her way and get to those clothes. "*Everyone* wants a peek into that closet. Mom once told me that in the old days they covered the eyes of all who went out there because of the treasures locked away in its depths." She slid Bridget a hopeful look. "Are you going to put a blindfold on me? Any Clayworth skeletons for me to find out there?"

Bridget chuckled. "No skeletons and no blindfolds. I trust you." She gunned the high-horsepower engine. "All right, then. Rest your eyes a while. We'll be there in about an hour. Dependin' on traffic."

Athena turned her head toward the window, but she couldn't close her eyes. Now that she was on her way to the family's top-secret fallout shelter, built beneath a farmer's field during the Cold War, which currently housed many of their treasures, including Bertha's priceless gowns, excitement made her feel warm all over, like it had her entire life. Like she'd felt when word came that the Clayworth family had agreed to the museum's request to examine the dresses for possible inclusion in the exhibit.

Why had they agreed? Guilt? For old times' sake?

Their tangled friendships were such old, old news. Yet since her dad's firing, the Clayworths and everything they'd meant to her filled her mind nearly every waking moment. She shoved them away *again,* determined to focus on her goal of doing provenance on the department store's impressive, never-before-seen collection of vintage couture clothing.

Warm and eager, she watched the city fade away into flat prairie. Travel on I90 appeared lighter than normal. Thirty minutes later, Bridget exited onto a two-lane highway. She seemed to know the road by heart, anticipating the bad patches and the sharp twists. Prairie gave way to slightly rolling cornfields. Bridget slowed and turned onto a one-lane black-tar road. She sped up, a clear, smooth stretch of road before them. All at once the tar turned to gravel and Bridget made a sharp right onto a bumpy dirt track leading into a soybean field.

She braked to a halt, and Athena, getting more eager by the second, sat up straighter. They were plop in the middle of Midwest farmland, surrounded by low soybean sprouts and rustling stalks of short young corn.

Athena pressed her nose to the window. "There's nothing here."

Bridget laughed. "They built it so it couldn't be seen from the air. Look again."

When she'd been a child whiling away the long, hot

summer afternoons, lying on the grass in their back yard in Lincoln Park, Athena's family would play the cloud game. She squinted her eyes looking for the secret. Once she'd been the best at spotting everything from her cat, Drusilla, to the Field Museum in the clouds, and once, absolutely, she still swore to this day, she saw Abraham Lincoln in his top hat.

In this case, at first she thought she must be simply gazing at good black Illinois dirt, but no.

I've found it!

A steel door big enough to back a semi trailer into. The rolling field of soybeans directly in front of her had to be the roof.

"I see it!" Athena quickly stepped out and followed Bridget to the enormous black wall. She paused to read the sign engraved into the steel: "When the alarm sounds, a blast has occurred. You have three minutes to get inside."

"Gives you the willies, doesn't it?" Bridget shuddered. "Wait until you see the rest." She punched a code into the panel on a smaller door, barely visible, and led Athena into silent blackness.

Athena blinked, allowing her eyes to adjust to the dim, vast cavern looming in front of her. She pulled off her glasses to get a better look.

The cooler air sent goose bumps crawling along her arms, and she rubbed them away. "This constant underground temperature is the best storage."

Beside her, Bridget chuckled. "You don't need to whisper. Let me turn on more lights so you can see the place. It's a real time capsule."

The harsh glare of fluorescent lights made Athena blink again. Now she could see they were standing in a small entrance to the huge cave that stretched out before her. To her right loomed an oven big enough to roast an ox.

"This is the decontamination chamber." Bridget moved briskly forward. "That oven is the incinerator where we would have burned our clothes." She glanced back, her wide smile splitting her pale face. "I guess they would have been naked as the day they were born until they got to the bedroom."

Athena burst out laughing. "The Clayworth men running around naked. Now, there's a sight half the women in Chicago have dreamed about seeing."

Bridget shook her head. "Those boys are too good-lookin' for their own good. I fear half of those ladies have had their dreams come true."

And I'm one of them.

She felt herself getting warmer.

Bridget shot her a sharp, inquisitive look. "Are you all right?"

"Great! Love it. What's next?"

"The bedrooms."

Athena followed Bridget into a room lined with rows of bunk beds and one appropriately green-tiled 1950s-style bathroom. Beyond she saw a kitchen with appliances in the same color and a Formica dinette set, straight out of a vintage television sitcom.

"What kind of clothes did you find here when they decided to turn it into their Secret Closet?" Athena asked. The curator in her was already planning an exhibit of what would have been worn in a fallout shelter like this one during the Cold War.

"Don't know. Back in the day they must have planned to have somethin' to wear while they were here." She pointed to a chain-link fence holding back small boulders stretching out for six yards beyond the kitchen. "The idea was to stay down here for two years. Then tear apart this fence holdin' back rocks. Dig their way out into what was left of the world." Bridget shook her head so hard the gold clip holding up her white-streaked strawberry curls came loose. With a yank she shoved it firmly back in place. "Whole thing was crazy. But the vault was the craziest of all."

Totally entranced, Athena followed her deeper into the cavernous underground shelter. They passed row after row of the store's famous glass-window wagons and a fleet of electric broughams, all with the famous John Clayworth and Company logo brazened in gold letters on the side.

They stopped in front of the largest safe door she'd ever seen, even in pictures of the U.S. Mint.

Using both hands, Bridget turned the giant tumbler. "They built this to keep the credit records of all the store's customers." She snorted. "Like anyone would care about their bills when the world's comin' to an end." She swung the door wide open. "Now all that foolishness is behind us, they store Bertha's gowns in here."

A golden glow fell out into the gloom. Light glistened off rhinestones, silver cord, and gold beads.

The four Bertha Palmer dresses beckoned Athena into their world, the way mythology had, when her father made it come alive. Her senses dazzled by the dresses worn by one of her mother's idols, dresses that when used properly could make her dreams come true, Athena rushed past Bridget into the vault.

Struck by a blast of warm air, she gasped. "The temperature in here should be better controlled. And these dresses shouldn't be on mannequins. They should be in their own specially built archival boxes."

"Good golly, you almost sound like your old self." Bridget laughed. "That's the spirit. You and your sisters used to give those boys hell when you were youngsters. They need to be put in their place once in a while."

Part of her would like nothing better than to tell the Clayworths what she thought of them for casting her father aside so cavalierly, but she had to put the past behind her to get what she needed.

Maybe I'm wrong again.

She slowly shook her head. "Maybe it's just me. It's probably cool enough. I'm just so thrilled to be here, I'm feverish with anticipation. It's an honor for the museum to have the opportunity to establish the provenance on these dresses."

Bridget cocked her head, slanting a long glance into Athena's deliberately blank face. "Sure you're all right with all of this?"

"Sure. Can't wait to get my fingers on these dresses." She tried to beam good cheer but felt naked not being able to hide behind the glasses she'd rammed into the lab coat pocket. She turned away to slip on the coat and rubber gloves. "I'll get to work. I don't want to keep you here all day."

"I'd best leave you to it, then." Bridget sighed. "If you need me, I'll be in the kitchen doin' paperwork."

Athena nodded without looking around. She sensed Bridget wanted to say more, but Athena couldn't discuss her dad now. It still felt too raw.

Determined to push away every thought except these dresses, she stepped in front of the first mannequin. Her breath caught in a tremble of excitement before she spoke into her tiny handheld tape recorder.

"I'm here in the Clayworth family Secret Closet to establish provenance on four Bertha Palmer gowns. I am starting with a dress of black corded grenadine with green and pink stripes over green taffeta. Trimmed with loops of narrow pink satin and green grosgrain ribbons."

Unable to resist, she delicately traced the bodice with her fingertips. "The bodice is made to look like a corselette of black satin with jet passementerie interlaced with narrow pink satin ribbon outlined with one-and-one-fourth-inch double-faced satin ribbon."

She dropped to her knees to peer up into the sleeves, again reverently touching the exquisite, delicate fabric. "The small leg-of-mutton sleeves are lined to the elbow with green taffeta."

Wanting to better view the workmanship, she stretched out on the concrete floor. The cold seeped through her lab coat, thin cashmere sweater, and cotton skirt.

Shivering, she carefully lifted the hem of the gown and peered up inside. "The skirt is gored with gathers at the back. Blind pocket of white taffeta lined with soft green fine rep silk taffeta. The construction is exquisite. There are twelve bones in the bodice. Each is sewn with stitches so tiny and fine I can barely see them."

Something kept irritating the back of her throat, and she stifled a cough. "Bertha Palmer wore this gown in the summer months, and it is reported to have been one of her favorites."

Her voice hoarse from holding back the cough, she slid out from beneath the gown to clear her throat. She brushed at her cheeks, trying to get rid of whatever tickled her skin.

The second mannequin, the one on her right, began to shimmer, giving it the sudden, odd appearance of movement.

She shook her head, trying to clear it. Instead the world spun slowly around and a rush of euphoria made her giddy. Happier than she'd felt in months. She didn't understand what was happening to her, but right now, here, she didn't care.

She giggled, doing a little dance to the gown. Her body tingled with recklessness, daring her to do something forbidden. Like the time she dared Drew to go skinny dipping with her in the pond at the far end of the Clayworth estate in Lake Forest.

She shook her head to clear her thoughts. *Away with you!* she commanded. But the memory wouldn't obey. She just kept swelling and swelling with the same excitement and fear she'd felt then, knowing if her parents found out she'd be sent to boarding school. She ripped off her gloves to stroke the heavy champagne silk satin gown with her bare fingers.

She'd seen countless pictures of this famous Worth gown when Mrs. Potter Palmer wore it at the Court of Saint James's in London, but the photos didn't do it justice. It mesmerized her. Totally irresistible.

Athena slid her fingertips down the elegant, heavy white velvet train and lifted it around her shoulders, wrapping herself in its beauty. Again and again she traced the white satin iris design, each flower done by hand, which made the dress so unique, so special. She turned the train over in her arms so the lining of silver tissue and rhinestone edging glistened back at her.

Seeing and touching this gown made her feel connected to her mom's passion for vintage haute couture fashion. She had been the epitome of beauty and had taught Athena to appreciate the grace of this lost world.

She ached to slide her body up and through the

princess-style dress the way Bertha would have done. She ran the old, soft silk tulle along her neck and arms, loving the feel of it.

Drawn by the exquisite detail of the double white net ruffle around the hem, she sank down upon her knees and then lay on her back. She scooted beneath the skirt to look up at the white taffeta lining. She brushed her hot cheek against the cool fabric and sighed.

It felt so cool, so comforting she didn't want to move. The dress fell around her like a wedding veil, beautiful yet protective. She felt content to merely lie beneath the gown, breathing in its history. She wanted to stay here forever, safe in Bertha's kinder, gentler world. She heard a string quartet playing a waltz like they would have done that afternoon in London for Bertha. Athena closed her eyes, lost in the music, lost in a world she adored. Far away from the reality of the last few months.

She floated in peace until the musicians started repeating the same stanza, over and over and over again. She opened her eyes, angry at this rude, discordant interruption of her bliss.

"Athena! Athena! Athena! Can you hear me? Athena! Athena!" Bridget called excessively. "Come out from under that skirt. You've been lyin' there for an hour!"

Athena tried to shake off Bridget's strong hands tugging at her ankle, but she couldn't. "No, I don't want to come out. I like it here," she shouted back.

"Athena, if you don't come out, I'm comin' in after you," Bridget called and gave another hard tug at Athena's foot.

Not wanting to be rude, Athena sighed and crawled out. After all, she *loved* Bridget—at this moment she *loved* everyone.

Blinking, she looked up.

It isn't Bridget!

Bertha Palmer, Chicago's proud social queen of the late 1800s and early 1900s, stood smiling down at her.

Athena screamed, scrambling to her feet. "This isn't a time capsule, it's a time warp! Bertha, you're really here!"

Joy exploded through her hot, throbbing body. She gripped Bertha's small, cool hands. "My mother *loved* you and what you did for Chicago. She loved powerful women of the past who blazed a trail for the rest of us."

Out of the corner of her eye, she caught a blur of movement, like someone else had come. She looked around but couldn't focus her eyes. She shook her head, trying to stop the slowly spinning world. "Is someone else here, too?" She looked toward the last shimmering mannequin and blinked. Jackie Kennedy, wearing her famous blue pillbox hat and coatdress, stood watching her.

"Jackie, you're here, too!" Athena called to her. "Mom said you were just like Bertha and knew the power of dress."

The world spun faster and faster, making Bertha blur and Jackie vanish. Fearful she'd lost both of them, Athena gripped Bertha's hand tighter. "Where did Jackie go?"

"Come with me, Athena. I saw Jackie go this way, toward the front."

She laughed in relief and joy, twining her fingers through Bertha's and running with her toward the harsh fluorescent lights in the decontamination chamber.

Outside, the sky looked so penetratingly blue its brightness hurt her eyes. She squeezed her lids closed. "I can't see Jackie anymore. Which way did she go?"

"I see her, Athena. This way. Climb into the back seat of the car and we'll follow her."

Athena opened her aching eyes the tiniest bit to glance up at Bertha. For a brief instant a vivid gold encircled Bertha's curls like a halo. Athena sighed. "You look just as beautiful as I knew you were. You were Mom's absolute favorite. She called you Chicago's angel."

"That's nice. In you go, Athena."

The back seat smelled like new leather. Athena's lids felt too heavy to leave open. She closed them just as she heard the loud, powerful car motor roar to life.

"Can you still see Jackie?" Athena whispered, so tired she couldn't lift her head.

"Yes. Don't you worry. Everythin' will be fine. You rest now. I'm turnin' on some nice, soothin' music for you."

Athena floated in a strange twilight contentment more profound than she'd experienced beneath Bertha's exquisite gown. This time when the music came, it had words. "God Bless the Child."

"I love this song." The words vibrated through her head, and she began to hum the tune to herself. A burst of energy and joy exploded through her blood. Her voice sounded so pure and true and golden, she let the words pour from her throat.

Holding the last note, she lost track of her breathing. The twilight world behind her eyes swirled crazily around, blue, purple, orange, and, at last, a cool blackness. She rested again, floating contentedly in silent bliss.

THE DISH

Where authors give you the inside scoop!

♥ ♥ ♥ ♥ ♥ ♥ ♥ ♥ ♥ ♥ ♥ ♥ ♥ ♥ ♥ ♥

From the desk of Sherrill Bodine

Dear Reader,

One of my favorite things about writing is taking real people and mixing and matching their body parts and personalities to create characters who are captivating and entirely unique. And of course, I always set my books in my beloved Chicago, sharing with all of you the behind-the-scenes worlds and places I adore most.

But in ALL I WANT IS YOU, I couldn't resist sharing one of my other passions: vintage jewelry.

Thanks to a dear friend I was able to haunt antique stores and flea markets all over the city, rescuing broken, discarded pieces of fine vintage couture costume jewelry and watching her repair, restore, and redesign them. She gave these pieces new life, transforming them into necklaces, bracelets, and brooches of her own unique creation, and it was an amazing thing to see.

I just knew my heroine, Venus Smith, had to do the very same thing, and thus her jewelry line, A Touch of Venus, was born.

And of course it seemed only fitting that Venus's designs end up in Clayworth's department store, the store I created in my previous book, *A Black Tie Affair*, which is a thinly veiled Marshall Fields, Chicago's late great iconic retailer. Of course, the most delicious part is that Clayworth's is run by Venus's archenemy, Connor Clayworth O'Flynn, the man who betrayed her father and ruined his reputation. And yes, you guessed it—sparks fly between them, igniting into a fiery passion.

But this book isn't just the product of my imagination. Readers have been so kind, telling me the most amazing stories that have transported me to fascinating places, and I want to take all of you with me!

When someone shared with me the legend of the "Angel of Taylor Street," I fell in love with the story and couldn't resist using it myself. The Angel of Taylor Street was a person or persons who for decades did good deeds for strangers without ever asking anything in return. I changed the character to the Saint of Taylor Street in ALL I WANT IS YOU, and now it's an important part of Venus and Connor's story.

But that isn't the only one. Did you know there's a private gambling club hidden beneath the parking lot of an old Chicago restaurant, one that's been in business since our gangster days? I didn't either, until someone tipped me off. Of course it is the site of a fabulous adventure for Venus and Connor. It is just a hint of Chicago's inglorious past, but this time it has a positive spin—I promise!

I hope you'll enjoy Venus and Connor's story in ALL I WANT IS YOU. Please come visit my website at www.sherrillbodine.com. I'd love to hear from you!

Xo, Sherrill

Sherrill Bodine

♥ ♥ ♥ ♥ ♥ ♥ ♥ ♥ ♥ ♥ ♥ ♥ ♥ ♥ ♥ ♥ ♥ ♥

From the desk of Kendra Leigh Castle

Dear Reader,

"Dogs and cats living together…mass hysteria!"

I heard the voice of Peter Venkman in my head a lot as I was writing MIDNIGHT RECKONING, the second book in my Dark Dynasties series. That's because his little quip there is the basis for the story. Well, maybe not the mass hysteria part. But I did want to see what would happen when one of my cat-shifting vampires met a gorgeous woman who wasn't just out of his reach, but out of his species entirely. This is a tale of cat vamp meets werewolf, and relationships don't come with more built-in baggage than theirs.

I love a good star-crossed relationship, as long as it works out all right in the end (I still suffer traumatic flashbacks from *Romeo and Juliet*), but writing one turned out to be more difficult than I'd imagined. I'm perfectly happy to torment my characters from time to time, but the deck was so stacked against these two that even I was sometimes left wondering how they could possibly work things out. You see, Jaden Harrison and Lyra Black are natural enemies. In their world, vampires and werewolves don't mix, period. While the vampires rule the cities, the wolf packs keep to more rural areas, and the enmity between the races is strong despite years of relative peace between them. The wolves think the vampires are arrogant, worthless bloodsuckers; and the vampires think the wolves are wild, unruly, violent beasts. Each race steers clear of the other, so the chances of

Jaden and Lyra ever meeting were incredibly slim. But they did...and it left quite an impression.

If you've read *Dark Awakening*, you'll remember the beautiful she-wolf who stalked off after Jaden insulted her. What she was doing in a vampire safe house was left a mystery, but in MIDNIGHT RECKONING, you'll discover that Lyra has much larger problems than one rude vampire. She's the only child of her pack's Alpha, and the natural choice to fill his shoes when he steps down. There's just one problem: Lyra is female, and werewolf society is patriarchal, with some archaic notions about a woman's place that would horrify most twenty-first-century women. But this is Lyra's family, Lyra's world, and rather than desert them she's determined to make them see her value. She wants to win the right to lead at the pack's Proving...but to do so, she'll need to learn to fight in a way that evens the playing field. Finding someone to teach her seems hopeless as the clock ticks down, until a chance encounter with an unpleasantly familiar face leads to unexpected opportunity...and a very unlikely teacher.

The wolf and the cat together are a volatile mix of confidence and caution, brashness and reserve, unrestrained ferocity and quiet intensity. Their interaction is frowned upon, and a relationship between them is strictly forbidden. But a blue-eyed Cait Sith is hard to resist for even the most stubborn she-wolf, and it isn't long before both Lyra and Jaden start to wonder if there might not be a way around the traditional "fighting like cats and dogs" arrangement. That is, if the forces working against them from within the pack don't end Lyra's chances, and her life, first.

How Lyra and Jaden find their way to each other, and whether Venkman was right about canine/feline love affairs being a harbinger of the apocalypse, is something you'll have to read the book to find out. But if you're a fan of the sparks that fly when opposites attract, you'll want to come along and visit the Pack of the Thorn, where a vampire cat without a cause has finally met his match.

Enjoy!

Kendra Leigh Castle

♥ ♥ ♥ ♥ ♥ ♥ ♥ ♥ ♥ ♥ ♥ ♥ ♥ ♥

From the desk of Rochelle Alers

Dear Reader,

You've just picked up a very special novel, one that has lingered in my heart for ages.

SANCTUARY COVE, the first book in the Cavanaugh Island series, not only comes from my heart, but connects me to my ancestral roots.

Set on a Sea Island in the Carolina lowcountry, SANCTUARY COVE envelops you with the comforting spirit of a small town, where the residents cling to old traditions that assure a slower, more comforting way of life. Drive slowly through quaint Main Street, and you'll sense a place where time seems to stand still. Step into Jack's Fish House and be welcomed with warm feelings and comfort food. Sit quietly by the picturesque harbor and listen to the natural ebb and flow of nature.

The Cove draws recently widowed Deborah Robinson into its embrace, offering a fresh start for herself, her teenaged son, and her daughter. Her grandmother's ancestral home reaches out to her, filled with wonderful childhood memories that give Deborah the strength she needs to face her future.

When Dr. Asa Monroe arrives at the Cove, he's at a crossroads. The loss of his wife and young son in a tragic accident has devastated his world, sending him on a nomadic journey to find faith and meaning. And as he spends the winter on the Cove, he discovers a world of peace that has eluded him for more than a year. When he meets Deborah, he realizes not only that they are kindred spirits, but that fate might grant him a second chance at love. When friendship gives way to passion, Deborah and Asa find their greatest challenge is hiding their love in a town where there is no such thing as a secret.

The residents of the Cove are loving, wonderful, and quirky, just like the relatives we love even when they embarrass us at family reunions. So come on home and meet Asa, Deborah and her children, and a town full of unforgettable characters that will make you laugh, cry, and long for island living. Sit down with a glass of lemonade, put your feet up, and let life move a little slower. Enjoy the magnificent sunsets, the rattle of palmetto leaves in the breeze, and the mouthwatering aroma of lowcountry home cooking. If you listen carefully, you'll even hear a few folks speak Gullah, a dialect that is a blend of English and African.

And don't forget to look for *Angels Landing*, the second novel in the Cavanaugh Island series, coming in the fall of 2012.

Read, enjoy, and do let me hear from you!

Rochelle Alers

ralersbooks@aol.com
www.rochellealers.com